Monstrous Compendium
Appendices I & II

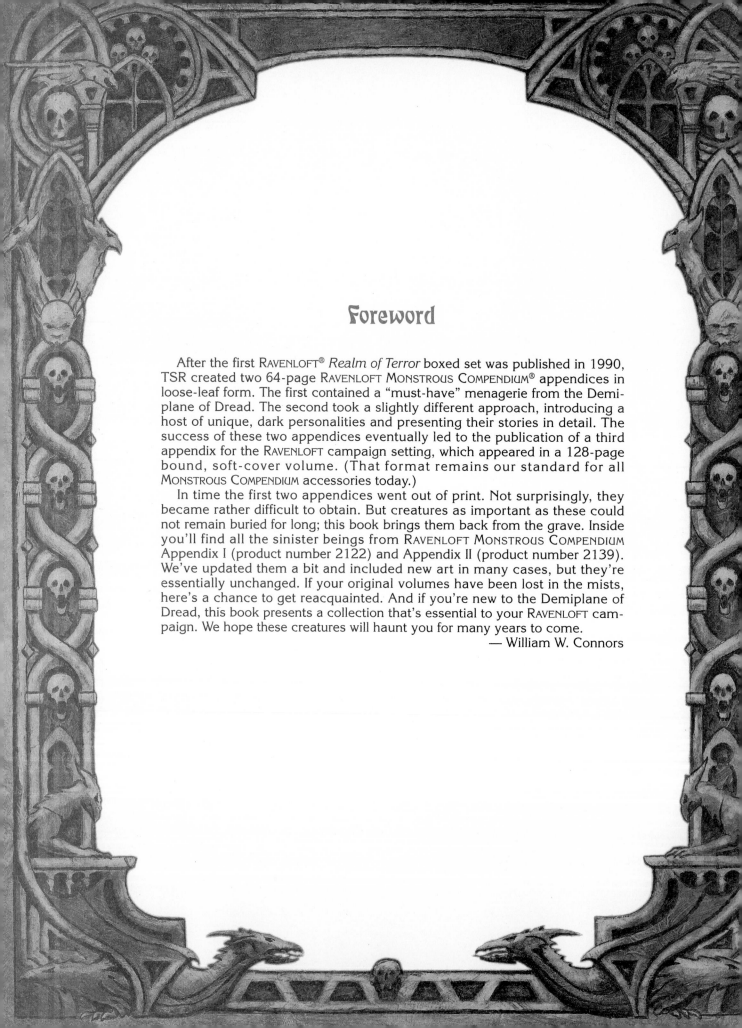

Foreword

After the first RAVENLOFT® *Realm of Terror* boxed set was published in 1990, TSR created two 64-page RAVENLOFT MONSTROUS COMPENDIUM® appendices in loose-leaf form. The first contained a "must-have" menagerie from the Demi-plane of Dread. The second took a slightly different approach, introducing a host of unique, dark personalities and presenting their stories in detail. The success of these two appendices eventually led to the publication of a third appendix for the RAVENLOFT campaign setting, which appeared in a 128-page bound, soft-cover volume. (That format remains our standard for all MONSTROUS COMPENDIUM accessories today.)

In time the first two appendices went out of print. Not surprisingly, they became rather difficult to obtain. But creatures as important as these could not remain buried for long; this book brings them back from the grave. Inside you'll find all the sinister beings from RAVENLOFT MONSTROUS COMPENDIUM Appendix I (product number 2122) and Appendix II (product number 2139). We've updated them a bit and included new art in many cases, but they're essentially unchanged. If your original volumes have been lost in the mists, here's a chance to get reacquainted. And if you're new to the Demiplane of Dread, this book presents a collection that's essential to your RAVENLOFT campaign. We hope these creatures will haunt you for many years to come.

— William W. Connors

Credits

Design: William W. Connors
Editing: C. Terry Phillips (Appendix I),
John D. Rateliff (Appendix II),
Karen Boomgarden and TSR staff (recompilation)
Cover Art: Jeff Easley
Interior Art: Tom Baxa and Mark Nelson (Appendix I),
Mark Nelson (Appendix II)
Graphic Design: Dawn Murin
Art Direction: Bruce Zamjahn

TSR, Inc.
201 Sheridan Springs Road
Lake Geneva
WI 53147
U.S.A.

TSR Ltd.
120 Church End
Cherry Hinton
Cambridge CB1 3LB
United Kingdom

How to Use this Book

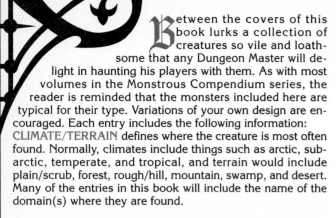

Between the covers of this book lurks a collection of creatures so vile and loathsome that any Dungeon Master will delight in haunting his players with them. As with most volumes in the Monstrous Compendium series, the reader is reminded that the monsters included here are typical for their type. Variations of your own design are encouraged. Each entry includes the following information:

CLIMATE/TERRAIN defines where the creature is most often found. Normally, climates include things such as arctic, subarctic, temperate, and tropical, and terrain would include plain/scrub, forest, rough/hill, mountain, swamp, and desert. Many of the entries in this book will include the name of the domain(s) where they are found.

FREQUENCY is the likelihood of encountering a creature in an area. Very rare is a 4% chance, rare is 11%, uncommon is 20%, and common is a 65% chance. Chances can be adjusted for special areas. As the traditional random encounters used in other campaigns are not generally found in Ravenloft, this entry can be taken as a guideline for adventure design.

ORGANIZATION describes the general social structure that the monster adopts. Common types are solitary, clan, pack, herd, flock, and such. In many cases, "solitary" includes small familial groups like mated pairs.

ACTIVITY CYCLE is the time of day when the monster is most animated. Those who tend to be busy at night may be active at any time in subterranean or similar settings. It is worth remembering that the "activity cycle" entry is a general guide and exceptions are fairly common.

DIET tells what the creature generally eats. Carnivores eat meat, herbivores eat plants, omnivores eat either, and scavengers dine mainly on carrion. Unusual entries, like *life energy* or *emotions,* will be listed from time to time and explained more fully in the text.

INTELLIGENCE is the equivalent of the Ability Score of the same name. Certain unintelligent monsters are instinctively cunning hunters and these are noted in the monster descriptions. Ratings correspond roughly to the following Intelligence Ability Scores:

0	Non-intelligent or not ratable
1	Animal intelligence
2–4	Semi-intelligent
5–7	Low intelligence
8–10	Average (human) intelligence
11–12	Very intelligent
13–14	Highly intelligent
15–16	Exceptionally intelligent
17–18	Genius
19–20	Supra-genius
21+	Godlike intelligence

TREASURE refers to the treasure tables in the *Dungeon Master® Guide* and indicates the type of wealth likely to be found on an individual monster. Treasure should be adjusted downward if few monsters are encountered. This may be further increased or decreased at the DM's discretion. These tables should not be used to place dungeon treasure, as numbers encountered underground will be much smaller. Intelligent monsters will use magical items present and try to carry off their most valuable treasures if hard pressed.

Major treasures are usually found in the monster's lair and will be enclosed in parentheses. As a rule, these should not be determined randomly but ought to be designed and placed by the DM. If the Dungeon Master does decide to assign such treasure randomly, he should roll for each type possible: if all rolls fail, no treasure of any type is found.

Unusually large or small treasures are noted by a parenthetical multiplier (×10, etc.), These should not be confused with treasure type X.

ALIGNMENT shows the general behavior of the average monster of that type. Exceptions, though uncommon, may be encountered, especially within the misty confines of Ravenloft.

NO. APPEARING indicates an average number of creatures that will be encountered in the wild. The DM should alter this to fit the circumstances as the need arises. In many cases, additional information on this topic will be presented in the **Habitat/Society** or **Ecology** section.

ARMOR CLASS is a rating of the monster's resistance to damage in combat. In many cases this will be due to the creature's natural defenses, but it can also indicate armor worn by humanoids or other creatures. In some cases, high speed, natural agility, or magical protection may play a part in the determination of a creature's Armor Class rating. Humans and humanoids of roughly man-size that wear armor will have an unarmored rating in parentheses. Listed ACs do not include any situational bonuses noted in the description.

MOVEMENT shows the relative speed of the creature with an unencumbered man having a rating of 12. Higher speeds may be possible for short periods. Human, demihuman, and humanoid movement rates are often determined by armor type (unarmored rates are given in parentheses). Movement through common media is abbreviated as follows:

Br	Burrowing
Fl	Flying
Sw	Swimming
Wb	Moving in a web

Flying creatures also have a Maneuverability Class from A to E that is indicated in parentheses. Complete information on Maneuverability Classes and their use can be found in the Aerial Combat rules in the *Dungeon Master Guide.*

HIT DICE indicates the number of dice rolled to generate the creature's hit points. Unless otherwise stated, Hit Dice are 8-sided. The Hit Dice are rolled and the numbers shown are added to determine the monster's hit points.

Some monsters will have additional points added to the total rolled on the Hit Dice. Thus, a creature with a rating of 4+4 has between 8 and 36 hit points. Monsters with a bonus of +3 or more to their rolled hit points are considered to have an extra Hit Die for the purposes of attack rolls and saving throws. Thus, a creature with 4+4 Hit Dice attacks and saves as if it had 5 Hit Dice.

In rare cases, a monster will have a hit point spread without a Hit Dice rating. In order to determine the number of Hit Dice that such creatures have for Attack and Saving Throws, divide the listed hit points by 4. Round the Hit Die rating up with remainders of .5 or greater and drop all other fractions.

THAC0 is the base roll that the monster needs to hit an enemy with an Armor Class of 0. This is a function of Hit Dice as described in the Combat section of the *DUNGEON MASTER Guide*. Modifiers to the creature's attack roll will be presented in the **Combat** section of the entry, but the listed THAC0 does not include any special bonuses.

NO. OF ATTACKS indicates the number of times that the monster can attack in a single round. Multiple attacks can usually be taken to indicate several attacking arms, raking paws, multiple heads, etc. In some cases, this does not include special attacks listed in the **Combat** section, but the text will make that clear. This number may be modified by hits that sever members, magic such as *haste* or *slow* spells, and so forth.

DAMAGE/ATTACK shows the severity of a given attack and is expressed as a spread of damage points. The number and type of dice rolled to determine the total number of hit points lost by the target of the attack will be listed in parentheses. If the monster uses weapons, the damage listed is for its favored weapon. Damage bonuses due to high strength, special abilities, and the like are listed in the **Combat** section of the entry.

SPECIAL ATTACKS details any unusual attack modes possessed by the creature such as breath weapons, spell use, poison, and the like. These are fully explained in the monster description.

SPECIAL DEFENSES provides information detailing any unusual resistances to harm that the monster might have. These commonly include an immunity to certain forms of attack or an invulnerability to non-magical weapons. These are fully detailed in the monster description.

MAGIC RESISTANCE is the percentage chance that magic cast upon the creature will fail to affect it, even if other creatures nearby are affected. If the spell penetrates this resistance, the creature is still entitled to any normal saving throws allowed. A creature may drop its magic resistance at any time and allow a spell to affect it normally if it so chooses.

SIZE is an indication of the overall dimensions of the creature. In the case of humanoids, it indicates the height of the monster. For other creatures (snakes and dragons, for example), it refers to the animal's length. Other measurements are possible and will be explained in the text.

T = tiny	under 2 feet tall
S = small	over 2 feet to 4 feet tall
M = man-sized	over 4 feet to 7 feet tall
L = large	over 7 feet to 12 feet tall
H = huge	over 12 feet to 25 feet tall
G = gargantuan	over 25 feet tall

MORALE is a general rating of how likely the monster is to persevere in the face of adversity or armed opposition. This guideline may be adjusted for individual circumstances. Morale ratings correspond to the following range:

2–4	Unreliable
5–7	Unsteady
8–10	Average
11–12	Steady
13–14	Elite
15–16	Champion
17–18	Fanatic
19–20	Fearless

XP VALUE is the number of experience points awarded for defeating (not necessarily killing) the monster. This value is a guideline that may be modified by the DM for the degree of challenge, encounter situation, and overall campaign balance.

PSIONICS gives a complete breakdown of the creature's innate psionic abilities, including sciences or devotions known and PSPs available. A complete understanding of this section requires *The Complete Psionics Handbook*. This entry is included only for those creatures that have psionic powers.

COMBAT provides all of the information that a DM will need to resolve a battle with the monster. Among other things, it details special combat abilities, arms or armor, and unusual tactics employed by the creature.

HABITAT/SOCIETY outlines the monster's general behavior, nature, social structure, and goals. Where the previous section provided the information needed for resolving skirmishes involving the creature, this entry provides information useful for role-playing encounters.

ECOLOGY describes how the monster fits into the campaign world, gives useful products or byproducts of the creature, and presents other miscellaneous information. This information can help the Dungeon Master to decide exactly when and where to best introduce the monster to his campaign.

CLOSE VARIATIONS of a monster are given in a special section after the main monster entry. For example, the *akik-age* entry also includes a brief discussion of the *ansasshia*, a closely related creature.

Calculating Experience Points

One of the things that game designers love to do is change things. As of this writing, it has been about seven years since the final touches were put on the ADVANCED DUNGEONS & DRAGONS® 2nd Edition game rules. In that time, a number of major and minor changes have been made to the game system.

One of the more important revisions is a change to the formula used to calculate experience point rewards for defeating the various monsters encountered during an adventure. This revision was introduced in the MONSTROUS MANUAL™ tome and has become the new standard for the calculation of experience points.

The experience point values for the monsters in this book have all been calculated using the new, revised rules. The table to the right, updating the one printed in the AD&D® 2nd Edition DUNGEON MASTER GUIDE, is provided in order to make the Dungeon Master's task easier when designing his own monsters.

It is worth noting that there are cases where DMs will want to deviate from the values given here. Some monsters are so powerful that the experience point rewards generated with these tables will be far less than a party might deserve. Some good examples of such creatures are the denizens of the Abyss and similar realms described in the PLANESCAPE™ campaign setting or the various lords of Ravenloft's domains.

What Has Changed?

None of these changes affect the general way in which experience points are calculated. A DM still begins by noting the number of Hit Dice that a monster has (Table 31) and then applying some modifiers based on the general powers and abilities of that creature. Only the modifiers (Table 32) have changed, although both tables have been printed here for easy reference.

Two new entries for psionic abilities have been added to the table. Thus, the possibility that a monster might have psionic disciplines or sciences (as detailed in *The Complete Psionics Handbook*) available to it has now been taken into account. Dungeon Masters who are not using psionic powers in their campaigns can simply ignore these additions.

Both the **magic resistance** and **breath weapon** entries have been split into two categories, reflecting the great range of possibilities within these classifications.

The bonus normally awarded for flight has been expanded to include other special forms of movement. Thus, a monster like a bulette or xorn, which can travel through the earth at great speed, would receive the same adjustment to its experience point value as a flying creature.

Of course, exceptions and unusual cases will still crop up. When this happens, Dungeon Masters will simply have to use a little common sense in the awarding of experience points.

Table 31:
Creature Experience Point Values

HD or Level	XP Value
Less than 1–1	7
1–1 to 1	15
1+1 to 2	35
2+1 to 3	65
3+1 to 4	120
4+1 to 5	175
5+1 to 6	270
6+1 to 7	420
7+1 to 8	650
8+1 to 9	975
9+1 to 10+	1,400
11 to 12+	2,000
13 or higher	2,000 +1,000 per additional Hit Die

Table 32: Hit Dice Value Modifiers

Modifier	Ability
+1	Armor Class 0 or lower
+1	Blood drain
+1	Breath weapon (up to 20 hp maximum damage)
+1	Can fly or has other special movement power
+1	Cause disease
+1	Employs psionic devotions
+1	Greater than normal hit points (over 6 hp/HD)
+1	Has and uses magical items or weapons
+1	High (13–14) or better Intelligence
+1	Hit only by magic or silver weapons
+1	Immunity to a spell
+1	Immunity to or half-damage from any weapon type
+1	Invisible at will
+1	Magic resistance (less than 50%)
+1	Missile weapons or ranged attack ability
+1	Multiple (four or more) attacks per round
+1	Regeneration
+1	Spell casting (level 2 or less)
+1	Unlisted special defense mode
+1	Unlisted non-magical special attack mode
+2	Breath weapon (over 20 hp maximum damage)
+2	Causes weakness or fear
+2	Employs psionic sciences
+2	Magic resistance (50% or better)
+2	Multiple attacks inflicting over 30 points of damage
+2	Paralysis
+2	Poison
+2	Single attack inflicting over 20 points of damage
+2	Spell casting (level 3 or greater)
+2	Swallows whole
+2	Unlisted special magical attack mode
+3	Energy drain (level or ability draining)
+3	Petrification

The environment (both mental and physical) in an AD&D game set in the dark domains of RAVENLOFT is not what it is in TSR's other fantasy campaign settings. While this is apparent in many places, it is perhaps most significant in the presentation of monsters and similar encounters. Before we begin to present the various monsters and minions of darkness that a party adventuring in Ravenloft is likely to encounter, let's take a few moments to go over some basic guidelines. By becoming familiar with these guidelines and making them a part of each encounter, the Dungeon Master will be better able to make the mysterious and macabre world of Ravenloft come alive for his players.

Random Encounters

Traditional random encounters, in which the DM checks a variety of tables periodically to determine if an encounter occurs and exactly what the party encounters, really have no place in a RAVENLOFT game. Nothing so simple as blind chance should drive the course of an adventure in Ravenloft. Each encounter, whether with man, beast, or monster, should be a premeditated and carefully controlled part of the scenario.

This is not to say that random events can never be used in a RAVENLOFT game—only that care must be taken and a little extra effort put into planning by the DM. It is perfectly all right to orchestrate a handful of encounters ahead of time, set up a chart to determine which one occurs with a given die throw, and then check periodically to see if one turns up. In such cases, however, each event should be a logical part of the scenario that has the effect of enhancing the game as a whole.

To illustrate this point, consider the following scenario: An elf vampire has been stalking the land, and the party has been trying to track it down and end a string of evil deaths attributed to it. The DM sets up six random encounters and decides that one will happen each day. A simplified encounter table might look something like this:

Die Roll	Encounter
1	Party finds body of new victim with clues to the location of the vampire's lair on the corpse.
2	Party finds diary that tells the story of the vampire's origin and hints at some of his personality.
3	Minions of the vampire, aware that the PCs are tracking their master, attack the party while they sleep.
4	A wandering Vistani woman is discovered. She consults the stars and provides the PCs with information about the vampire's weaknesses.
5	Party comes across a local citizen who remembers a story his grandfather used to tell him. Using this information, the PCs can learn how to protect themselves from one of the vampire's special attacks.
6	PCs come across the vampire while it is attacking another victim. The vampire is not interested in engaging in a prolonged fight and flees the encounter after only a brief skirmish.

As you can see, each of these encounters provides a random event that serves a role in the evolution of the game. In addition, the DM can prepare these encounters in advance, devoting the time to make them each unique and interesting to the party. Thus, these encounters become far more than a chance to trade blows with some faceless monsters for no readily apparent reason.

A Typical Encounter

In a FORGOTTEN REALMS® campaign, for example, it might be perfectly all right for a DM to describe an encounter to his players in terms that are absolute and clear. Assume that a party in Faerûn is traveling to Calaunt when the dice indicate a random encounter. The Dungeon Master checks his tables quickly and finds that the party has come across a pair of ogres. Thinking quickly, he decides to present the party with a bridge that spans the narrow river they have been following. A pair of ogres have taken to robbing those who would use the bridge, and the party will have to deal with them. The DM's description of the encounter might be as follows:

Your party comes to a bend in the path. With some concern, you notice that the singing of the birds in this gentle forest has suddenly been stilled. Ahead, the path comes to a solidly built, but poorly tended, wooden bridge that crosses a wide length of the river you have been following. The water beneath it looks cold and swift, as do the pair of ogres who stand atop the bridge. With cruel smiles, they each pick up a heavy axe and lumber toward the party. "Before humanscum go over bridge they must give us shineygold!" rumbles one of the creatures in a voice heavy with menace.

The intent of this scene is obvious: The party is being challenged to either pay the toll demanded by the ogres or engage the monsters in combat and win their way across the bridge by force of arms. The scene plays no part in any greater adventure, but is a well-presented and probably entertaining encounter that everyone should enjoy (as it presents possibilities for both role-playing and combat).

Further, the text contains enough descriptive elements (the silent birds, the cold water, etc.) to make the narrative seem fairly vivid to most players. In short, the DM has done a perfectly fine job of setting out for his players what they have encountered and what they must do to get past it. For their part, the players understand that they are faced with ogres and can decide on their course of action based upon the relative wealth, strength, and cleverness of their characters. A carefully calculated decision can be made and play can proceed from there.

A Ravenloft Encounter

To repeat the example above, in a fashion more appropriate to Ravenloft, assume that the party is investigating the disappearances of a number of local farm families. The cause of these strange happenings is simply that an ancient curse on the newly cleared lands they are farming has been triggered. The nature of the curse is such that it has transformed these people into ogres and bound them into the protection of the lands they would have exploited. Thus, the heroes are again traveling down a path beside a river when they encounter a pair of ogres.

The narrow path makes a gradual turn toward the river. It snakes around a dark and brooding pine copse to open out at the foot of a wide bridge. The bridge, built of stout-looking wooden logs and assembled in a most professional manner, shows signs of neglect and unrepaired damage, marring its otherwise picturesque appearance. Clearly, no effort has been made to maintain this once fine construction.

The water moving under the bridge is gray and looks cold. Here and there, dark shadows flicker just beneath its surface, moving too quickly for you to discern their source. The water flows swiftly past this point, filling the air with churning, splashing sounds as it passes over the rocky shallows along the bank.

Encounters in Ravenloft

As you take in this scene, a sense of uncertainty fills your party. One by one, you begin to realize that the birds overhead have grown silent. The sunlight, which had been streaming in brilliant pillars through the scattered branches overhead, is blocked off by a single dark cloud that seems to have swallowed the fiery sphere. Even the faint humming of insects and chirping of crickets have faded away. The air is heavy with the scent of wet earth, yet alive with expectation.

Suddenly, two dark figures rise up from the shadows under the bridge. As they step into the light, a gasp escapes the lips of all in your company. Each of these foul-looking creatures towers above even the tallest of you. Although humanoid, these brutes are clearly not men. Their skin is dark and mottled, and their cold eyes gleam with barely restrained bloodlust. The taut muscles of their hulking bodies ripple smoothly as they move toward you. Their mouths gape slightly as they draw heavy, rasping breaths through yellow, jagged teeth. A foul odor, like that found in the ruins of a violated crypt, smothers the sweet smell of pine in this part of the forest. With low growls that sound like warning snarls of vicious dogs, the horrid things stride toward your wary group.

Obviously, the second example goes into more detail than the first one. The scene is largely the same, but the second is more graphic and lavish in its particulars. Despite this, however, the reader will note that it deprives the players of or clouds much factual information. Consider the following points:

1. **The Environment:** Note that both descriptions touch on the environment in which the encounter takes place. In each case, the players are able to picture the area around them and use the information presented to them in deciding how their characters will act.

In the Ravenloft example, however, the environment becomes more ominous and potentially threatening. Dark shapes drift beneath the surface of the water below the bridge—are they harmless fish or lurking horrors? The sun, which was so recently shining brightly in the sky, has been covered by a dark cloud—is magic involved? The crickets and birds have grown silent—is it because of the ogres or is something else lurking in ambush?

By making the most of the description of the environment in which an encounter takes place, the DM can inject a level of suspense not normally found in AD&D games.

2. **The Mood:** Notice that the mood in the first encounter is fairly upbeat. The ogres are clearly a danger to be faced, but the scene is presented in such a way as to elevate the party members to the status of equals. That is, while the ogres are clearly dangerous monsters, the characters are brave heroes who have the strength and determination to stand against them.

In the Ravenloft example, the mood of the text is darker. The party is presented with information in a way that makes it seem to them that everything around them is more powerful than they are. The ogres are described as hulking creatures with rippling muscles and wicked fangs. An air of the supernatural hangs about the scene that will make any party think twice before feeling too cocky.

3. **The Monsters:** An observant reader will note that the word "ogre" does not appear in the Ravenloft encounter. It's all well and good to tell characters in a typical fantasy campaign that they are fighting an ogre, since it's a part of the everyday world they live in. For adventures in Ravenloft, however, the DM must play up the macabre and alien aspects of the supernatural. By describing the monsters only as hulking humanoid creatures, the party is left unclear as to what they are facing. Could these be hill giants? If they are ogres, are they common ogres, or might they be ogre magi? Maybe they're bugbears or some form of evolutionary throwback—or something altogether new and unknown? Without a solid base from which to draw conclusions about the nature of their enemies, the party members will have to be careful about their choice of tactics and weapons.

A side benefit of this use of descriptive text is that it prevents the "rules lawyers" among us from instantly selecting the best attack mode against a given creature. For example, everyone knows to use burning oil and flame attacks against trolls. A DM who describes such creatures in loose terms, playing up their supernatural aspects, makes it far more difficult for the player to decide that he is, in fact, faced with trolls and not some other loathsome menace.

4. **Potential Solutions:** Lastly, the first scene makes it clear to the players what is expected of them: They must battle the ogres or forfeit their hard-won gold. The second presents no such hard and fast solutions to the players. The players may well assume that these beasts mean them no good, but can they be certain of it? It could be that direct confrontation will rob the characters of vital information or place them in direct conflict with creatures far more powerful than they are (remember, they aren't sure that these are ogres).

By not handing out obvious solutions to the problems encountered, the DM leaves the players free to make their own decisions and assumptions. Not only is this good role-playing, it can lead to a far more exciting and challenging game. By never allowing the players to have all the information they need, the DM is making the world around their heroes mysterious and uncertain.

Storytelling

Try to remember that a DM running a RAVENLOFT game is under a special obligation to his players. While each and every DM refereeing an AD&D game has accepted the challenge of entertaining his players, the judge in a Ravenloft game must go beyond even that formidable task. To properly run a campaign in Ravenloft, the DM must become a true storyteller.

Mood and description are the keys to success here. While each of the monsters in this book has been designed to fit well into a gothic horror setting, they can easily be used too loosely and freely—transforming them into nothing more than sword practice for a party of adventurers. Conversely, almost any monster can be transformed into a horrifying nightmare with just a little storytelling by the DM. If kobolds are described as "a cowardly, sadistic race of short demihumans," it is easy to use them for comedy relief or nuisance encounters. If, instead, they are described as looking like "twisted mockeries of children with cruel eyes and snarling, dark voices," they become far more interesting and, potentially, horrific.

By keeping the points above in mind, the DM can go a long way toward making each and every RAVENLOFT game session an exciting one. Obviously, many other factors must be sewn together to make the unique fabric of the Ravenloft gaming environment whole. The importance of properly presenting and using the monsters provided in this book may, however, be the make-or-break point in an enjoyable campaign in Ravenloft.

8

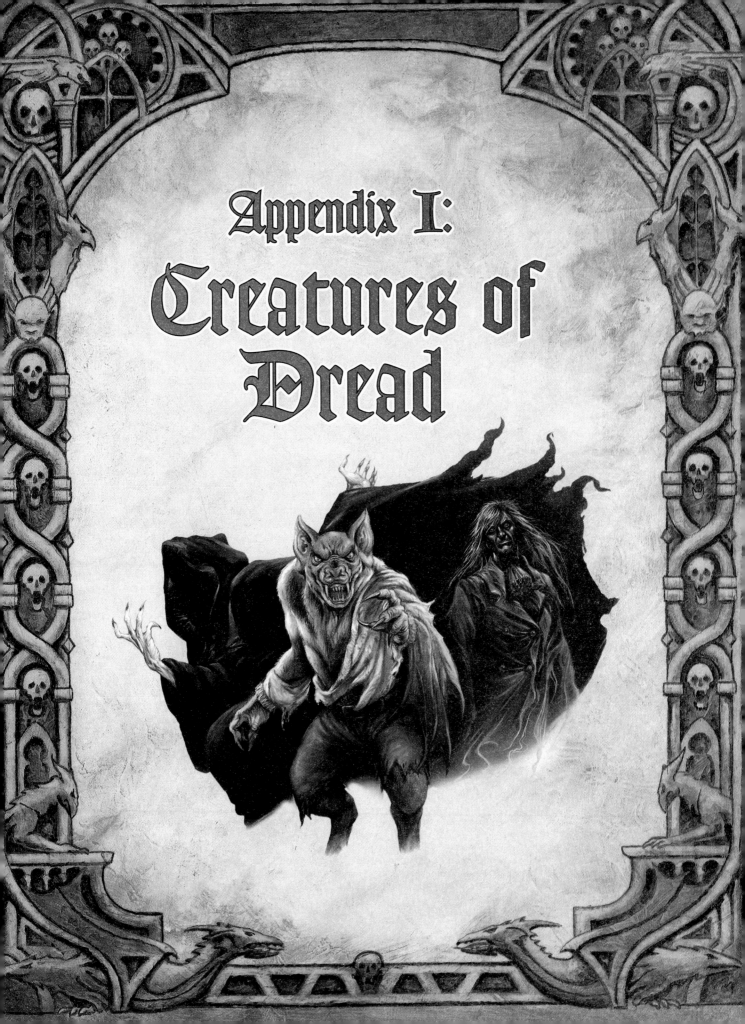

Appendix I:
Creatures of Dread

Bastellus

CLIMATE/TERRAIN:	Any city or village
FREQUENCY:	Very rare
ORGANIZATION:	Solitary
ACTIVITY CYCLE:	Night
DIET:	Dream essences
INTELLIGENCE:	Average (8–10)
TREASURE:	Nil
ALIGNMENT:	Neutral evil

NO. APPEARING:	1
ARMOR CLASS:	0
MOVEMENT:	Fl 15 (A)
HIT DICE:	4
THAC0:	17
NO. OF ATTACKS:	1
DAMAGE/ATTACK:	Nil
SPECIAL ATTACKS:	Sleep
SPECIAL DEFENSES:	+3 or better weapons to hit; spell immunity
MAGIC RESISTANCE:	Nil
SIZE:	M (6' tall)
MORALE:	Unsteady (5–7)
XP VALUE:	6,000

The bastellus is a haunting undead creature that comes in the night to feed upon the dream energies of helpless sleepers. In many cultures, it is known simply as a nightmare or dream stalker.

The bastellus is seldom seen, for it only appears in the presence of sleeping beings. Reports of the creature's true form, however, have been gathered from those who came across one while it was feeding. From these accounts, it is known that the bastellus looks like a hulking humanoid shadow. Utterly featureless, it feeds by placing its outstretched hand upon the victim's brow. When feeding, it always has its head thrown back as if in ecstasy, for the absorption of dream energy causes it great pleasure.

No recorded attempt to communicate with a bastellus has ever succeeded, so its language (if any) is unknown to mortal man. It is assumed, however, that a bastellus can impart messages to others through manipulation of their dreams, for many incidents have occurred in which previously unknown facts were available to someone after a visitation from a bastellus.

Combat: The eerie and spectral nature of the bastellus makes it largely invulnerable to physical harm. Only magical weapons of +3 or better can strike the creature, and even they do only half damage to it. Like most undead, it is immune to *charm, sleep,* or *hold* spells. Spells that depend on cold, heat, or electricity to inflict damage cannot injure bastelli and, as they have no physical bodies, they are immune to all manner of poisons. Holy water and the like cause no damage to bastelli, but they can be turned (as if they were ghosts) by powerful priests and clerics. A *dispel evil* cast directly at a bastellus is the only sure way to destroy it, and even then it is allowed to a save vs. spell to avoid annihilation.

The bastellus can move about in dimly lit or shadowy places without detection 95% of the time. Even persons on their guard for a dark form moving through the shadows have little hope of spotting the horror: a percentage chance equal to the higher of their Intelligence or Wisdom scores.

A *protection from evil* spell prevents the bastellus from entering a given area or attacking a given individual, but it is not harmed by these spells. A *negative plane protection* spell is fully effective against a bastellus and also breaks the creature of its desire to feed again on the same victim. (Although it may do so out of chance or proximity, it is no longer compelled to do so as described below.)

If it desires to move into an area with awake beings in it, the bastellus can employ a powerful *sleep* spell that affects all beings within 50 feet. A saving throw vs. spell is permitted by those in range, but this roll is made at a –4 penalty. This spell is so powerful that elves are only 30% resistant to it and half-elves are only 10% resistant.

Once all the persons in a given area are asleep, the bastellus picks out a target and moves in to feed. Since the sleep it induces in others is a magical and dreamless one, it does not attack those who have been affected by its power. Thus, only someone who was asleep before its spell was cast will be targeted. In addition, the bastellus is unable to feed on the spirit essences of elves and half-elves, so they are safe from its predation as well.

To attack, the bastellus moves close to its victim and reaches out an arm to touch the target's brow. As soon as it makes contact, the dreams of the sleeper become twisted. Whatever scene he or she might have been imagining turns dark and evil. The only common thread in these visions of terror is that they will be drawn from the darkest part of the dreamer's mind—the id—and will reflect his or her greatest fears.

For example, if a paladin is worried about his chaste love for a sweet princess and is dreaming of an evening rendezvous with his cherished one, he might find that she has suddenly turned into a sultry temptress. Her actions might be so alluring that in his dream he cannot turn away from her, even though he knows that to yield to her invitations spells certain doom. In the end, he is forced to embrace the twisted mockery of his betrothed and his soul seems to fade to absolute darkness.

When the dreamer awakes, he feels shaken and distraught. The night's sleep proves to be unrestful, and the memory of the horrible dream burns in his mind. No hit points are recovered from a sleep interrupted by a bastellus, and the character will awake too disturbed to be able to memorize new spells or perform any act of great mental concentration. In addition, the victim will find that he has been reduced by one level due to the feeding of the dark creature.

Any being reduced to below level 0 by the predation of a bastellus dies in its sleep, seemingly of a heart attack. If the body is not destroyed (via cremation, immersion in acid, or similar means), its spirit will rise in a number of days equal to the number of levels it lost to the bastellus. Thus, a 14th-level wizard would rise up in two weeks. The new spirit is also a bastellus, but it has no connection with the monster that created it.

If caught unawares, the bastellus can be forced into actual combat—although it will always try to flee from such confrontations. In these cases, it is very limited in power, for its *sleep* spell does not work on those who can see it. Other powers enable it to escape in such cases, but they are not nearly so fearsome as its energy draining dreams. The bastellus can invoke an area of *darkness* within 50 feet of itself (often to cover its escape) and pass through any solid object without resistance.

As creatures of darkness, bastelli will shun brightly lighted areas. While their natural ability to create *darkness* is able to overcome magical light sources of less than 3rd level (a normal *light* spell, for example), it cannot darken an area illuminated by more powerful spells. Thus, a *continual light* spell will provide enough luminescence to prevent the bastellus from entering the lighted area. Note that bright light does not harm the creature but merely serves to keep it at bay. Further, the presence of a bright light will not prevent the bastellus from employing its sleep spell on those in the illuminated area if it can draw near enough to them to do so.

Should the bastellus be forced to attack, it does so by moving through a living being (requiring a normal attack roll to do so). If the bastellus can do this, the victim must save vs. spell or be driven into an extreme state of paranoia. The victim's companions become (to him) his greatest enemies, as drawn from his own subconscious by the touch of the bastellus, and he will attack them without mercy. Although these delusions last only 1d4 rounds, the chaos that usually ensues during this time provides more than enough cover to allow the bastellus to escape.

If the bastellus is reduced to 0 hit points but is not destroyed by the casting of *dispel evil*, it will rise again to plague the world. When the last blow is struck to the creature, it will seem to boil away into nothingness like the cloud of steam rising above a pot of boiling water. At the same time, it throws its head back and unleashes a telepathic cry of anguish and pain that causes all within 50 feet to make a fear check. If the creature was in contact with a victim when it was struck down, the shock to the dreamer is so intense that he or she must save vs. death magic or be instantly slain. On the next night, the bastellus will rise again at the place where it was first created to renew its dreadful preying.

The bastellus passes the day in a pocket dimension of shadows and nightmares (see below). Because of the regenerative effects of its slumber here, the creature is always returned to full hit points before the coming of night and its return to the Prime Material Plane.

Habitat /Society: The bastellus is drawn to places where large numbers of people dwell and, thus, dream. Because of this, it frequently appears in cities and towns.

While in a given location, it seeks out those who have the most vivid dreams. Usually, this includes highly passionate or motivated individuals and those rare creative minds who can find true freedom of expression only in their nightly flights of fantasy. Because these people tend to be the most extroverted and well known persons in their area, their sudden and mysterious deaths often cause quite a stir. Before long, it becomes all too clear that some foul creature is stalking the citizenry and feeding on those who provide its fire and life.

Once the bastellus has fed upon a given person's dreams, it becomes obsessed with that person and will return to taste his or her essences nightly until the victim dies. As soon as this fate befalls its chosen prey, the creature moves on in search of another energetic mind upon which to feast.

As mentioned earlier, those who die from the predation of a bastellus may well become one themselves. On the night that the disembodied spirit returns from the dead, it feels a burning hunger. Having no memory of its past life, the spirit knows only that it must seek out the dreams, aspirations, and loves of others in order to fill the aching void within it. Before the night is done, it must taste the dream essences of another or fade away, never to return. Usually, this is not a problem as the victim probably died in a city and the spirit will reappear at the site of its death.

The pocket universe in which the bastellus passes the day is believed to be associated with an unusual conjunction of planes. Many luminaries have postulated that it must contain aspects of both the Negative Material Plane and the dreaded demiplane of Ravenloft. As these creatures are encountered only in the latter realm, such an explanation seems likely.

Ecology: There are those who would argue that the bastellus is a creature from beyond the grave and, therefore, has no place in the biology of the natural world. In fact, there is a great deal of speculation that this is not the case. Numerous scholars have put forth the theory that the bastellus is actually a product of the unrecognized hopes and aspirations of living creatures. If this is true, then the bastellus is very much a byproduct of the living world and at least nominally important to it. This debate has raged for countless centuries, however, and it seems that the scholars who put forth both arguments are no closer to a resolution of the issue than they were when the debate began.

The dream essences of the bastellus, while hard to obtain, are of almost incalculable value to necromancers and illusionists in the crafting of magical items. It is said that an illusionist who uses even the tiniest fraction of such a creature's substance as a material component in the creation of an illusion will find that the images created are drastically more vivid than they might otherwise be—making it almost impossible for victims to convince themselves that such images are not real.

Bat, Ravenloft

	Sentinel	Skeletal
CLIMATE/TERRAIN:	Any land	Any land
FREQUENCY:	Very rare	Rare
ORGANIZATION:	Solitary	Solitary
ACTIVITY CYCLE:	Night	Night
DIET:	Carnivore	Nil
INTELLIGENCE:	Avg (8–10)	Non- (0)
TREASURE:	Nil	Nil
ALIGNMENT:	Special	Neutral
NO. APPEARING:	1	3–12
ARMOR CLASS:	6	5
MOVEMENT:	3, Fl 18 (C)	1, Fl 15 (C)
HIT DICE:	1	1–1
THAC0:	19	20
NO. OF ATTACKS:	1	1
DAMAGE/ATTACK:	1d4	1d3
SPECIAL ATTACKS:	Powers of master	Nil
SPECIAL DEFENSES:	Powers of master	See below
MAGIC RESISTANCE:	Nil	Nil
SIZE:	T (1′)	T (1′)
MORALE:	Fearless (20)	Fearless (20)
XP VALUE:	65	65

Bats are more common in the dark realms of Ravenloft than they are anywhere else in the known universe. All of the traditional varieties of bat (common, large, giant, huge, mobat, and so forth) are represented in one domain or another, but two distinct species of bat are found only in Ravenloft.

Sentinel Bat

A sentinel bat is a strange form of bat that is drawn to powerful undead and serves them as familiars serve wizards. While they look much like common bats, being roughly the same size and coloration, they are often marked in some way by their masters. Thus, a sentinel bat that is serving a vampire whose family crest is a silver crown might develop a gray crown-shaped patch of fur.

The eyes of a sentinel bat are normally deep black, but when their master wishes to see through them, their eyes glow like pinpoints of fiery red light.

Through a series of clicks and ultrasonic whistles they are able to speak with and command other species of common (or even giant) bats. In this way, a single sentinel bat can provide its master with a vast intelligence network composed wholly of bats.

Combat: Sentinel bats are unusual enemies. They seldom engage in direct combat, preferring to flee any potentially dangerous situation. Often, they will call upon other bats in the area and command them to cover their escape. When they do attack, they will swoop down upon a victim and bite them, inflicting 1d4 points of damage per successful attack. In addition, they have the traditional powers of their masters available to them. Thus, a sentinel bat who is serving a wight has the ability to drain 1 level of life energy with each strike, is hit only by silver or +1 or better magical weapons, and is immune to *sleep, hold,* and *charm* spells. They never have the ability to create undead, however, so any creature slain by a sentinel bat serving a wight would not rise up as a wight itself. The life energy drain (if any) of a sentinel bat is less potent than that of its master, however; lost levels are regained at a rate of 1 per day or by the casting of a *remove curse* or *atonement* spell upon the victim.

Habitat/Society: Sentinel bats are to undead what familiars are to wizards. When any free-willed, intelligent undead creature in Ravenloft desires a companion, it can call upon the Mists to deliver to it a sentinel bat. Such a request can be made but once every decade, and only one bat serves an undead individual at any given time. The request for a bat must be made near a bat lair at midnight, on a night when the moon is full. During the next full moon, the undead creature returns to the lair and one of the bats, now transformed into a sentinel, will fly to join him. Thereafter the bat's master can look through the eyes of its pet whenever it desires and see what the bat sees. In all other regards, however, the link between the two creatures functions as if the two were linked by a *find familiar* spell. Because the death of a sentinel bat can result in the death of its master, these creatures are seldom sent into dangerous situations.

Ecology: Sentinel bats are normal creatures who have been empowered by the Mists of Ravenloft. Like their mundane kin, they have an acute natural sonar, keen eyesight, and subsist on a diet of insects and such.

The body of a sentinel bat has been used with great success in the creation of devices and potions intended to convey power over the undead.

Skeletal Bat

Skeletal bats are created by the use of an *animate dead* spell and are often associated with necromancers or evil priests. They are to bats what traditional skeletons are to humans—mindless animated remains.

Skeletal bats attack with their bony claws (inflicting 1 to 3 points of damage) and are often used as guardians by those who create them. In addition, they radiate an aura of fear that causes all creatures who view them to make a fear check. A bonus of +1 is allowed on the check for every 3 full Hit Dice that the victim has. Thus, a 5th-level character looking upon a skeletal bat is entitled to a +1 on his fear check.

Skeletal bats are nothing more than puppets who will obey simple instructions given to them by their creator. These cannot be overly long (two or three concepts is the most one of these monsters can understand) and must be very clearly worded. Because of this, their assigned tasks are usually quite simple.

The bones of skeletal bats can be used in the creation of bone golems (described elsewhere in this book).

CLIMATE/TERRAIN:	Any ocean or sea
FREQUENCY:	Very rare
ORGANIZATION:	Solitary
ACTIVITY CYCLE:	Night
DIET:	Special
INTELLIGENCE:	Average (8–10)
TREASURE:	Nil
ALIGNMENT:	Chaotic evil

NO. APPEARING:	1
ARMOR CLASS:	10
MOVEMENT:	18
HIT DICE:	4+3
THAC0:	15
NO. OF ATTACKS:	1
DAMAGE/ATTACK:	1–6 (1d6)
SPECIAL ATTACKS:	Haunting
SPECIAL DEFENSES:	See below
MAGIC RESISTANCE:	Nil
SIZE:	M (6′ tall)
MORALE:	Fearless (20)
XP VALUE:	975

The bowlyn (or sailor's demise, as it is often called) is a strange and dreadful spirit that haunts oceangoing vessels. In many ways, the creature has been likened to a poltergeist or similar restless spirit that haunts the place of its death.

Like the poltergeist, a bowlyn is typically invisible. Unlike the former, however, it can become visible when it wishes to. When visible (or invisible and viewed by someone who can see such things), the bowlyn appears as a gaunt and skeletal seaman. Although the creature's features are torn and twisted by the trauma of its death, it is often possible for those who knew it in life to recognize their former shipmate. Such individuals are entitled to an ability check on Wisdom to see if they can identify their former companion. Those who do are instantly required to make a horror check and may, at the DM's discretion, be called upon to make a fear check as well.

Bowlyns do not communicate with the living in any way, although they do constantly moan and wail in agony as they seek to exact vengeance upon those they blame for their deaths.

Combat: Bowlyns generally engage only in indirect combat. When they do opt to use their deadly touch in melee, however, they inflict 1d6 points of damage and cause the victim to successfully save vs. paralysis or instantly be overcome with nausea. Individuals so affected suffer a –4 penalty on all attack rolls, saving throws (including fear and horror checks), and proficiency checks until they are cured with any form of healing magic. Any healing spell, even one as minor as *goodberry* or *cure light wounds*, will remove the nausea from the character.

When a bowlyn chooses to attack through indirect means, it generally does so by causing accidents aboard the ship on which it died. These accidents will often begin as minor mishaps (a secured line coming loose, or damage to a minor navigational instrument) and gradually grow into severe hazards (the crow's nest breaking free with a sailor in it, or the destruction of all navigational charts). More often than not, the latter stages of a bowlyn haunting result in men being hurled overboard to drown (see the *Player's Handbook* for rules on this).

The bowlyn can be successfully attacked only with magical weapons or spells. It has the traditional spell immunities associated with undead and cannot be affect by *charm, sleep, hold,* or similar spells. Because it is not solid, spells that are meant to bind a physical form (like *web*) will not affect it. Bowlyns are immune to the damaging effects of holy water, but can be turned as if they were ghasts by priests or similar characters.

Because the bowlyn is a spirit tied directly to the sea, it can be destroyed without combat by any captain wise (or foolish) enough to run his ship aground while the bowlyn is haunting the vessel. In such cases, the creature is instantly annihilated and the mysterious accidents it has been causing cease. Of course, if the bowlyn learns that a captain or crew mean to do this, it takes preventative measures.

Over the course of its "visit" to the ship, the creature will stage one mishap per night. If possible, it will arrange accidents similar to the one in which it died, or incidents related to its former duties on the ship. Thus, a bowlyn that was once a navigator might arrange for a fire in the ship's chart room.

On the last night of its haunting, the bowlyn will attempt to sink, cripple, or destroy the ship. In order to spread fear and panic among the crew, the bowlyn will arrange for those near the scene of an accident to catch fleeting glimpses of its being.

Habitat/Society: Bowlyns are undead spirits who, like the poltergeist, do not rest easily in their graves. Without exception, they were sailors on oceangoing vessels who died due to an accident at sea. In life, they were cruel or selfish persons; in death they blame their shipmates for the mishap that took their lives. Thus, they return from their watery graves to force others beneath the icy waves.

Typical hauntings do not occur immediately after the death of the sailor fated to become a bowlyn. It takes the spirit of the seaman 1 to 10 years to return from the grave. The first appearance of a bowlyn always takes place on the anniversary of its death, and the initial haunting lasts 1 to 6 weeks. Subsequent hauntings occur every 6 months to 1 year later, and last for 2 to 4 weeks.

Ecology: The bowlyn is a dangerous creature. Since it exists only to torment those it blames for its death, it has no place in the natural world. While the accidents arranged by a bowlyn often affect persons it never knew in life, the focus of its attacks will always be those it served with prior to death.

Broken One

	Common	Greater
CLIMATE/TERRAIN:	Any land	Any land
FREQUENCY:	Rare	Very rare
ORGANIZATION:	Pack	Pack
ACTIVITY CYCLE:	Any (night)	Any (night)
DIET:	Varies	Varies
INTELLIGENCE:	Low (5–7)	High (13–14)
TREASURE:	I, K, M	I, K, M (Z)
ALIGNMENT:	Neutral evil	Neutral evil
NO. APPEARING:	3–12 (3d4)	1–4 (1d4)
ARMOR CLASS:	7 (10)	5 (8)
MOVEMENT:	9	9
HIT DICE:	3	5
THAC0:	17	15
NO. OF ATTACKS:	1	1
DAMAGE/ATTACK:	1d6 (or by weapon)	1d8 (or by weapon)
SPECIAL ATTACKS:	See below	See below
SPECIAL DEFENSES:	Regeneration	Regeneration
MAGIC RESISTANCE:	Nil	Nil
SIZE:	M (4'–7' tall)	M (4'–7' tall)
MORALE:	Unsteady (5–7)	Steady (11–12)
XP VALUE:	175	420

Broken ones (or animal men) are the tragic survivors of scientific and magical experiments gone awry. While they were once human, their beings have become mingled with those of animals and their very nature has been forever altered by the shock of this event. It is rumored that some broken ones are the result of failed attempts at *resurrection, reincarnation*, or *polymorph* spells.

While broken ones look more or less human, they are physically warped and twisted by the accidents that made them. The characteristics of their nonhuman part will be clearly visible to any who see them. For example, a broken one who has been infused with the essence of a rat might have horrific feral features, wiry whiskers, curling clawed fingers, and a long, whiplike tail.

Broken ones know whatever languages they knew as human beings; 10% of them can communicate with their nonhuman kin as well. It is not uncommon for the speech of a broken one to be heavily accented or slurred in accordance with the deformities of its body.

Combat: Broken ones tend to be reclusive creatures; combat with them is rare. Still, they are strong opponents. Broken ones are almost always blessed with a greater-than-human stamina, reflected in the fact that they always have at least 5 hit points per Hit Die. Thus, the weakest broken ones has at least 15 hit points. In addition, broken ones heal at a greatly accelerated rate, regenerating 1 hit point each round.

A broken one will often wield weapons in combat, inflicting damage according to the weapon used. Many broken ones have also developed claws or great strength, which makes them deadly in unarmed combat. Hence, all such creatures inflict 1d6 points of damage in melee. Unusually strong strains might receive bonuses to attack and damage rolls.

Many broken ones have other abilities (night vision, keen hearing, etc.) that are derived from their animal half. As a general rule, each creature will have a single ability of this sort.

Habitat/Society: Broken ones tend to gather together in bands of between 10 and 60 individuals. Since they seldom find ac-

ceptance in human societies, they seek out their own kind and dwell in secluded areas of dense woods or rocky wastes far from the homes of men. From time to time they will attack a human village or caravan, either for supplies, in self-defense, or simply out of vengeance for real or imagined wrongs. If possible, they will try to seek out their creator and destroy him for the transformations he has brought upon them.

When a society of these monsters is found, it will always be tribal in nature. There will be from 10 to 60 typical broken ones with one greater broken one for every 10 individuals. The greater broken ones (described below) act as leaders and often have absolute power over their subjects.

Ecology: Broken ones are unnatural combinations of men and animals. Their individual diets and habits are largely dictated by their animal natures. Thus, a broken one who has leonine characteristics would be carnivorous, while one infused with the essence of a horse would be vegetarian. There are no known examples of a broken one who has been formed with the essence of an intelligent nonhuman creature.

Broken ones manufacture the items they need to survive. These are seldom of exceptional quality, however, and are of little or no interest to outsiders. Occasionally, broken ones may be captured by evil wizards or sages who wish to study them.

Greater Broken Ones

From time to time, some animal men emerge who are physically superior. While they are still horrible to look upon and cannot dwell among men, they are deadly figures with keen minds and powerful bodies. Their twisted and broken souls, however, often lead them to acts of violence against normal men.

These creatures regenerate at twice the rate of their peers (2 hit points per round) and inflict 1d8 points of damage in unarmed combat. When using weapons, they gain a +3 to +5 bonus on all attack and damage rolls. Like their subjects, they often have special abilities based on their animal natures. Such powers, however, are often more numerous (from 1 to 4 additional abilities) and may be even better than those of the animal they are drawn from. For example, a greater broken one created from scorpion stock might gain a chitinous shell that gives it AC 2 and have a poisonous stinger.

CLIMATE/TERRAIN:	Any
FREQUENCY:	Very rare
ORGANIZATION:	Solitary
ACTIVITY CYCLE:	Any
DIET:	Nil
INTELLIGENCE:	Very (11–12)
TREASURE:	Nil
ALIGNMENT:	Neutral evil

NO. APPEARING:	1
ARMOR CLASS:	N/A
MOVEMENT:	9
HIT DICE:	N/A
THAC0:	Special
NO. OF ATTACKS:	N/A
DAMAGE/ATTACK:	N/A
SPECIAL ATTACKS:	Despair
SPECIAL DEFENSES:	See below
MAGIC RESISTANCE:	See below
SIZE:	M (6′ tall)
MORALE:	Fearless (20)
XP VALUE:	0

Bussengeists are the spectral forms of those who died in a great calamity brought on by their own action or inaction. They look much as they did in life, save that they are partially transparent. Over time, the gloom and suffering the spirit is forced to witness takes its toll, and the creature's visage becomes sad and tired. Thus, these harbingers of doom often appear far older than they were at the time of their death.

The bussengeist is a ghostlike creature that finds itself drawn to scenes of great disasters or tragedies. With a slow, sad pace it walks the countryside, traveling from crisis to crisis. As a rule, the bussengeist does not cause the disaster to occur, but is drawn to it for some reason. Once present, however, the *aura of despair* that surrounds the creature can certainly make an already bad situation worse.

Bussengeists are able to communicate with those around them via a limited form of telepathy. More often than not, however, they will convey only gloomy tidings of impending doom, not information that might be used to avert the coming catastrophe.

Combat: Bussengeists do not engage in combat directly. Their lot in life (or death, as the case may be) is simply to witness time and time again the type of disaster that killed them.

When a bussengeist arrives to view a scene of destruction, it radiates an aura of despair. This aura will affect only one side in a battle, generally the side most akin to "good." All creatures within 120 feet of the bussengeist suffer a penalty of –4 on all attack and damage rolls, saving throws, and proficiency checks. Other die rolls may be negatively affected as well, at the DM's option. The effects of this aura can be avoided by characters who make a successful save vs. spell.

While a bussengeist cannot be harmed by physical weapons, it may be confronted, driven off, and even destroyed by some spells. Attempts to turn undead, however, will prove fruitless.

A bussengeist can be forced away from a place by a wizard or priest who employs a *control undead, holy word, limited wish,* or *dismissal* spell. A bussengeist driven away in this manner will return in 2 to 12 hours, however, and will be immune to further casting of the same spell by the same wizard. The *forbiddance* spell can be cast to prevent a bussengeist from entering a given area for the duration of the spell.

While these means provide temporary protection from the bussengeist, destroying one is another matter entirely. The only way to annihilate a bussengeist is with a *wish* or *dispel evil*.

Habitat/Society: Bussengeists are solitary wanderers. Unlike the typical nomad or vagabond, however, they have no control over their movements. They are constantly drawn from tragedy to tragedy and forced to witness scenes of destruction similar to that which ended their own lives. As a rule, only those persons who feel remorse for their actions will become bussengeists. For example, a traitor who allowed an invading force to gain access to a walled city and was himself slain in the ensuing battle might become a bussengeist. If he was killed without warning and felt no pity for those his actions had brought misery to, he would not be transformed. If, on the other hand, he knew that he was about to die and had reason to feel that he had acted in error, he might well become a bussengeist. In his afterlife, he would visit cities in the process of being raided by barbarians, castles being overrun by monsters, and similar scenes.

Bussengeists travel from place to place in an insubstantial—though not invisible—state. On reaching their destination, they begin to radiate their *aura of despair*. Once the catastrophe that drew them has occurred, they will feel a need to move on. Walking with a slow, methodical stride they will seek out another place where a tragedy is about to unfold.

Bussengeists generally arrive at the scene of a disaster 1 to 6 days before it is due to occur. Thus, the inhabitants are given some warning that a crisis is at hand (if they are wise enough to recognize the tragic, spectral figure of the bussengeist for what it is).

Ecology: As an unnatural creature, the bussengeist has no real place in the ecology of the world it has left behind. The same is not true, however, of the course of history. There are many scholars who can point out great battles which, they claim, can only have been decided by the influence of these tragic souls.

The essence of these creatures, if captured in some way, can be a powerful magical component. It is rumored that many cursed magical weapons are forged in fires fanned by the breath of a bussengeist and that their powers are harnessed in the creation of *drums of panic* or a *harp of discord*.

15

Darkling

CLIMATE/TERRAIN:	Any land
FREQUENCY:	Very rare
ORGANIZATION:	Solitary
ACTIVITY CYCLE:	Any
DIET:	Omnivore
INTELLIGENCE:	Very (11–12)
TREASURE:	J, K, M, (A)
ALIGNMENT:	Chaotic evil

NO. APPEARING:	1
ARMOR CLASS:	8 (10)
MOVEMENT:	12
HIT DICE:	2
THAC0:	19
NO. OF ATTACKS:	1
DAMAGE/ATTACK:	1d4 (or by weapon)
SPECIAL ATTACKS:	Foreseeing, evil eye
SPECIAL DEFENSES:	Foreseeing
MAGIC RESISTANCE:	Nil
SIZE:	M (6')
MORALE:	9
XP VALUE:	420

The darkling is a member of the Vistani (see the RAVENLOFT Campaign Setting) who has been cast out from his people. No longer tied to the fabric of the demiplane in the same way that he once was, the darkling becomes more and more evil with the passing of time. In the end, he or she is utterly corrupted by the gloom of the surrounding land.

Darklings look much like their distanced Vistani cousins, save that their skin tends to be even darker and they are almost uniformly gaunt. Their features are sunken and worn, making them look as if they had been far too long without nourishment. They dress much like other Vistani, save that they lose their taste for bright colors and tend to wear drab earth tones.

Darklings want as little to do with true Vistani as possible, but often prey on normal men and their societies. They speak the common tongue of men and are generally familiar with a handful (3 to 6) of other languages or dialects.

Combat: The darkling still clings to a portion of the power that was once his. As such, he is a dangerous and clever opponent. Perhaps the most important of his abilities is that of *foreseeing*. Because the darkling has an innate sense of what his enemies are about to do, he is never surprised and makes all saving throws automatically. In addition, the darkling imposes a –2 penalty on all opponents' surprise rolls. For this reason, the darkling often strikes from ambush.

In melee combat, the darkling will generally rely on light arms like daggers and short swords, doing damage according to the weapon employed. The use of lethal poisons on bladed weapons is a darkling trademark, however, so those who suffer even a minor scratch from a darkling blade may be in deadly peril. The toxin created by darklings is similar to type E poison (injected, immediate, death/20). They will share the secrets of its creation with no one. It is rumored that even the Vistani cannot duplicate the poisons of their distanced kin.

If a darkling attains surprise when it attacks someone, it will often employ its *evil eye*. This curse is a variant on the traditional Vistani enchantment and causes its victims to suffer a –2 on all attack rolls and saving throws unless they successfully save vs. spell.

Habitat/Society: Having been cast out of the Vistani society for some crime or wrongful act, the darkling often gathers a band of human thugs around him and takes up a life of heinous crime and wandering brutality. While unable to cross the misty borders between the domains of Ravenloft, a darkling is said to know every stone and tree in the domain he dwells in. This imprisonment in a single domain is quite painful to a people as full of wanderlust as the Vistani and serves to fuel the evil desire for vengeance that burns in the darkling's heart.

Often, a darkling will work toward some grand scheme which he feels will allow him to escape from the domain he is imprisoned in (or even from Ravenloft itself) and strike back at his former people in some way. Since the Vistani are in far better harmony with the environment than their darkling outcasts, such plans of vengeance are seldom anything but failures.

Darklings often claim to retain more of their fortune telling powers than they truly do. Predictions offered by them, therefore, are either lies or educated guesses.

Ecology: The darkling lives either alone or as the leader of a small band of thugs and ruffians. He looks upon the Vistani as cruel people who have done him wrong and upon normal men as pawns and prey. To the darkling, the world has committed a great wrong and now owes him a massive debt. Thus, he looks upon all material things as his rightful property and takes what he needs without regard for the consequences of his actions.

The death of a darkling usually (90%) draws the attention of the nearest Vistani group. Within a week, they arrive at the location of the demise, bury the body (if such is still available), and perform an ancient rite designed to soothe the spirit of their tortured brother and allow him to rest in eternal peace. If this ritual is not completed, there is a 90% chance that the darkling will return in 1 to 6 weeks as a ghast (if the body is intact) or as a wraith (if the body has been destroyed). This undead creature then hunts down those men who served it in life and kills them, transforming them into ghouls (if the darkling returns as a ghast) or wights (if it is a wraith). Thus, its evil band will again plague the lands.

Doom Guard

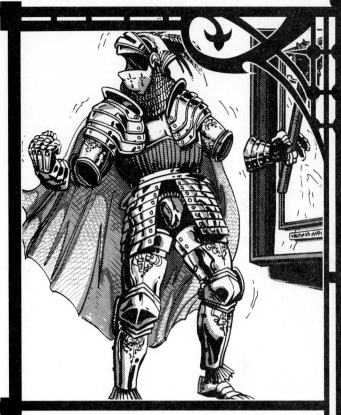

CLIMATE/TERRAIN:	Any castle or ruin
FREQUENCY:	Rare
ORGANIZATION:	Solitary
ACTIVITY CYCLE:	Any
DIET:	Nil
INTELLIGENCE:	Low (5–7)
TREASURE:	Nil
ALIGNMENT:	Neutral

NO. APPEARING:	1–6
ARMOR CLASS:	2
MOVEMENT:	9
HIT DICE:	5
THAC0:	15
NO. OF ATTACKS:	1
DAMAGE/ATTACK:	1d8 (by weapon)
SPECIAL ATTACKS:	Nil
SPECIAL DEFENSES:	See below
MAGIC RESISTANCE:	Nil
SIZE:	M (6′ tall)
MORALE:	Fearless (20)
XP VALUE:	2,000

Originally nothing more than a suit of armor, the doom guard is now an animated creature similar in nature to a golem. Created by a series of arcane enchantments, these frightening automatons are often used as guards in the castles and towers of those who create them. Doom guards are found in both western and eastern (oriental) styles as well as a variety of others.

Doom guards never speak and, thus, have no language of their own. They are able to obey simple commands from their creator, but these are generally limited to one or two rudimentary concepts. Typical orders include "Stay in this room and attack anyone but me who enters," or "Kill each person who opens this chest until I tell you otherwise."

Combat: Doom guards are unsubtle and straightforward opponents. When their instructions call for them to engage in combat, they simply move toward their intended target and strike with their weapons. Subtle planning can often enable a party to outwit doom guards without having to battle them one-on-one.

Most doom guards are armed with some manner of sword, axe, or bludgeon. In almost every case their blows with these weapons will inflict 1 to 8 (1d8) points of damage. In rare cases (about 1 in 10), they are equipped with heavier or lighter weapons (50% chance of either) and can inflict 1d10 or 1d6 points of damage respectively.

Doom guards are not undead, although they are often mistaken for creatures of this type. They cannot be turned or affected by spells that are intended for use against the living dead (*control undead*, etc.)

Spells such as *charm, hold, sleep,* or other mind-affecting magics have no power over doom guards because of their mindless nature. Similarly, the fact that they are not true living beings makes them immune to spells that depend on biological function (*cause light wounds* or *cause blindness*, for example). For like reasons, poisons do not harm them.

Heat- and cold-based attacks inflict only half damage to doom guards, with successful saving throws (when applicable) indicating that no harm is done. Lightning- or electricity-based spells inflict full damage when used against these unnatural foes. A *transmute metal to wood* or *crystalbrittle* spell is instantly fatal to doom guards, transforming them and destroying the delicate balances of the spells that keep them animated.

Habitat/Society: Clearly, doom guards are not natural creatures and have no society. They dwell only in those places where they have been created and stationed, and have no means of reproducing themselves.

Ecology: The creation of a doom guard is an interesting process, for it runs contrary to the idea of an "enchanted suit of armor." The reason for this is simply that the suit of armor is never actually subjected to a spell cast directly upon it. Rather, the doom guard is fashioned using an enchanted *anvil of darkness*, and it is this device that gives the creature its magical aura.

The first step in the creation of an *anvil of darkness* is the building of the *anvil* itself. The raw materials used in the creation of this object must be attained from the body of a slain iron golem. When the *anvil* is cast, it must have either a *scarab versus golems* (of any type) or a pristine, unread *Manual of Golems* set at its heart. Before the hot metal of the *anvil* cools, it must be enchanted by a powerful wizard. The first step in this enchantment is the weaving of an *enchant an item* spell over the anvil to make it ready for further wizardry. A *fabricate* spell is cast next, in order to the give the *anvil* the creative essence that will be so important to it in later years. Subsequently, a binding spell is employed to capture the last essences of the spirit that once animated the anvil in its iron golem form. Finally, a *permanency* spell is used to bind these magics into a single, cohesive enchantment that will enable the *anvil* to carry out its function.

Once the *anvil of darkness* is created, it can be used by a skilled armorer to create one doom guard every 20 weeks. Once work on a specific doom guard is begun, the armorer must work at least 8 hours out of 24 on his creation. Work cannot be halted or delayed for any reason or the enchanting process fails. The raw materials must be discarded and the work begun anew. The *anvil* is unaffected by this failure.

Doppleganger Plant

	Doppleganger Plant	Podling
CLIMATE/TERRAIN:	Any warm, temperate land	
FREQUENCY:	Very rare	Very rare
ORGANIZATION:	Patch	Band
ACTIVITY CYCLE:	Any	Any
DIET:	Special	Nil
INTELLIGENCE:	Genius (17–18)	Genius (17–18)
TREASURE:	Nil	Varies
ALIGNMENT:	Chaotic evil	Chaotic evil
NO. APPEARING:	1 or 2	1–20
ARMOR CLASS:	10 (vines) or 6 (pods)	Varies
MOVEMENT:	Nil	Varies
HIT DICE:	11–18	Varies
THAC0:	Nil	Varies
NO. OF ATTACKS:	1	Varies
DAMAGE/ATTACK:	0	Varies
SPECIAL ATTACKS:	Mind bondage	Varies
SPECIAL DEFENSES:	See below	Varies
MAGIC RESISTANCE:	Nil	Varies
SIZE:	G (10' wide/hp)	M (6' tall)
MORALE:	Fanatic (17–18)	Fanatic (17–18)
XP VALUE:	25,000	Varies

The origins of this horrific plant are utterly unknown, as is much important information about it. The reasons for this are numerous, but center around the difficulty of coming into contact with the creature to study it and living to record one's observations.

In appearance, the doppleganger plant looks much like any of a variety of melon-bearing crops. It spreads out in a tangle of vines and broad, glossy leaves. Scattered throughout its mass are a number (1 per Hit Die) of pods, each measuring between 4 and 8 feet long. These pods are the source of the wicked creature's intelligence. They also serve as its main form of self defense, as they are able to dominate the minds of others and make them serve the plant's will.

The doppleganger plant cannot communicate with those it does not control, but is able to instantly exchange information and instructions with those it has taken over. In this manner, the doppleganger plant knows and experiences all that its minions do and see.

Combat: The doppleganger plant itself is unable to attack or defend itself except with its unusual *mind bondage* power. Thus, in physical combat, it depends on its minions to fight for it.

Doppleganger plant patches are unusually resistant to fire and lightning, suffering only half damage from all flame- or electricity-based attacks. Cold-based attacks do normal damage, as do most other forms of magical attack. Weapons employed against the plant's vines and leaves inflict but 1 point of damage per successful attack roll, but those directed against the pods themselves inflict normal damage.

Only 20% of the creature's hit points are represented by the tangle of vines and leaves that makes up the majority of its mass. The remaining hit points are divided evenly among each of its pods. Destruction of all the hit points in the vines does not kill the plant, but gives it the appearance of being slain. Conversely, destruction of the pods without the elimination of the vines and leaves will not kill the plant either. Thus, many doppleganger plants that are left for dead eventually sprout up again, to reap their harvest of horror anew.

Once each round, the doppleganger plant can attempt to use its *mind bondage* power on any sleeping or unconscious creature within a 1-mile-per-Hit-Die radius of its patch. The intended victim is located via mystical means and the plant need not be able to see its target; neither does the plant have to be aware of its victim's existence prior to the use of this power. Although this power may be employed any number of times per day, only one new slave may be obtained in a given 24-hour period. Thus, once the plant has taken control of another creature, it cannot dominate a second being for at least one full day.

The *mind bondage* power of the doppleganger plant acts much like a combined *trap the soul* and *domination* spell. Victims of the *mind bondage* attack are entitled to a saving throw vs. spell to avoid its affects. Success indicates that they have escaped the influence of the doppleganger plant but are aware that something evil has just tried to attack their minds. Elves and half-elves have the same resistance to this power that they do to *charm* spells, as do all other races with similar defenses. Those who fail their saving throws become podlings (see below). Once a being becomes a podling, it can go anywhere (even crossing over to another plane of existence) and still be in instant contact with and under the absolute control of the plant that created it.

Habitat/Society: Doppleganger plants are found only in warm, moist climates and generally appear after some natural prophecy of doom (usually a comet or a meteor shower) has shown itself in the heavens. The connection between these two events has never been fully understood.

The doppleganger plant apparently feeds upon its podlings and thus is constantly seeking new ones to enslave. Because there is no range restriction on the plant's power to control its minions, it will often send them abroad in an effort to lure more victims into its grasp. It is not unknown for whole towns to fall beneath the shroud of evil spread by a single one of these creatures.

In cases where more than one plant is encountered, they will often cooperate. These highly intelligent creatures have never been known to turn against each other, despite their foul alignments. A pair of doppleganger plants working in concert will often use their agents in seemingly conflicting roles to keep potential victims off balance until they can be defeated.

Doppleganger plants have been known to allow some of their minions to be destroyed without true resistance. In much the same way that a masterful chess player will sacrifice a pawn to take a more valuable piece, the doppleganger plant will often arrange for one of its lesser minions to be lost in order to improve the position of one of its other puppets. ("Don't be silly, Derodd can't be a podling—she's the one who discovered that two of the town guards were acting under *mind bondage*, remember?")

Ecology: Doppleganger plants sustain themselves by drawing away the vital essences of their podlings (see below). They require nothing else (not even sunlight or water) to survive. Their appearance only in warm and temperate regions remains a mystery, but may be linked more to reasons of comfort than environmental need.

The sap from a doppleganger plant's vines as well as the flesh from the inside of its pods have both proven to be useful in the creation of magical potions and devices that influence the minds of others in some way. In many cases, the latter material results in the creation of magical powers twice as great as those found in devices crafted with other materials. Thus, a *potion of human control* created with the heart of a doppleganger pod allows the imbiber to control a total of no fewer than 64 levels or Hit Dice worth of humans or demihumans.

Podlings

These tragic creatures are the victims of a doppleganger plant's *mind bondage* spell. In addition to providing the plant with nourishment at the cost of their own life essences, podlings also act as the plant's eyes and hands. Although podlings are mentally dominated by the plants they serve, their actions are in no way stiff or unnatural. Any casual observer will almost certainly assume that there is nothing unusual about the podling.

A podling is created when the life force of a being under *mind bondage* is drawn into one of the plant's pods, where it remains until that pod is destroyed. Any given pod's hit points are determined as described above, and any pod that is destroyed will release the soul trapped within it. Freed spirits will attempt to return to their bodies. This can be done only if the body has not been slain or destroyed and requires the character in question to make a resurrection survival check. This counts toward the number of times a character can be resurrected and is handled in all ways as if it were an actual resurrection attempt. A successful return to the body leaves the character dazed and helpless for roughly one hour while he throws off the effects of the imprisonment.

A podling retains all knowledge and abilities it had in its previous existence, but now serves the needs of the doppleganger plant exclusively. It is no longer alive in the sense that

it once was. Any basic medical check will reveal no respiration (except as needed to speak or smell), no heart beat, and no response of the pupils to light. Similarly, podlings have no need (or desire) to eat, drink, or sleep. It is through these differences that they are most often found out when they move among men. However, the average person has only a 10% chance per hour spent with the podling of noticing anything amiss about it. Even then, only those who knew the individual before it was enslaved have a chance of detecting something specifically wrong. ("Derodd didn't want any chocolates? Strange, I've never known her to turn one down before.")

In addition, podlings usually weigh far less than they did when they were "alive." This factor can be accidentally or purposefully discovered by those with whom a podling comes into contact. Starting 24 hours after it has been placed under *mind bondage* by the doppleganger plant, a podling will begin to waste away. They will lose 1d4 hit points a day as the plant feeds upon their essences. This wasting occurs at the center of the body and gradually works its way outward with all manner of tissues, bones, and bodily fluids being consumed. When the podling finally dies from the feedings of its master, it will be nothing more than a hollow shell of flesh with some muscle tissue and subcutaneous fat. The creature gradually becomes lighter as more and more of its mass is absorbed by the plant. Thus, for every 25% of its hit points lost to the plant, the podling weighs 20% less than it did before its transformation. A 200-pound man would, therefore, be reduced to a shell weighing only 40 pounds (20% of its original weight) when he finally died.

Anyone fighting a podling with a slashing or piercing weapon has a 5% chance per hit point inflicted upon it of noticing something unusual about the creature. Following that, there is a 10% chance per point of damage inflicted on subsequent rounds of discovering that the podling is partially hollowed out. If the attacker has no reason to suspect that this is the case, he will be forced to make a horror check as soon as the truth about the creature is uncovered. Any examination of the corpse of a podling killed with such weapons will instantly reveal the nature of the beast.

When called upon to defend the doppleganger plant, the podling will not hesitate. It draws upon all of the knowledge and power it had prior to its transformation (including spells, special abilities, or familiarity with the enemy's tactics, weaknesses, and capabilities) to defeat the enemies of the plant. Thus, the actual statistics used for an individual podling will vary greatly. Most, however, are ordinary men, women, and demihumans who have fallen under the influence of the evil doppleganger plant.

Podlings will often lure unsuspecting victims within range of the plant's *mind bondage* spell. They will then attempt to knock the victims unconscious or convince them to sleep so that new podlings can be created.

Elemental, Ravenloft

General Information

Ravenloft elementals are not dissimilar to their more mundane cousins. However, they are created because of an unusual interaction between the Mists of Ravenloft and the fabric of the elemental planes. Thus, they tend to absorb some of the dark aspects common throughout the land and take on an aura of the macabre not found in elementals elsewhere.

Unlike true elementals, those formed in conjunction with the mists have no native plane to return to when their tasks in Ravenloft are done. The essences that animate them, however, are found in the mists that surround the dark domains of Ravenloft. Like true elementals, they can exist outside of the mists only in a shell of material drawn from the environment into which they are summoned.

As a rule, elementals are not very intelligent. They are aware, however, that they have been snatched away from their normal lives and forced into physical shells to do the bidding of another creature. As such, they are foul-tempered and violent when encountered and will seek, if possible, to avenge themselves upon their summoner (see below).

Combat: All Ravenloft elementals share a number of common features, many of which apply to combat situations. First, they are harmed only by magical +2 or better weapons. Similarly, creatures with fewer than 4 Hit Dice and no magical abilities are unable to harm an elemental in any way. Thus, a band of goblins would be helpless to fend off the attacks of an elemental unless they had access to a +2 or better weapon.

Unlike normal elementals, Ravenloft elementals are not held off by spells like *protection from evil* that ward off extraplanar creatures, for they are on their own plane in Ravenloft. In addition, the fact that many spells intended for use against elemental creatures function differently in Ravenloft than they do in other realms makes these creatures doubly difficult to overcome.

All elementals are immune to attacks that draw on their basic natural element to inflict damage. Thus, a pyre elemental (which is a variant fire elemental) is unharmed by spells like *fireball*, and a grave elemental would remain unharmed by a *transmute rock to mud spell.*

Summoning an Elemental

There are three ways by which an elemental can be called into existence (conjured or summoned) by a wizard. These are detailed in the basic Elementals entry and will not be repeated here. The following information, however, supersedes the data presented earlier and applies only to the conjuration of elementals in Ravenloft. Much of this information is collected from various points in the RAVENLOFT Campaign Setting.

The dark powers of Ravenloft restrict the free travel of planar creatures into and out of their domain. Thus, any attempt to summon a traditional elemental (air, earth, fire, or water) has a 20% chance of creating a Ravenloft elemental instead. If the materials needed to form such a creature are not close at hand, the dark powers provide them. Ravenloft elementals summoned by accident cannot be controlled by their conjurer and will be free-willed, angry forces when they arrive. For additional information on this, see "Controlling an Elemental" below.

Although most appearances of Ravenloft elementals are the result of a failed attempt to conjure a traditional elemental, this is not always the case. A specific attempt to conjure a Ravenloft elemental is possible, provided the caster has the materials required to form the creature's shell (soil from a grave, a funeral pyre, etc.). In fact, it is only through the purposeful summoning of a Ravenloft elemental that such a creature can be controlled by its conjurer. Such deliberate uses of the dark powers of Ravenloft require a Ravenloft powers check by the summoner, with the level of the check being determined by the purpose for which the summoned creature is used.

In all other ways, the process of conjuring an elemental in Ravenloft is similar to that employed elsewhere.

Controlling an Elemental

As stated in the basic elemental entry, absolute concentration is required to control a summoned elemental. In Ravenloft, however, it is even more difficult to control elementals than it is in other planes. Because of this, all conjured elementals receive a saving throw versus spell at –2 to escape control on the round they arrive in Ravenloft. If this spell fails, they are not allowed another attempt unless a new person tries to take control of them (see below). Ravenloft elementals that are conjured by accident are automatically uncontrolled (or free-willed).

A free-willed elemental will use its first action to attempt a return to its home 25% of the time. Otherwise, it will attack the character that conjured it. Since escaping from Ravenloft is not easy, those elementals who attempt to leave instantly will fail and will then turn on their creator as well.

Spells like *dismissal* or *banishment* do not work the same way in Ravenloft that they do in other domains. The exact effects of these and other spells are described in the RAVENLOFT Campaign Setting, but it should suffice to say that they are seldom able to send a summoned elemental out of Ravenloft.

In all other ways, control of elementals is handled the same way that it is in other realms. The exception to this, obviously, is that a summoned elemental cannot return to its home plane (as most will do after no more than 3 rounds of combat). Trapped in Ravenloft, they will do everything in their power to destroy those who brought them into that place.

A Ravenloft elemental that is successfully controlled will, of course, break free of the caster's influence at the end of the duration of a conjuration spell. Since it is unable to return to its home at this time, it will become free-willed (see below).

Stealing Control of an Elemental

This is handled just as it is with normal elementals, save for one thing. Any successful attempt to break another's control of an elemental allows it to make a new saving throw (albeit with a –2 penalty) to avoid the control of its new master.

Free-willed Ravenloft Elementals

A free-willed Ravenloft elemental will seek to destroy the one who created it, for only by so doing can it be freed from servitude. As soon as the conjurer is slain, the Ravenloft elemental dissipates, ending any threat it might pose to others. If the summoner flees the area, it will find itself stalked by the monster until one or the other is destroyed. Because of the bond created between the two beings at the time of the summoning, the elemental will always know the location of its intended victim and can follow him no matter where he goes or what wards he erects around himself.

	Blood	Grave
CLIMATE/TERRAIN:	Any Ravenloft	Any Ravenloft graveyard
FREQUENCY:	Very rare	Very rare
ORGANIZATION:	Solitary	Solitary
ACTIVITY CYCLE:	Any	Any
DIET:	Special	Special
INTELLIGENCE:	Low (5–7)	Low (5–7)
TREASURE:	Nil	Nil
ALIGNMENT:	Neutral	Neutral
NO. APPEARING:	1	1
ARMOR CLASS:	0	0
MOVEMENT:	12	6
HIT DICE:	8, 12, or 16	8, 12, or 16
THAC0:	8 HD: 13	8 HD: 13
	12 HD: 9	12 HD: 9
	16 HD: 5	16 HD: 5
NO. OF ATTACKS:	1	1
DAMAGE/ATTACK:	3d6	4d10
SPECIAL ATTACKS:	See below	Sink
SPECIAL DEFENSES:	See below	See below
MAGIC RESISTANCE:	Nil	Nil
SIZE:	——— 8 HD: L (8′ tall) ———	
	———12 HD: L (12′ tall) ———	
	———16 HD: L (16′ tall) ———	
MORALE:	——— 8 HD: Champion (15–16)	
	———12 HD: Champion (15–16)	
	———16 HD: Fanatic (17–18) —	
XP VALUE:	8 HD: 3,000	8 HD: 3,000
	12 HD: 7,000	12 HD: 7,000
	16 HD: 11,000	16 HD: 11,000

Blood Elementals

A blood elemental can be called forth only from a large quantity of blood or from water drawn from the lungs of drowned men. Because of the difficulty in obtaining these materials, they are the rarest of the Ravenloft elementals.

A blood elemental apears as a roughly humanoid creature composed entirely of blood. Blood dries in a trail behind it, and the air around it reeks with the scent of iron. A pair of fluid tentacles whip about the creature, enabling it to manipulate objects and attack enemies.

Combat: A blood elemental will attack in one of two ways. The first and most common means of attack is a blow from one of its tentacles. Each such strike inflicts 3d6 points of damage. Further, the victim of such an attack must make a successful saving throw versus spell or have a portion of his own blood drawn from his body and added to that of the elemental. The amount of blood lost in this way is equal to the damage done by the initial blow. Thus, an attack that inflicts 12 points of damage is followed by a potential blood drain that inflicts an additional 12 points of damage. Hit points lost to the blood drain are added directly to the elemental's own hit point total (to a maximum of 8 hit points per Hit Die). When striking at a target that has no blood of its own (a golem, say), the blood elemental cannot employ its blood drain attack and suffers a –2 penalty per die on all damage rolls (to a minimum of 1 point per die).

In any round that the elemental chooses not to attack, it may attempt to smother an opponent. To do so, the elemental makes a normal attack roll to hurl itself onto the target of the attack. If it succeeds, the victim of the attack must make a successful saving throw versus death magic or find that the elemental has filled his nose, mouth, and lungs with blood. The victim of this attack has a very good chance of drowning

(as described in the AD&D *Player's Handbook*). On the next round, the elemental is free to move away from this victim and attack another character, leaving the first target for dead. Attacks on the elemental while it is smothering do full damage to the elemental and half damage to the victim (who is unable to lash out at the elemental while being smothered).

Curiously, although they are a variant on water elementals, blood elementals are unable to enter or cross open water. If forced into such a situation, they begin to dissipate—suffering 1d10 points of damage per round—until such time as they break contact with the water.

Grave Elemental

The grave elemental is a variant earth elemental drawn from the soil of a graveyard or similar resting place of the dead. It appears as a towering, man-shaped mass of earth studded with bones and the shattered remnants of coffins.

Combat: A grave elemental cannot travel through water but can move effortlessly through earth and stone. It often uses this ability to lurk beneath the surface of the ground while would-be victims draw near. When they are right above it, it explodes upward and attacks, imposing a –4 penalty on all surprise rolls made by its adversaries.

When grave elementals engage in combat, their preferred means of attack is simply a blow from their mighty fists. The damage they inflict with such an attack is dependent on their size, with 8 HD elementals delivering 4d8 points of damage, 12 HD elementals causing 4d10 points of damage, and the massive 16 HD elementals inflicting a crushing 4d12 points of damage.

Grave elementals are less effective when striking at targets who are air- or waterborne. Obviously, they cannot employ their *sink* power (see below) against such creatures, and any physical damage they inflict on them is reduced by 2 points per die (to a minimum of 1 point per die).

In lieu of attacking with brute force, they may employ a magical power that functions as the *sink* spell of a wizard

21

Elemental, Ravenloft

	Mist	Pyre
CLIMATE/TERRAIN:	Any Ravenloft	Any Ravenloft land
FREQUENCY:	Very rare	Very rare
ORGANIZATION:	Solitary	Solitary
ACTIVITY CYCLE:	Any	Any
DIET:	Special	Special
INTELLIGENCE:	Low (5–7)	Low (5–7)
TREASURE:	Nil	Nil
ALIGNMENT:	Neutral	Neutral
NO. APPEARING:	1	1
ARMOR CLASS:	0	0
MOVEMENT:	Fl 36 (A)	12
HIT DICE:	8, 12, or 16	8, 12, or 16
THAC0:	8 HD: 13	8 HD: 13
	12 HD: 9	12 HD: 9
	16 HD: 5	16 HD: 5
NO. OF ATTACKS:	1	1
DAMAGE/ATTACK:	2d10	3d8
SPECIAL ATTACKS:	Infuse evil	See below
SPECIAL DEFENSES:	See below	See below
MAGIC RESISTANCE:	Nil	Nil
SIZE:	8 HD: L (8′ dia.)	8 HD: L (8′ tall)
	12 HD: L (12′ dia.)	12 HD: L (12′ tall)
	16 HD: H (16′ dia.)	16 HD: H (16′ tall)
MORALE:	——8 HD: Champion (15–16) ——	
	——12 HD: Champion (15–16) ——	
	——16 HD: Fanatic (17–18) ——	
XP VALUE:	8 HD: 4,000	8 HD: 3,000
	12 HD: 8,000	12 HD: 7,000
	16 HD: 12,000	16 HD: 12,000

(. . . continued from previous page)

whose level is equal to their Hit Dice. They may cast this spell but once per hour and may only use it against creatures or objects standing on an earthen or stone surface. Although this is an innate power and has no casting time or components, the elemental is unable to undertake any other action in the round that it attempts to *sink* an opponent.

Grave elementals share the earth elemental's ability to lash out at buildings with earthen or stone foundations. Their attacks against such structures can be devastating and are far more effective than those made by other creatures of similar power due to the elemental's affinity for the building materials used.

Mist Elemental

A mist elemental is a relative of the traditional air elemental who has been formed from the essences of the Ravenloft Mists themselves. Once conjured, the mist elemental appears as a drifting cloud of white vapor that looks like nothing more than a patch of fog. Because of this, a mist elemental moving about in a region of fog or mist is treated as if it were invisible.

Combat: When a mist elemental chooses to attack, it does so with its chilling, evil touch. Moving with a speed one would never expect from a being that seems to drift about at the mercy of the wind, the elemental moves toward (and then through) its target. In so doing, the creature has the ability to employ one of two attack modes. The first is a simple, straightforward attack that inflicts 2d20 points of damage from the creature's chilling presence.

In lieu of inflicting damage, however, the mist elemental may seek to *infuse evil* into the victim. When it does so, the creature seems to enter the body of the victim and then pass

on through it without harm. However, anyone subject to such an attack must successfully save vs. spell or suffer an alignment shift to chaotic evil. In addition, a character who has been infused is also *charmed* by the elemental and will not act against it. The elemental may not infuse evil twice in a row. That is, it may not *infuse evil* again until after it attacks and attempts to inflict damage. This attack may be against the same character or another one. All of the normal penalties associated with an involuntary alignment change are in effect following an attack by a mist elemental. In order to regain their original alignment and break the *charm* upon them, infused characters must receive a *remove curse* spell cast by an individual of their true alignment.

Pyre Elementals

The wild and dancing pyre elemental is drawn from the flames of a funeral pyre or some large burning associated with a burial rite. A pyre elemental appears as a slender column of intense flame with tendrils of fire licking away from it like the waving arms of a dancer.

Combat: A pyre elemental attacks those it encounters with unmatched savagery, taking delight in the destruction and death it causes. Anyone who is struck by one of the lashing streams of fire that it wields whiplike in combat suffers 3d8 points of damage. Their armor (including shields and magical items of protection) must make item saving throws vs. magical fire. Suits of armor that fail their saves lose one level of AC. Thus, a suit of brigandine armor that fails its saving throw is reduced from AC 6 to AC 7. AC-enhancing shields and magical devices that fail their saves are destroyed.

CLIMATE/TERRAIN:	Any Borca
FREQUENCY:	Rare
ORGANIZATION:	Solitary
ACTIVITY CYCLE:	Any
DIET:	Omnivore
INTELLIGENCE:	Very (11–12)
TREASURE:	W (I)
ALIGNMENT:	Lawful evil

NO. APPEARING:	1
ARMOR CLASS:	10
MOVEMENT:	15
HIT DICE:	4
THAC0:	17
NO. OF ATTACKS:	1
DAMAGE/ATTACK:	Special
SPECIAL ATTACKS:	See below
SPECIAL DEFENSES:	See below
MAGIC RESISTANCE:	Nil
SIZE:	M (6′ tall)
MORALE:	Champion (15–16)
XP VALUE:	650

The ermordenung are a dark and evil people found almost exclusively in the domain of Borca. Here, they act as elite agents of Ivana Boritsi, the ruler of that dread domain. On rare occasions, they are sent on missions outside of Borca to further the interests of their mistress.

Ermordenung appear as normal human beings of surpassing attractiveness. The men are tall, normally no less than six feet in height, and smoothly muscled. They seem to radiate an inner power from their finely set, classical features. The women are tall, often only an inch or two shorter than the men, and have the perfect features that every artist tries to create. Both sexes are marked by raven hair and penetrating dark eyes that, it is said, are almost hypnotic. Their complexion, however, is rather more pale than that common to most of the people in Borca and contrasts greatly with their dark hair and eyes.

The ermordenung speak the common language of the people of Borca. Their dialect, however, is marked by an aristocratic manner and they carry themselves with a noble bearing that sets them apart from all but the ruling family.

Combat: In combat, an ermordenung will attempt to grasp an exposed area of flesh on an opponent's body so that its deadly touch can do its work. Any successful attack roll indicates that the target has been touched and must save vs. poison (with a +4 bonus on their roll). The effects of the ermordenung toxins are felt within seconds—those who fail their saves are instantly slain, while those who succeed suffer 10 points of damage.

If the attack roll is a natural 20, the ermordenung has managed to get a firm grip on his enemy. In such cases, the victim must make a saving throw vs. poison (with no modifiers). While failure to save still results in death, success indicates that 20 points of damage are inflicted. Targets unable to pull free of the grip (see below) are subject to the same saving throw each round until they are slain or they escape.

In noncombat situations, the ermordenung will often use their great physical beauty and overwhelming charisma to lure would-be victims of the opposite sex close. Once their victims are at ease, they draw them into a deadly embrace and slay the hapless souls with their toxic kiss. Victims of this "kiss of death" are entitled to a saving throw vs. poison (with a –4 penalty to their die roll). As usual, failure indicates

instant death. Success, on the other hand, indicates that the victim suffers 30 points of damage. Those who survive this horrid attack may attempt to break free of the embrace (see below), but will be kissed again on the next round if they fail to do so.

Breaking the grasp or embrace of an ermordenung is very difficult, for they are considered to have an 18/90 strength if male or an 18/50 strength if female. Weaker enemies must make a successful saving throw versus paralysis (with a –4 penalty to their roll) in order to pull away from their attackers. Those of equal strength need only make a successful unmodified save, while those who are stronger than the ermordenung must save successfully with a +4 bonus to their roll.

Ermordenung are immune to nearly all forms of toxins themselves. The only variety to which they have no natural resistance is that of their peers—any ermordenung is as vulnerable to the deadly touch of its own kind as a normal man.

Habitat/Society: The ermordenung live as members of the ruling elite in Borca. They seldom mix with "the common folk" unless acting on behalf of their mistress, Ivana Boritsi.

The fact that the ermordenung cannot touch another living creature without causing it to wither and die causes them endless heartache. They have been forever denied the physical pleasures—the caress of a lover's hand, the embrace of a close friend, the affectionate hug of a child—that mean so much to mortal men. Their inner suffering and agony has been marshaled to make them cruel and heartless agents who carry out the orders of Ivana Boritsi without question.

Ecology: The ermordenung are normal humans who have been transformed, at the command of Ivana Boritsi, mistress of Borca, into nightmarish creatures. The process by which these creatures are created is dark and mysterious, but is believed to be so brutal to its subjects that only the most physically fit can survive it. Because of her own passionate nature, Ivana Boritsi selects only the most physically beautiful of her people for the "honor" of transformation.

Ghoul Lord

CLIMATE/TERRAIN:	Any land
FREQUENCY:	Very rare
ORGANIZATION:	Solitary
ACTIVITY CYCLE:	Night
DIET:	Corpses
INTELLIGENCE:	High (13–14)
TREASURE:	Q, R, S, T, (B)
ALIGNMENT:	Chaotic evil

NO. APPEARING:	1
ARMOR CLASS:	4
MOVEMENT:	15
HIT DICE:	6
THAC0:	15
NO. OF ATTACKS:	3
DAMAGE/ATTACK:	1d6/1d6/1d10
SPECIAL ATTACKS:	Paralysis, disease
SPECIAL DEFENSES:	Evil aura
MAGIC RESISTANCE:	Nil
SIZE:	M (6′ tall)
MORALE:	Elite (13–14)
XP VALUE:	3,000

It is hard to imagine a more frightening creature than the dreaded ghoul lord. Lurking in places thick with the stench of death, the ghoul lord feasts upon the flesh of living and dead alike, often surrounding itself with a band of lesser undead that obey its every command.

The ghoul lord looks much like the common ghoul or ghast. It retains some semblance of its human form, but its skin has turned the sickly gray of rotting meat, its tongue has grown long and rasped, and its teeth and nails have become sharp and wicked instruments ideal for rending flesh and cracking bone.

Ghoul lords can speak the languages they knew prior to their death and transformation into the undead. When commanding their ghoul and ghast minions, however, they do not speak, but employ a telepathic sense that defies mortal languages.

Combat: The ghoul lord looks so much like a ghoul that it is 90% likely that it will be mistaken for such a creature even by those familiar with the undead. The true nature of these beasts becomes apparent, however, as soon as they spring into combat.

When a ghoul lord strikes with its long, cruel claws it inflicts 1d6 points of damage with each blow that lands. In addition, it can also bite with its deadly teeth, scoring 1d10 points of damage with each hit. Those hit by the creature's claws must save vs. paralysis or become unable to move for 1d6+6 rounds. Even elves are not immune to this effect.

The bite of a ghoul lord causes the victim to contract a horrible rotting disease unless a successful saving throw vs. poison is made. Those afflicted with this illness lose 1d10 hit points and 1 point from their Constitution and Charisma scores each day. If either ability score or their hit point totals reach 0, they die. If the body is not destroyed, they will rise as a ghast on the third night after their death. In such a state, they are wholly under the command of the creature that made them until such time as that horror is destroyed. At that point, they become free-willed creatures.

The rotting disease can be cured by nothing less than a *heal* spell. Once the progression of the disease is halted, the victim's Constitution score will return to its original value at the rate of 1 point per week. Their Charisma, however, will remain at its reduced level because of the horrible scars this ailment leaves on both body and soul.

Like other undead of their ilk, ghoul lords are immune to the effects of *sleep* and *charm* spells. They are not harmed by holy water or by contact with holy symbols, but can be turned as if they were 7 HD monsters. Ghoul lords are immune to damage from all but magical weapons or those forged of pure iron. A *circle of protection* has no effect on these creatures unless pure iron is used in its casting. Even then, the ghoul lord has a 10% chance per round of overcoming the effects of the spell and striking freely at those allegedly protected by it.

Ghoul lords do not radiate the foul odor associated with ghasts, but they do fairly reek of evil. In fact, this effect is so potent that those of good alignment suffer a –4 on all attack rolls when within 30 feet of these creatures. In addition, all persons who are forced to make a fear or horror check because of an encounter with a ghoul lord must do so with a –2 penalty on their die roll because of the creature's evil nature. A *remove fear* spell negates the effects of this foul aura.

Habitat/Society: The ghoul lord is a foul creature found, thankfully, only in the demiplane of Ravenloft. It tends to dwell in isolated places rife with the odor of death; graveyards and ruins are its favorite haunts.

Ghoul lords always have a following of lesser undead with them. These minions act under telepathic command from the ghoul lord and are absolute in their loyalty to him. A ghoul lord's band comprises 2 to 12 (2d6) ghasts, each of which commands 2 to 8 (2d4) ghouls.

Ecology: Ghoul lords are unique to the demiplane of Ravenloft. It is rumored that they were first created at the hands of an insane necromancer in some other dimension, but that they were so evil as to instantly draw the attention of the dark powers. The Mists of Ravenloft absorbed all of the existing ghoul lords and scattered them across the domains.

There are those who insist that the necromancer has also been transported to Ravenloft and that it is his twisted soul that rules the Nightmare Lands. Of course, no proof of this has ever been found.

CLIMATE/TERRAIN:	Any
FREQUENCY:	Rare
ORGANIZATION:	Servant
ACTIVITY CYCLE:	Any
DIET:	Carnivore
INTELLIGENCE:	Low (5–7)
TREASURE:	Nil
ALIGNMENT:	Neutral evil

NO. APPEARING:	3–24 (3d8)
ARMOR CLASS:	4
MOVEMENT:	12
HIT DICE:	4+4
THAC0:	15
NO. OF ATTACKS:	2 or 1
DAMAGE/ATTACK:	1d6/1d6 or 2d6
SPECIAL ATTACKS:	Special
SPECIAL DEFENSES:	Nil
MAGIC RESISTANCE:	10%
SIZE:	M (4'–6')
MORALE:	Special/Fearless (20)
XP VALUE:	975

G oblyns are hideous creatures with slightly bloated heads, pointed ears, and glowing red eyes. Their long, mangy hair grows only on the back of their head and neck. A wide mouth full of needle-sharp teeth occupies nearly half a goblyn's face.

Powerful evil magical items and spells transform humans into these twisted beings. This transformation causes them to become very evil and totally submissive to their master's every whim.

Goblyns have a telepathic link with their master and, through him, with all of the other goblyns he controls.

Combat: Goblyns are very nimble creatures, causing a –2 adjustment to their opponent's surprise roll. Furthermore, when a goblyn is unexpectedly encountered, it flashes its teeth and leers at its opponent in a terribly frightening manner. A fear check is required the first time this sight is encountered. In any event, this action causes a –4 penalty to surprise. Those surprised will be so stricken with fear that they will be unable to move that round.

Goblyns seldom attack with weapons. Instead, they strike at their victim's throat with their clawed hands. Each successful claw attack inflicts 1d6 points of damage. If both claws hit, the goblyn is assumed to have gotten a solid hold on the target's neck. On each subsequent round, the victim will be bitten (usually in the face) for an additional 2 to 12 (2d6) points. In addition, the victim will have difficulty breathing and must make a successful saving throw versus spell or suffer an additional 1d4 points of suffocation damage. Both attacks are assumed to be automatic hits. The goblyns refer to this as "feasting," and it is so frightening to observe that all who see someone attacked in this manner must make a horror check.

In addition, for every 10 points of feasting damage done, the victim suffers a permanent –1 adjustment to Charisma due to facial scars and deformities.

Any attacks made by someone with a goblyn at his throat suffers a –3 penalty on all attack or damage rolls and saving throws. Others who are striking at a "feasting" goblyn gain a +2 on their attack and damage rolls while its attention is focused on its victim.

Goblyns are similar to undead creatures in that they never check morale.

All goblyns have the ability to move silently (80%), hide in shadows (70%), and climb walls (25%). They have infravision which functions at a range of 90 feet.

Habitat/Society: Goblyns are totally controlled by their master's desires. If they are told to attack another of their kind, they will do so without pity. They never instigate combat on their own, but eagerly leap to the attack if challenged or instructed to do so. Goblyns have no apparent desires other than to fulfill their master's every whim with an emotionless devotion.

Goblyns do not sleep, tire, or become bored. Furthermore, they can go for a considerable amount of time without food or drink.

Ecology: Goblyns are strict carnivores. They will eat only freshly killed meat, in addition to drinking the blood of their victims.

Goblyns are often sought after by certain wizards and priests, for they are useful as components in spells and magical items that control humans.

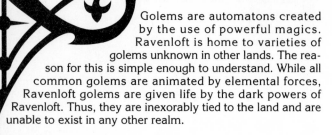

Golem, Ravenloft

Golems are automatons created by the use of powerful magics. Ravenloft is home to varieties of golems unknown in other lands. The reason for this is simple enough to understand. While all common golems are animated by elemental forces, Ravenloft golems are given life by the dark powers of Ravenloft. Thus, they are inexorably tied to the land and are unable to exist in any other realm.

Background

The origin of the first golems created in Ravenloft dates back to a time when the land itself was young. Their story is tied to the "lives" of two of Ravenloft's most powerful lords.

In the land of Barovia, Azalin (the current lord of Darkon) was engaged in magical studies under the yoke of Strahd Von Zarovich. At Strahd's command, he was examining a number of Strahd's minions—undead zombies and skeletons—who had been slain in mysterious ways. Strahd demanded to know who had done this and by what means. Azalin was able to give Strahd the information he wanted, but also learned something more. He found that there was some essence of life left in these fragmentary remains.

For the next several weeks, Azalin locked himself away in his laboratory, experimenting with powers he had never dealt with before. When Strahd sought him out and demanded to know what he was working on, Azalin answered honestly (if incompletely) and said that he had found something unusual in the mystical fabric of this demiplane that needed more study. Strahd, satisfied that this work was related to Azalin's assigned duties of finding an escape from Ravenloft, bade him continue and left the lich to his work. Azalin never related to Strahd the fact that he had learned how to create two new species of golem using the essences of Ravenloft.

When Azalin assumed his place as Lord of Darkon, he brought with him the knowledge of these new possibilities. Although he now found it impossible to learn new magical spells, he had already laid out the process required to create his new breeds of golem. Before long, he had produced the first zombie and bone golems ever created in the land.

In the years since that time, others have learned the secrets first unearthed by Azalin and used them to create new golems. Each is unique to Ravenloft, and all require the creator to make a mystical pact with the dark powers that, for many, has led to their final demise.

Common Characteristics

There are eight known varieties of Ravenloft golem, each with its own strengths and weaknesses. While these are described in detail on the following pages, they all share some common characteristics.

Ravenloft golems can be damaged in combat only by magical +2 or better weapons. They are immune to all manner of mind- or life-affecting spells (such as *charm, sleep, hold,* or *finger of death*) and cannot be harmed by poisons of any sort. They are all vulnerable to the effects of a *dispel magic*. If the caster of such a spell is equal to the level of the golem's creator, then the monster will collapse, seemingly dead, and be inanimate for a number of turns equal to the caster's level. A *dispel magic* cast on a "stunned" golem will reveal that it still has an aura of power about it and that it is gradually growing stronger as the monster "recharges" itself. If the caster of the *detect magic* is of a higher level than the golem's creator, however, the golem falls inanimate and is slain.

Lastly, the creation of any Ravenloft golem requires such close contact with the dark powers that a Ravenloft powers check is required for each month of research into or actual work on the fashioning of such a creation.

Theory

The creation of any manner of Ravenloft golem is a dark and dangerous process for the creature's master. The creature must be created with loving care and special magical spells woven over the body to bring it to life. The exact materials and magics required to create each type of golem are detailed below.

As with traditional golems, those fashioned with the aid of the dark powers of Ravenloft have a great hatred of all living things. They are kept in check only by the will of their creator, who faces death at their hands if they ever escape his domination and become free-willed creatures. While the spells used to create the golem usually enslave it so that it cannot refuse to obey its creator, there is a 10% chance that any Ravenloft golem will break free of that control. Thereafter, it will devote all of its time and energy to the destruction of its creator. Once a golem is created, it is entitled to a saving throw vs. spell once per month (on the full moon). Failure indicates that it must serve for another month, while success indicates that it has become free-willed.

The rituals to animate the body once it has been built require one full month (from full moon to full moon) and cannot be interrupted in any way or the entire enchantment process must be started anew. In all cases, the spells used may come from any source (including devices or scrolls). If a spell is cast on behalf of the golem's creator by a second individual, that spell must contain special alterations to make it sympathetic to the creature's intended master. There is no additional cost for these alterations.

Bone Golem

Only powerful wizards (of at least 18th level) can create these evil creatures. The body of a bone golem is assembled wholly from the bones of animated skeletons who have been defeated in combat. Any manner of skeletal undead will do, from traditional skeletons to Strahd skeletons, but all must have been created and slain in Ravenloft. Only 10% of the bones from any given skeleton can be used, so the final product is a compilation of bones from many creatures. Often, there will be animal, monster, and human bones in the same golem, giving the creature a nightmarish appearance.

Various spell components, costing a total of roughly 25,000 gold pieces, must be acquired and are consumed by the assembly process. The following spells are woven over the body: *animate dead, symbol of fear, binding,* and *wish*.

Doll Golem

Only a priest of at least 15th level can create a doll golem. These creatures resemble a child's toy—often a baby doll or stuffed animal. Doll golems can serve as either the guardians of children or as murdering things too foul to contemplate.

Construction of the doll's body takes only two weeks, but the cost of components and enchanted elements of the golem reaches 15,000 gold pieces. The spells needed to complete the animation are *imbue with spell ability, Tasha's uncontrollable hideous laughter, (un)holy word, bless,* and *prayer*.

The first known examples of this type of golem turned up in the land of Sanguinia in the hands of a traveling priest. While his name has been lost to memory, it is believed that he researched and built the doll to protect his wife and daughter as they traveled around this dark land. History does not record the final fate of that pilgrimage. It is rumored that the doll survived and still haunts the realms of Ravenloft today, but there is no solid evidence that this is the case.

Gargoyle Golem

This creature is fashioned in the image of a real gargoyle and is often placed as a warden atop a building, cathedral, or tomb. It is most similar to the stone golem, save that it is built only by priests of at least 16th level. The body must be carved from a single slab of granite (weighing 3,000 pounds and taking 2 months to complete) and prepared with components costing 75,000 gold pieces. Of this amount, 15,000 gold pieces pay for vestments that can be reused once, so a second golem could be created for only 60,000 gold pieces. The spells required to complete the process are *bless, exaction, (un)holy word, stone shape, conjure earth elemental,* and *prayer.*

The first gargoyle golem was fashioned at the command of Vlad Drakov, Lord of Falkovnia, as a means of defending his castle. Eventually, the secret of their construction leaked out and others began to build them. It is rumored that none of these creatures can attack Drakov, and even that they may all secretly serve him. This may or may not be true. Although none can report ever having seen Drakov challenged by such a creature, it seems unlikely, however.

Glass Golem

Fashioned by either priests or wizards (of at least 14th level), the glass golem is composed entirely of stained glass. Perhaps the most artistic of all the known Ravenloft golems, its creation takes 3 months and requires an outlay of 100,000 gold pieces. In addition to the materials required, the following spells must be used: *glassteel, animate object, prismatic spray, rainbow,* and *wish.* Because of the mixture of spells, this type of golem is usually built by multi- or dual-classed characters or with the aid of a powerful assistant.

While the origins of some types of Ravenloft golems are firmly established, the first appearance of glass golems is not recorded with certainty in any known record. It is believed that they were created by a spellcaster who fancied himself an artist (hence their eerie beauty), but the identity of that sorry individual cannot be guessed. Some say that he was the lord of a small domain (one of the so-called Islands of Terror) who died at the hands of a brave band of adventurers.

Mechanical Golem

A nightmare of technology, the mechanical golem is an intricate device that depends on both magic and machinery to operate. It is the only known manner of golem that can be built by any class of character, even those without spellcasting ability, if they meet the requirements listed below. Construction of the body requires a full year of work (with no more than 2 interruptions, each no longer than 30 days, permitted in that time) and an outlay of 125,000 gold pieces. Almost half of that money (60,000 gold pieces) is spent on the creation of a properly equipped laboratory, and additional golems may be built for only 65,000 gold pieces using this existing equipment. The person building the body must have an Intelligence score of not less than 16 and either experience with fine workmanship (training as a watchmaker) or a Dexterity score of not less than 17. In the animation of the golem, the following spells are required: *animate object, fabricate, grease, chain lightning,* and either *major creation* or *wish.*

The first of these horrors was created at the order of Easan the Mad, Lord of Vechor. A twisted man fascinated by technological devices, Easan is said to have foreseen the elements of this creature in a study of a falling star. While most doubt that this is anything but more proof of Easan's dementia, few can challenge the obvious conclusion that these evil creatures are a mix of sorcery and technology that must surely have come from the mind of a lunatic.

Zombie Golem

One of Azalin's two original Ravenloft zombies, these dark creatures can be created only by wizards of at least 16th level. They are fashioned from the body parts of animated corpses (zombies, animal zombies, Strahd zombies, etc.) that have fallen in combat. In many ways, they are similar to bone golems. As with bone golems, only 10% of any individual zombie's body will be suitable for reanimation, so the zombie golem will often be composed of parts from many types of zombies, making the construction look awkward and alien.

Sewing together the parts of the body requires a full month and an outlay of 50,000 gold pieces (all of which pays for items consumed in the animation process). The spells needed are *wish, polymorph any object, strength, control undead,* and *stinking cloud.*

Manuals of Ravenloft Golems

According to rumor, there are magical tomes that detail the procedures used in the creation of Ravenloft golems. Like the traditional *Manuals of Golems* found in other realms, each of these books describes how to fashion and animate one type of golem. In addition, the dark powers of Ravenloft favor the creation of these golems over their more mundane cousins, so that any *Manual of Golems* brought into Ravenloft has a 75% chance of transforming into a *Manual of Ravenloft Golems* when the tome enters Ravenloft. Such books do not revert to normal when removed from Ravenloft, but the creation of the golems they describe is not possible outside of that domain, making these tomes all but worthless in other lands. When a *Manual of Golems* is found in Ravenloft, roll percentile dice on the following table to determine the type of golem it can create:

Die Roll	Golem Type	Creator	Construction Time	GP Cost
01–20	Bone	Wizard	2 months	35,000
21–27	Clay	Priest	1 month	65,000
28–37	Doll	Priest	2 months	20,000
38–45	Flesh	Wizard	2 months	50,000
46–55	Gargoyle	Priest	4 months	100,000
56–63	Glass	Priest/Wizard	6 months	125,000
64–66	Iron	Wizard	4 months	100,000
67–76	Mechanical	Any	18 months	125,000
77–80	Stone	Wizard	3 months	80,000
81–00	Zombie	Priest	2 months	60,000

These works function as normal *Manuals of Golems* in all ways, except that the *Manual of Mechanical Golems* can be used by a character of any class so long as he meets the requirements listed in the "Mechanical Golem" text above.

Golem, Bone and Doll

	Bone	Doll
CLIMATE/TERRAIN:	Any	Any
FREQUENCY:	Very rare	Very rare
ORGANIZATION:	Solitary	Solitary
ACTIVITY CYCLE:	Any	Any
DIET:	Nil	Nil
INTELLIGENCE:	Non- (0)	Non- (0)
TREASURE:	Nil	Nil
ALIGNMENT:	Neutral	Neutral
NO. APPEARING:	1	1
ARMOR CLASS:	0	4
MOVEMENT:	12	15
HIT DICE:	14 (70 hp)	10 (40 hp)
THAC0:	7	11
NO. OF ATTACKS:	1	1
DAMAGE/ATTACK:	3d8	3d6
SPECIAL ATTACKS:	Laugh	Bite
SPECIAL DEFENSES:	Spell immunity	See below
MAGIC RESISTANCE:	Nil	Nil
SIZE:	M (6′ tall)	T (1′ tall)
MORALE:	Fearless (20)	Fearless (20)
XP VALUE:	18,000	7,000

Bone Golem

As already mentioned, the bone golem is built from the previously animated bones of skeletal undead. These horrors stand roughly 6 feet tall and weigh between 50 and 60 pounds. They are seldom armored and can easily be mistaken for undead, much to the dismay of those who make this error.

Combat: Bone golems are no more intelligent than other forms of golem, so they will not employ clever tactics or strategies in combat. Their great power, however, makes them far deadlier than they initially appear to be. There is a 95% chance that those not familiar with the true nature of their opponent will mistake them for simple undead.

Bone golems attack with their surprisingly strong blows and sharp, clawlike fingers. Each successful hit inflicts 3 to 24 (3d8) points of damage. They can never be made to use weapons of any sort in melee.

In addition to the common characteristics of all Ravenloft golems (described previously), bone golems take only half damage from those edged or piercing weapons that can harm them.

Bone golems are immune to almost all spells, but can be laid low with the aid of a *shatter* spell that is focused on them and has the capacity to affect objects of their weight. If such a spell is cast at a bone golem, the golem is entitled to a saving throw vs. spell to negate it. Failure indicates that weapons able to harm the golem will now inflict twice the damage they normally would. Thus, edged weapons would do full damage while blunt ones would inflict double damage.

Once every three rounds, the bone golem may throw back its head and issue a hideous laugh that causes all those who hear it to make fear and horror checks. Those who fail either check are paralyzed and cannot move for 2 to 12 rounds. Those who fail both checks are instantly stricken dead from fear.

Doll Golem

The doll golem is an animated version of a child's toy that can be put to either good uses (defending the young) or evil uses (attacking them). It is often crafted so as to make it appear bright and cheerful when at rest. Upon activation, however, its features become twisted and horrific.

Combat: The doll golem is, like all similar creatures, immune to almost all magical attacks. It can be harmed by fire-based spells, although these do only half damage, while a *warp wood* spell affects the creature as if it were a *slow* spell. A *mending* spell restores the creature to full hit points at once.

Each round, the doll golem leaps onto a victim and attempts to bite it. Success inflicts 3d6 points of damage and forces the victim to save versus spell. Failure to save causes the victim to begin to laugh uncontrollably (as if under the influence of a *Tasha's uncontrollable hideous laughter* spell) and become unable to perform any other action. The effects of the creature's bite are far worse, however. The victim begins to laugh on the round after the failed save. At this time, they take 1d4 points of damage from the muscle spasms imposed by the laughter. On following rounds, this increases to 2d4, then 3d4, and so on. The laughter stops when the character dies or receives a *dispel magic*. Following recovery, the victim suffers a penalty on all attack rolls and saving throws of −1 per round that they were overcome with laughter (e.g., four rounds of uncontrolled laughter would equal a −4 penalty on attack rolls/saving throws). This represents the weakness caused by the character's inability to breathe and is reduced by 1 point per subsequent turn until the character is fully recovered.

	Gargoyle	Glass
CLIMATE/TERRAIN:	Any	Any
FREQUENCY:	Very rare	Very rare
ORGANIZATION:	Solitary	Solitary
ACTIVITY CYCLE:	Any	Any
DIET:	Nil	Nil
INTELLIGENCE:	Non- (0)	Non- (0)
TREASURE:	Nil	Nil
ALIGNMENT:	Neutral	Neutral
NO. APPEARING:	1	1
ARMOR CLASS:	0	4
MOVEMENT:	9	12
HIT DICE:	15 (60 hp)	9 (40 hp)
THAC0:	5	11
NO. OF ATTACKS:	2	1
DAMAGE/ATTACK:	3d6/3d6	2d12
SPECIAL ATTACKS:	See below	See below
SPECIAL DEFENSES:	See below	See below
MAGIC RESISTANCE:	Nil	Nil
SIZE:	M (6' tall)	M (6' tall)
MORALE:	Fearless (20)	Fearless (20)
XP VALUE:	16,000	6,000

Gargoyle Golem

The gargoyle golem is a stone construct designed to guard a given structure. It is roughly the same size and weight as a real gargoyle (6 feet tall and 550 pounds). Although it is winged, it cannot fly. However, a gargoyle golem can leap great distances (up to 100 feet) and will often use this ability to drop down on enemies nearing any building protected by it.

Gargoyle golems cannot speak or communicate in any way. When they move, the sound of grinding rock is audible to anyone near them. In fact, it is often this noise that serves as a party's first warning that something is amiss in an area.

Combat: When a gargoyle golem attacks in melee combat, it does so with its two clawed fists. Each fist must attack the same target and inflicts 3d6 points of damage. Anyone hit by both attacks must successfully save versus petrification or be turned to stone. On the round after a gargoyle golem has petrified a victim, it attacks that same target again. Any hit scored by the golem against such a foe indicates that the stone body has shattered and cannot be resurrected. *Reincarnation*, on the other hand, is still a viable option.

Gargoyle golems are, like most golems, immune to almost every form of magical attack directed at them. They are, however, vulnerable to the effects of an *earthquake* spell. If such a spell is targeted directly at a gargoyle golem, it instantly shatters the creature without affecting the surrounding area. The lesser *transmute rock to mud* spell will inflict 2d10 points of damage to the creature while the reverse (*transmute mud to rock*) will heal a like amount of damage.

On the first round of any combat in which the gargoyle golem has not been identified for what it is, it has a good chance of gaining surprise (–2 on opponent surprise checks). Whenever a gargoyle golem attacks a character taken by surprise, it will leap onto that individual. The crushing weight of the creature delivers 4d10 points of damage and requires every object carried by that character in a vulnerable position (DM's decision) to successfully save vs. crushing blow or be destroyed. In the round that a gargoyle golem pounces on a character, it cannot attack with its fists.

Glass Golem

The glass golem is very nearly a work of art. Built in the form of a stained glass knight, the creature is often built into a window fashioned from such glass. Thus, it usually acts as the guardian of a given location—often a church or shrine.

Glass golems, like most others, never speak or communicate in any way. When they move, however, they are said to produce a tinkling sound like that made by delicate crystal wind chimes. If moving through a lighted area, they strobe and flicker as the light striking them is broken into its component hues.

Combat: When the stained glass golem attacks, it often has the advantage of surprise. If its victims have no reason to suspect that it lurks in a given window, they suffer a –3 on their surprise roll when the creature makes its presence known.

Once combat is joined, the stained glass figure (which always has the shape of a knight) strikes with its sword. Each blow that lands delivers 2d12 points of damage.

Once every three rounds, the golem can unleash a *prismatic spray* spell from its body that fans out in all directions. Any object or being (friend or foe) within 25 feet of the golem must roll as if struck by a wizard's *prismatic spray* spell (see the *Player's Handbook*).

Glass golems are the most fragile of any type of Ravenloft golem. Any blunt weapon capable of striking them (that is, a magical weapon of +2 or better) inflicts double damage. Further, a *shatter* spell directed at them weakens them so that all subsequent melee attacks have a percentage chance equal to twice the number of points of damage inflicted of instantly slaying the creature.

Anyone casting a *mending* spell on one of these creatures instantly restores it to full hit points. In addition, they regenerate 1 hit point per round when in an area of direct sunlight (or its equivalent).

Golem, Mechanical and Zombie

	Mechanical	Zombie
CLIMATE/TERRAIN:	Any	Any
FREQUENCY:	Very rare	Very rare
ORGANIZATION:	Solitary	Solitary
ACTIVITY CYCLE:	Any	Any
DIET:	Nil	Nil
INTELLIGENCE:	Non-(0)	Non- (0)
TREASURE:	Nil	Nil
ALIGNMENT:	Neutral	Neutral
NO. APPEARING:	1	1
ARMOR CLASS:	–2	2
MOVEMENT:	12	6
HIT DICE:	13 (75 hp)	18 (60 hp)
THAC0:	7	4
NO. OF ATTACKS:	1	2
DAMAGE/ATTACK:	4d10	3d6/3d8
SPECIAL ATTACKS:	Shock, lightning aura	Odor
SPECIAL DEFENSES:	See below immunity	Spell
MAGIC RESISTANCE:	Nil	Nil
SIZE:	M (7' tall)	M (6' tall)
MORALE:	Fearless (20)	Fearless (20)
XP VALUE:	15,000	17,000

Mechanical Golem

The mechanical golem is a nightmare combination of magic and technology first woven together in the mind of a madman. They come in many sizes, but are generally manlike in shape. In most cases, they have some manner of melee weapon built onto one of their arms.

A mechanical golem moves with a variety of whirs, clicks, and other mechanical sounds. It occasionally releases a hissing sound and a cloud of steam. Despite the creature's jury-rigged appearance, however, it is a smoothly functioning and deadly machine.

Combat: In melee combat, the mechanical golem attacks with whatever weapon has been built into it. In most cases, this weapon inflicts 4d10 points of damage, although examples of these creatures capable of inflicting greater or lesser injuries have been found.

When the golem's weapon strikes an enemy with a natural attack roll of 20, it delivers a powerful electrical shock. This attack inflicts an additional 6d6 points of damage (half that if a successful save versus spell is made). The victim of this attack is entitled to a saving throw versus paralysis to avoid being incapacitated for 2d4 rounds due to the effects of the electrical current on his muscles.

Anyone attacking the mechanical golem with a metal weapon (whether or not it is capable of harming the golem) suffers the same electrical attack upon rolling a natural 20 on their attack die. The same saving throw vs. paralysis is required to avoid incapacitation as well.

On every other combat round, the golem can engage its *lightning aura*. This field causes all those within 20 feet of the creature to be hit with small lightning bolts that inflict 3d6 points of damage. Saving throws vs. breath weapons are allowed for half damage and no paralysis is inflicted by this

attack. Exposed items carried by anyone struck by the *lightning aura* must successfully save vs. lightning or be destroyed.

Zombie Golem

First created by Azalin from information he gleaned while in the employ of Strahd von Zarovich of Barovia, these foul creatures look much like flesh golems. Unlike those traditional golems, however, these creatures are composed of rotting body parts and carry the stench of death about them wherever they go.

Unlike flesh golems, which are able to emit a guttural roar when they engage in combat, zombie golems are utterly silent. They move slowly and without thought, attacking in a lackluster manner retained from their undead status.

Combat: The zombie golem attacks with its powerful fists twice per round, inflicting 3d6 points of damage each. Because of the creature's slow movements, however, it always acts last in any given combat round with no initiative check being required. Further, the zombie golem never attains surprise.

The odor of decay and corruption that surrounds a zombie golem is so strong that it causes all those who move within 30 feet of it to successfully save vs. poison or be overcome with nausea. Such individuals suffer a –2 penalty on all attack rolls and saving throws while within the area of the stench. Characters who save successfully are unaffected unless they move out of the area and then reenter it (in which case they must make another save).

Zombie golems are immune to most magical spells, although a *resurrection* spell will instantly slay them. On the other hand, an *animate dead* spell will restore them to full hit points as if it were some manner of healing magic.

CLIMATE/TERRAIN:	Any Ravenloft
FREQUENCY:	Very rare
ORGANIZATION:	Solitary
ACTIVITY CYCLE:	Any
DIET:	Special
INTELLIGENCE:	High (13–14)
TREASURE:	Nil
ALIGNMENT:	Neutral

NO. APPEARING:	1
ARMOR CLASS:	0
MOVEMENT:	Fl 9 (A)
HIT DICE:	5
THAC0:	15
NO. OF ATTACKS:	1
DAMAGE/ATTACK:	See below
SPECIAL ATTACKS:	See below
SPECIAL DEFENSES:	See below
MAGIC RESISTANCE:	See below
SIZE:	M (7′ tall)
MORALE:	Fearless (20)
XP VALUE:	4,000

The grim reaper (or death spirit) is a creature from the Negative Material Plane that appears only in Ravenloft. It is drawn to the ebbing life energies of a creature on the verge of death (i.e., at or below 0 hit points) and seems, in some way, to feed upon those essences. Despite its apparent nature, a death spirit is not undead.

A grim reaper has the appearance of a bleached skeleton well over 6 feet tall, shrouded in a dark robe. It always carries a scythe in its bony hands.

No death spirit has ever been known to speak to the living on their own terms, but rumors persist that such a creature can be contacted by the use of *speak with dead* spell. In such cases, language does not seem to be a factor.

Combat: A death spirit has little need to enter combat in most cases. Typically, it will be drawn into battle only when an attempt is made to prevent it from feeding on the spirit of a dying person. In such cases, its wrath is great, its power terrible.

When the spirit arrives to feed, it is invisible and can thus be attacked effectively only by those able to see invisible objects. In addition, it is hit only by +3 or better magical weapons and is immune to all mind- and life-affecting spells (including *sleep, charm, suggestion, fear, finger of death, cause light wounds,* etc.).

As already mentioned, the death spirit is not truly undead; it is, therefore, immune to any attempts to turn it as well as the effects of spells like *control* or *detect undead.* Similarly, it is immune to all manner of cold-, fire-, or electricity-based spells. A *negative plane protection* spell cast upon the intended victim of the death spirit prevents the feeding and damages the reaper normally.

When the death spirit attacks a creature other than the one it has come to feed upon, it does so in three ways. On the first round of any combat, it strikes with its scythe (if possible). This ethereal weapon hits as if it were a normal polearm, but inflicts only 1d4 points of physical damage. Anyone hit by this blade must, however, successfully save vs. death magic or be instantly slain. In the second round, it

will fix its gaze on one of its attackers, forcing him to make a horror check or be overwhelmed by the creature's aura of death. On the third round, it strikes again with its scythe, this time using the shaft as if it were a quarterstaff. Anyone hit by this attack suffers 1d4 points of damage and is affected as if by a *feign death* spell. The effects of this spell fade if the creature is driven off. On the next round, this cycle begins again with the normal scythe attack.

If, at any time during the combat, the creature is able to strike at its intended victim, it does so with its scythe. No attack roll is required and no physical damage is done; rather, the life essence of the victim is drained away. As soon as this is done, the spirit fades away into the Mists of Ravenloft. Any attempt at *resurrection* or *reincarnation* of the victim is doomed to fail unless the powers attempting it are divine in nature.

If the reaper is reduced to 0 hit points, it is driven off. The intended victim benefits from this and instantly regains 10% of his original hit point score. Similarly, if healing magic is used on the dying person at any point during the encounter, he is rescued from the brink of death and the reaper is driven off.

Habitat/Society: According to some, death spirits are agents of the dark powers of Ravenloft and thwarting them earns the wrath of these mighty forces. No evidence exists to support that claim, but some connection between the two seems almost a certainty.

The chance that any mortally wounded individual (one reduced to 0 or fewer hit points) will attract the attention of a death spirit is equal to 5% per character experience level. Thus, a 15th-level character on his death bed has a 75% chance of being visited by a grim reaper.

Ecology: Being creatures of the Negative Material Plane, these nightmares seem to have no place in the physical world. Some, however, contend that they form a vital link in the balance between life and death that is central to all neutral-aligned philosophies.

Imp, Assassin

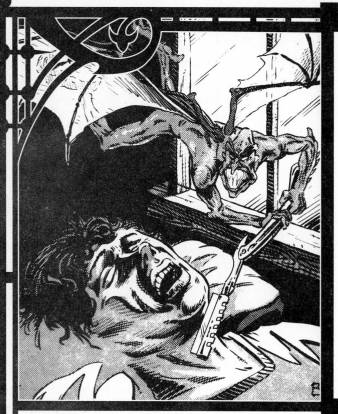

CLIMATE/TERRAIN:	Any Ravenloft
FREQUENCY:	Rare
ORGANIZATION:	Solitary
ACTIVITY CYCLE:	Any (night)
DIET:	Carnivore
INTELLIGENCE:	Very (11–12)
TREASURE:	O
ALIGNMENT:	Lawful evil

NO. APPEARING:	1
ARMOR CLASS:	0
MOVEMENT:	6, Fl 18 (B)
HIT DICE:	3
THAC0:	17
NO. OF ATTACKS:	1
DAMAGE/ATTACK:	1d4
SPECIAL ATTACKS:	See below
SPECIAL DEFENSES:	See below
MAGIC RESISTANCE:	50%
SIZE:	T (1′ tall)
MORALE:	Average (8–10)
XP VALUE:	975

The assassin imp is a clever and evil creature that, like the more common quasit or traditional imp, serves the cause of darkness.

Assassin imps are tiny creatures, seldom standing over 1 foot in height. Their coloration, normally black, varies in some individuals to as light as slate gray. Two batlike wings fan out from the creature's back and enable it to fly, while a long, slender tail dangles behind it. The tail, which is almost constantly in motion, ends in a scorpionlike stinger. Its keen eyesight is augmented with 60-foot infravision.

Assassin imps are able to communicate with others of their kind by means of a language that some describe as purely evil in sound and expression.

Combat: As its name implies, the assassin imp often strikes without warning. The spell-like abilities of the imp are obviously useful in such practices. At will, an assassin imp can become *invisible, detect magic,* or *find traps.* Three times per day the imp can employ a *knock* or *cause light wounds* spell, and once per day it may cast a *command* spell.

When an assassin imp attacks a target that has not yet detected it, it imposes a –3 penalty to that creature's surprise roll. Often, the imp avoids detection by remaining *invisible* until its victim draws near and then diving at them from above.

Assassin imps generally try to kill their victims in some way that is linked to their professions. Thus, a weaponsmith might be impaled on one of his own swords or a thief could be slain by a poisoned needle cleverly concealed in his own home.

An assassin imp's stinger is not nearly as dangerous as that of a true imp. While it inflicts the same 1d4 points of damage with each successful attack, the poison it injects does not cause death. Rather, it forces those who fail to save against its effects into a deep state of hibernation (as a *feign death* spell) that lasts for 2d4 days. Assassin imps often linger near the body of an affected individual in hopes of seeing them buried alive by their companions. When this happens, the imp always arranges for the character's friends to discover what they have done after it is too late.

Assassin imps are immune to all fire-, cold-, or electricity-based attacks. They have a basic 50% immunity to all other spells and save as if they were 7 HD monsters. They can be hit only by magical weapons of +2 or better enchantment and are immune to all poisons and toxins. They regenerate lost hit points at the rate of 1 per melee round.

Habitat/Society: Whenever a wizard of lawful evil alignment employs a *find familiar* spell in Ravenloft, there is a base 10% chance per level that he or she will receive an imp as a servant. If that individual has already failed at least one Ravenloft Powers check, then the imp is an assassin imp.

The imp serves its master faithfully, but cannot leave Ravenloft. If its lord leaves Ravenloft causing it to remain behind, it is instantly slain (invoking the normal penalties for losing a familiar). As with a normal imp, however, the assassin will attempt to lead its master into greater and greater acts of darkness. Its final goal in all this is to cause the wizard it serves to fall to the dark powers and (with luck) to become another lord in the Domain of Dread.

The master of an assassin imp is telepathically linked to it whenever the two are within one mile of each other. This enables the wizard to receive all the sensory input from his familiar (including infravision). The master also acquires the imp's natural magic resistance (50%) and, when within one mile of the creature, can cast spells as if he were 1 level higher than he actually is. When the imp moves beyond this range, the wizard reverts to his normal level. The death of an assassin imp causes its master to instantly lose 4 levels of experience (in addition to all other penalties for losing a familiar).

The assassin imp will ruthlessly kill those that it feels are a threat to its master—whether or not its master desires it to do so. Thus, the creature will often act on its own in "defending" its lord and may actually draw unwanted attention to its master. Thus, a wizard may well find that everyone (including his loved ones) who has dangerous information about him has become a target for the murderous attentions of his familiar.

Ecology: The assassin imp is a tool of the dark powers of Ravenloft that seeks to lead the already evil into acts that will eventually trap him in the Demiplane of Dread forever.

CLIMATE/TERRAIN:	Any wetlands or subterranean
FREQUENCY:	Rare
ORGANIZATION:	Solitary
ACTIVITY CYCLE:	Any
DIET:	Blood
INTELLIGENCE:	Semi- (2–4)
TREASURE:	Varies
ALIGNMENT:	Neutral evil

NO. APPEARING:	1
ARMOR CLASS:	8
MOVEMENT:	3
HIT DICE:	5 + 2
THAC0:	15
NO. OF ATTACKS:	1
DAMAGE/ATTACK:	1d4
SPECIAL ATTACKS:	See below
SPECIAL DEFENSES:	See below
MAGIC RESISTANCE:	Nil
SIZE:	S (4′ diameter)
MORALE:	Average (8–10)
XP VALUE:	13,000

The strange life form known as an impersonator lurks in swamps, wetlands, and caverns, waiting for its chance to drain the blood from a living creature.

In its natural form, an impersonator appears to be nothing more than a pool of thick, stagnant water. In actuality, it is far more dense than water and its body has the viscosity of heavy oil. When the creature decides to attack, however, it assumes the form of one of its past victims.

In their natural forms, there is no evidence that these creatures can communicate with each other or with outsiders in any way. When they assume the form of another being, however, they communicate by any means available to the victim whose shape they have taken.

Combat: An impersonator usually uses its power of *replication* to assume a form that will make it welcome among others. It then lures one or more individuals into a situation where they feel safe and are either helpless or asleep. It then returns to its true form and attacks them. While the impersonator can engage in battle in its assumed form, it is loath to do so. For one thing, damage inflicted on its victims in this state means less blood to be consumed later. In addition, the assumed form has only the statistics of the impersonator. Thus, while it may appear to be a powerful knight in field plate, it is actually only a 5 HD monster with AC 8. Any attack from the impersonator in its assumed form inflicts 1d4 points of damage. The impersonator does not gain any of its form's special abilities (like infravision or magical spells), although it does have access to all of the knowledge that its new form possessed.

The impersonator feeds by drawing blood out of its victims. However, the process it uses to do this is quite slow and, therefore, the creature must first immobilize its prey. This is accomplished by physical contact with its natural form. Anyone who touches the impersonator while it is in its true form must successfully save vs. poison (with a +4 bonus to the roll) or become unable to move. The effect of this toxin wears off 1d4 rounds after contact with the creature is broken.

While its victim is helpless, however, the impersonator flows over him and begins to siphon off his blood. Each round, the victim suffers 1d4 points of damage. Although the blood drain itself is painless, the victim eventually begins to feel a bone-numbing cold as death draws ever closer.

Impersonators seldom have the chance to attack in their natural forms, so they use their special ability of *replication* to lure victims near. This power allows an impersonator to assume the form of any creature whose blood it has tasted. It takes one round to assume the new form; once this is done, it can remain in that state for 1 turn (10 minutes) per point of damage it inflicted on that particular victim. Thus, if it had drained 50 hit points from a 9th-level fighter, it could assume the form of that fighter for 50 turns (8.3 hours) before reverting to its natural form. The impersonator can abandon its disguise at any time by taking 1 round to melt back into its true state. An impersonator can assume a form of a victim only once per feeding; in order to take that shape again, the creature must effect another blood drain on that victim. However, the typical impersonator will have from 3 to 12 (3d4) forms available to it at any given time, and the order in which it fed upon victims has no bearing on the order in which it assumes their forms.

Habitat/Society: The impersonator possesses an unusually evil and cunning nature. While not truly sentient, it has a natural ability to sense the least offensive forms (among those available to it) to take on before entering a new feeding area. Thus, it never appears before a band of elves in the form of a growling orc.

Once the impersonator has located a rich feeding ground (say, near a small village) it attempts to attack and kill an unsuspecting member of that community. Then, using the form it has just acquired, it will move into that group and begin to seek new prey. By constantly assuming new forms as it feeds, it is often able to stay one step ahead of those who would kill it, leaving a trail of pale, bloodless bodies behind.

Ecology: The origins of the impersonator are unknown. If it is a natural creature, which most sages doubt, then it is possibly a relative of the mimic. The majority of scholars, however, believe that the impersonator is either a creature from the lower planes or the result of twisted magical experiments.

Lycanthrope, Werebat

CLIMATE/TERRAIN:	Temperate woodlands
FREQUENCY:	Rare
ORGANIZATION:	Flock
ACTIVITY CYCLE:	Night
DIET:	Blood
INTELLIGENCE:	Average (8–10)
TREASURE:	B
ALIGNMENT:	Neutral evil

NO. APPEARING:	1–4
ARMOR CLASS:	5
MOVEMENT:	9, Fl 15 (D)
HIT DICE:	4+2
THAC0:	17
NO. OF ATTACKS:	3
DAMAGE/ATTACK:	1d4/1d4
SPECIAL ATTACKS:	See below
SPECIAL DEFENSES:	See below
MAGIC RESISTANCE:	Nil
SIZE:	M (6′ tall)
MORALE:	Steady (11–12)
XP VALUE:	420

Like the other species of lycanthrope found in Ravenloft, two varieties of werebat exist: natural (or true) and infected. True werebats are those creatures who have been born to werebat parents. The parents may be either true or infected werebats themselves, but the offspring of any two werebats is a true werebat. In those rare cases when a child is born with one werebat and one human parent, there is a 50% chance that it will be a true werebat and a 25% chance that it will be an infected werebat.

True werebats have three forms: normal human, vampire bat, and hybrid. In the first form, it is marked by batlike features and traits (an aversion to bright lights, keen night vision, a taste for blood or raw meat, etc.). In its vampire bat form, it looks just like a common vampire bat. By far the most feared of its forms, however, is that of the hybrid. In this form, it retains its humanoid shape but takes on the added features of a bat. The arms extend to become willowy and leather wings form under them, the teeth sharpen into deadly fangs, and the snout protrudes from the face. The nails stretch into deadly claws and the eyes spawn an inner glow when light strikes them.

Infected werebats have only two of the three forms listed above. Most (75%) have a human and hybrid form, while the rest have only a human and true bat form.

Combat: The type of attacks employed by a werebat depend upon its form. In human form, it depends upon weapons to inflict damage, for its bare hands inflict a mere 1d2 points per attack. If at all possible, the creature avoids combat in this form.

In bat form, werebats attack as if they were bats. Each round, they may attack once and inflict but a single point of damage with any successful strike. The bitten victim, of course, stands a chance of contracting lycanthropy (see below), even from this meager wound. Opponents of a werebat in this form will find that it is unusually resilient, for it has its full human-form hit points.

In hybrid form, the werebat lacks the manual dexterity to employ weapons effectively. However, its deadly sharp claws

and needlelike teeth make it far from helpless. In each round it can strike twice with its claws (inflicting 1d4 points of damage each). If both of these attacks hit, it can follow with a vicious bite causing 2d4 points of damage. Werebats can fly in their hybrid form and often use this ability to their advantage in combat.

Anyone damaged by a werebat's natural attacks stands a chance of contracting lycanthropy and becoming an infected werebat. Every point of damage done indicates a flat 2% chance per point that the victim will become infected. The procedures for curing an infected lycanthrope are given in the RAVENLOFT Campaign Setting.

Werebats can be harmed only by silver or +1 or better magical weapons. Any wound inflicted by another type of weapon knits as quickly as it is inflicted, hinting at the creature's true nature.

Habitat/Society: Werebats favor caves in lightly wooded, temperate regions as their homes. From here, they can fly out and seek prey from which they can draw the blood necessary to satisfy their thirst.

Werebat caves are commonly home to only one family of werebats (two parents and 1 to 4 young). The young remain in true bat form until they reach 3 years of age. At this time, they mature into adults and, within a single year, become fully grown. This time of transformation brings out a great hunger in the creature, which forces it to spend most of its time hunting and feeding. Human villages near a werebat cave are certain to lose many citizens to the feasting of the ravenous creatures at this time.

In addition to the werebat family, each cave will contain 20 to 200 (20d10) common bats and 1 to 10 giant bats. All of these lessers are under the command of the adult werebats and act as their sentinels and companions.

Ecology: Although werebats favor humans and demihumans as prey, they have been known to feed on the blood of other mammals (like cattle and horses) when preferred prey is not available. Interestingly, such animals seem to be immune to the lycanthropy that these dark creatures spread.

While werebats do look upon humans and demihumans as animals to be devoured, they are not cruel or evil in their attacks. They simply regard such beings as having a lower place in the food chain. Werebats will, typically, refer to themselves as "predators of the night."

Lycanthrope, Wereraven

CLIMATE/TERRAIN:	Temperate woodlands
FREQUENCY:	Uncommon
ORGANIZATION:	Flock
ACTIVITY CYCLE:	Day
DIET:	Omnivore
INTELLIGENCE:	Genius (17–18)
TREASURE:	Q×10
ALIGNMENT:	Neutral good

NO. APPEARING:	2–8 (2d4)
ARMOR CLASS:	6
MOVEMENT:	1, Fl 27 (C)
HIT DICE:	4+2
THAC0:	17
NO. OF ATTACKS:	1
DAMAGE/ATTACK:	2–12 (2d6)
SPECIAL ATTACKS:	See below
SPECIAL DEFENSES:	See below
MAGIC RESISTANCE:	Nil
SIZE:	M (5′ tall)
MORALE:	Elite (13–14)
XP VALUE:	420

Wereravens are a race of wise and good-aligned shape changers who seem to have migrated to Ravenloft from another realm (probably the GREYHAWK® Campaign Setting) centuries ago. While they are no longer found on their plane of origin, they have managed to survive in the demiplane of dread.

Natural wereravens have three forms, that of a normal human, a huge raven, and a hybrid of the two. Infected wereravens can assume only two of the above forms. While all infected wereravens can take the human form, roughly half are able to turn into hybrids while the others can transform into huge ravens.

The hybrid form of these creatures looks much like that of a werebat. The arms grow long and thin, sprouting feathers and transforming into wings. The mouth hardens and projects into a straight, pecking beak, and the eyes turn jet black. A coat of feathers replaces the normal body hair of the human form.

Combat: Wereravens are deadly opponents in close combat, although they seldom engage in it. Because they can be hit only by silver weapons or those with a +2 or better magical bonus, these creatures do not fear most armed parties.

When in human form, a wereraven retains its natural immunities to certain weapons but has no real attack of its own. If forced to fight unarmed, it inflicts a mere 1 to 2 points of damage. For this reason, wereravens in human form often employ weapons, doing damage appropriate to the arms they wield.

In raven form, the wereraven attacks as if it were a common example of that creature. Thus, it inflicts but 1 to 2 points of damage but has a 1 in 10 chance of scoring an eye peck with each successful attack. Any eye peck will cause the target to lose the use of one eye until a *heal* or *regeneration* spell can be cast on the victim. Half-blinded persons (those who have lost 1 eye) suffer a –2 on all attack rolls. A second eye peck results in total blindness until the above cure can be affected.

In hybrid form, the wereraven's arms have grown into wings, making them almost useless in combat. However, the muscles in their mouths/beaks strengthen, giving them a savage bite. Each attack made with the creature's beak inflicts 2d6 points of damage.

Anyone bitten or pecked by the wereraven has a 2% chance per point of damage inflicted of becoming an infected wereraven. Infected lycanthropes are discussed in the RAVENLOFT Campaign Setting.

Wereravens are strong flyers and often use this ability to their advantage in combat.

Habitat/Society: A wereraven family will be found only at the heart of a dense forest. Here, they live in the hollowed out body of a great tree. Entrance to their lair is possible only from above (if one does not wish to cut or break through the trunk itself). Curiously, the wereravens are able to keep the tree in which they nest from dying even after they have hollowed it out, so it is difficult to distinguish from the normal trees around it.

Wereravens recognize that they are bastions of good in a land dominated by evil. They have managed to survive by avoiding large populations or overt acts of good that would draw the attention of the reigning lords to them. Thus, a wereraven flock will generally have no more than 2 to 8 adults in it. Of course, such groups have young with them (1 to 4 per 2 adults), but these are seldom encountered for they remain in a true raven state until they are old enough to fend for themselves. In addition, a typical wereraven lair will draw 10 to 100 (10d10) common ravens to nest in the trees about it. These wise birds will serve the wereravens, doing their bidding and striving to protect them from harm.

Wereravens are not opposed to helping out the cause of good in Ravenloft, but they do so reluctantly. This is not because they do not wish to do good, but because they fear the wrath of the dark powers. It is said that the wereravens have come to the aid of endangered Vistani clans on several occasions and that close ties exist between these two races, but neither will admit this openly.

Ecology: Wereravens are omnivores who prefer to maintain a vegetarian diet. They enjoy berries and nuts, but will eat carrion or kill for fresh meat from time to time in order to maintain good health.

Men (Abber Nomads)

CLIMATE/TERRAIN:	The Nightmare Lands
FREQUENCY:	Common
ORGANIZATION:	Tribe
ACTIVITY CYCLE:	Day
DIET:	Omnivore
INTELLIGENCE:	Average (8–10)
TREASURE:	Nil
ALIGNMENT:	Neutral

NO. APPEARING:	10–40 (10d4)
ARMOR CLASS:	8 (10)
MOVEMENT:	12
HIT DICE:	2
THAC0:	19
NO. OF ATTACKS:	1
DAMAGE/ATTACK:	1d2 or by weapon
SPECIAL ATTACKS:	Nil
SPECIAL DEFENSES:	Resist illusion
MAGIC RESISTANCE:	Nil
SIZE:	M (6½' tall)
MORALE:	Average (8–10)
XP VALUE:	65

The Abber nomads are a stoic and proud people who dwell in the dreaded Nightmare Lands. Considered by outsiders to be barbarians, the Abber nomads have an unusually sophisticated outlook on life that, not surprisingly, is almost as alien as the bizarre realm that they inhabit.

The typical Abber nomad male stands roughly 6½ feet tall, the typical female being only an inch or so shorter. They are generally well muscled survivors, as befits their nomadic society and the harsh land with which they must contend.

The language of the Abber nomads is absolutely unique; no scholar has ever been able to liken it to any tongue spoken by any other race in any known land. Further, there seems to be little in their culture to link these people with any other human race, making them seem all the more outcast and alien to the visitor.

Combat: When hunting or making ready for battle, Abber nomads paint their faces and bodies with traditional symbols that they feel will give them power over the animals they are stalking or the enemies they are confronting. Most wear tanned skins and carry wooden shields that provide them with AC 8 protection. In all regards, save the following, they fight as normal men.

In melee combat, they employ long, slender, stone-tipped spears that function as javelins. These weapons could be thrown, but the nomads seldom use them in that manner and make no effort to balance them for flight.

In missile combat, the Abber nomads use short bows. They often coat their arrowheads in a mild toxin (Class C, 2 to 5 minutes, 25/2d4) to aid in hunting larger animals. As a rule, 1 in 3 nomads will have poisoned arrows in any encounter.

The Abber nomads live in a wild land of chaos and uncertainty. Because of this, they have developed a natural immunity to all manner of illusions and hallucinations. Any spell designed to fool any of an Abber nomad's senses has a 25% chance of failing. Even if the spell manages to get past their inherent resistance to it, they are entitled to a +4 bonus on any saving throws required to negate enchantments of this type.

Habitat/Society: The Abber nomads, as their name implies, make no permanent structures. They travel about from place to place in search of the basic elements of survival.

They work no metals but are skilled at woodworking and have some interest in stone carving (usually for the design and construction of minor tools and hunting implements).

While the Abber nomads might seem to be a fairly typical aboriginal culture, nothing could be further from the truth. Their strange surroundings have convinced them that the universe is a wild and unpredictable place—leaving them with no understanding of science or the traditional concepts of cause and effect. In the Nightmare Lands, a device or spell that works one day might cease to function the next.

Because of the strange happenings of the Nightmare Lands, the nomads have developed a philosophy that, greatly paraphrased, says that anything they cannot perceive themselves does not exist. Thus, someone who walks out of their sight ceases to exist until they are again visible. While this can make outsiders uncomfortable and efforts to deal with the nomads very difficult (the nomads will make no long range plans or commitments), it enables them to cope with life in a wild place that seems oblivious to the natural laws that rule the rest of the universe. In addition, the nomads have no faith in the permanency of anything, including ideas or memories. In short, they accept what is and make no efforts to change it or participate in it. They are, perhaps, the universe's most withdrawn and disinterested occupants.

Each tribe of nomads will be composed of 10 to 40 adults (roughly half male and half female). In addition, there will be another 25% of this number who are young children that do not fight or hunt. Among adults, men and women hunt and share all labors equally. One in ten of the adults will be a leader with 5 HD (THAC0 15). There may be more than one leader in any given tribe. None of the Abber nomads will employ any manner of spells, for they practice no magic.

Ecology: As the Nightmare Lands have no natural ecosystem, any judgment about the nomad's place in it is difficult to make. Still, it is clear that, even if the wild lands about them were not constantly in flux, they would have little impact upon them. They are a simple people who survive as hunters and gatherers.

Men (Lost Ones, Madmen)

	Lost Ones	Madmen
CLIMATE/TERRAIN:	Any Ravenloft	Any urban
FREQUENCY:	Very rare	Very rare
ORGANIZATION:	Solitary	Solitary
ACTIVITY CYCLE:	Any	Any (usually night)
DIET:	Omnivore	Omnivore
INTELLIGENCE:	Low (5–7)	Average (8–10)
TREASURE:	Nil	Varies
ALIGNMENT:	Neutral	Chaotic evil
NO. APPEARING:	1	1
ARMOR CLASS:	10	Varies
MOVEMENT:	6	9
HIT DICE:	1–1	2
THAC0:	20	19
NO. OF ATTACKS:	1	1
DAMAGE/ATTACK:	1d2 or by weapon	1d3 or by weapon
SPECIAL ATTACKS:	Rage	Surprise
SPECIAL DEFENSES:	Nil	Nil
MAGIC RESISTANCE:	Nil	Nil
SIZE:	M (6' tall)	M (6' tall)
MORALE:	Unsteady (5–7)	Average (8–10)
XP VALUE:	15	35

Lost Ones

In a land as filled with nightmares and unspeakable horrors as Ravenloft, there are persons who have seen more evil than they can possibly bear. These shattered and broken souls are know throughout the demiplane as "the lost ones."

Almost mindless, the lost ones have no interest in the outside world. They often stay in a single place where they feel safe and spend most of their time in an almost catatonic state. The enormity of the things they have seen is written in their tortured features and the blankness of their eyes, which seem to have lost the very spark of life.

Lost ones seldom speak or communicate in any way. They often emit nothing more than muttered warnings or periodic cries of alarm and terror.

Combat: Lost ones will take no actions to defend themselves from attack and will not normally engage others in combat. The only time they have been known to do so is when they are reminded of the terrors they have seen. For example, a woman who has seen her children destroyed by a vampire might go into a berserk fit and attack someone who looks much like the monster that took her family (and sanity) from her. In such cases, they attack with whatever weapons are nearby (usually just their hands). The ferocity and suddenness of their rage, however, imposes a –1 penalty on their opponents' surprise rolls.

Habitat/Society: Lost ones can be found anywhere in Ravenloft. As a rule, their wanderings will carry them to towns and villages where they become pitied and shunned creatures who survive only by the kindness of others. The only known way to return a lost one to sanity is to force him to confront the horrors that destroyed him. If a lost one witnesses the death of the thing that drove him to mental destruction, there is a 25% chance that he will be able to begin the recovery process—a process that may take many months. Because of the special link these people have with the dark powers, they are immune to magical attempts to cure them.

Ecology: Lost ones have given up all links with reality. As such, they produce nothing useful and play no important role in the world.

Madmen

For some, the horrors of Ravenloft are too much to bear. While those too weak to cope with the things they have seen are destroyed (see Lost Ones), others are driven into absolute madness. Twisted to evil, they prowl the night looking for fresh victims—often their own friends and neighbors—to slaughter.

Combat: Typically, madmen will depend on smaller weapons—knives, hand axes, garrotes, etc.—that they can conceal until they strike. Madmen normally present a pleasing front that lures their would-be victims into a false sense of security before they strike. When a madman strikes in this fashion, he imposes a –2 penalty on his victim's surprise roll. In addition, those surprised by the madman's attacks take triple damage as if they had been backstabbed by a 5th-level thief. If confronted with actual resistance to their attack, the madman will generally flee.

Habitat/Society: In many cases, madmen appear normal. They may even lead a normal life and go about in public without notice. Thus, their dress and behavior are dictated by their surroundings. When something sparks the insanity that burns within them, however, they transform into brutal killers who seek to drive the horrors from their memory in a torrent of blood.

Some madmen have special "calling cards" to mark their kills. In this way, they begin a dangerous game of cat-and-mouse with the local constabulary. A madman's calling card might be anything from a particular style of murder (cutting the throat, a single wound to the heart, etc.) to an unusual item left behind at the scene of each killing (a crimson silk handkerchief knotted about the wrist, perhaps). The subconscious mind of these twisted murderers often causes them to leave clues to their identity or that of their next victim in their "calling cards."

Ecology: In many cases, madmen continue to lead normal lives, interacting with society just as before witnessing the horrors that drove them over the edge.

Mist Horror

	Common	Wandering
CLIMATE/TERRAIN:	Ravenloft mists	Ravenloft mists
FREQUENCY:	Common	Uncommon
ORGANIZATION:	Solitary	Solitary
ACTIVITY CYCLE:	Any	Any
DIET:	Nil	Nil
INTELLIGENCE:	Low (5–7)	Average (8–10)
TREASURE:	Nil	Nil
ALIGNMENT:	Neutral evil	Chaotic evil
NO. APPEARING:	1	1
ARMOR CLASS:	2	0
MOVEMENT:	15	15
HIT DICE:	5	5
ThAC0:	15	15
NO. OF ATTACKS:	2	2
DAMAGE/ATTACK:	2d6/2d6	2d6/2d6
SPECIAL ATTACKS:	See below	See below
SPECIAL DEFENSES:	See below	See below
MAGIC RESISTANCE:	50%	50%
SIZE:	Varies	Varies
MORALE:	Steady (11–12)	Steady (11–12)
XP VALUE:	3,000	5,000

Mist horrors lurk in the swirling banks of fog that encompass all of Ravenloft. Any creature who lingers too long in the mist is sure to draw the attentions, and earn the wrath, of these horrid creatures.

While their presence is often sensed as they move by a party just outside of visual range—an unusual ripple in the vapors to one side, a strange sensation of some lurking presence—they do not allow themselves to be seen until they attack. When they do make their presence known, their forms can be greatly varied, though they always appear to be made of mist. While a horror is generally man-size, it can take any shape it desires, usually taking on a form that it knows (from an empathic probe of the victim's mind) will cause terror. Thus, persons afraid of wolves would find themselves facing a six-foot-long wolf composed of billowing fog.

Mist horrors appear to be able to communicate telempathically with anyone moving through the Ravenloft Mists. Thus, when they are about to attack or are stalking someone, they will send feelings of dread and fear into their minds. In addition, they often use this power to entice persons outside of the mists to enter them. Communication in this manner consists of feelings and impressions rather than solid understanding. Someone being called into the mists by these foul spirits might begin to feel an mild fascination with the billowing clouds of vapor. Eventually, this interest grows into a consuming need to enter the mists.

Combat: It takes a mist horror some time (generally 1d4 turns) to assemble its physical form and attack someone traveling through the mists. Thus, those who keep moving are safe from harm as a mist horror is very restricted in its own movement and must remain within a small area. A mist horror will often use its telempathic powers to make travelers feel that they are safe and can rest without danger. Once they stop moving, of course, it attacks.

When a mist horror attacks, it is likely to catch its victims off guard. This is largely due to the fact that it can spring out of the swirling vapors (in which it is treated as if it were invisible) without warning. Once a mist horror assumes its combat shape (whatever form that may be), it is easy enough to detect, although it can, at will, break off from combat and return to the mists, effectively becoming invisible again. When a mist horror opts to do this (or before it assumes a combat form), it is protected from any attack as its essence disperses through the mists. However, it requires 1d4 turns to reform.

When in combat, the horror will attack in whatever manner seems appropriate for its form. Because of the mystic nature of this being, however, the number of attacks it is entitled to and the damage it inflicts remain constant (two attacks at 2d6 points each.) Thus, if the horror appears as a vast, six-tentacled creature only two of its limbs would strike each round.

Because of its almost insubstantial nature, the mist horror can be hit only by +2 or better magical weapons. Further, it has an innate magic resistance (50%) that not only protects it, but radiates into an area 20 feet around it, canceling the effects of all spells cast in its presence. Because this magic resistance takes the form of a mental wave that affects the minds of spell casters and upsets their ability to properly direct magical influences, it has no effect on magical items. Thus, a *fireball* spell directed at a mist horror has a 50% chance of failure, while a *wand of fireballs* will work normally. Magical effects already in place (such as infravision) do not falter when they enter this aura. Spells cast within the aura must overcome both the magical resistance of the target and the effects of the spell disruption field.

Mist horrors are, in a sense, a form of undead. They can be turned as if they were "special" creatures by high-level priests and paladins. They suffer no damage from spells designed to affect undead (*negative plane protection*, for example) and are immune to the effects of holy water. They cannot be charmed or controlled in any way and have no physical forms to be affected by spells like *cause blindness* or *cause light wounds*.

Habitat/Society: Mist horrors are the spirits of evil beings who, while not foul enough to receive their own domain, attracted the attention of the dark powers with their diabolical acts during life. Upon their deaths, their spirits leave their bodies to enter the mists. Throughout Ravenloft, there is a superstition that anyone buried on a foggy day will become a mist horror. This may or may not be true, but the Vistani themselves seem to take this belief very seriously and that lends great credence to it in the eyes of many.

Once it becomes a mist horror, the evil spirit is unable to move about freely. Like the various lords scattered throughout Ravenloft, the mist horror must remain in one area. As a rule, this region is very small. Thus, as mentioned earlier, the time required for the horror to assume a dangerous form makes it possible for explorers moving through the Ravenloft Mists to avoid attack if they do not linger too long in any one place.

Because mist horrors know that they were judged to be less important than the lords of even the smallest domain, they envy them their comparative freedom and power. This hostility burns within them, making them more and more evil as time goes by. Thus, when a mist horror is encountered, it is a foul and spiteful spirit that seeks only to cause pain and suffering. If a party traveling through the mists is bearing wounded, infirm, or otherwise defenseless beings with them, these will often be the first target of a mist horror's attack. By destroying the persons who have entrusted their well being to the might of other party members, the horrors hope to shatter the morale of the entire group.

Ecology: As mentioned above, mist horrors are the spirits of evil beings who did not merit a place as lord of their own domain. The Vistani say they serve a vital role in maintaining the structure of Ravenloft and that the very land itself could not exist without their lingering presence. Whether this is true or not, no outsider can say.

Wandering Horrors

The wandering horror is an even more dangerous, though thankfully rarer, version of the mist horror. Unlike the traditional mist horror, it is not rooted in a given place and can travel through the Ravenloft Mists at will in search of victims. When it attacks, it is every bit as evil and malicious as its kindred spirit.

Wandering horrors appear as dark shapes that can be seen as they move through the mists. Unlike mist horrors, they are locked into a single shape: one that is based on the evil deed they did in life. For example, a cruel baron who ordered those he considered disloyal beheaded might well appear as a wandering figure without a head while a woman who murdered her lover with a poisonous spider might appear as a giant black widow. The wandering horror looks much like a heat mirage, for its body seems to ripple and shift from second to second. This effect is a reflection of its spiritual nature and the twisted shape of its soul.

Wandering horrors employ the same telempathic communication used by their lesser cousins but are also able to use this power to implant a *suggestion* (once per day) in the minds of their victims. In order to be affected by this power, the target must be within 120 feet of the horror.

Combat: When moving through the mists in an effort to position itself for an attack, the wandering horror is 75% unlikely to be detected. Once it attacks, however, it is fully visible to all its opponents. If it wishes to break away from combat, it may do so by attempting to vanish into the mists again (75% chance of success). Thereafter, it returns to its virtually undetectable state. When a wandering horror attacks a person that has not detected it, it imposes a –3 penalty on the victim's surprise check.

In combat, the wandering horror has the same attacks and defenses as the traditional mist horror (two attacks for 2d6 points of damage each). It can also send out a *wave of fear*

with its telempathic power. While this can be attempted only once per day, it causes all those within 120 feet to make a fear check. Since a failed fear check often has the result of scattering a party that might otherwise destroy the wanderer, it will always use this power (if possible) on the first round of combat (or the second if it makes a surprise attack).

The wandering horror can only be hit by +2 or better magical weapons and has the same magical resistance as the mist horror. This magic resistance functions in the same way, affecting spell casters but not magical items, except that it has a greater area of effect (30 feet).

A wandering horror can be turned by priests and paladins as if it were a "special" undead creature. If a character attempts to turn it and fails, however, they are subject to a special telempathic backlash that causes them to make a fear check at a –2 penalty.

Wandering horrors suffer no damage from spells designed to affect undead (*negative plane protection* for example) and are immune to the effects of holy water. They cannot be charmed or controlled in any way and have no physical forms to be affected by spells like *cause blindness* or *cause light wounds*.

Habitat/Society: The wandering horror is an evolutionary step above the mist horror. In essence, a mist horror is the evil soul of a being foul enough to draw the attention of the dark powers, but not so evil as to be rewarded/cursed with their own domain. After a period of time as a mist horror, however, this spirit may have caused enough fear and suffering (in short, done enough evil) to be elevated to the status of wandering horror.

Wandering horrors share the same vile and sadistic mannerisms as their lesser brethren. If anything, in fact, they are far more evil and dangerous as they generally hope to prove themselves dark and foul enough to earn their own domain and escape the limbo in which they now dwell.

Ecology: Wandering horrors seem to be as much a part of the fabric of Ravenloft as mist horrors. There are those who say that the destruction of a wandering horror weakens all of the evil things in Ravenloft slightly. Of course, as evil things are constantly dying and becoming mist horrors, this less-than-significant drop in power is quickly replenished.

Pseudo Horrors

In addition to the true mist horrors that lurk in the boiling vapors that surround Ravenloft, there are the pseudo horrors. These are simply beings traveling through the mists for one reason or another. In most cases, they have wandered in through a portal from some other land and are seeking escape. Because the temporary, one-way entrances to Ravenloft often appear near an evil thing, and then close again behind it, the number of pseudo horrors in the mists can be quite large.

A pseudo horror is, therefore, not a distinct creature but rather any monster that has become trapped in the Ravenloft Mists and is seeking either prey or escape. Most often, they are spectral things (like ghosts, wraiths, and shadow fiends) although occasional physical monsters (ghouls, vampires, mind flayers, and the like) are encountered. As a rule, nearly all (85%) of the things a party of explorers encounters in the Mists of Ravenloft can be assumed to be evil, for such creatures are naturally drawn into the demiplane of terror. Those creatures that are not evil, however, are almost certain to be hostile to or wary of strangers, for one seldom comes across friends in the dreaded Mists of Ravenloft.

Mummy, Greater

CLIMATE/TERRAIN:	Any desert or subterranean
FREQUENCY:	Very rare
ORGANIZATION:	Solitary
ACTIVITY CYCLE:	Night
DIET:	Nil
INTELLIGENCE:	Genius (17–18)
TREASURE:	V (Ax2)
ALIGNMENT:	Lawful evil

NO. APPEARING:	1
ARMOR CLASS:	2
MOVEMENT:	9
HIT DICE:	8 + 3
THAC0:	11
NO. OF ATTACKS:	1
DAMAGE/ATTACK:	3d6
SPECIAL ATTACKS:	See below
SPECIAL DEFENSES:	See below
MAGIC RESISTANCE:	Nil
SIZE:	M (6' tall)
MORALE:	Fanatic (17–18)
XP VALUE:	8,000

Also known as Anhktepot's Children, greater mummies are a powerful form of undead created when a high-level lawful evil priest of certain religions is mummified and charged with the guarding of a burial place. It can survive for centuries as the steadfast protector of its lair, killing all who would defile its holy resting place.

Greater mummies look just like their more common cousins save that they are almost always adorned with (un)holy symbols and wear the vestments of their religious order. They give off an odor that is said to be reminiscent of a spice cupboard because of the herbs used in the embalming process that created them.

Greater mummies are keenly intelligent and are able to communicate just as they did in life. Further, they have an inherent ability to telepathically command all normal mummies created by them. They have the ability to control other mummies, provided that they are not under the domination of another mummy, but this is possible only when verbal orders can be given.

Combat: Greater mummies radiate an *aura of fear* that causes all creatures who see them to make a fear check. A modifier is applied to this fear check based on the age of the monster, as indicated on the Age & Abilities Table at the end of this section. The effects of failure on those who miss their checks are doubled because of the enormous power and presence of this creature. The mummy's aura can be defeated by a *remove fear, cloak of bravery,* or similar spell.

In combat, greater mummies have the option of attacking with their own physical powers or with the great magics granted to them by the gods they served in life. In the former case, they may strike but once per round, inflicting 3d6 points of damage per attack.

Anyone struck by the mummy's attack suffers the required damage and becomes infected with a horrible rotting disease that is even more sinister than that of normal mummies—for it manifests itself in a matter of days, not months. The older the mummy, the faster this disease manifests itself (see the Age & Abilities Table at the end of this entry for

exact details). The disease causes the person to die within a short time unless proper medical care can be obtained. Twenty-four hours after the infecting blow lands, the character loses 1 point from his Strength and Constitution due to the effects of the virus on his body. Further, 2 points of Charisma vanish as the skin begins to flake and wither like old parchment. No normal healing is possible while the disease is spreading through the body, and the shaking and convulsions that accompany it make spellcasting or memorization impossible for the character. Only one form of magical healing has any effect: A *regenerate* spell will cure the disease and restore lost hit points, but not ability scores. All others healing spells are wasted. A series of *cure disease* spells (one for each day that has passed since the rotting was contracted) will temporarily halt the infection until a complete cure can be affected. Regaining lost ability score points is impossible through any means short of a *wish*.

The body of a person who dies from mummy rot begins to crumble into dust as soon as death occurs. The only way to resurrect a character who dies in this way is to cast both a *cure disease* and a *raise dead* spell on the body within 6 turns (1 hour) of death. If this is not done, the body (and the spirit within it) are lost forever.

Greater mummies can be turned by those who have the courage and conviction to attempt this feat; however, the older the mummy, the harder it is to overcome in this fashion. Once again, the details are provided on the Age & Abilities Table. They are immune to damage from holy water, but contact with a holy symbol from a nonevil faith inflicts 1d6 points of damage on them. Contact with a holy symbol of their own faith actually restores 1d6 hit points.

Perhaps the most horrible aspect of these creatures, however, is their spell casting ability. All greater mummies were priests in their past lives and now retain the spell casting abilities they had then. They will cast spells as if they were of 16th through 20th level (see below) and will have the same spheres available to them that they did in life. Greater mummies receive the same bonus spells for high Wisdom scores that player characters do. Dungeon Masters are advised to select spells for each greater mummy in an adventure before the adventure starts. For those

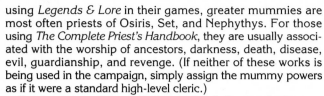

using *Legends & Lore* in their games, greater mummies are most often priests of Osiris, Set, and Nephythys. For those using *The Complete Priest's Handbook*, they are usually associated with the worship of ancestors, darkness, death, disease, evil, guardianship, and revenge. (If neither of these works is being used in the campaign, simply assign the mummy powers as if it were a standard high-level cleric.)

Greater mummies can be harmed only by magical weapons, with older ones being harder to hit than younger ones. Even if a weapon can affect them, however, it inflicts only half damage because of the magical nature of the creature's body.

Spells are also less effective against greater mummies than they are against other creatures. Cold-based spells are useless against the mummy, but fire-based ones inflict normal damage. Unlike normal mummies, these foul creatures are immune to nonmagical fire. The enchanting process that creates them, however, leaves them vulnerable to attacks involving electricity; all spells of that nature inflict half again their normal damage. In addition, older mummies develop a magic resistance that makes even those spells unreliable.

Greater mummies, like vampires, become more powerful with the passing of time in Ravenloft. The following table lists the applicable changes to the listed statistics (which are for a newly created monster) brought on by the passing of time:

Age and Abilities Table

Age	Ench	AC	HD	THAC0
99 or less	+1	2	8+3	11
100–199	+1	1	9+3	11
200–299	+2	0	10+3	9
300–399	+2	–1	11+3	9
400–499	+3	–2	12+3	7
500 or more	+4	–3	13+3	7

Age	Align	Wis	Magic	Disease
99 or less	LE	18	Nil	1d12 days
100–199	LE	19	5%	1d10 days
200–299	LE or CE	20	10%	1d8 days
300–399	CE or LE	21	15%	1d6 days
400–499	CE	22	20%	1d4 days
500 or more	CE	23	25%	1d3 days

Age	Level	XP	Fear	Mummies
99 or less	16	8,000	–1	1d4
100–199	17	10,000	–2	2d4
200–299	18	12,000	–2	3d4
300–399	19	14,000	–3	5d4
400–499	20	16,000	–3	6d4
500 or more	20	18,000	–4	7d4

Ench(antment) indicates the magical plus that must be associated with a weapon before it can inflict damage to the mummy.

AC is the Armor Class of the monster.

HD are the number of Hit Dice that the mummy has. Greater mummies are turned as if they had one more Hit Die than they actually do, so a 250-year-old (10+3) is turned as if it had 11 Hit Dice. Any mummy 300 years old or older is turned as a "special" undead.

THAC0 is listed for the various Hit Dice levels of the mummy to allow for easy reference during play.

Align(ment) may change with age. As the mummy grows older, it becomes darker and more evil. If two alignments are listed, there is a 75% chance that the mummy will be of the first alignment and a 25% chance that it will be of the second. Thus, a 300-year-old mummy is 75% likely to be chaotic evil.

Wis is the creature's Wisdom score. When employing their spells, greater mummies receive all of the bonus spells normally associated with a high Wisdom. Further, as they pass into the higher ratings (19 and beyond) they gain an immunity to certain magical spells as listed in the *Player's Handbook*.

Magic is the creature's natural magic resistance. As can be seen from the table, old mummies can be very deadly indeed.

Disease is the length of time it takes for a person infected with the mummy's rotting disease to die.

Level indicates the creature's level as a priest. Older mummies have access to far greater magics than younger ones and are thus more dangerous than younger ones.

XP lists the number of experience points awarded to a party for battling and defeating a greater mummy of a given age.

Fear indicates the penalty to those making fear checks due to the evil influence of the greater mummy's foul aura.

Mummies indicates the number of normal mummies that the creature will have serving it when encountered.

Habitat/Society: Greater mummies are powerful undead creatures that are usually created from the mummified remains of powerful, evil priests. This being the case, the greater mummy now draws its mystical abilities from evil powers and darkness. In rare cases, however, the mummified priests served non-evil gods in life and are still granted the powers they had in life from those gods.

Greater mummies often dwell in large temple complexes or tombs where they guard the bodies of the dead against the disturbances of grave robbers. Unlike normal mummies, however, they have been known to leave their tombs and strike out into the world—bringing a dreadful shroud of evil down upon every land they touch.

When a greater mummy wishes to create normal mummies as servants, it does so by mummifying persons infected with its rotting disease. This magical process requires 12 to 18 hours (10+2d4) and cannot be disturbed without ruining the enchantment. Persons to be mummified are normally held or charmed so that they cannot resist the mummification process. Once the process is completed, victims are helpless to escape the bandages that bind them. If nothing happens to free them, they will die of the mummy rot just as they would have elsewhere. Upon their death, however, a strange transformation takes place. Rather than crumbling away into dust, these poor souls rise again as normal mummies. Obviously, this process is too time consuming to be used in actual combat, but the greater mummy will often attack a potential target in hopes of capturing and transforming it into a mummy. All mummies created by a greater mummy are under its telepathic command.

Ecology: The first of these creatures is known to have been produced by Anhktepot, the Lord of Har'akir, in the years before he became undead himself. It is believed that most, if not all, of the greater mummies he created in his life were either destroyed or drawn into Ravenloft with him when he was granted a domain. A number of these creatures are believed to serve Anhktepot in his domain, acting as his agents in other lands he wishes to learn what is transpiring in other portions of Ravenloft. The process by which a greater mummy is created remains a mystery to all but Anhktepot. It is rumored that this process involves a great sacrifice to gain the favor of the gods and an oath of eternal loyalty to the Lord of Har'akir. If the latter is true, then it may lend credence to the claim of many sages that Anhktepot can command every greater mummy in existence to do his bidding. If this is indeed the case, it makes the power of this dark fiend far greater than is generally supposed.

Quevari

CLIMATE/TERRAIN:	Any land
FREQUENCY:	Uncommon
ORGANIZATION:	Village
ACTIVITY CYCLE:	Any
DIET:	Omnivore
INTELLIGENCE:	Average (8–10)
TREASURE:	A,B,C, or D (Z)
ALIGNMENT:	Lawful good or chaotic evil

NO. APPEARING:	1–8
ARMOR CLASS:	10 or 7
MOVEMENT:	17
HIT DICE:	1
THAC0:	19
NO. OF ATTACKS:	1
DAMAGE/ATTACK:	1d2 or by weapon
SPECIAL ATTACKS:	Nil or see below
SPECIAL DEFENSES:	Nil
MAGIC RESISTANCE:	Nil
SIZE:	M (6′ tall)
MORALE:	Average (8–10) or Fanatic (17–18)
XP VALUE:	15 or 65

The quevari are a race almost indistinguishable from normal humans. As a rule, they are friendly and helpful people who seem to go about their lives without concern for the evils that abound in the land around them. Their true nature is revealed only on the three nights of the full moon-when they become foul creatures of the night.

The quevari, as mentioned above, look just like normal humans. They are fond of bright colors in their clothes and flowers in their hair. Many observers will quickly notice that the quevari might well be taken as a light-skinned offshoot of the Vistani.

The quevari language is a sweet and mild sounding one, filled with musical sounds and a poetic grammar. Those fluent in it marvel at the easy way its words can be linked together to form enchanting songs and delicate verse. In addition to this, most quevari can speak one or two other languages, making communication with them an easy matter in all but the most unusual of cases.

Combat: The quevari shun combat when they are in their pacifistic phase. At such times they can be counted on to defend themselves and little more. Their primary weapons in such situations are those they use to hunt—short bows and slings—or those they use in their labors: sickles and knives. Their natural reluctance to enter into battle against intelligent opponents, however, imposes a –2 penalty on all attack rolls.

On the three nights of the full moon, however, the quevari become bloodthirsty killers who strike with the skill and finesse of trained assassins. The quevari call this time "the rising of the bloodmoon" and accept it as an inescapable part of their nature. Those who are unaware of this side of the quevari personality (but who have had dealings with them while they were in their timid phase) suffer a –2 penalty on their initiative rolls for the first round of any combat with these supposedly peaceful people.

Their agility becomes greatly heightened at this time, dropping their natural armor class from 10 to 7. This increase in agility also gives them a +2 bonus on all missile fire

attack or initiative rolls, and allows them to move silently, hide in shadows, and hear noise 75% of the time, as if they were thieves. Further, they can climb sheer surfaces with a 95% chance of success at these times.

While the weapons the quevari bring to play in combat do not change, their skill with them does. During the bloodmoon, the quevari always strike with a +2 bonus on their attack rolls when using a weapon familiar to them (as described earlier). If they are using weapons not found in their daily lives (a war hammer or polearm, perhaps), they strike normally.

Habitat/Society: Quevari villages tend to be small, farm communities with not more than three or four score inhabitants in any town. The community will decide on all issues important to their populations by simple votes or with the aid of an elected town council. There is nothing about a quevari community that makes it seem at all different from any other small village—until the full moon rises. Because of this, most of the people who enter or travel through a quevari town have no reason to suspect that it is not a human village. For their part, the quevari are unlikely to mention the fact that they are not strictly "human" unless asked directly. Even in this case, however, the quevari will not spell out the nature of their dark and cyclical psyches.

During the three nights of the full moon, the quevari metabolism and psychology changes. Some scholars liken this to a form of lycanthropy that affects their minds. The quevari themselves never speak of this time (thus, they never warn strangers to leave before the full moon rises) and have learned to block out those three nights from their lives. While this means nothing to them (it's just the way things are, after all) travelers who are staying in a quevari town at the time of the bloodmoon will be in for a great surprise.

Ecology: Normally the quevari are a people who live by gathering nuts and berries, tending their modest farms, and hunting or fishing for the meat they need in their diet. When they are under the spell of the bloodmoon, however, they are ravenous cannibals who feast upon the flesh of their victims.

Quickwood (Spy Tree)

CLIMATE/TERRAIN:	Any/Forests
FREQUENCY:	Very rare
ORGANIZATION:	Solitary
ACTIVITY CYCLE:	Any
DIET:	Soil nutrients and water
INTELLIGENCE:	Very (11–12)
TREASURE:	Special
ALIGNMENT:	Neutral

NO. APPEARING:	1(90%), 2–4 (10%)
ARMOR CLASS:	5
MOVEMENT:	1 (3 for roots)
HIT DICE:	5–10
THAC0:	5–6HD: 15
	7–8HD: 13
	9–10HD: 11
NO. OF ATTACKS:	1d6+12 and mouth
DAMAGE/ATTACK:	Nil and 3d4
SPECIAL ATTACKS:	Roots
SPECIAL DEFENSES:	Spell channeling
MAGIC RESISTANCE:	Special
SIZE:	L (12'+)
MORALE:	Champion (15–16)
XP VALUE:	Variable

This great hardwood tree appears to be an oak, although close inspection reveals that it has a visage and sensory organs that resemble a distorted human face. It is 90% unlikely that the "face" is noticed unless the observer is within 10 feet of the quickwood.

Combat: As it is very difficult for a quickwood to move its massive trunk, the creature usually remains still if at all possible. It can, however, send out thick roots that move 30 feet per round through the loose top soil (90-foot range). These roots can seize and hold immobile any creature under 1,000 pounds of weight (the creature is then drawn to the maw in one round to be chewed upon). The roots are too strong to be broken, and blunt weapons do not damage them, but an edged weapon may be used to sever one. Treat roots as large-size creatures, with 10 hit points each. Note that damage inflicted upon roots does not count toward destruction of the quickwood proper. The creature allows only six of its roots to be severed before it withdraws the other 1d6+6 to safety. The roots cause no damage.

The limbs of the creature are too stiff to serve as offensive members, but a quickwood has a mouthlike opening that can clamp shut for 3d4 points of damage. The victim must be touching the trunk or forced into position by a nearby grasping root where the maw can inflict damage before this is an actual danger, however. The visual, auditory, and olfactory organs (resembling large human eyes, ears, and nose) are slightly superior to the human norm, and the creature's infravision extends to 120 feet. The quickwood has numbers of lesser roots it spreads to sense approaching creatures. Its sensitive leaves can detect air movements and changes in pressure.

It is possible to use plant-affecting spells against a quickwood, but most others do not work. The creature is able to perspire, drenching itself in water so fire does not harm it. Lightning is harmlessly channeled off into the ground, and poisons and gases do not harm a quickwood. A *disintegrate* spell will certainly destroy one of these things, if successful. However, if under spell attack, a quickwood uses the spell energy to radiate *fear* in a radius equal to 10 feet per level of spell energy. If the caster fails his saving throw, the quickwood has channeled off all of the spell energy into fear; otherwise the fear is only a side effect of the spell use, and the magic has standard effects on the spy tree (saving throws are still permitted, of course). Mind-affecting spells do not affect a quickwood.

In addition to its own attacks and defenses, a mature spy tree is able to cause 2d4 other normal oaks to serve as its hosts. These trees resemble the quickwood while so possessed, having visages and sensory organs through which the master tree actually controls the hosts and gains information. Such control extends up to one mile.

Habitat/Society: These creatures may be found in any habitat that supports normal oak trees, including the warmer regions where live oaks are found.

Ecology: It is said that quickwoods grow only through the magical offices of some great wizard (or possibly druid) who planted mandragora roots after imbuing them with mighty spells. Others claim that these weird trees are a natural progression of vegetable life toward sentience and mobility. In any case, quickwoods are certainly sentient, unlike most of the vegetation found in the world.

Quickwoods are sometimes charmed or otherwise convinced to serve as repositories for treasure or as guardians of an area. In the former role, the treasure guarded is typical of the creature having placed it there. Such items are always stored within the trunk orifices of the quickwoods. As guardians, the creatures spy for intruders and upon sighting them send out a hollow drumming sound that can be heard for a mile or more.

43

Ravenkin

CLIMATE/TERRAIN:	Temperate lands
FREQUENCY:	Very rare
ORGANIZATION:	Flock
ACTIVITY CYCLE:	Day
DIET:	Omnivore
INTELLIGENCE:	Exceptional (15–16)
TREASURE:	U (Communal), I (Individual)
ALIGNMENT:	Neutral good

NO. APPEARING:	3–12 (3d4)
ARMOR CLASS:	6
MOVEMENT:	3, Fl 27 (C)
HIT DICE:	1
THAC0:	19
NO. OF ATTACKS:	1
DAMAGE/ATTACK:	1d3
SPECIAL ATTACKS:	Eye peck, spell use
SPECIAL DEFENSES:	Not surprised
MAGIC RESISTANCE:	Nil
SIZE:	M (5' wingspan)
MORALE:	Elite (13–14)
XP VALUE:	175

The ravenkin are an avian race that have been trapped within the misty confines of Ravenloft. They are one of the few forces for good in this otherwise dark land of evil.

Ravenkin look much like huge versions of the common raven or crow with a wingspan that averages 5 feet in width. They are shrouded in black feathers and have long, straight beaks. To set themselves apart from normal ravens, they often wear small items of sparkling jewelry.

The ravenkin speak their own language, which sounds like a collection of squawks and shrieks to those who do not know it. Most (fully 80%) of these creatures will also speak the common language in use by the human or demihuman inhabitants of their lands.

Combat: The ravenkin will always try to flutter around a victim's head in combat, waiting for a chance to strike at his eyes. They will often land briefly on a would-be target before striking, using their talons to stay in place while they peck with their beaks. But, as the small talons inflict no damage, the creatures have only one pecking attack that inflicts but 1d3 points of damage. On any natural attack roll of 19 or 20, however, the ravenkin has scored a hit on one of the victim's eyes (assuming they are not wholly protected). Such an injury will blind that eye, imposing a –2 penalty on all attack rolls made by the character. A second such hit indicates loss of the other eye and, thus, total blindness. Injuries of this nature cannot be cured save by spells like *heal* or *regeneration*.

All ravenkin have a limited spell casting ability. Most (75%) are able to employ any three first-level spells per day. They need neither material or somatic components, but always cast their spells verbally. Ravenkin are required to memorize their spells ahead of time, just as human casters. An additional 20% of these creatures have the ability to employ two second-level spells per day in addition to their first-level spells. Lastly, 5% of the ravenkin population can invoke one third-level spell per day.

Habitat/Society: The ravenkin are a long-lived race with many of their elders claiming to be "a hundred winters" old. As a rule, an individual's name includes his age, so a recently hatched chick might be "Kareeka Twomoons" and a wise old elder might be known as "Shreeaka Fiftyautumns:'

Ravenkin are slow breeders. It is believed that the evil of Ravenloft has been corrupting their eggs and making them sterile. Whether this is the case or not, fully 8 in 10 ravenkin eggs fail to hatch. A ravenkin community generally consists of 155 to 200 individuals (150+5d10). Of these, half will be females (who fight just as if they were males), and 10% will be young (who do not fight). They will nest in family groups, each claiming a copse of trees as their own territory. In addition, the area around a ravenkin community tends to be filled with mundane crows, generally about 500 in number. While the ravenkin cannot directly command them, they are able to train the crows with great effectiveness and employ them as sentries and hunting animals.

Ravenkin tend to ignore travelers unless these actively seek out contact with the avians. In the latter case, they are wary and untrusting until the strangers prove themselves to be friends. Once someone has earned the trust of the ravenkin, though, they have won a great prize, for these creatures are able to provide a wealth of information about the evils of Ravenloft. The Vistani say that ravenkin can see through the eyes of every raven in the land; from the vast knowledge these folk seem to be able to amass on even the shortest notice, that seems to be only a minor exaggeration.

Ecology: The ravenkin exist on a diet of insects, berries, and carrion. In short, they will eat almost anything put before them—truly proving themselves to be omnivorous. They find the act of hunting bothersome, however, and delight in the taste of slightly rotted meat, making carrion the main element of their diet.

CLIMATE/TERRAIN:	Sea of Sorrows
FREQUENCY:	Rare
ORGANIZATION:	School
ACTIVITY CYCLE:	Any
DIET:	Carnivore
INTELLIGENCE:	Low (5–7)
TREASURE:	(A)
ALIGNMENT:	Chaotic evil
NO. APPEARING:	2–12 (2d6)
ARMOR CLASS:	4
MOVEMENT:	6, Sw 18
HIT DICE:	4+3
THAC0:	15
NO. OF ATTACKS:	3
DAMAGE/ATTACK:	2d6/2d6/2d4
SPECIAL ATTACKS:	Grapple
SPECIAL DEFENSES:	Cutting scales
MAGIC RESISTANCE:	Nil
SIZE:	M (7′ tall)
MORALE:	Steady (11–12)
XP VALUE:	420

The race of reavers are an evil and dark people who live beneath the waves on Ravenloft's western shore. Here, they lurk in hopes of attacking swimmers, fishermen, and small ships. Few indeed are the coastal communities in Lamordia, Mordent, Dementlieu, and Darkon that do not have stories of past encounters with these foul aquatic creatures.

Individual reavers look like tall humanoid creatures covered with scales. They have large, fishlike eyes and webbed hands and feet. Their fingers end in short but deadly sharp claws that can rip through flesh and tissue with ease. Their mouths are wide and filled with rows of needlelike teeth.

Reavers speak with a lisping, hissing language that is very difficult for other creatures to match. In addition, many of the sounds they use to communicate are ultrasonic, so men cannot even hear them. No reaver has ever been known to speak a human tongue.

Combat: The reaver is not noted for clever tactics and intricate strategies. As a rule, it is a brutal and savage opponent that tears its victims into pieces.

In melee, a reaver strikes three times: twice with its claws and once with its deadly bite. The former attack mode, which combines the great strength of the monster with the cutting edge of its claws, inflicts 2d6 points of damage. The latter attack combines the crushing might of the creature's jaws with its deadly, piercing teeth and inflicts 2d4 points of damage.

If both of the claw attacks hit, the reaver has managed to grapple its opponent and drag him along its scales. The edges of these small, natural plates are razor sharp, however, making such close physical contact with the reaver very dangerous. Attackers who grapple with or are grappled by a reaver will take 1d6 points of damage each round. Attempting to escape from the grip of the creature requires a 3d6 ability check against the victim's Strength. Failure to escape indicates that an additional 1d6 points of damage is taken while a successful escape reduces the damage to 1d4 points. Anyone who enters into unarmed combat will take 1d3 points of damage for each blow he lands on the reaver. Attacks from weapons that are unusually soft, like whips, will result in the breaking of the weapon on a natural attack roll of 1, 2, or 3.

Habitat/Society: Reavers tend to gather in schools of a dozen or so individuals. They are territorial in the extreme and will often regard any human settlement near their lairs (even those that predate the lair's establishment) as an intrusion upon their territory. Such "violations" are rewarded with nightly raids on the homes of the humans. each of these raids is marked by violent acts of terror targeted at individual households. In this way, the reavers hope to drive the "invaders" from the lands that border on their ocean realms.

A reaver lair is often hidden beneath a coral reef or at the heart of a thick forest of sea weed. In such isolated regions, the reavers are masters of stealth and hunting. Those who stumble upon these evil places seldom have time to see the creatures as they seem to spring out of nowhere to attack and destroy all intruders.

Ecology: Reavers feed on the raw flesh of their victims. They are strictly carnivorous and, oddly enough, feed only on land dwelling creatures and sea mammals. Reavers look upon intelligent prey as far more worthy than simple animal life. Thus, they will often pass up other targets to strike at a wandering band of humans or demihumans. After they have feasted on the bodies of their victims, they often leave behind a grisly scene of blood and death—to mark their successful hunt and warn off those who might seek to hunt them down in a quest for vengeance.

Outcasts

From time to time, an individual reaver is exiled from his people for one reason or another (usually failure in an important task). These outcasts leave the salty sea water behind and find a fresh water lake or river in which to live. Thus, even inland communities are not always safe from these evil creatures. Outcasts have the same statistics as other reavers.

Scarecrow

CLIMATE/TERRAIN:	Any farmland
FREQUENCY:	Very rare
ORGANIZATION:	Solitary
ACTIVITY CYCLE:	Night
DIET:	Nil
INTELLIGENCE:	Non-(0)
TREASURE:	Nil
ALIGNMENT:	Neutral evil

NO. APPEARING:	1
ARMOR CLASS:	8
MOVEMENT:	9
HIT DICE:	3
THAC0:	17
NO. OF ATTACKS:	1
DAMAGE/ATTACK:	1d4 or by weapon
SPECIAL ATTACKS:	See below
SPECIAL DEFENSES:	See below
MAGIC RESISTANCE:	Nil
SIZE:	M (6′ tall)
MORALE:	Fearless (19–20)
XP VALUE:	420

The Ravenloft scarecrow is a magically animated creature that moves about under the influence of an evil force. Usually found only in agricultural regions, it is often the chosen form of a vengeful farmer's spirit.

The appearance of these creatures varies, since the bodies they enter and animate are all built by different people and reflect the artistic talents and tastes of their creator. As a rule, however, the scarecrow's body is an assemblage of old clothes, stuffed with leaves, straw, or some other filling material and braced up on a wooden support. Some manner of gourd or melon is generally placed atop the body after being hollowed out and carved to resemble a haunting, frightening face. When the creature is animated, the face glows from within as if a candle or lantern were placed inside its hollow head.

Scarecrows are able to speak any language they knew in life. There is even a small chance (10%) that anyone who in life knew the individual whose spirit inhabits the scarecrow will recognize and identify that evil soul when listening to the creature's eerie, haunting voice.

Combat: The scarecrow exists only to exact vengeance on those who wronged it in life. As such, it tends to avoid combat with others and will often flee from encounters with those it does not know. When it finally comes across someone it blames for an act committed against it in life, it attacks quickly and savagely, refusing to retreat until either it or its victim is slain.

The scarecrow's main hand-to-hand attack is made with its flailing arms. This attack is only mildly harmful, however, because the creature is not noted for great strength. Each successful attack will inflict but 1d4 points of damage. From time to time, a scarecrow will attack with some manner of farm implement (usually a pitch fork or scythe). In such cases, it does damage according to the weapon employed.

The real danger presented by a scarecrow is the fact that anyone it strikes must save vs. death magic. Failure to make the save will find the victim cursed with an magical odor that draws biting and stinging insects to him from miles away. On the round after the failed saving throw, the victim takes 1d4 points of damage from bites and stings. On the next round, the victim takes 2d4 points of damage, then 3d4, and so on. This affect can be negated only by the casting of a *remove curse* spell. In addition to the damage sustained, a cursed character suffers a penalty of –1 on all attack rolls for each die of damage inflicted by the insects on that round. For example, on the first round in which the character is bitten and stung, he is at a –1 penalty on all attacks rolls and takes 1d4 points of damage. Four rounds later, he takes 5d4 points of damage and suffers a –5 penalty on his attack rolls.

Scarecrows are immune to the effects of cold-based spells and take only half damage from all lightning- or electricity-based spells. They suffer full damage from all nonmagical fire attacks. All magical flame attacks receive a +1 bonus on their attack roll and a +1 bonus per die on their damage roll. Nonmagical weapons can hit them, but these inflict only 1 point of damage per blow landed. Magical weapons not employing fire inflict half damage while those using fire (i.e., a *Flame Tongue*) gain a +1 bonus on all attack rolls and a +1 bonus per die on all damage rolls.

While they are similar to undead creatures, scarecrows cannot be turned. They are, however, immune to *sleep, charm, hold,* or similar mind-based magical influences.

Habitat/Society: The Ravenloft scarecrow is an animated form of the mundane farm construct. The spirit that drives it to commit acts of evil is often that of a local resident who feels that he was wronged by one or more of his neighbors in life. Unable to attain justice while he was alive, his spirit lingers on after his death and becomes a powerful force for evil.

Ecology: Ravenloft scarecrows are magically animated constructs. Although they are fashioned out of organic materials, there is no evidence to support a belief that they have any role in the ecosphere around them.

CLIMATE/TERRAIN:	Lower planes
FREQUENCY:	Very rare
ORGANIZATION:	Solitary
ACTIVITY CYCLE:	Any
DIET:	Special
INTELLIGENCE:	Very (11–12)
TREASURE:	Nil
ALIGNMENT:	Chaotic evil

NO. APPEARING:	1
ARMOR CLASS:	9, 5, or 1
MOVEMENT:	12 (see below)
HIT DICE:	7+3
THAC0:	13
NO. OF ATTACKS:	3
DAMAGE/ATTACK:	ld6/ld6/ld8
SPECIAL ATTACKS:	Spell use
SPECIAL DEFENSES:	Immune to fire, cold, electricity
MAGIC RESISTANCE:	See below
SIZE:	M (6' tall)
MORALE:	Champion (15–16)
XP VALUE:	2,000

The shadow fiend is a dark and dangerous creature from the most dreaded of the lower planes. Lurking in regions of darkness, it attacks only to satisfy its desire to do evil, for it never hungers or thirsts.

The shadow fiend looks like a tall, slender humanoid with small batlike wings and a body composed wholly of darkness. Both the long fingers and slender toes of the creature end in terrible claws that can inflict great wounds on enemies.

Shadow fiends have no known language, although it is said that they can communicate with other creatures from the lower planes when they encounter them. No mortal being has ever been able to attest to this, however, and it may be mere speculation.

Combat: The unusual nature of these creatures is evident in their combat tactics. Like the shadows, which many believe (wrongly) to be related creatures, these horrors are 90% undetectable when they move through dimly lit or shadowy areas. When they attack those who have not spotted them, they always attain surprise. Each round, the monster is able to strike with two of its wicked claws (inflicting 1d6 points of damage each) and its horrible bite (inflicting 1d8 points of damage).

Once engaged in combat, the power of the creature depends upon the lighting in the area of battle. In brightly lit areas (open sunlight, a *continual light* spell, and such), the shadow fiend is greatly weakened. Here, its Armor Class is 9 and all attacks that strike it do double damage. Because of this, shadow fiends will normally flee from opponents in bright light.

In dimmer lighting, that created by a torch, lantern, or light spell, the shadow fiend is somewhat better off. Here, it has an armor class of 5, though it still suffers normal damage from attacks. When it strikes in these conditions, however, it gains a +1 bonus on its attack rolls.

In darkness, anything up to candle or moonlight, the creature is at its deadliest. Here, it gains a +2 bonus on all attack rolls and is Armor Class 1. Further, all damage done to the creature is halved.

Regardless of the lighting around it, the shadow fiend is immune to all damage from fire, cold, and electricity (whether magical or mundane in nature.) A *light* spell cast directly at the creature inflicts 1d6 points per level of the caster, although this damage may be reduced (or enhanced) by the lighting in the area.

Whenever the shadow fiend gains surprise, it will spring onto its victim. Because of the small wings on its back, it can leap up to 30 feet and strike with four claws (each doing 1d6 points of damage). When it leaps, it cannot employ its bite attack.

Once per day, the shadow fiend may cast a *darkness, 15' radius* spell or subject all persons within a 30 foot area to a *fear* spell. Once per week, it can cast a *magic jar* spell at a single target (provided that it has a suitable receptacle for the victim at hand). If the victim of the *magic jar* attack makes his saving throw, however, the shadow fiend is stunned for 1d3 rounds during which time it cannot act.

Shadow fiends can be turned by clerics as if they were "special" creatures on the undead turning chart.

Habitat/Society: The shadow fiend is called into Ravenloft by the use of magical gate spells and similar incantations. Once summoned to the demiplane of terror, however, they find themselves bound to the land and unable to leave (as is the case with all summoned beings). Thus, over the centuries, a number of these creatures have been trapped in Ravenloft.

Already creatures of evil, their imprisonment only serves to increase their hatred of the world around them. Thus, they often attempt to pass their time by inflicting pain and suffering on those few mortals they encounter.

Ecology: It is doubtful that the shadow fiend is important to the overall ecology of Ravenloft. However, there are those who say that the dark powers have close ties to these foul creatures, claiming that the Powers are able command the fiends to do their bidding at any time. Since none can even pretend to predict the actions or guess the desires of the dark powers, it seems possible that this is the case.

Skeleton, Giant

CLIMATE/TERRAIN:	Any
FREQUENCY:	Rare
ORGANIZATION:	Solitary
ACTIVITY CYCLE:	Any
DIET:	Nil
INTELLIGENCE:	Non-(0)
TREASURE:	Nil
ALIGNMENT:	Neutral

NO. APPEARING:	2–8 (2d4)
ARMOR CLASS:	4
MOVEMENT:	12
HIT DICE:	4+4
THAC0:	15
NO. OF ATTACKS:	1
DAMAGE/ATTACK:	1d12
SPECIAL ATTACKS:	Nil
SPECIAL DEFENSES:	See below
MAGIC RESISTANCE:	Nil
SIZE:	L (12′ tall)
MORALE:	Fearless (20)
XP VALUE:	1,400

Giant skeletons are similar to the more common undead skeleton, but they have been created with a combination of spells and are, thus, far more deadly than their lesser counterparts.

Giant skeletons stand roughly 12 feet tall and look to be made from the bones of giants. In actuality, they are simply human skeletons that have been magically enlarged. They are normally armed with long spears or scythes that end in keen bone blades. Rare individuals will be found carrying shields (and thus have an Armor Class of 3), but these are far from common. A small, magical fire burns in the chest of each giant skeleton, a byproduct of the magics that are used to make them. These flames begin just above the pelvis and reach upward to lick at the collar bones. Mysteriously, no burning or scorching occurs where the flames touch the bone.

Giant skeletons do not communicate in any way. They can obey simple, verbal commands given to them by their creator, but will ignore all others. In order for a command to be understood by these animated skeletons, it must contain no more than three distinct concepts. For example, "Stay in this room, make sure that nobody comes in, and don't allow the prince to leave" is one type of command these creatures could obey.

Combat: In melee combat, giant skeletons most frequently attack with their bone-bladed scythes or spears. Each blow that lands inflicts 1d12 points of damage.

Once per hour (6 turns), a skeleton may reach into its chest and draw forth a sphere of fire from the flames that burn within its rib cage. This flaming sphere can be hurled as if it were a fireball that delivers 8d6 points of damage. Because these creatures are immune to harm from both magical and normal fires, they will freely use this attack in close quarters.

Giant skeletons are immune to *sleep, charm, hold,* or similar mind-affecting spells. Cold-based spells inflict half damage to them, lightning inflicts full damage, while fire (as has already been mentioned) cannot harm them. They suffer half damage from edged or piercing weapons and but 1 point of damage per die from all manner of arrows, quarrels, or missiles. Blunt melee weapons inflict full damage on them.

Being undead, giant skeletons can be turned by priests and paladins. They are more difficult to turn than mundane skeletons, however, being treated as if they were mummies. Holy water that is splashed upon them inflicts 2d4 points of damage per vial.

Habitat/Society: The first giant skeletons to appear in Ravenloft were created by the undead priestess Radaga in her lair within the domain of Kartakass. Others have since mastered the spells and techniques required to create these monsters; thus, giant skeletons are gradually beginning to appear in other realms where the dead and undead lurk.

Giant skeletons are employed as guards and sentinels by those with the power to create them. It is said that the dark powers can see everything that transpires before the eyes of these foul automatons, but there is no proof supporting this rumor.

Ecology: Like lesser animated skeletons, these undead things have no true claim to any place in nature. They are created from the bones of those who have died and are abominations in the eyes of all who belief in the sanctity of life and goodness.

The process by which giant skeletons are created is dark and evil. Attempts to manufacture them outside of Ravenloft have failed, so it is clear that they are in some way linked to the dark powers themselves. In order to create a giant skeleton, a spell caster must have the intact skeleton of a normal human or demihuman. On a night when the land is draped in fog, they must cast *animate dead, produce fire, enlarge,* and *resist fire* (in that order) over the bones. When the last spell is cast, the bones lengthen and thicken and the creatures rise up. The creator must make a Ravenloft powers check for his part in this evil undertaking.

CLIMATE/TERRAIN:	Any Barovia
FREQUENCY:	Very rare
ORGANIZATION:	Solitary
ACTIVITY CYCLE:	Night
DIET:	Nil
INTELLIGENCE:	Non-(0)
Treasure	Nil
ALIGNMENT:	Neutral

NO. APPEARING:	1–10
ARMOR CLASS:	7
MOVEMENT:	18
HIT DICE:	3 +1
THAC0:	17
NO. OF ATTACKS:	3
DAMAGE/ATTACK:	1d6/1d6/1d4
SPECIAL ATTACKS:	See below
SPECIAL DEFENSES:	See below
MAGIC RESISTANCE:	Nil
SIZE:	L (8′ tall)
MORALE:	Fearless (19–20)
XP VALUE:	270

Strahd's skeletal steeds are magically animated undead horses, created as guardians and warriors by the master vampire Strahd Von Zarovich.

Completely stripped of flesh, skeletal steeds are held together by magic. They wear the tattered remains of whatever saddles or blankets may have been on them when they died. Thus, many will wear nothing at all while rare individuals might actually wear the remnants of barding (improving their armor class accordingly). Any horse shoes they may have had in life are still on their hooves; however, the enchantment that raised these creatures from the dead gives those shoes a magical aura that causes illusory flames to flicker around the steed's hooves when it breaks into a gallop.

Unlike normal, living horses, which are rarely still and always shifting and twitching, Strahd's skeletal steeds are completely motionless until they need to act. Many times they are encountered as a mere pile of dusty horse bones. If given a command by Strahd or upon the activation of some trigger magic, they can rise up and assemble. The mere sight of this is enough to require those viewing it to make a horror check.

They have no strong odor, other than a faint trace of dust and mold. They sound hollow and light when in motion and the clatter of their hooves sounds more like a rattle of sticks than the pounding of horses.

Combat: Strahd's skeletal steeds fight like normal war horses. Each round, the creature rears up and can both strike with its hooves and bite. On the second round of combat, and every other round thereafter, they can breathe a cloud of noxious gas in an area five feet wide and deep in front of them. Anyone caught in it must successfully save vs. breath weapon or be frozen to the spot for 2 to 8 (2d4) rounds.

Like all undead, they are immune to *sleep, charm, hold,* and other mind-controlling spells. Piercing weapons such as spears and arrows do no damage to them, for they just slide between the bones. Edged weapons, like swords and axes, will inflict only half damage, while blunt weapons (including polearms and the like used as quarterstaves) can inflict normal damage.

Strahd's skeletal steeds are totally immune to cold- or fire-based attacks, but take full damage from lightning- and electricity-based spells. Further, their creator has greatly strengthened their ties to the negative plane. This makes them harder to turn (they are turned as wraiths), but also makes them vulnerable to the damaging effects of a *negative plane protection* spell.

Habitat/Society: Strahd's skeletal steeds are found in the dark catacombs beneath Barovia's surface, on old battlefields, or anywhere within Castle Ravenloft. Strahd has been known to post them as sentries throughout Barovia. He never uses them as mounts, but has been known to use them as couriers. Thus, such a creature might well be encountered while on an important mission to deliver some vital message or object for the Lord of Barovia.

As mindless undead creatures, skeletal steeds have no society. They obey any orders given to them by Strahd. The commands must be simple, a single sentence of no more than a few words. They only obey Strahd Von Zarovich unless some magical means (like a *control undead* spell) is used to usurp command of a specific creature. In this case, however, Strahd will know at once that something has happened to one of his steeds.

Ecology: As undead things, Strahd's skeletal steeds are not a part of nature. Further, only Strahd Von Zarovich knows the arcane ritual necessary to make them. He can make them only from horse skeletons where 90% of the bones and the skull are present. It is not known if other animals can be animated from the same spell, but given the power of the Lord of Barovia, and his ties to the evil forces of necromancy, this seems probable.

Treant, Evil

CLIMATE/TERRAIN:	Any forest
FREQUENCY:	Very rare
ORGANIZATION:	Grove
ACTIVITY CYCLE:	Any
DIET:	Carnivore
INTELLIGENCE:	Very (11–12)
TREASURE:	Q (×5), X
ALIGNMENT:	Chaotic evil

NO. APPEARING:	1–20
ARMOR CLASS:	0
MOVEMENT:	12
HIT DICE:	7–12
THAC0:	7–8 HD: 13
	9–10 HD: 11
	11–12 HD: 9
NO. OF ATTACKS:	2
DAMAGE/ATTACK:	Variable
SPECIAL ATTACKS:	Nil
SPECIAL DEFENSES:	Nil
MAGIC RESISTANCE:	Nil
SIZE:	H (13′–18′)
MORALE:	Elite (13–14)
XP VALUE:	2,000 (+1,000/HD)

The peaceful race of treants, found on many worlds and in many lands, is also represented in Ravenloft. Sadly, the dark waters and corrupting evil of the land has twisted them into evil and foul things. The treants of Ravenloft despise good and innocent things as much as their counterparts hate evil; they go to great lengths to torment and terrorize travelers in their domains. The only trait they seem to share with the true treant is a hatred of unchecked or unrestricted use of fire.

Evil treants look much like normal trees—so much so, in fact, that when standing in a grove or forest they have a 90% chance of being mistaken for common flora. Their bark is thick and gnarled, providing them with protection from physical damage. While they have a face that looks unsettlingly human when they are speaking, it vanishes into patterns of grooves and knots when the creature wishes to remain stationary. Evil treants come in three age groups: young (13 to 14 feet tall), mature (15 to 16 feet tall), and elder (17 to 18 feet tall). In combat, the amount of damage inflicted by a treant is determined by its age and size.

Evil treants can speak their own language and can usually communicate with the animals in the forest around them. They are also often capable of speaking a fair number (14) of other languages.

Combat: Young treants can lash out with their powerful branches to strike twice in combat, inflicting 2d8 points of damage per blow landed. Mature treants are able to inflict even more dangerous wounds, inflicting 3d6 points of damage with each attack. Elder treants have amassed so much physical power that their attacks deliver fully 4d6 points of damage each. Few and far between are the creatures that can stand against them in combat.

Despite the thick bark that provides them with protection against physical assaults, treants are unusually vulnerable to fire. Any weapon or attack based on fire (magical or normal) receives a +4 bonus on its attack roll. Further, such attacks score an additional 1 point per die to all damage inflicted. Saving throws required for fire-based attacks and

spells are made at a –4 penalty.

Like their good counterparts, evil treants can animate and command living trees. Each treant can animate two trees. This power has a range of 60 yards, and any animated tree that moves beyond that limit is instantly returned to its normal state. After spending one round to uproot itself, an animated tree is able to move about and attack as if it were a mature treant.

Because of their mass and strength, treants are quite effective in combat against structures and fortifications—especially those made from wood. Exact details on this aspect of combat are provided in *The Castle Guide* and BATTLESYSTEM® miniatures rules, where they are considered to be identical to good treants.

Habitat/Society: Evil treants live in secluded forests like those found in the mountains of southwestern Ravenloft. Here, they warp the nature of what might otherwise be peaceful and picturesque woodlands, turning them into evil, haunted forests.

Evil treants have no interest in treasures, magical or monetary, although items of value are sometimes found on the ground where they have claimed the lives of past victims. Only in very rare cases will an evil treant attempt to use any of these artificial items, as they prefer to leave them where they fell and use them as bait to lure curious explorers to their deaths.

Ecology: Unlike good treants, who feed wholly by photosynthesis, evil treants are carnivorous. In fact, they favor the flesh of intelligent creatures (usually humans and demihumans) over all other prey. Their chosen delicacy, when they can obtain it, is the flesh of innocents, who they torment and horrify before devouring. Evil treants rarely kill their prey before consuming it, for they believe that this makes it unfit for digestion. Thus, victims who are accidentally slain during the tortures inflicted upon them by hungry treants are discarded and left to feed the scavengers of the forest.

The sap of an evil treant, when smeared over the entire body, is reported to provide humans and demihumans with protection equivalent to that granted by a *barkskin* spell.

CLIMATE/TERRAIN:	Any forest
FREQUENCY:	Very rare
ORGANIZATION:	Copse
ACTIVITY CYCLE:	Night
DIET:	Blood
INTELLIGENCE:	High (13–14)
TREASURE:	Nil
ALIGNMENT:	Chaotic evil

NO. APPEARING:	1-4
ARMOR CLASS:	0
MOVEMENT:	12
HIT DICE:	15
THAC0:	5
NO. OF ATTACKS:	2
DAMAGE/ATTACK:	5d6/8d6
SPECIAL ATTACKS:	See below
SPECIAL DEFENSES:	See below
MAGIC RESISTANCE:	Nil
SIZE:	H (20′ tall)
MORALE:	Champion (15–16)
XP VALUE:	15,000

When an evil treant sees that its many years are soon to come to an end, it seldom accepts this fate quietly. For most, this means a final, wild orgy of violence and death. For a few, however, it means death and resurrection as a thing so dark and evil that even the Vistani will not speak of it.

An undead treant looks much like any other deciduous tree in the winter. It has no leaves and a lusterless, almost brittle, look to its bark. Like living treants, its face is hidden until it chooses to speak or make its presence known. When a creature of this sort stands amid a grove or copse of similar leafless trees, it is 90% likely to go unnoticed by those passing near.

Undead treants speak the language of evil treants and generally know many (2d4) other tongues. Despite their linguistic skills, however, they seldom converse with the living and seem unable to speak with the animals of the forest around them.

Combat: Undead treants lash out with their powerful branches, striking twice per round and inflicting 5d6 points of damage with each successful blow. On any natural roll of 19 or 20, they are assumed to have knocked their opponent prone and stunned them for 1 round per 5 points (or fraction thereof) of damage inflicted. Thus, a blow delivering 18 points of damage would stun a character for 4 rounds.

If the treant is not otherwise engaged in combat, it will move beside the fallen form and feed upon the blood of the victim. To do this, the treant must remain stationary for 1 round. On the second round, it sprouts 3d4 rootlike appendages that snake out and bury themselves in the victim's flesh. These inflict 1 point of damage each and allow the monster to begin feeding on the third round. Starting then, and on each subsequent round, the creature will drain 1d3 points of blood for each root sunk into the victim.

Anyone being drained of blood by the treant is rendered immobile as the coils of roots encircle his body. Individuals so entrapped can only escape the deadly embrace of these vampiric trees with the aid of a third party. In order to end the blood draining, the treant's roots must be cut away. They are treated as armor class 5 and any successful attack will break the tendril. If all of the tendrils are cut, the victim can work

his way free in 2 rounds (1 with outside help). When an undead treant stops feeding, either because it has drained its victim of blood or because all of its tendrils have been severed, it requires a full round to become mobile again. During this time, or whenever it is feeding, all attacks against the creature gain a +2 bonus.

Like other treants, the undead variety are vulnerable to fire. All fire-based attacks gain a +4 bonus on their attack rolls and inflict an extra 2 points per die of damage.

Undead treants are unable to animate other trees, but they are known to employ magic. All undead treants have the spellcasting powers of a level 2 to 6 (2d3) druid. Because of their own vulnerability to flames and fires, however, they will never employ any spells that use any kind of fire. Undead treants require the same verbal and somatic components that other spellcasters do, but never need to employ material components unless they are vital to the operation of the spell (a *goodberry*, for example).

Undead treants are immune to spells like *sleep, charm,* or *hold,* as are all undead, but also have several other immunities that set them above the rest of the living dead. Holy water, for example, has no effect on them, and they cannot be turned by priests or paladins. They are also untouched by sunlight and cannot be affected by spells like *control undead* or *control plants.*

Habitat/Society: Undead treants tend to live in small copses of dead trees with no more than four individuals in any given area. Their foul aura permeates the copse around them, making the woods they inhabit dark and evil places.

It is not uncommon for individual undead treants to still be members the evil treant community they once lived in. When this is the case, the undead treant will be treated with the respect due to a powerful leader and will clearly be in command of the others.

Ecology: Undead treants seem to be a natural stage in the life cycle of some evil treants. No doubt this is given as a "reward" for their evil lives by the dark powers.

Valpurgeist

CLIMATE/TERRAIN:	Any land
FREQUENCY:	Very rare
ORGANIZATION:	Solitary
ACTIVITY CYCLE:	Any
DIET:	Nil
INTELLIGENCE:	Average (8–12)
TREASURE:	Nil
ALIGNMENT:	Chaotic evil

NO. APPEARING:	1
ARMOR CLASS:	4
MOVEMENT:	9
HIT DICE:	15
THAC0:	5
NO. OF ATTACKS:	2
DAMAGE/ATTACK:	1d6/1d6
SPECIAL ATTACKS:	Strangulation
SPECIAL DEFENSES:	See below
MAGIC RESISTANCE:	Nil
SIZE:	M (6′ tall)
MORALE:	Average (8–10)
XP VALUE:	650

The valpurgeist, or hanged man, is an undead creature that is sometimes manifested when an innocent man or woman is wrongly hanged for a crime. Unable to prove its innocence in life, the spirit returns after death to claim the lives of those who sent it to the gallows.

Valpurgeists are clearly human in appearance, although they are far from able to pass as normal men. Their necks have clearly been broken, causing the head to hang at an awkward angle and flop about loosely as the creature moves. Further, the skin of the creature has taken on the pallor of the dead and an odor of decay hangs heavy in the air around the thing.

The valpurgeist cannot speak and seems unwilling or unable to listen to the words of others. Attempts at communication that do not involve magic (a *speak with dead spell*, for example) are doomed to failure. Those who do manage to speak with the creature will find that it is wholly obsessed with exacting revenge and destroying those who have wronged it.

Combat: The valpurgeist attacks with its two powerful fists. The essence of darkness that has animated it has given it incredible strength, so that each blow it lands inflicts 1d6 points of damage.

If both of its fists strike the target, it is assumed to have gotten a solid grip on the throat of its victim and will begin to strangle him or her. Escaping from the creature's grip requires a successful roll to bend bars.

Beginning on the round after its viselike grip has locked onto its victim, the creature automatically inflicts 1d8 points of damage without making another attack roll. Further, the victim must make a successful saving throw vs. paralysis or fall unconscious from lack of oxygen. Those who do fall unconscious will die on the next round, suffering a crushed windpipe and broken neck if they are not freed by a third party. The only ways to free a character who is being strangled from the deadly grip of the valpurgeist are to pry the choking hands from their throat (a roll to bend bars is required) or distract the monster from its current victim. The latter method is very diffi-

cult, for there is but a 1% chance per point of damage inflicted that the monster will release someone in its grip and attack another character. If it does release its hold, it will always attack the person that distracted it.

Cutting the arms off of the monster will not cause them to release their victim, for their muscles will remain locked and the hands will continue to strangle the character.

Valpurgeists can be turned as if they were ghasts and suffer 1d4 points of damage per vial of holy water splashed on them. They are immune to *sleep, charm, hold,* and similar spells, but can be affected normally by all spells that are intended for use against undead.

A valpurgeist can be freed of its burden of guilt (and thus allowed to rest in peace) if evidence can be found that will prove the being's innocence in the case for which it was hanged. If the monster's spirit is not appeased in this way, it will return to plague its accusers time and time again, no matter what steps are taken to destroy it or its physical form. Thus, even if the entire body of the valpurgeist is destroyed with acid, it will reassemble itself and begin its quest for vengeance anew. Returning to life after being destroyed requires 2d4 days if the body is intact or twice that if the body is destroyed in some way.

Habitat/Society: Valpurgeists are lonely souls who have felt the cold injustice of a world that would not believe their pleas of innocence. Because of this, they will have no kinship with any living thing in their afterlife.

While the valpurgeist is no more or less intelligent than he was in life, all of his mental faculties are now centered on revenge. Thus, he will work methodically, and often quite shrewdly, to arrange for the demise of those he considers his enemies.

Even the death of all those involved with the creature's trial and execution cannot free the spirit from its agony. Once it has slain all those who wronged it, the creature simply begins to widen the scope of its evil. The only way to free the world of a valpurgeist's cursed presence is to prove its innocence, thus removing the anger that taints its spirit.

Ecology: Like all undead, valpurgeists have no place in the natural world. They are simply products of evil and darkness.

Vampires in Ravenloft

Of all the dark and evil things that move about in the mists of Ravenloft, none is more feared than the vampire. These creatures can often move freely about in the world of men and, as such, are all the more dreadful. Their unexpected attacks often target the innocent and helpless, leaving little hope that a victim will survive to lead would-be vampire hunters to the monster. All in all, they are certainly the darkest of the dark.

Ravenloft is home to many vampires, some of whom are even lords of their own domains. Strahd Von Zarovich, the master of Barovia, is one such creature. His darkness is so great that many believe the land itself to be tied directly to him. This may or may not be true, but the Vistani and Lord Azalin of Darkon certainly seem to believe it. Other vampire lords, like Duke Gundar of Gundarak, are certainly powerful—but none can compare to the might or the evil that is Strahd's.

Becoming a Vampire

As described in the RAVENLOFT boxed set, there are three ways to become a vampire. Each of these paths to darkness has its own unique character, but the end result is always a creature of unsurpassed evil and power.

The first path, generally known as that of deadly desire, is perhaps the most awful. In this case, the individual who is destined to become a vampire actually wishes to cross over and become undead. While it has been said that they must sacrifice their lives to attain this goal, a greater cost is often paid. Those who desire to live eternally and feed on the life essences of their fellow men must give up a portion of their spirits to the dark powers themselves. In this way, they are granted the powers of the undead, but also stripped of the last vestiges of their humanity. In the centuries to come, many find this loss too great to bear and seek out their own destruction.

The second path, that of the curse, is often the most insidious of the three. In this case, the individual is often unaware that he or she is destined to become a thing of the night. The transformation into "unlife" might occur because of a potent curse laid down by someone who has been wronged by the victim. Occasionally, an individual might find that he or she has inherited (or found) a beautiful and alluring magical ring—only to find that it cannot be removed and that the character is slowly . . . changing. There are those who accept this curse and embrace their new existence as a vampire, while others despise the things they have become. In nearly every case, these are the most passionate and "alive" examples of this evil race.

The final, and surely most tragic, path to vampirism is that of the victim. This is the route most commonly taken to vampirism, for it is the way in which those slain by a vampire become vampires themselves. Vampires created in this way almost always detest themselves and the creature that made them what they are. More information on this type of vampire is presented in the next section, which details the relationship of such creatures to their masters. All in all, the victims of other vampires are unhappy in their new lives, for few ever accept their fates happily—and many do not have the strength of character to seek an end to their wretched "unlives."

Vampire Masters & Slaves

When a vampire decides to create new slaves, it does so by taking their lives in some special way. For most, it is simply the draining of their life energies or the drinking of their blood. Whatever the end result, if the victim dies from the feeding of the beast, he or she rises again as a vampire. At this point, the victim of the attack is enslaved by the vampire that created it.

The newly created monster seldom has any fraction of its master's power and is thus unable to challenge its master's authority. Further, the master exerts a powerful form of charm over its subjects that prevents them from acting to destroy it. This does not, however, mean that the vampire's minions cannot act to undermine the vampire's plans in minor ways, only that they must do as they are ordered by their lord. Unlike the limitations of a traditional *charm,* the vampire's power enables him to order his slaves to destroy their loved ones or act against their own self interest without resistance.

Vampire Companions

As the years pass, vampires often find that their greatest enemies are not would-be heroes, but time and boredom. The immortality they may once have craved now looks like a bleak and endless chain of suffering that they must wear eternally. To ease their misery, many vampires seek out a special companion. The most commonly encountered form of this is regarded, by those unfamiliar with the depth of the bond to be established, in the same way that they might look upon any normal person taking a wife or husband. In truth, there is far more to this process.

The process of vampiric bonding is as murky as the fog that often shrouds the vampire's movement. When the vampire decides to take a companion, it generally (although not always) seeks out an individual of the opposite sex that reminds him of someone he loved in life. The vampire repeatedly visits the victim, feeding on him until he is at the point of death. At the last, when all hope seems lost, the vampire draws away the last vestiges of the companion's life and infuses him with its own energies. The process is both traumatic and passionate, for this mingling of essences is far more intimate than any purely physical act of love.

When the bonding is completed, both the vampire and its victim are exhausted and all but helpless for upwards of an hour. At the end of that time, the victim has become a vampire.

While the newly created companion is as much a slave of its master as any vampire spawned from an act of violence, there is something special about it. The companion shares a special metaphysical link with its master. Both can experience the other's senses at certain times of day or under the influence of certain charms and enchantments. In many cases, this bond is fleeting and exists only briefly, at dawn and dusk for example, while for others it is a continuous exchange that cannot be broken without the death of one or the other. In many cases, a vampire's companion also has the ability to command its master's slaves, so long as no action is ordered that would place them in direct confrontation with their creator.

From the point of their bonding on, the two vampires are utterly loyal to each other. While the master might willingly sacrifice its other minions as pawns, it will protect its companion as if it were a king or queen. Likewise, the companion will take no action against its master and will do all that it can to protect him or her from harm. Both will even give up their own lives to save that of their companion. In fact, the bond between the two is so intense that if the master is slain, its companion retains the ability to command its slaves as if he or she were the vampire that had created them.

Vampire, Dwarf

CLIMATE/TERRAIN:	Any subterranean
FREQUENCY:	Very rare
ORGANIZATION:	Solitary
ACTIVITY CYCLE:	Any
DIET:	Special
INTELLIGENCE:	Very (11–12)
TREASURE:	F
ALIGNMENT:	Neutral evil
NO. APPEARING:	1
ARMOR CLASS:	0
MOVEMENT:	9
HIT DICE:	9+3
THAC0:	11
NO. OF ATTACKS:	1
DAMAGE/ATTACK:	1d4 or by weapon (+ STR bonus)
SPECIAL ATTACKS:	See below
SPECIAL DEFENSES:	See below
MAGIC RESISTANCE:	Nil
SIZE:	S (4' tall)
MORALE:	Elite (13-14)
XP VALUE:	3,000 (+1,000 per 100 years of age)

Dwarves are a long lived race with an intense cultural hatred of the undead and their evil work. They regard death as the just rewards of a warrior and undeath as cheating a hero of his glorious end. For this reason, a dwarf vampire is perhaps the most awful of things, for its natural hatred of what it has become leads it to do great acts of evil.

Dwarf vampires, like all vampires, look much as they did in life. They are short and stocky, with long, white or silver beards, and heavy, rounded features. In most cases, they retain the trappings of the profession they held in life; a dwarf vampire who was a warrior is often found in full armor with a heavy battle axe or war hammer close at hand.

Dwarf vampires retain the knowledge of languages that they had in life. There is no language specific to these creatures save the dwarven tongue that served them before their deaths.

Combat: Dwarf vampires retain the courage and vigor that marked them in life. As such, they are deadly warriors who will often battle opponents for the sheer love of combat. Often, they will wield the weapons they loved in life, doing damage based on the type of weapon employed. Further, their status as undead has greatly magnified their physical power in most cases, so that all dwarf vampires are assumed to have a Strength score of 18/76. This gives them a natural bonus of +2 on all melee attack rolls and +4 on all melee damage rolls. Vampire dwarves retain their natural combat advantage (+1 bonus on all attack rolls) when battling orcs, goblins, hobgoblins, and so forth. Similarly, large creatures (like ogres and trolls) suffer a –4 penalty on their attack rolls against these smaller creatures. This ability exactly matches that presented in the *Player's Handbook*.

The most feared attack mode of these dark creatures, however, is their vitality drain. Each successful unarmed melee attack allows the vampire to drain 2 points of Constitution from its victim. This loss is permanent and will instantly modify the character's hit points and other related scores. Any character reduced to a Constitution score of 0 is instantly slain and rises again as a vampire of the appropri-

ate type after three days (see Ecology).

Dwarf vampires have the natural racial abilities of dwarves: detecting grades, slopes, or newly constructed stonework 5 times in 6, detecting sliding or shifting walls or rooms 4 times in 6, and detecting stonework traps (including pits and deadfalls) or determining their approximate depth underground 3 times in 6.

Like their strength, the natural Constitution and inherent magic resistance of these creatures have also been increased by their contact with the Negative Material Plane. While this gives dwarf vampires a +5 bonus on all saving throws vs. wands, rods, staffs, and spells, it also makes it impossible for them to employ magical items. Being undead, of course, they cannot be poisoned.

Dwarf vampires do not have the natural charm ability of human vampires, but are able to strike fear into the hearts of their enemies with but a gaze. In any combat round, the creature may employ this attack on any single foe, requiring them to make a fear check. Failure indicates that they have met the monster's gaze and been filled with supernatural fear and revulsion. Due to the power of this enchantment, the victim suffers a –2 penalty on this check.

While the vampire dwarf had a natural infravision in life, death has rewarded him with a far greater sense of sight. In addition to his normal 60-foot infravision, the vampire dwarf can see in all but absolute darkness as if in full daylight.

Vampire dwarves are even more resistant to physical and magical attacks than normal vampires. They can be hit only by +2 or better magical weapons, with all others passing harmlessly through them as if they were no more than vapor. Even if struck and harmed by weapons or spells, a vampire dwarf regenerates 4 hit points per round when in any subterranean area. Above ground, they regenerate only 1 point per round. If reduced to 0 hit points, a vampire dwarf is not slain. Rather, it is forced to employ its stonewalking ability and flee the combat. If it is unable to reach its coffin within 12 turns, the vampire merges with the stone around it and is destroyed. If it does reach its coffin, the foul vampire enters it and, after resting for eight hours, is restored to full health and power.

Holy water has no effect on these creatures, but water of a natural spring bums them for 2d4 points of damage per round. Immersion in a pool of water fed wholly by natural springs utterly destroys the vampire when it reaches 0 hit points. Holy symbols keep the creature at bay, although they do no damage to it (even if pressed against the vampire's flesh).

Like all other vampires, these creatures are immune to all manner of mind-affecting spells. These include, but are not limited to, *sleep, charm,* and *hold.* As undead things, they are immune to any type of poisons or toxins and cannot be suffocated or drowned. Spells that do damage with cold or electricity do only half damage to the monster, but those employing fire have their normal effect. Unlike most other vampires, dwarf vampires are not harmed by sunlight. They are unable to regenerate when in full sunlight, however, and will go to great lengths to avoid entering it, for they find it painfully bright.

Dwarf vampires cannot assume the forms of wolves or bats as some other vampires can, but are able to summon any form of burrowing or subterranean creature to their aid. When they opt to do this, 10d10 Hit Dice worth of such animals will arrive within 2d6 rounds. The exact type of animals called depends on the area in which the vampire is encountered, but each vampire has its favorite type of animal.

Vampire dwarves have the ability to stonewalk at will. With this power, they are able to enter and walk through any thickness of stone or earth as if it were nothing more than air. It is not unknown for a vampire dwarf to lurk just beneath the surface of the earth and then spring up to attack those walking above it. The vampire can extend the magical aura of this power to allow it to bring any object it can carry with it when it stonewalks. Thus, a dwarf vampire could grab a victim and then employ its stonewalking power to sink straight into the earth and escape anyone in pursuit. A dwarf vampire affected by a *dispel magic* spell is unable to stonewalk for 2d4 rounds or until reduced to 0 hit points and forced into a stonewalking state. If a character manages to attack the dwarf vampire while it is employing this power, there is no change to the creature's natural defenses or vulnerabilities.

Dwarf vampires cannot cross a line of powdered metal (even if they are stonewalking). They can take action to indirectly break the line, summoning rats to scamper through it, for example, but the dwarf vampire may never directly affect it. If there is even the slightest break in the line, however, the vampire can move past it with ease.

Dwarf vampires are unable to enter a structure that is not made in some part of stone or earth. Thus, a yeoman's home in the woods built wholly of logs would offer complete protection from the intrusions of a dwarf vampire while a mighty stone castle could be entered with ease.

Dwarf vampires can be turned as if they were normal vampires. As the years pass, however, and their contact with the Negative Material Plane strengthens and, when combined with their own natural resistance to all manner of magics, they become harder and harder to turn away. The most powerful and ancient of these creatures are reported to be almost impossible to drive away, no matter how strong the faith of the turning priest may be.

Killing a vampire dwarf is a difficult proposition at best. The most sure way of ending the creature's dark unlife is to impale it through the heart on a natural stalactite or stalagmite. The body of the vampire can either be forced onto the stone or the stone driven through the body of the creature. Once the vampire has been killed in this way, however, it can be revived simply by removing the impaling object. In order to assure that the creature remains dead, its heart must be cut out, soaked in oil for three days, and then set alight. When the last flames of the fire have faded away, so too has the essence of the vampire.

Habitat/Society: Dwarf vampires seek out the deepest and darkest of subterranean lairs. They shun all contact with their kind, perhaps out of disgust or embarrassment over what has become of them. The only time they will seek out

other dwarves is when they wish to create a vampire companion or are in need of slaves for some evil deed.

Dwarf vampires are the most introverted of all the racial vampire types. They tend to keep to themselves and do not seek to amass power as do human vampires. This does not mean that they will become utterly isolated, however, for they are drawn to feed on the essences of the living.

Age	HD	Save	Ench	Fear	Turn
0–99	10 + 3	+5	+2	–2	Vampire
100–199	11 + 3	+5	+2	–2	Vampire
200–299	12 + 3	+5	+3	–3	Ghost
300–399	13+ 2	+6	+3	–4	Ghost
400–499	14 + 1	+6	+3	–5	Lich
500+	15	+7	+4	–5	Special

HD indicates the number of Hit Dice that the vampire has at a given age.

Save shows the bonus to the vampires saving throws versus wands, rods, staffs, and spell.

Ench(antment) indicates the magical plus that must be associated with a weapon before it can harm the vampire.

Fear indicates the penalty that is applied to the fear check of those targets being attacked by the vampire's gaze attack.

Turn indicates the row on the Turning Undead table that is consulted for attempts to drive away these monsters.

Ecology: The dwarf vampire is a thing of darkness and evil that has no place in the natural world. It moves about, spreading death and suffering in an attempt to ease the misery it feels over having been doomed to an eternal life that it detests.

Those dwarves that fall prey to the undead will often become themselves undead. Three days after any character dies from the vampire's vitality draining, they will rise again if certain conditions are met. First, and most importantly, the victim must have been a dwarf. Vampire dwarves who kill elves or humans will not create new vampires, for only their own kind can be brought back to unlife by them. Further, the body must be intact. Second, the body must be placed in a stone coffin or sarcophagus and then entombed in some subterranean place. A typical burial service will meet this requirement, while placement in a crypt on the surface will not. Finally, the dwarf vampire must visit the body of its victim on the third night after burial and sprinkle the body with powdered metals. As soon as this is done, the new vampire is born. As with all vampires, it is now a slave to its creator.

Because they realize the torment that transformation into a vampire causes to dwarves, the vampire dwarf is reluctant to create others of its kind. Thus, it does this only when it feels that it need minions to help it carry out its acts of evil.

In many cases, the vampire will kill its minions after they have served it for a few months, freeing them from the suffering that it must endure. Such kindness and compassion seems out of place for these creatures, but many scholars believe that they still retain the last vestiges of their love for other dwarves and cannot bear to spread their suffering to others of their proud race. In most cases, the free-willed dwarf vampires of Ravenloft were created by masters who were slain before they could destroy their minions, leaving their creations to suffer in their place.

Both the MONSTROUS MANUAL tome and the RAVENLOFT boxed set go into great detail about vampires. The information presented in this overview is intended to complement, clarify, and enhance the text presented elsewhere.

Vampire, Elf

CLIMATE/TERRAIN:	Nonarctic forest
FREQUENCY:	Very rare
ORGANIZATION:	Solitary
ACTIVITY CYCLE:	Day
DIET:	Charisma
INTELLIGENCE:	Genius (17–18)
TREASURE:	F
ALIGNMENT:	Lawful evil

NO. APPEARING:	1
ARMOR CLASS:	2
MOVEMENT:	15
HIT DICE:	7+3
THAC0:	13
NO. OF ATTACKS:	1
DAMAGE/ATTACK:	1d4 or by weapon (+ STR bonus)
SPECIAL ATTACKS:	Charisma drain
SPECIAL DEFENSES:	Struck only by magical weapons; spell immunity
MAGIC RESISTANCE:	Nil
SIZE:	M (5'–6' tall)
MORALE:	Champion (15–16)
XP VALUE:	3,000 (+1,000 per 100 years of age)

The elf vampire is a tragic creature indeed, for when someone from a race that so loves life and goodness turns to evil and death the world has lost much. The evil that lurks within the elf vampire is so overwhelming that it forces the creature to transform the vital, living forests around him into places of death and decay.

Unlike all other types of vampire, the elf variety cannot move among others of its kind freely. The evil that has twisted the creature's spirit has also wrought havoc on its fair features. Thus, elf vampires appear as twisted and scarred mockeries of their beautiful and graceful race. Because of this, they often dress in dark robes and wear garments designed to hide their appearance from the world.

Elf vampires tend to speak their own language and a handful of others—whatever they had learned in life. It is rumored (and there is much evidence to support this) that they can converse with the animals of the forest and learn from them all that is occurring in their realms.

Combat: When they engage in melee combat, elf vampires are very dangerous opponents. While they do not have the same physical power that vampires of other types might possess, their Strength score of 18/01 is still enough to merit a +1 bonus on all attack rolls and a +3 bonus on all damage rolls. They will often employ weapons in combat, favoring swords and daggers above all other weapons.

Elf vampires retain the knowledge they had in life, including their racial, class, and magical abilities. Thus, all elf vampires have an extra +1 bonus on attack rolls made with long swords or bows, can move silently when not in metal armor, and see fully 60 feet with keen infravision. Further, they remain able to detect secret and concealed doors with great skill and often employ this power to gain entrance into places where their prey might be hiding.

These undead are also master archers and will employ all manner of bows in combat. Their undead status removes from them the disrupting effects of breathing, muscle fatigue, and heartbeats, and grants them a +4 bonus on all missile fire attack rolls. The arrows these foul creatures employ are almost always carved from the bones of living, intelligent creatures and may (20% chance) be magical in some way.

Elf vampires feed by drawing the vital, creative energies out of their prey. Any successful unarmed melee attack allows the vampire to drain 2 Charisma points from its victim. The resulting lack of vibrancy and personal leadership ability is also accompanied by a disfiguring scar that will never leave the body of the victim. A victim of several blows from such a creature may well become so horribly scarred as to be unrecognizable to all but his closest friends. Any elf or half-elf who dies from the vampire's essence draining attack will become a vampire as described in Ecology.

Those who see the scarred and twisted face of an elf vampire must successfully save vs. paralysis or be unable to move until 1d4 rounds after they have lost sight of the vampire. If the saving throw attempt results in a natural die roll of 1, the character is instantly struck dead. Those who die in this way will not become vampires and can be resurrected normally.

Elf vampires can be struck only by +1 or better magical weapons. All lesser arms will not bite into the creature but will pass through it as though the monster were not there. Even those weapons that harm the vampire may not be strong enough to destroy it, for the creature regenerates 2 hit points per combat round.

All manner of *sleep, charm,* or *hold* spells will not affect the vampire. Likewise, the creature cannot be harmed by poisons, toxins, or diseases for it is no longer a living thing. Magical spells that inflict damage with fire or cold will do only half damage to the vampire, but those employing lightning or electricity will do full damage.

A vampire driven to 0 hit points is not destroyed but is forced to flee the combat at once by using its transport via plants ability (see below) to enter a nearby plant and escape its enemies. If the vampire cannot do this within 2 combat rounds, its body will crumble into dust and will be forever destroyed.

At will, the elf vampire can make use of a power almost identical to the *transport via plants* spell. With this power, the vampire may simply walk into any man-size or larger plant and walk out of another plant (of the same type) anywhere else in the world. In Ravenloft, it cannot use this power to cross domain borders or leave the demiplane itself. As soon as the vampire has used this power, both of the plants involved are killed. Within a week, they will lose all of their

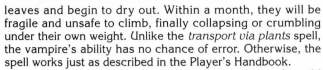

leaves and begin to dry out. Within a month, they will be fragile and unsafe to climb, finally collapsing or crumbling under their own weight. Unlike the *transport via plants* spell, the vampire's ability has no chance of error. Otherwise, the spell works just as described in the Player's Handbook.

An elf vampire may, at will, assume the form of a wild eagle. In this guise, it retains all of its natural vampiric powers, immunities, and vulnerabilities, but has the characteristics listed for such creatures in the MONSTROUS MANUAL tome. Once per week it may take on the form of a giant eagle, again conforming to the statistics presented in the MONSTROUS MANUAL tome.

Elf vampires can command the creatures of the forest to come to their aid when they are in peril. As a rule, they will call upon wolves (3d6), birds of prey (5d6), or small mammals like badgers, porcupines, or the like (6d6). In all cases, these animals arrive within 1d6 turns and will remain with the vampire until dismissed.

Elf vampires have a number of natural abilities that make them very dangerous in their natural environment. At will, they can pass without trace or become invisible to animals. They seldom use the latter power, however, for they can command any creature of the forest to obey them, as described above. Thrice per day they may employ the following spell-like abilities: *entangle*, *warp wood*, *snare*, *spike growth*, and *anti-animal shell*. Once per day they may create a *wall of thorns*, change *sticks to snakes*, or manifest a *giant insect*.

Sunlight does not harm the elf vampire. In fact, they live their unlives by day and shun the night. As soon as the sun falls behind the horizon, the elf vampire must be in his coffin. Each round that the monster lingers outside after sunset inflicts 1d4 points of damage, ultimately killing the creature. An elf vampire that dies in this manner is forever dead.

The cruelest card that fate has dealt the elf vampire is that of its black thumb. Any plant that the creature touches withers and dies. In small plants, like flowers, this effect is instantaneous. In larger plants, like shrubs or hedges, it takes about a day for the plant's death to become obvious. The largest of plants, trees and such, will take over a week to die, during which time the elf feels the agony they are experiencing. This curse does not travel through clothing, so elf vampires wearing boots do not leave a trail of dead footprints in the grass they walk through. They can also handle flowers if they wear gloves. The intimate relationship that the elf had with living things when he was alive, however has been shattered and this is a psychological blow that drives many elf vampires over the brink of madness when they are first created.

Although the powers of the elf vampire are many and varied, they are not without weaknesses. Like all vampires, they can be turned by priests or paladins with the courage to do so. In fact, the elf vampire's link to the Negative Material Plane is not as strong as those of other vampires, causing it to be turned as if it were a spectre instead of a vampire.

Elf vampires can travel beneath the earth's surface only at great physical risk to themselves. For each round spent in such a setting, the creature must suffer 1d4 points of damage (as if it were moving about after nightfall). Further, the creature cannot regenerate or employ any of its magical abilities when underground. If the vampire dies or is reduced to 0 hit points while underground, it is destroyed.

An elf vampire is unaffected by holy water, but can be burned by contact with sap from any deciduous tree. If the sap is fresh (drawn within the last 6 hours) it can be smeared on the vampire with a successful attack roll. As soon as it hits the creature's skin, it causes the vampire extreme pain and inflicts 2d4 points of damage.

Elf vampires cannot be held at bay by mirrors, holy symbols, or garlic, but they cannot cross a line of flower petals.

The petals must be fairly fresh—plucked from their plants within the last 24 hours—and the line must be unbroken in order for this defense to be effective. The vampire cannot take direct action to break the line of petals, but can command some animal or other servant to break the line for him.

Destroying an elf vampire is as difficult as destroying any other vampire, for they are crafty and deadly foes. The surest way to accomplish this feat, however, is to impale the creature with a charcoal stake. In order to be effective, the stake must be driven through the creature's heart with a single blow from a wooden mallet. If the vampire is incapacitated in some way, this does not normally present a problem, but in combat it is almost impossible to accomplish.

While a charcoal stake through the heart will kill the creature, it will rise again as soon as the stake is removed unless the vampire's head is cut off and burned in a fire made of flowers and flowering shrubs. In order to completely destroy the skull and brain, which is vital to the destruction of the vampire, the fire must burn for no less than 24 hours.

Habitat/Society: Elf vampires despise the living world that they have left behind. The sight of thriving woods and blooming flowers that once thrilled them has now been replaced by a hatred of all that is vital and fair. The areas they inhabit reflect this, for they will always be groves or forests with diseased trees, dying plants, and infertile soil. No attempt to raise crops or cultivate the land near an elf vampire's lair will be tolerated by the creature.

As time goes by, elf vampires can become even more powerful than they are initially. The following table list the modifications associated with the aging of the monster.

Age (Yrs.)	HD	Ench	Bows	Resist
0–99	7+3	+1	+4	0%
100–199	8+2	+1	+4	5%
200–299	9+1	+1	+5	5%
300–399	10	+2	+5	10%
400–499	11	+2	+6	15%
500+	12	+3	+6	25%

HD is the number of Hit Dice that a vampire has at any given age.

Ench(antment) indicates the magical plus that must be associated with a weapon in order for it to harm the vampire.

Bows lists the attack roll bonus that the creature gains when it is employing any form of noncrossbow.

Resist lists the magic resistance that the vampire acquires as time goes by.

Ecology: Like all undead, the elf vampire is not a part of the living world. It has no place in the land of the living and, knowing this, seeks to corrupt or destroy all that it encounters. Because of this, even the dreaded drow fear these creatures greatly.

Any elf or half-elf who falls to the essence-draining attack of an elf vampire will rise again as an elf vampire so long as the body is intact after three days. If the body has been destroyed or mutilated, the transformation is averted, and the dead character may rest in peace. However, any attempt to revive the slain character (with a *resurrection* spell, for example) has a flat 50% chance of transforming the character into a vampire once the spell is cast.

Editor's Note: Jandar Sunstar, a blood-sucking elf featured in the novel *Vampire of the Mists*, does not fit this description precisely. He is unique.

Vampire, Gnome

CLIMATE/TERRAIN:	Any subterranean
FREQUENCY:	Very rare
ORGANIZATION:	Solitary
ACTIVITY CYCLE:	Any
DIET:	Special
INTELLIGENCE:	Genius (17–18)
TREASURE:	F
ALIGNMENT:	Chaotic evil

NO. APPEARING:	1
ARMOR CLASS:	0
MOVEMENT:	9
HIT DICE:	6+3
THAC0:	13
NO. OF ATTACKS:	1
DAMAGE/ATTACK:	1d4
SPECIAL ATTACKS:	Smile
SPECIAL DEFENSES:	Struck only by metal magical weapons; spell immunity
MAGIC RESISTANCE:	Nil
SIZE:	S (3'–4' tall)
MORALE:	Elite (13–14)
XP VALUE:	3,000 (+1,000 per 100 years of age)

While the race of gnomes is little understood by many surface dwellers, the deadly breed of vampire that these creatures spawn are even more alien. Moving about far beneath the world's surface, they are seldom encountered by humans or other demihumans. When they are found, however, they are terrible foes indeed.

Gnome vampires are shorter and slighter of build than dwarvish vampires. Unlike other undead, however, the passage of time is visible in the features of a gnome vampire. Thus, their features are grooved and worn, showing the full burden of the years that have passed them by.

Gnome vampires are still able to understand the languages they spoke in life, but are unable to speak themselves. There is no known reason for this curse of silence, save that it robs them of the ability to joke and sing that they so loved in life. Because of this, most communications with gnome vampires require written messages.

Combat: Physical combat with any form of vampire is dangerous indeed. When the opponent is a gnome vampire, however, the penalty for defeat may be a horrible life as a helpless cripple.

The gnome vampire gains no bonus for strength in combat, for its ties to the Negative Material Plane have not infused it with great physical power. Thus, an unarmed blow from the creature will inflict but 1d4 points of damage. Because their hand-to-hand attack is so ineffective, they will often employ flails or other weapons in combat.

While the hand-to-hand blows of gnome vampires are weak, however, they are not without a powerful debilitating affect. Those struck by such attacks will begin to feel the painful arthritic attack of the creature instantly, for each successful attack drains 2 points of Dexterity from the victim. The result is a painful stiffness in the joints and muscles that can, if the victim suffers several attacks, be crippling or even fatal. Those reduced to a Dexterity score of 0 will be slain as the creeping paralysis spreads through their lungs and heart, making it impossible for them to survive. Gnomes who die in

this fashion may themselves become undead (see Ecology) if steps are not taken to prevent this foul transformation.

The gnome vampire is able to add a +1 bonus to its attack rolls against creatures such as kobolds or goblins. Similarly, creatures like ogres, trolls, and bugbears are unable to effectively battle such an agile creature, suffering a –4 penalty on their attack rolls.

The natural 60-foot infravision of living gnomes still exists in their vampiric form, but is augmented by their dark nature. Like dwarf vampires, they are able to see in even the dimmest of lighting as if it were full daylight.

Once per turn, the gnome vampire can twist its features into a horrible smile. Those who look upon the gnome at this time must successfully save vs. spell or begin to laugh. The effects of this grin are the same as those of a *Tasha's uncontrollable hideous laughter* spell, save that the duration is doubled and the character suffers 1d4 points of damage per round of laughing. As the vampire ages, this power becomes even more horrible, inflicting greater damage and becoming more difficult to save against.

Gnome vampires can be hit only by metal weapons, and then only by those that are magical and have a +1 or better enchantment. Nonmetal magical weapons are utterly useless against the creature. Gnomes also have the traditional vampiric immunity to such spells as *charm, sleep,* or *hold* and cannot be harmed by poisons or disease. They are immune to the effects of all spells from the illusion/phantasm school and take only half damage from magical attacks that depend on lightning, cold, or fire.

Gnome vampires that are driven to 0 hit points by spells or weapons are not destroyed. Rather, they are driven into their spectral form (see below) and forced to flee from combat. While in this form they must fly as quickly as possible to the cavern that holds their sarcophagus. If they are unable to reach their final resting place within 12 rounds, they will break up and be utterly destroyed.

Gnome vampires have the ability to assume a spectral form. In this guise, they appear to be nothing more than spheres of light—much like will o'wisps. While in this glowing shape, the creature can pass through solid stone walls or similar barricades. It cannot, however, pass through any living or once-living material in this shape, so a wooden wall is impassable to it.

Gnome vampires are unable to change their shapes as some other undead creatures can. Still, they are not unable to disguise themselves when the need arises, for they can cast a *change self* spell at will and can maintain the deception provided by this spell for an unlimited period of time.

When they wish to, gnome vampires are able to command any animal they encounter. They cannot, however, summon such creatures to them and must rely on those that arrive by chance. Once they have commanded a specific creature to do their bidding, it remains with them for 2d4 days before moving on.

Gnome vampires can employ an ability similar to that of the *spider climb* spell. This power, however, permits them to scale only surfaces built of stone or earth; they are unable to cling to surfaces of wood or other substances. This power can be invoked at will.

The creature retains the special abilities that it had in life, just as all other types of vampires do. Thus, gnome vampires are able to employ all of their class and magical abilities long after they have become undead.

Like dwarf vampires, these creatures are unusually resistant to magic. Any saving throw they are required to make vs. spell, rod, wand, or staff is made at a +5 bonus. As the creature ages, it becomes even more resistant to magic as described in Habitat/Society, below. Because of this, gnome vampires are greatly hindered when they attempt to employ magical devices. Whenever they seek to use such items, there is a 35% chance that the device will malfunction. This does not apply to weapons, armor, shields, or those items that duplicate the effects of illusionist spells. If the creature was a thief in life, it can also employ those devices used by such characters without penalty.

These creatures' natural familiarity with the underground environment gives them many special abilities in life, and all of these are manifested in the creature after death. Thus, the gnome can determine approximate directions when underground 3 times in 6, sense their approximate depth underground 4 times in 6, detect slopes or grades 5 times in 6, and detect unsafe walls or floors 7 times in 10.

Gnome vampires can be held at bay in several ways. They cannot turn away from any jewel (see Gems in the *Dungeon Master Guide*) presented to them for 2d4 rounds. If they are attacked during that time, they are freed of this enchantment and can act normally. Similarly, they can be turned aside by priests or paladins who present a holy symbol to them with conviction. As they grow older, though, it becomes more and more difficult to turn them in this fashion.

Gnome vampires can be burned by holy water or contact with holy symbols, but suffer only 1d4 points of damage per vial splashed upon them or successful attack roll. They cannot approach someone who displays a holy symbol and has strong convictions about the validity of their beliefs, but neither are they driven away from such persons.

The surest way to destroy a gnome vampire is to impale it on a spike made of purest silver and enchanted with a *bless* spell. As soon as the spike is driven into the body of the creature, its material form is destroyed and it will collapse dead. While the creature is truly lifeless at this point, it can be revived simply by removing the spike. In order to assure that the creature remains dead a number of things must be done. First, the hands must be cut from the corpse and boiled in a natural volcanic hot spring for 24 hours. Second, the body must be placed in a wooden casket that will be sealed at the end of the destruction process. Lastly, when the

body lies in the coffin, its eyes must be removed and replaced with precious gems. Stones of higher quality may be used, but those of lesser value will allow the creature to be revived. Finally, the lid of the casket is hammered into place and the nightmare is ended.

Daylight is devastating to these creatures, destroying them utterly and instantly when it falls upon them. Magical spells that duplicate sunlight, even those that normally harm undead, do not affect these creatures, however, for their natural magical resistance protects them from such things.

Habitat/Society: Gnome vampires live in the deepest of caverns, hiding like hermits from all surface dwellers. Where they were charismatic and mischievous in life, now they are dour and reclusive. They only seek out others when they need to feed and will gladly prey on the energies of any human, demihuman, or humanoid they encounter.

As gnome vampires age, they become more dangerous and more powerful. Very old vampires are, of course, among the most deadly beings found in Ravenloft or any other realm.

Age	HD	Laugh	Ench	Saves	Turn
0–99	6+3	0/1d4	+1	+5	Vampire
100–199	7+3	–1/1d6	+1	+5	Vampire
200–299	8 +3	–2/1d8	+1	+6	Ghost
300–399	9+3	–3/1d8	+2	+6	Ghost
400–499	10+2	–4/1dl0	+2	+7	Lich
500+	11+2	–5/1dl0	+3	+8	Special

HD indicates the number of Hit Dice that the creature has at any given age.

Laugh lists the saving throw modifiers and the damage inflicted by its deadly grin.

Ench(antment) is the minimum magical plus that must be associated with a metal weapon. Nonmetal weapons cannot harm the vampire regardless of its age.

Save indicates the modifier to the creature's saving throws versus spell, rods, staffs, or wands.

Turn shows the row on the Turning Undead table that is consulted when a priest or paladin attempts to drive away the creature with a holy symbol.

Ecology: The gnome vampire sustains itself by drawing the youthful vigor from the bodies of those it touches. While this resembles the aging attack of a ghost, it is not truly the same, for the person is not actually aged, their body is just robbed of its youthful vitality. While the difference is fine, it is important; many believe that the vampire's attack is far worse than that of the ghost.

Gnome vampires seldom create others of their kind. When they opt to do so, however, the process is not without risk. The vampire must first slay a victim with its debilitating touch and then move the body to the sarcophagus in which the vampire itself sleeps. For the next three days, the body must lie in the coffin while the vampire rests atop it, allowing its essences to seep slowly into the evolving vampire. At the end of this time, the slain gnome rises as a fully functioning vampire, completely under the control of its creator. While the gnome vampire rests atop its coffin, it is unable to regenerate any lost hit points or employ any of its spell-like abilities. Thus, the creature is far more vulnerable to attack at this time than it normally might be. In addition, it cannot interrupt the creation process once it has begun, or both the would-be vampire and its creator will die.

Vampire, Halfling

CLIMATE/TERRAIN:	Temperate woodlands
FREQUENCY:	Very rare
ORGANIZATION:	Solitary
ACTIVITY CYCLE:	Night
DIET:	Special
INTELLIGENCE:	High (13–14)
TREASURE:	F
ALIGNMENT:	Chaotic evil

NO. APPEARING:	1
ARMOR CLASS:	3
MOVEMENT:	9
HIT DICE:	6+3
THAC0:	13
NO. OF ATTACKS:	1
DAMAGE/ATTACK:	1d4
SPECIAL ATTACKS:	Lethargy aura
SPECIAL DEFENSES:	Spell immunity
MAGIC RESISTANCE:	Nil
SIZE:	S (4′–5′ tall)
MORALE:	Steady (11–12)
XP VALUE:	3,000

Few races enjoy life and the basic comforts of a quiet, peaceful existence more than the halflings. Thus, when one of these fine creatures is driven into a life of evil by the preying of some sinister vampire, the world suffers a great loss.

Halfling vampires have the same physical characteristics of living halflings: slightly plump, only about four feet high, and florid of complexion, with tufts of hair on the backs of their hands and tops of their feet. They tend to dress in dark clothes, however, shunning the happy and colorful garb of their living kin.

Halfling vampires are most often familiar with half a dozen or so languages (including their native tongue). Nearly all of them spoke common in life (and thus retain that knowledge in death) as well as the elvish, dwarvish, and gnomish languages.

Combat: The strength of halfling vampires is not exceptional as it is for most other vampire races. Thus, they gain no additional bonus to their melee attack or damage rolls. They employ melee weapons frequently, favoring the short sword, dagger, and similar small weapons. Should the halfling vampire elect to strike without benefit of weaponry, it inflicts a mere 1d4 points of damage. While this is not greatly threatening in itself, the vampire's strong connection with the Negative Material Plane allows him to drain a portion of the victim's life energy with each successful attack. Thus, any character hit by the vampire suffers the required damage and instantly loses 1 point each of Strength and Constitution. The resulting loss in hit points, combat ability, and so forth is calculated immediately. Halflings who die from this life-draining attack become vampires themselves, as described in Ecology, below.

The halfling vampire is able to radiate an aura that affects all persons within 20 yards. Any creature that comes within this distance while the vampire is radiating its aura must successfully save vs. spell or become fatigued. Those who make their save are unaffected and will remain so for the duration of the encounter. If they meet the vampire again, however, a new save will be required to resist this enchantment.

Those who fail their saving throw are overcome with a feeling of lassitude and torpor. This state lasts for 1d6 rounds, during which time they attack with a –4 penalty, inflict half damage with all weapons, and are unable to summon the mental stamina required to cast spells or make proficiency checks. As the vampire ages, the duration of its terrible lethargy aura becomes greater, although its effects remain largely the same.

The natural resistance to magic of all halflings, coupled with the increased immunity to spells of the undead, makes attacking the halfling vampire very difficult. Any weapon of less than +2 enchantment cannot harm the creature, passing harmlessly through the vampire. As the vampire ages, it becomes more and more difficult to strike.

Halfling vampires retain all natural abilities of halflings in their undead state. Thus, they have an improved saving throw vs. spells, rods, staffs, or wands employed against them. This begins at +5, but improves with the passing of time until the vampire is almost impossible to destroy with such attacks. Similarly, they retain their natural affinity for thrown weapons, gaining a +1 bonus on all attack rolls made with them. Halfling vampires are still able to move silently (as an elf) in their afterlife, allowing them to sneak up on opponents with ease. These undead can always employ the backstabbing ability of a 1st-level thief; vampires who were thieves in life may have better backstabbing abilities.

All halfling vampires have infravision out to 60 feet, regardless of their subracial stock (Hairfoot, Tallfellow, Stout) or infravision ability in life. Further, they all have the ability (75% chance) to tell whether a passage has any natural grade or slope to it, no matter how minor the slope might be. They also have a 50% chance of determining directions (north, south, etc.) when underground.

The vampire is immune to all manner of *sleep, charm, hold,* or other mind-affecting spells. Further, it is immune to all manner of poisons, toxins, or diseases and has no need to breathe. Spells based on lightning or fire inflict only half damage to the halfling vampire, while those based on cold have their full effect.

If the vampire is reduced to 0 hit points, either by magical spells or physical attack, but is not properly destroyed (as dictated below), it is not slain. Rather, it is forced to assume its smoking form and flee from the combat. If it is unable to return to its coffin within 12 rounds of this forced transformation, its smoking form breaks up and it is forever destroyed.

At will, the halfling vampire can transform itself into any manner of small woodland mammal. While in this form, the vampire takes on all of that creature's abilities and senses, but retains its own intelligence, immunity to spells or non-magical weapons, and similar powers. The most commonly employed forms are those of badgers, beavers, skunks, and other like animals.

Just as halfling vampires can assume the shape of woodland mammals, so too can they command them. Within 2d6 rounds after the vampire issues its mental summons, 10d6 Hit Dice worth of such creatures arrive to do its bidding. These animals remain throughout the night on which they were summoned, returning to their homes with the coming of the dawn.

In addition to its natural animal guises, the vampire can transform itself into a smoking form at will. In this state, it appears as a drifting cloud of smoke such as might be made by a small campfire or burning pipe. It radiates a familiar and pleasing odor, one that will remind those within 10 yards of pipeweed and a comfortable inn. In this state, the vampire is immune to all damage from melee attacks and suffers no injury from magical spells. Even the smallest opening—a keyhole or cracked pane of glass, for example—affords enough space for a halfling vampire in this shape to pass through.

Halfling vampires have the ability to *create food and drink* up to three times per day. When they invoke this power, the food they create is always of the highest quality and certain to please even the most discriminating palate. In addition, they can cast a *purify food and drink* or *putrefy food and drink* at will, often using the former powers to lure potential victims into a sense of security and safety that makes them more vulnerable to attack.

Despite its great power, the halfling vampire is not without weaknesses of its own. It cannot, for example, stand the odor of a smoking pipe, for the aroma reminds it of the physical pleasures it has left behind. While the scent of burning pipeweed will not drive the vampire away, it does prevent the creature from coming within 20 yards of the smoker until the offending device is removed. Similarly, the vampire cannot enter any room where a fire is burning in the hearth. Again, the association with the halfling's past life is too strong for the creature to bear, and it will turn away from such memories. In both cases, the vampire can take no action to directly counter the offending items. The vampire may, however, instruct one of its minions to enter the room and extinguish the pipe or smother the fire, allowing the undead creature to come freely into the chamber.

Halfling vampires can be held at bay by anyone who presents a lawful good holy symbol to them strongly and with conviction. As with the pipe smoke, this does not drive them away, but does keep them from approaching a character so equipped. Holy water or lawful good holy symbols that touch the vampire's flesh inflict the same damage that they do to human vampires (1d6+1 points), burning the creature's body. Halfling vampires can be turned normally.

Halfling vampires regenerate damage very quickly. Each combat round they regain 2 hit points of damage. If they are standing in the light of the moon, this is increased to 3 points of damage. Under a full moon, this is further improved to 4 points of damage.

Falling rain is deadly to the halfling vampire, for it is nature's way of driving away taints from the atmosphere and revitalizing all living creatures. Damage is based on the severity of the weather and the duration of exposure. A vampire destroyed by rainfall is forever dead.

Snow does not harm the vampires as rain does, but they are loath to move into a cold climate and thus seldom encounter it.

Severity of Rain	Damage Per Round
Light	1d6
Heavy	1d8
Torrential	1d10

Just as the presence of a burning hearth can hold halfling vampires at bay, so too can it destroy them. The surest way to destroy a vampire of this type is to impale him with a piece of wood that burns with a hearth's fire. The wood must be ignited directly from the hearth itself, not from a fire transferred to it via some third item. This "weapon" must be employed within 12 rounds to be effective. Not all of the wood need be ablaze, but the part driven into the vampire must be burning for the attack to have its desired effect.

Although the vampire is instantly slain by this attack, the creature can be revived simply by removing the wooden stake from its body. In order to complete the destruction of the being, the creature's hands and feet must be cut off and cast into a hearth fire. If the fire is maintained for 3 hours, the rest of the vampire's body will smolder away into smoke and dissipate, never to rise again.

Sunlight is very dangerous to halfling vampires, as it is to most such creatures, and can destroy them. For each round a halfling vampire is exposed to the direct rays of the sun, it suffers 3d6 points of damage and is filled with such pain that it can neither attack nor defend itself. Further, it cannot transform into any of its other shapes until it removes itself from the direct light of the sun. Magical spells that imitate the light of the sun, such as *continual light*, will not harm the creature, but sources like a *sunblade* will have the sunlight effect.

Habitat/Society: Halfling vampires shun the comforts of physical life that were so dear to them before their transformations. They live in dark and dreary places that do not serve to remind them of the happiness they have left behind. Their loss of happiness and contentment has led them to despise all those who are able to curl up before a crackling fire with a good story and a mug of ale, driving them to do what they can to shatter the complacent lives of other halfling whenever they are able.

As with other demihuman vampires, halfling vampires become more powerful with age, as represented by the table below.

Age	HD	Save	Ench	Aura
0–99	6+3	+5	+2	–0
100–199	7+3	+5	+2	–1
200–299	8+2	+6	+2	–2
300–399	9+2	+6	+3	–3
400–499	10+1	+7	+3	–4
500 +	11+1	+8	+3	–5

HD indicates the creature's Hit Dice as it ages.

Save shows the bonus to the creature's saves when attacked with spells, rods, staves, or wands.

Ench(antment) indicates the magical bonus that must be associated with the weapon to enable it to affect the vampire.

Aura is the penalty to applied to the saving throws of those caught in the vampire's fatigue aura.

Ecology: The halfling vampire has no place in the natural world, a fact demonstrated by its aversion to rain and the earthly purity it represents.

The vampire can make more of its kind only by slaying other halflings with its energy-sapping attack. The halfling vampire need do nothing more than keep the body of its victim intact for 7 days after death and a new vampire will arise.

Vampire, Kender

CLIMATE/TERRAIN:	Sithicus
FREQUENCY:	Very rare
ORGANIZATION:	Solitary
ACTIVITY CYCLE:	Night
DIET:	Special
INTELLIGENCE:	Average (8–10)
TREASURE:	Nil
ALIGNMENT:	Lawful evil

NO. APPEARING:	1
ARMOR CLASS:	2
MOVEMENT:	9
HIT DICE:	4+3
THAC0:	15
NO. OF ATTACKS:	1
DAMAGE/ATTACK:	1d6
SPECIAL ATTACKS:	Spiritrend, laugh
SPECIAL DEFENSES:	Struck only by +1 or better weapons, regeneration
MAGIC RESISTANCE:	Nil
SIZE:	S (2′–4′ tall)
MORALE:	Elite (13–14)
XP VALUE:	4,000

From the dark land of Sithicus comes word of a breed of vampire only recently released on the demiplane of Ravenloft: the kender vampire. While not truly the equal of the other species of vampire, these monsters are no less evil.

Kender vampires retain the same general physical properties that they did in life. Thus, they stand somewhat under 4 feet in height and are very slightly built. Their eyes and ears give them an impish, elven look, and their slender bodies are finely muscled, like those of gymnasts. Upon closer examination, however, the foul corruption of the undead is obvious. The skin is pale and withered, stretched tight across the bones in a manner similar to that found on mummified corpses. The teeth are long and sharp, giving the face a feral look that cannot be easily forgotten. The fingers have been reduced to little more than bones with a thin covering of flesh, and their nails have stretched into claws.

Kender vampires are able to speak only in hissing whispers. Since it is clearly quite painful for them to talk, however, they seldom do so. Their knowledge of languages seems unchanged from what it was in life, however, so they often understand a small number of other tongues.

Combat: The kender vampire moves slowly and stiffly when it attacks. Thus, the great agility and dexterity that served it so well in life have been lost in its transition to darkness. Because of this, kender vampires always act last in any combat round and never surprise their opponents. The loss of agility is somewhat compensated for by an increased physical strength and the growth of dangerous claws. Thus, they inflict 1d6 points of damage in any hand-to-hand attack.

Kender vampires often use the hoopak, a combination staff sling and bo staff. When employed as a sling, it enables the creature to hurl stones that inflict 1d4+1 points of damage to small or man-size opponents and 1d6+1 points to larger foes. If used as a bo staff, it causes 1d4 points of damage to man-size or smaller foes and 1d6 points of damage to larger ones.

Anyone struck by the claws of the kender vampire feels far more than the pain of a physical wound. Their attacks reach beyond the mortal body of their victim and strike directly into his spirit. The shock and pain caused by this attack is great, requiring the victim to make a successful saving throw vs. paralysis or be unable to act on the next combat round. Whether or not they pass their saving throw, they suffer a loss of 1 point each from their Intelligence and Wisdom scores. Those kender who die from the spiritrending attack of the kender vampire are in no danger of becoming vampires themselves, however, for these foul creatures are the product of dark sciences and magical experimentation that can only be duplicated with the direct intervention of Lord Soth of Sithicus.

The kender vampire has the ability to throw back its head once per hour and release a hideous laugh. Those within 20 yards of the vampire when it cackles must successfully save vs. spell or be affected as if they had looked upon a symbol of insanity. Those under the influence of a *remove fear* or similar spell are immune to this attack.

The kender vampire can be hit only by +1 or better weapons. Nonmagical wooden weapons that strike the creature are instantly rotted and destroyed; magical wooden weapons are entitled to an item saving throw vs. acid to avoid this effect.

The mystical nature of the vampire's physiology is such that it is able to regain lost hit points very rapidly. Thus, the creature regenerates 2 hit points per combat round. A *raise dead* spell cast upon the monster will restore it to full hit points at once.

A kender vampire that is driven to 0 hit points in combat is not truly destroyed. Rather, its body is slain and it is forced to assume its spiritual form. Because this new form is very easily destroyed (see below), the kender vampire will immediately try to flee from the combat area and return to its coffin. If it is unable to reach its coffin within 12 turns, the creature will become trapped in this form and remain a poltergeist until slain.

At will, the kender vampire is able to transform itself into a purely spiritual creature similar to a poltergeist. While in this form, it is invisible and has all of the characteristics, strengths, and weaknesses of a common poltergeist. If the creature is slain while in this form, it is forever dead, and the world is free of its evil machinations.

Kender vampires are immune to *sleep, charm,* or *hold* spells and can never be influenced by any form of mind-affecting magic. They are wholly unaffected by all manner of toxins, poisons, and diseases. Spells or other attacks that rely on cold or heat (including ice and fire) inflict only half damage to kender vampires, but lightning- or electricity-based attacks inflict full damage.

Holy water splashed on kender vampires is somewhat harmful to them, inflicting 1d4 points of damage per vial that strikes their flesh. Holy symbols pressed against their skin inflict a like amount of damage and cause the creatures such pain that they must make a successful morale check or flee from the battle at once if possible.

Kender vampires are unable to leave the domain of Sithicus. The strange and foul magics that created them have forged an unbreakable bond between them and the realm of Lord Soth. Any attempt to cross the borders of this domain (whether voluntary or not) instantly destroys a kender vampire. Within seconds, its body will crumble into dust and the thing will be gone. Even drawing near to the border is painful for these creatures, and they will seldom come within a mile of it for fear or being forced across it and destroyed.

Kender vampires are unusually easy to turn. It is thought that this is due to the fact that their inner spirit is unbroken by their transformation into an undead thing and, thus, they do not have the mental stamina that similar undead do when confronting devoutly religious individuals. Whether or not this is the case, kender vampires are turned as if they were only wraiths.

Kender vampires are not as hard to destroy as many other types of undead, for they are greatly vulnerable to their own hoopaks. Any vampire hunter who is able to snatch a vampire's hoopak from him and then turn that weapon against its owner will find that it inflicts full damage. Further, any natural attack roll of 19 or 20 indicates that the attacker has been able to impale the creature on the end of the weapon, killing it instantly. As soon as the creature dies (either from wounds inflicted with the hoopak or by being impaled upon it) the body bursts into flames. In the next few seconds, both it and the weapon are consumed by fire and irrevocably destroyed.

The kender vampire cannot stand the sight of shimmerweed (a crystalline plant that grows on Krynn and in some secluded areas of Sithicus). The mere sight of these flowers is enough to keep the vampire from drawing within 10 yards of them. If moonlight is falling on these flowers, the prismatic display they release is enough to actually harm the creature, inflicting 1d4 points of damage for each round that the plants are within 20 yards of the vampire.

Habitat/Society: The kender vampire is a solitary creature that exists only to do the bidding of Lord Soth of Sithicus. He is the father of their race, and although they despise him for what he has done to them, they are unable to turn against him or act in any way contrary to his interests.

Knowing the revulsion that the elves who live in his domain feel for all manner of unnatural things, Soth felt that he could find no better slaves than a band of undead. Aware that undead elves might pose a threat to his own power, Soth set about the creation of a new breed of undead. Drawing a small kender village through the misty veils of Ravenloft and into his domain, he had them killed one by one so that he could study their sufferings and invoke carefully designed magical rituals over their bodies in attempts to make them rise as undead. By the time he had finished with these sad kender, fully half of them had died horrible deaths and suffered unspeakable torment at the hand of the dreaded deathknight. The results of his experiments were, however, satisfactory to Soth, for he discovered a formula that would create a race of vampires utterly loyal to him. Soth is believed to have created no fewer than 10 and no more than 30 such monsters, although hard evidence to support any given estimate is hard to come by.

The typical kender vampire heads a small band of undead who also serve Lord Soth. As a rule, each such creature commands 3d4 other creatures, drawn from the chart below.

2d6 Roll	Undead Type
2	Undead Beast (Stahnk)
3	Spectre
4–5	Ghast
6–8	Ghoul
9–10	Ghast
11	Spectre
12	Skeletal warrior

In addition to the forces generated above, the creature will have 4d6 Hit Dice worth of lesser undead (zombies and skeletons) acting under its command as well.

Ecology: Kender vampires can exist only within the confines of Lord Soth's domain of Sithicus. They are tied to that dark land in some mystical way that, no doubt, relates to the evil magic used in their creation. It is possible that Lord Soth was required to invoke the favor of the dark powers in his creation of these dreaded monsters and, thus, that he has paid some horrible price for their loyalty to him.

Despite their links to Sithicus, the vampire kender are not natural creatures and, therefore, have no place in the biology of the world around them. The elves in Sithicus can sense the presence of one of these creatures whenever it comes within 100 yards of them. At first, the elves feel only a curious sense of concern or dread, but as the monster draws nearer, the feeling intensifies into one of loathing and horror. The elves describe these sad creations as vile pollutants that foul the living by their mere presences. It is unclear why only those elves native to Sithicus can sense the kender vampire so easily.

Unlike the other vampires in Ravenloft, these creatures do not grow more powerful with the passing of time. It is a part of their curse that they must forever remain as they are, denied the pleasures of curiosity or the wanderlust that once gave their lives meaning. It is said that the rising of the full moon reminds these tragic souls of what they have lost and that, on that one night each month, they are unable to do anything but sit and weep beside the coffin that now serves them as both home and prison.

Vampyre

CLIMATE/TERRAIN:	Any urban
FREQUENCY:	Very rare
ORGANIZATION:	Pack
ACTIVITY CYCLE:	Night
DIET:	Blood
INTELLIGENCE:	Exceptional (15–16)
TREASURE:	F
ALIGNMENT:	Chaotic evil
NO. APPEARING:	3d4
ARMOR CLASS:	4
MOVEMENT:	12
HIT DICE:	8+3
THAC0:	11
NO. OF ATTACKS:	3
DAMAGE/ATTACK:	1d4/1d4/1d6
SPECIAL ATTACKS:	Charm toxin
SPECIAL DEFENSES:	Charm toxin
MAGIC RESISTANCE:	Nil
SIZE:	M (6′ tall)
MORALE:	Steady (11–12)
XP VALUE:	2,000

The vampyre is a foul creature that, like the much-feared nosferatu, exists on the blood of its victims. Unlike the nosferatu or its vampiric cousins, however, the vampyre is not undead. Thus, while it gains none of the powers of the undead, neither does it have any of the undead weaknesses.

Vampyres look much like normal humans or half-elves. They stand just under 6 feet tall and are, as a rule, of exceptional physical beauty. Some rare examples are less handsome, and a few are actually repulsive to look upon, but these are by far in the minority. Vampyres favor the dark and somber dress of the dead or their mourning kin, although females often employ the wanton garb of a harlot to lure victims into their clutches. Vampyres are generally slender of build—though their appearance hides exceptional physical strength—and have burning, dark eyes. Their skin is very pale, almost white, and their features are slightly feline, giving them a wild and exotic look. Their fingers end in deadly, curving claws; their teeth are long and sharp, with the canines showing clearly as fangs to anyone close enough to see them plainly.

Vampyres have no native language, but communicate in the tongue of those humans they live among. As a rule, any given vampyre will know from 1d4 human or demihuman languages.

Combat: The vampyre typically attacks only helpless or surprised prey. Often, a single vampyre moves out into a crowd of humans at a tavern or similar gathering place to seek out a victim of the opposite gender. Once a suitable person is found, the vampyre lures the prey back to its lair with teasing promises of romance and companionship. No sooner does the door close behind the couple, however, than the vampyre's companions spring to the attack. The foul and evil nature of these creatures might mean the victim will linger on the edge of death for days, satisfying the hunger of these monsters as they drink only enough blood to keep their captive too weak to escape.

In combat, the vampyre can strike with its two ripping claws, inflicting 1d4 points of damage with each strike; it also bites with its jagged, tearing teeth for an additional 1d6 points of damage. The saliva of a vampyre carries a foul toxin that requires those bitten by the monster to make a successful saving throw vs. poison or become charmed. This saving throw is modified by a –1 penalty for every 2 points of damage done in the biting attack. Thus, a vampyre who strikes for 3 points of damage with its bite causes its victim to save at –2. Charmed victims will not resist the attack of the vampyre that bit them, but they will fight against other vampyres.

Habitat/Society: Vampyres live in packs, usually consisting of no more than a dozen individuals (evenly mixed between males and females) and a half dozen young. They seldom encounter other packs, but when they do the two bands will join together in a few days of murderous feasting and horrific slaughter of victims.

At these times, the vampyres mate with members from the other group and, in 6 months, new vampyres are born. The young are virtually helpless until they reach the age of 5 years, at which time they are able to fight as half-strength adults. When they reach the age of 10, they are fully grown and must undergo a ritual to prove that they are no longer children. Usually, this means making an unassisted kill.

The lair of a pack of vampyres may seem to be a completely normal human home—until the creatures spring their trap and lash out at those in their presence. On rare occasions, a pack of vampyres will actually work to pass themselves off as members of a community, holding down jobs and keeping their bloody feeding habits a dark secret.

Ecology: Vampyres are fierce hunters who fill the same ecological niche as tigers or wolves—save that their prey is human. Long ago, before man was an intelligent and social animal, they had their place. Now, they are nightmarish creatures that stalk the weak and innocent, fulfilling a task no longer needed.

CLIMATE/TERRAIN:	Any temperate land
FREQUENCY:	Very rare
ORGANIZATION:	Solitary
ACTIVITY CYCLE:	Any
DIET:	Blood and bodily fluids
INTELLIGENCE:	High (13–14)
TREASURE:	W (Z)
ALIGNMENT:	Neutral evil

NO. APPEARING:	1
ARMOR CLASS:	4
MOVEMENT:	9, Wb 12
HIT DICE:	6+3
THAC0:	13
NO. OF ATTACKS:	1
DAMAGE/ATTACK:	1d3
SPECIAL ATTACKS:	Poisonous bite, webbing
SPECIAL DEFENSES:	Nil
MAGIC RESISTANCE:	Nil
SIZE:	M (5′–6′ tall)
MORALE:	Average (8–10)
XP VALUE:	3,000

The red widow, or spider queen, is an evil and deadly shape changer. Spinning a web of evil to all the lands about its lair, this foul creature derives a vile pleasure from murdering those lured to it by its many charms and promises of delight.

The red widow has two physical forms. The first, in which it is most commonly encountered, is a phenomenally beautiful and alluring human woman with long, flowing red hair. The creature's dress will vary to enable it to blend in with the human society around it, but will always be provocative and inviting. In this form, the creature is treated as a 0-level human, for the statistics listed above are those for its spider form (see below).

The red widow adopts its true form—that of a giant spider—only when it is about to make a kill. In this shape, the creature has a bright crimson body with a black hourglass pattern on its back. In effect, it looks like a giant version of the common black widow spider, save that the colors are reversed.

Red widows seem to have no natural language of their own, but are always fluent in the languages of those cultures with which they come into contact.

Combat: Red widows seldom engage in open combat. Rather, they lure unsuspecting victims near and draw them into a passionate embrace. Once this is done, they transform into their true form. Those who witness this change (usually only the doomed victim) must make an immediate horror check. The transformation into a giant spider takes a full round, during which the creature never releases its hold on its victim. Attempting to escape the powerful grip of the red widow requires the victim to attempt a roll to bend bars. Failure indicates that escape is impossible at this time, although a new attempt is allowed each round.

Once in its spider shape, the red widow bites its victim. While the bite itself inflicts only 1d3 points of damage, it allows the creature to inject a deadly poison (Class E, Immediate, Death/20). If the creature is striking at someone it is holding, it automatically hits. If it is trying to kill someone who has eluded its deadly embrace, the red widow must make a successful normal attack roll.

The red widow is capable of releasing a jet of webbing when in its spider form. DMs should treat this as if the creature were casting a *web* spell.

When the creature is in its spider form, it has the ability to climb sheer surfaces (just as if using a *spider climb* spell) and to command spiders. In the latter case, it will be able to summon 10d10 spiders. Of these, 65% will be normal spiders, 20% will be large spiders, 10% will be huge spiders, and 5% will be giant spiders. These creatures adore the red widow and will do all that they can to protect her from harm, even at the cost of their own lives; no morale checks are ever required of them.

Habitat/Society: The red widow often makes its home in the cities and towns of men. Here, it moves about in its human guise and seduces its victims under cover of darkness. It is not uncommon for a red widow to woo and destroy a new victim every week.

Ecology: Red widows live by draining the blood and other bodily fluids from those they kill. A slain lover is hidden away somewhere in the creature's lair and can supply the widow with nourishment for up to a week. When the monster finishes with a corpse, it discards the partially decomposed and dehydrated body far from its lair. In this way, it hopes that its home will escape detection.

The red widow breeds by mating with a normal human. Following the consummation of their "love," the widow kills her mate and implants the now-fertilized eggs in his body. Within a week, the eggs hatch and consume the fluids in the corpse. Each brood of spiders comprises 2d4 young. These remain in spider form (being treated as large spiders) for one year. At the end of that time, they gain the ability to assume a human form and become adults. Only in rare cases will young remain with their mother at this time.

Assuming it does not die through violence or accident, the average red widow lives to be 20 to 30 years old.

Wolfwere, Greater

CLIMATE/TERRAIN:	Any/Forest
FREQUENCY:	Very rare
ORGANIZATION:	Solitary
ACTIVITY CYCLE:	Any (especially night)
DIET:	Carnivore
INTELLIGENCE:	Exceptional (15–16)
TREASURE:	20% U (B)
ALIGNMENT:	Neutral evil

NO. APPEARING:	1–4
ARMOR CLASS:	2
MOVEMENT:	18
HIT DICE:	8+2
THAC0:	13
NO. OF ATTACKS:	1, 2, or 3
DAMAGE/ATTACK:	2d8, 1d6/1d6/2d6, or 2d6/weapon +6 (see below)
SPECIAL ATTACKS:	See below
SPECIAL DEFENSES:	See below
MAGIC RESISTANCE:	50%
SIZE:	M–L (4′–9′ feet)
MORALE:	Champion (15)
XP VALUE:	8,000

Greater wolfweres are a bane to all who live. They are able to assume three shapes at will, taking only a single round to alter forms. Their natural shape is that of a giant dire wolf standing a full 5 to 6 feet tall at the shoulder. They can also assume a half-wolf/half-human form. In this state they are 8 to 9 feet tall with massive long arms equipped with talonlike nails. Finally, they may assume the form of any humanoid of either gender which is between 4 and 9 feet in height.

Greater wolfweres speak common, as well as the languages of forest animals.

Combat: Greater wolfweres often employ the same strategies used by typical wolfweres when hunting. They will change into a humanoid of opposite gender to that of their victim. Then, using their Charisma and singing ability, they will get close to their victim and sing their special song. Anyone failing a save versus spell is overcome with lethargy. The effects of this are the same as those for a *slow* spell and last for 1d6+4 rounds.

In dire wolf form, they bite with their savage jaws, inflicting 2d8 points of damage with each successful attack.

In demi-wolf form, they can strike with each of their clawed hands (causing 1d6 points of damage each) and also bite for 2d6 points. In lieu of their claw attacks, greater wolfweres in this form may employ weapons (gaining a bonus of +6 on their damage rolls).

In humanoid form, they are forced to fight with weapons only and are assumed to have a strength of 18/00 (+6 to damage).

Greater wolfweres have infravision with a 120-foot range, and in all forms except human, their eyes glow red in the dark.

Greater wolfweres have all the abilities of a first-level bard and can climb walls (55%), detect noise (25%), pick pockets (15%), and read languages (10%).

Some exceptional individuals may be of greater level. As a rule, 1 in 10 creatures will be of level 2 to 5, and 1 in 20 will be of level 6 to 11.

Iron weapons (or those of a +1 enchantment) are required to harm a greater wolfwere. However, unless the blow is instantly fatal, the wound quickly repairs itself as the wolfwere is able to regenerate all of its lost hit points at the end of any given round. It is important to note, however, that severed limbs and such are not regenerated in this fashion.

Greater wolfweres are somewhat more resistant to wolfsbane than their lesser cousins, able to stand the presence of that herb if they make a successful saving throw vs. poison. If they fail, they must avoid wolfsbane at all costs.

The howl of a greater wolfwere can summon 4d6 wolves or 2d6 dire wolves to its aid, if such creatures are in the area. These wolves fight most loyally on behalf of the greater wolfwere with a +2 morale bonus.

Habitat/Society: Greater wolfweres are nearly indistinguishable from typical wolfweres. They often team up with the latter (assuming positions of leadership), but seldom travel with others of their own breed. When more than one greater wolfwere is encountered, they will be working together on some scheme that requires their combined efforts.

Ecology: Greater wolfweres were originally the offspring of Harkon Lukas, Lord of Kartakass. So great was his evil power that the children he had by female wolfweres turned out to possess incredible abilities. Greater wolfweres never mate with each other; rather, they mate with typical wolfweres. Only 10% of the children produced by such matings result in a greater wolfwere, the others being typical.

When the victims of a greater wolfwere attack are left to rot and not eaten or buried properly, 50% of the time a meekulbern plant sprouts from the corpse. The berries from this bush are used in making meekulbrau, a special wine of Kartakass.

Greater wolfweres seem to have a near empathic link with wolves of all types but despise werewolves and will attack them on sight.

CLIMATE/TERRAIN:	Any Ravenloft land
FREQUENCY:	Very rare
ORGANIZATION:	Solitary
ACTIVITY CYCLE:	Night
DIET:	Carrion
INTELLIGENCE:	Average (8–10)
TREASURE:	A
ALIGNMENT:	Neutral evil

NO. APPEARING:	1
ARMOR CLASS:	6
MOVEMENT:	6
HIT DICE:	6
THAC0:	15
NO. OF ATTACKS:	2
DAMAGE/ATTACK:	2d4/2d4
SPECIAL ATTACKS:	See below
SPECIAL DEFENSES:	See below
MAGIC RESISTANCE:	Nil
SIZE:	M (6' tall)
MORALE:	Average (8–10)
XP VALUE:	650

Zombie lords are living creatures that have taken on the foul powers and abilities of the undead. They are formed on rare occasions as the result of a *raise dead* spell cast in the demiplane of Ravenloft.

Zombie lords look as they did in life, save that their skin has turned the pale gray of death, and their flesh has begun to rot and decay. The odor of vile corruption and rotting meat hangs about them, and carrion-feeding insects often buzz about them to dine on the bits of flesh and beads of ichor that drop from their bodies.

Zombie lords can speak those languages they knew in life and seem to have a telepathic or mystical ability to converse freely with the living dead. Further, they can *speak with dead* merely by touching a corpse. Thus, for them at least, dead men tell many tales.

Combat: When the zombie lord is forced into physical combat, he relies on the great strength of his crushing fists. Striking twice per combat round, the monster inflicts 2d4 points of damage from each blow that finds its mark.

The odor of death that surrounds the zombie lord is so potent that it can cause horrible effects in those who breath it. On the first round that a character comes within 30 yards of the monster, he must successfully save vs. poison or be affected in some way. The following results are possible:

d6 Roll	Effect
1	*Weakness* (as the spell)
2	*Cause disease* (as the spell)
3	–1 point of Constitution (permanent)
4	*Contagion* (as the spell)
5	Character unable to act for 1d4 rounds due to nausea and vomiting
6	Character dies instantly and becomes a zombie under control of the zombie lord

All zombies within sight of the zombie lord will be subject to its mental instructions. This includes monster and ju-ju zombies, but not Strahd or yellow musk creeper zombies.

Further, the creature can use the senses of any zombie that is within one mile of it and, thus, know all that is happening within a very large area.

Once per day, the zombie lord can use an *animate dead* spell to transform dead creatures into zombies. This works just as described in the *Player's Handbook*, except that it can also be used on the living. Any single living creature with fewer Hit Dice than the zombie lord can be attacked in this manner in lieu of the casting of this spell in its normal fashion. A target who fails a saving throw vs. death magic is instantly slain. In 1d4 combat rounds, the slain creature rises again as a zombie under the foul zombie lord's command.

Zombie lords have the same immunities to spells (*sleep, charm, hold,* and the like) that normal zombies do. In addition, they suffer the same 2d4 points of damage from contact with holy water or holy symbols. They are turned as vampires, however.

Habitat/Society: Zombie lords seek out places of death as lairs. Often, they choose to live in old graveyards or on the sites of tremendous battles—any place that contains many bodies to animate and feast upon.

The mind of a zombie lord tends to focus on death and the creation of more undead. The regions around their lairs are littered with the decaying bodies, often half-eaten, of those who have tried to confront the foul creature. They seldom have grandiose schemes like those undertaken by vampires or liches, but will frequently plan to take over a small town and turn its entire populace into living corpses.

Ecology: The zombie lord comes into being by chance, and only under certain conditions. First, an evil human being (the soon-to-be zombie lord) must die at the hands of an undead creature. Second, an attempt to raise the slain individual must be made. Third, and last, the individual must fail his *resurrection* survival roll. It is believed that zombie lords can be created only in Ravenloft, but this is not proven absolutely for they have been encountered in other lands from time to time.

Appendix II:
Children of the Night

Introduction

There is a tendency in Ravenloft adventures to focus only on the lords of the various domains. When a group of heroes enters the forests of Barovia, they expect to run afoul of the machinations of Strahd von Zarovich.

Should their travels bring them into the wilds of Kartakass, they gather wolfsbane and stand ready to face the challenge of Harkon Lukas and his lycanthropes.

While this certainly makes for an exciting adventure, it does tend to limit the scope of the Dungeon Master's imagination. In addition, the lord of a domain tends to be a very powerful creature. Lower-level adventurers are sometimes hard-pressed to meet the challenges presented by such encounters.

Thus, this appendix deals not with Ravenloft's lords, but with many of the other evil creatures that dwell amid the mists. None of the fiends presented here is the master of his or her own domain, although many are connected in some way to those most evil of Ravenloft's inhabitants.

Variations on a Theme

One of the subjects that the RAVENLOFT design team spends an awful lot of time talking and writing about is the fine art of refereeing a RAVENLOFT game. We write articles about it for DRAGON® magazine and POLYHEDRON® newszine and spend an incredible amount of time answering questions and hosting seminars about it at conventions. We offer hints on designing adventures and creating the horror mood, and we listen to the comments of our fans.

We encourage people to pay attention to the creation of unique villains. While this certainly applies to the most powerful of creatures, like the lord of a domain, it also holds true for lesser characters. After all, no two player characters will ever be exactly alike—why shouldn't the same be true for the monsters they face?

The creatures in this appendix can be divided into the following three general categories.

Old Familiar Faces

Some of the monsters presented in upcoming pages are based upon existing AD&D game creatures. Some are drawn from the pages of previous MONSTROUS COMPENDIUM volumes and some from earlier RAVENLOFT adventures and supplements.

In every case, however, the monster has been given a unique background and motivation that sets it apart from the others of its ilk. In the first half of this book, for example, statistics were presented for the vile ermordenung. In this section, we explore the secret origins of Nostalia Romaine, the first of the deadly ermordenung to be created and certainly the most evil of their kind.

Newly Recognized Terrors

Some of the other creatures in this appendix are unique examples of races that have not been previously defined. For example, you'll be introduced to the Voodan, a mysterious offshoot of humanity that may well be distantly related to the Vistani. The statistics presented are those of a single individual but can certainly serve as a model for Dungeon Masters who might wish to add other Voodan to their campaigns.

Freaks and Outcasts

The last type of entry in this particular appendix is the unique creature. These individuals are exemplified by entries like the Living Brain or the horribly cursed Jacqueline Montarri. Thankfully, there is only one of each such creature in existence, for they are terrible indeed. These entries can be the most interesting of all to run in a campaign because players won't know what it is that they are encountering.

Other Encounters

The Mists of Ravenloft do not transport characters exclusively; at times creatures native to other worlds may find themselves in the demiplane. The lists below include monsters from other MONSTROUS COMPENDIUM appendices that may appear in Ravenloft (at the DM's option).

Generic MONSTROUS COMPENDIUM Appendices

(MC1 & MC2)
Bat (common)
Bat (large or giant)
Bat (huge or mobat)
Carrion Crawler
Doppleganger
Elf, Drow
Gargoyle
Ghost
Ghoul
Ghoul (lacedon)
Ghoul (ghast)
Golem, Lesser (flesh)
Golem, Lesser (clay)
Golem, Greater (stone)
Golem, Greater (iron)
Groaning Spirit (banshee)
Guardian Daemon (least)
Guardian Daemon (lesser)
Guardian Daemon (greater)
Hag (annis)
Hag (green)
Hag (sea)
Haunt
Hell Hound
Heucuva
Homonculous
Imp
Jackalwere
Lich
Lich (demilich)
Lycanthrope, Werefox (foxwoman)
Lycanthrope, Wererat
Lycanthrope, Werewolf
Mind Flayer
Mummy
Poltergeist
Rakshasa
Rat (common)
Rat (giant)
Shadow
Skeleton
Skeleton (animal)
Skeleton (monster)
Spectre
Vampire
Vampire (oriental)
Wight
Will o'wisp
Wolf
Wolf (worg or dire)
Wolf (winter)
Wolfwere
Wraith
Zombie

Zombie (monster)
Zombie (ju-ju)

FORGOTTEN REALMS® Appendix I (MC3)
Claw, Crawling
Cloaker
Darkenbeast
Death, Crimson
Revenant
Web, Living

DRAGONLANCE® (MC4)
Beast, Undead (stahnk)
Beast, Undead (gholor)
Dreamshadow
Dreamwraith
Fetch
Fire Minion
Fire Shadow
Haunt, Knight
Imp, Blood Sea
Knight, Death
Spectral Minion
Warrior, Skeleton
Wichtlin
Yaggol

GREYHAWK® (MC5)
Crypt Thing
Hound, Yeth
Kyuss, Son of
Necrophidius
Raven (ordinary)
Raven (huge)
Raven (giant)
Scarecrow
Shadow, Slow
Wraith (swordwraith)
Wraith (soul beckoner)
Zombie, Sea

KARA-TUR™ (MC6)
Buso (tigbanua Buso)
Buso (tagamaling Buso)
Chu-u
Con-tinh
Gaki (jiki-ketsu-gaki)
Gaki jiki-niku-gaki)
Gaki (shikki-gaki)
Gaki (shinen-gaki)
Goblin Rat
Goblin Spider
Hannya
Hengeyokai (fox)
Hengeyokai (racoon dog)
Hengeyokai (rat)
Hu Hsien
Ikiryo
Kaluk
Krakentua
Kuei
Memedi
Oni (common)
Oni (go-zu-oni)
Oni (me-zu-oni)
P'oh Gohei
Spirit, Stone
Yuki-on-onna

FORGOTTEN REALMS Appendix II (MC11)
Bat, Deep
Cat (all)
Harrla
Inquisitor
Lhiannan Shee
Manni
Naga, Dark
Orpsu
Phantom
Plant, Carnivorous (Black Willow)
Skuz
Tempest

SPELLJAMMER® Appendix I (MC7)
Ancient Mariner
Spiritjam

SPELLJAMMER® Appendix II (MC9)
Allura
Dreamslayer
Dwep,erbprm
Fore;ocj
Skullbird
Spirit Warrior
Undead, Stellar

FORGOTTEN REALMS Appendix II (MC11)
Bat, Deep
Cat (all)
Harrla
Inquisitor
Lhiannan Shee
Manni
Naga, Dark
Orpsu
Phantom
Plant, Carnivorous (Black Willow)
Skuz
Tempest

DARK SUN® Appendix (MC12)
Banshee, Dwarf
Beetle Agony
Bog Wader
Dune Runner
Elemental (all)
Golem (all)
Id Fiend
Plant, Carnivorous (all)
Sand Bride
Thrax
Zhackal
Zombie Plant

FIEND FOLIO® Appendix (MC14)
Apparition
Coffer Corpse
Dark Creeper
Dark Stalker
Grimlock
Hellcat
Iron Cobra
Mephit (all)
Penanggalan
Phantom Stalker
Sheet Ghoul/Sheet Phantom

Brain, Living (Rudolph Von Aubrecker)

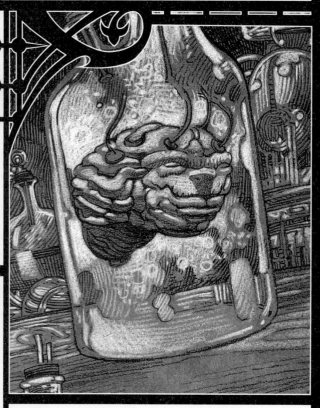

CLIMATE/TERRAIN:	Dementlieu (Port-a-Lucine)
FREQUENCY:	Unique
ORGANIZATION:	Solitary
ACTIVITY CYCLE:	Any
DIET:	Special
INTELLIGENCE:	Supra-genius (20)
TREASURE:	Nil
ALIGNMENT:	Neutral evil

NO. APPEARING:	1
ARMOR CLASS:	10
MOVEMENT:	Special
HIT DICE:	1 (8 hp)
THAC0:	19
NO. OF ATTACKS:	1
DAMAGE/ATTACK:	See below
SPECIAL ATTACKS:	See below
SPECIAL DEFENSES:	See below
MAGIC RESISTANCE:	Nil
SIZE:	Tiny (about 8″ diameter)
MORALE:	Average (9)
XP VALUE:	975

The Living Brain is a horrible result of Victor Mordenheim's early experiments in the creation and artificial sustenance of life. Like many of his other projects, the gods looked upon this as a violation of their sacred tenets. Mordenheim has long since forgotten this experiment, but the evil that he created on that stormy night years ago lives on in the Demiplane of Dread.

Externally, the Living Brain looks exactly as one might expect of a disembodied brain. The only difference that might be noticed by a careful and knowledgeable observer is an unusual enlargement of the frontal lobes and a "capping off" of the brain stem by a network of cells not unlike those that generate and store an electric eel's shocking attack.

In order to remain alive, the brain must be maintained at a temperature of between 95° and 105° Fahrenheit. Further, it must remain immersed in a nutritive saline solution which is artificially oxygenated by means of a mechanical pump. This fluid (and thus the brain itself) is contained in a thick glass jar.

The vessel which holds the brain is connected by a pair of thick conduits to a two-foot-wide cube that contains the apparatus which keeps it alive. Inside the sealed black cube is the pumping machine that circulates the solution upon which the brain depends for life. There is no known power source associated with this mechanism; many sages speculate that Mordenheim was actually able to create a perpetual motion machine for his experiment. If this is indeed the case, the secret behind such a wondrous device has been lost during Mordenheim's descent into madness.

The brain is able to communicate with any sentient creature (that is, any being with low Intelligence or better) by means of a limited telepathy. This transcends language barriers but allows only the most simple of concepts to be conveyed. Although the brain is able to take control of others via its terrible psychic powers, it is unable to converse with those it dominates. Attempts have been made by Mordenheim and others to construct speech machines for the brain, but these have always failed. When communication is vital to its plans, the brain simply uses its mental powers to dominate someone and then speak through that person.

Combat: Obviously, the Living Brain is utterly helpless in all physical matters. However, the isolation of this terrible organ from all physical concerns has enabled it to focus wholly on its mental powers. Further, the addition of various chemicals to the nutrient bath and the mild electrical current running through the solution which houses the brain have stimulated its development. Combined, these factors make the brain one of the most dangerous creatures in Ravenloft.

The actual appearance of the brain can give characters quite a shock. While the sight of a brain floating in a jar is probably not enough to inspire fear or horror in the average adventurer, the realization that the brain is a living, sentient thing is far more unsettling. At the DM's discretion, anyone who has the true nature of the Living Brain thrust upon him or her might well be required to make a fear, horror, or even madness check.

The primary weapon of the brain is a simple bolt of mental energy that does damage based on the Intelligence of the victim. Because the attack turns the target's own mind against itself, creatures with lower intelligences are far less vulnerable to it. Against highly intelligent creatures, however, the attack can be devastating. When employing its mental blast, the brain must make a normal attack roll. The "Armor Class" of the victim is determined not by armor worn but by the mental fortitude, or Wisdom, of the target. This mental

Armor Class is assumed to begin at 10, just as normal Armor Class does. However, every 3 full points of Wisdom provides a −1 reduction to this base. Thus, a character with a Wisdom of 15 has a mental Armor Class of five (15÷3=5; 10−5=5). Obviously, Dexterity will not modify the mental Armor Class of a target. At the Dungeon Master's option, however, other factors might. Any psionic defense mode will double the natural Wisdom bonus if employed.

Once a target has been hit by the mental attack, the damage inflicted by the attack is determined by rolling dice. The damage done varies according to the target's Intelligence, as indicated in the following chart:

Intelligence	Damage Done
Non- (0)	Nil
Animal (1)	1d4
Semi- (2–4)	1d6
Low (5–7)	1d8
Average (8–10)	1d10
Very (11–12)	2d6
High (13–14)	2d8
Exceptional (15–16)	2d10
Genius (17–18)	3d8
Supra-genius (19–20)	3d10
Godlike (21+)	4d10

The various psionic defense modes, magical spells like *mind blank*, and certain magical items will provide protection from this attack.

In addition to this simple attack, the Living Brain is able to employ special mental powers that mimic a number of magical spells. Three times per day it may duplicate the effects of a *charm person*, *command*, or *sleep* spell. Twice per day, the brain may employ *forget*, *hold person*, and *suggestion*. Once per day, the foul thing may also make use of *demand*, *domination*, *emotion*, or *mass suggestion*. In all cases, normal language requirements are waived for the purposes of the brain's special abilities, and all powers are employed as if by a 15th-level wizard. All normal ranges for these abilities are waived as well, as they are assumed to function within a 50-foot radius around the brain.

The brain maintains a low-level empathic field at all times. Because this aura senses any aggressive intent within 50 feet, it is impossible for anyone to achieve surprise when attacking the brain from within this range. This field also enables the brain to estimate the Intelligence, character class, and experience level of anyone entering it with great precision.

In addition to this rudimentary defense, the brain can invoke a protective shell three times per day. This shell combines the effects of both a *globe of invulnerability* and a *wall of force*, making it a most effective defense.

Even if its mental defenses are somehow bypassed or negated, the brain is not utterly without protection. While it is helpless to ward off any physical attack, the Living Brain regenerates 1 hit point per round so long as it is immersed in its fluid bath.

Habitat/Society: The Living Brain was once Rudolph Von Aubrecker, youngest son of the political ruler of Lamordia. The boy had grown up in the pampered lifestyle that one associates with nobility and was by all accounts a spoiled brat. While not truly evil, he was extremely selfish and spiteful.

When Rudolph turned 18, he decided to celebrate with a week of shameless debauchery aboard his caravel, the Haifisch. As the revelers descended into drunken stupor, a fierce storm blew in from the Sea of Sorrows. Without a capable crew to respond to the deadly gale, the Haifisch was hurled against the rocky coast and shattered. There were no survivors—or so it seemed.

In actuality, Rudolph's still-living body was found by a young man named Alexis Wilhaven, a young medical student who at the time was studying under Doctor Victor Mordenheim. Wilhaven carried the body to nearby Schloss Mordenheim (the doctor's manor) for emergency medical care. Despite their best efforts, however, it became clear to the doctor that there was no hope for the dying young Aubrecker.

At this point in his life, Mordenheim was deeply involved in the first stages of his experiments into the origins of life. He was particularly interested in studying the problem of brain tissue degeneration and decided to remove the man's brain prior to the death of the body and try to keep it alive in a tank. When Mordenheim told Wilhaven of his intent, the young man was horrified. He argued with the doctor, trying to dissuade him from the experiment. In the end, however, Mordenheim was able to calm his assistant's fears enough to obtain his reluctant cooperation for the delicate operation.

As the storm raged outside, the pair did their butchers' work and then destroyed the body. Despite Wilhaven's pleas, Mordenheim made no effort to inform the Baron about his son's true fate. Instead, he allowed the old man to believe that his youngest boy was simply lost at sea.

Mordenheim placed the brain in a glass container which he had filled with a saline solution. He circulated and aerated the fluid with a pump that was driven by a simple battery of his own design. Over the course of the next few weeks, he studied the brain and did all that he could to sustain it.

Horrified at what he had done, Wilhaven planned to leave Schloss Mordenheim and take word of the doctor's madness to the Baron. Before leaving, he made a final impassioned plea to Mordenheim, demanding that he destroy the brain and end this blasphemous experiment. Not only did he fail to convince the scientist, he found himself swayed by Mordenheim's own assertion that he was as deeply involved in the experiment as the doctor himself. Struck by the seed of truth in this argument, Wilhaven realized that he would be judged just as harshly as Mordenheim should news of his son's fate ever reach the Baron's ears. Reluctantly, Wilhaven agreed to remain with Mordenheim and see the experiment through to its end.

Eventually, it became clear that the brain was not only living, but aware. Mordenheim began to make attempts at communication with the brain. He built all manner of mechanical devices that he hoped would enable the brain to speak. At one point, he even hoped to establish some manner of psychic contact with the thing and connected the brain directly to a trickle current of electricity to give it more energy for psychic communication. Lacking any real training in or understanding of psionics, however, he failed yet again and abandoned this effort.

When Mordenheim despaired of communicating with the brain, he began to lose interest in it. He had learned all he felt he needed to know about the degeneration of tissue, for he had not only halted the brain's decay but reversed it. The brain was actually growing in some ways, for the frontal lobes had become unusually swollen and a new membrane had closed off the severed brain stem.

Mordenheim decided that it was time to end this experiment and get on with his other work, to disconnect the brain's life-support systems and let it die the natural death he had denied it nearly a year earlier. To his horror, he found that he could not destroy the brain. His every effort in that direction met with failure as he either lost his resolve or found that his body simply refused to obey his will. Indeed, the thing seemed to have acquired the ability to control him.

As weeks and then months passed, Mordenheim found himself building a new pumping mechanism to support the brain. He would spend hours laboring away with no idea what his final goal was. Only the brain, with its intelligence boosted by side effects from Mordenheim's experiments, knew what the device would do when completed. After nearly half a year of labor, Mordenheim put the finishing touches on a life-support system that appeared to be fully self-contained.

Then, less than a week after he had finished this device, the brain and all its supporting equipment vanished, as did young Wilhaven. It didn't take the doctor long to deduce that the boy had fallen under the brain's spell just as he had. While Mordenheim was forced to construct the brain's mechanism, Wilhaven must have been directed to plan the brain's departure from remote Schloss Mordenheim to some other location.

Mordenheim made inquiries, attempting to discover what had happened to the sinister thing that he created, but was able to learn only that a man matching the description of his young assistant had been seen in the harbor at Ludendorf, directing the placement of several large crates aboard a ship bound for Dementlieu. The man had then boarded the ship, which left the harbor and sailed into the mists that roll eternally across the surface of the Sea of Sorrows. More than that, he was unable to learn.

Indeed, Mordenheim quickly lost interest in the affair. While he had no doubt that the brain would do evil wherever it went, he soon found himself absorbed in his own work again. Still, the scientist did not forget the lessons that he learned from this tragedy. As he began again to examine the question of life and its origins, he vowed that he would allow no future experiments to go as far astray as had this one. . . .

The process which turned Rudolph Von Aubrecker into the Living Brain gave Mordenheim's creation tremendous mental powers and a greatly increased intelligence. The brain recognizes that it can never again be a part of the human world but is little distressed by this fact. Instead, it considers itself quite superior to those "mere humans" around it, due to the ease with which it can manipulate and control them.

When it left Lamordia, the creature had great plans, desiring nothing less than the total domination of all it encountered. While it found controlling a man of Dr. Mordenheim's brilliance very taxing, the doctor's young assistant proved to be a far more pliable slave. It used the youth to leave Mordenheim and Lamordia behind and seek a new land to claim for its own.

By the time its ship dropped anchor in Port-a-Lucine, the entire crew was under the brain's horrible control. Under its direction, its new lackeys quickly arranged for the purchase of an abandoned warehouse on the waterfront. Here, it ordered its hapless servants to began assembling a collection of scientific apparatus that eventually grew into a formidable laboratory.

At the same time, the Living Brain began to mentally enslave more and more people in pursuit of its long-range goal. But when it tried to take control of Marcel Guignol, the Lord Governor of Dementlieu, it discovered he was already under someone else's control, the man's mind filled with hypnotic blocks and mental suggestions—and that the sophistication of these techniques exceeded even its own powers. Looking further into the matter, it eventually deduced the identity of this mysterious rival: mesmerist Dominic d'Honaire, the lord of this domain.

In the years since its arrival in Dementlieu, the Living Brain has clashed with d'Honaire several times. The two are now hated enemies who play an incredibly subtle game of cat and mouse as they each strive to destroy the other. The fact that d'Honaire has not yet been able to destroy his enemy is directly attributable to the cunning intelligence of Aubrecker and the care that it takes to protect itself from discovery. Further, d'Honaire has never seen the Living Brain and does not yet understand the nature of his enemy. Indeed, the lord of Dementlieu is fairly certain that he opposes a man who, like himself, is a master of the hypnotic arts. That his enemy might be the result of an unhallowed operation by a brilliant mad scientist in another land has not occurred to him.

The brain has created a network of informants, most of whom do not realize the nature of the thing they serve. Thus, although they frequently refer to their hidden master as "The Brain," they have no idea that this is anything other than a nickname. So extensive is the intelligence network set up by the Living Brain that it knows almost everything that happens in the domain nearly as soon as d'Honaire himself does.

The Living Brain has several lairs in the waterfront district of Port-a-Lucine, Dementlieu's largest city, and can easily be moved to a place of hiding on short notice. Its main base of operations, secured with the help of young Wilhaven and the crew of the ship that carried it out of Lamordia, is an old warehouse building indistinguishable from the many other such edifices in this part of the city.

Inside, crates and barrels fill the large structure to the roof, and laborers seem to be always at work bringing in new cargoes and hauling out old ones. In actuality, these poor creatures are totally under the control of the brain and spend their entire lives moving things from one place in the building to another. If the brain is ever attacked, these men form its first line of defense. Each of them is nothing more than a lst-level fighter, but there are upwards of 20 available at any time.

Behind the warehouse and connected to it by both a narrow alleyway and a secret underground tunnel is an old two-story house. This smaller building is used as a home by the brain's most important minions. These are people who know the true nature of the creature they serve and act willingly on its behalf. To the outside world, they are the owners and operators of the warehouse. In actuality, they are murderers and assassins. They have been permitted to retain their free will only because the brain has searched their minds and found their loyalty to be beyond question.

Below the warehouse, in a secret sub-basement whose very existence is known only to a trusted few, lies the Living Brain's lair and laboratory.

Ecology: The Living Brain is free of the burdens imposed upon natural creatures. It has no need of food, save for the nutrients that are carried in its fluid bath, or most other biological requirements. It does require *sleep,* however, for only in dreams can it experience the physical sensations it requires to remain sane.

Although the pumping mechanism and electrical generator that keep the brain alive are perpetual and have no need of recharging or, at least to date, repair, it is not an utterly closed system. As the disembodied brain extracts chemicals and nutrients from the solution in which it floats, the mixture must be replenished. While the brain itself is unable to do this, this simple task is one that it can easily command any of its minions to do. The procedure takes one hour, during which period the brain is effectively helpless and comatose. During this time, player characters might be entitled to a saving throw to escape the brain's influence over them. Few, if any, NPCs should gain such a saving throw, however, as the brain's hold over a minion strengthens with time.

Young Wilhaven, the poor lad who found the body of the dying Aubrecker, has become the absolute slave of the Living Brain. Years of mental domination by the fiend have left the man's soul a desiccated husk. When the brain is not directly instructing him to act in some way, he generally sits listlessly looking out over the Sea of Sorrows. From time to time, a tear rolls from his eye—the result of some lingering fragment of his personality? Or merely a speck of dust carried in the air? None can say.

Adventure Ideas: The inherent dichotomy of d'Honaire and the Living Brain is a natural source of drama, one which places the player characters squarely in the middle of the endless struggle between the Living Brain and its rival, Dominic d'Honaire. Furious at his inability to root out and destroy this enemy, the master of Dementlieu arranges a meeting with a group of adventurers (that is, the PCs).

Through mundane or macabre means, d'Honaire convinces them to seek out and destroy his enemy. His own assumption that his foe is nothing more than a man, albeit a talented and intelligent one, will no doubt be passed on to the players. As they look deeper into the matter and the true nature of the Living Brain becomes apparent to them, they find themselves facing something far more horrible than anything they might have imagined. Even if they fail to destroy Aubrecker, d'Honaire would be very interested in learning that his enemy is a disembodied monster.

This scenario could easily be reversed, with the PCs being hired through one of the brain's agents to investigate the secret master of Dementlieu. As they explore the mysterious land, they discover the intricate web of deceit and hypnosis that d'Honaire has sown about the domain. Having run afoul of his plans, they might well find themselves forced to seek protection from their mysterious patron, only to discover its horrifying true nature.

Ermordenung (Nostalia Romaine)

CLIMATE/TERRAIN:	Borca
FREQUENCY:	Unique
ORGANIZATION:	Solitary
ACTIVITY CYCLE:	Any
DIET:	Omnivore
INTELLIGENCE:	Very (12)
TREASURE:	W (I)
ALIGNMENT:	Lawful evil

NO. APPEARING:	1
ARMOR CLASS:	10
MOVEMENT:	15
HIT DICE:	4 (27 hp)
THAC0:	17
NO. OF ATTACKS:	1
DAMAGE/ATTACK:	1d4+1
SPECIAL ATTACKS:	Poison; charm
SPECIAL DEFENSES:	Immune to poison
MAGIC RESISTANCE:	Nil
SIZE:	M (5'11")
MORALE:	Fanatic (17)
XP VALUE:	1,400

Nostalia Romaine is the head of Ivana Boritsi's dreaded ermordenung. She is as evil as she is ravishing, and utterly loyal to her evil mistress. A series of elixirs keeps her eternally young and maintains her alluring beauty, which is perhaps her most deadly weapon.

Like all ermordenung, Nostalia is in perfect physical condition. Slender and elegant, she moves with the grace and agility of a dancer. She stands just under six feet in height, with crisp dark eyes that stand out from the unnaturally pale complexion of her skin. Her ebony hair, which she wears in a thick braid, falls almost to her knees. She often decorates herself by braiding flowers into her hair, selecting blooms that are both beautiful and poisonous. Nostalia carries a slender jeweled dagger on her hip but employs no other armor or weapons. She always wears long, elegant gloves, removing them only when preparing to kill someone with her poisoned touch.

Nostalia speaks the language of Borca, as well as that of several neighboring domains. Her aristocratic tones come across clearly, whatever the language.

Combat: Like all ermordenung, Nostalia has the ability to kill with her touch. Because her body has been infused with deadly toxins, the slightest unprotected contact with her exposed skin is life-threatening. In combat, a normal attack roll is required for her to touch exposed skin. Anyone touched must make a saving throw vs. poison (with a +4 bonus) at once. Those who fail their saves succumb instantly to her deadly touch. Those who save successfully suffer 10 points of damage.

A natural roll of 20 on the attack indicates that Nostalia has gotten a firm grip on her enemy. When this happens, the victim must make an unmodified saving throw vs. poison: failure indicates instant death, while a successful save results in the loss of 20 hit points. If the victim is unable to break her iron grip, a new save must be made again on each subsequent round.

In noncombat situations, Nostalia strikes by luring male victims into a deadly embrace. Her natural charisma, intoxicating beauty, and seductive manner make this a simple task in most cases; in addition, her deep, husky voice acts as a *charm* spell. Once she has taken her victim into her arms, she delivers a passionate, and utterly deadly, kiss. Anyone kissed by Nostalia must make a saving throw vs. poison (with a –4 penalty to the roll) or be instantly slain. Success at the saving throw results in a mere 30 points of damage. Anyone caught in the ermordenung's embrace who fails to break free will be kissed again on the next round.

Breaking away from Nostalia is not an easy task. Like all ermordenung, she has a Strength score of 18/50. Anyone whose Strength score is lower must make a successful saving throw vs. paralysis (again, at a –4 penalty) in order to pull away. Persons of equal strength must succeed on an unmodified roll; those who are stronger gain a +4 bonus.

When she opts not to use her natural attacks, Nostalia strikes with her bejeweled dagger. This is her preferred means of attacking female victims, for she finds the touch of other women repulsive. This weapon is actually a *dagger of venom* that she keeps filled with a solution mixed from her own blood. Anyone stabbed by this +1 weapon must make a successful saving throw vs. poison with a –4 penalty or die instantly (success on the save means the toxin was not injected). The dagger holds enough poison for six attacks.

Nostalia's system is so infused with deadly toxins that she herself is immune to almost any manner of poisonous attack. The only toxin to which she is vulnerable is the touch of another ermordenung.

Habitat/Society: Nostalia was born near the city of Levkarest in Borca. Her parents were aristocrats, loyal followers of the dread Camille Dilisnya, the lord of the domain at that time.

As a young girl, Nostalia and Ivana Boritsi were close friends. When Ivana, who was the elder by some two years, began to plan her ascension to the throne of Borca, Nostalia was her loyal assistant and confidant. Nostalia had no great dislike of Camille, but her devotion to Ivana was such that she would do anything her friend asked of her.

When Ivana perfected her mysterious method of toxic infusions that she believed would grant the recipient a poisoned touch at will, she asked Nostalia to be the first to receive this dire and deadly gift. Nostalia agreed and underwent the horrible transformation. As the process was completed, she fell into a coma and remained all but lifeless for a fortnight. When she awoke at last, she was an ermordenung, the living embodiment of venom.

The first act that Nostalia was called upon to undertake as an ermordenung was the destruction of Ivana's mother, Camille. Ivana planned to poison her mother, just as Camille had poisoned so many others, and Nostalia would be her weapon.

On a warm, bright day some two weeks after she had completed her transformation, Nostalia went to visit the unsuspecting monarch in her chambers in the Boritsi Manor. Here, she professed her loyalty and love, saying that she had come to warn her monarch about Ivana's foul plot to assassinate her and usurp the domain. Even now, Nostalia warned, hired thugs were on their way to Camille's chambers to murder her, unless she fled immediately. Camille believed her story and, hearing noises outside that sounded like a mob breaking down the outer door, panicked and fled through a secret passage with Nostalia.

Together, the two women navigated the dark, narrow, cobweb-filled tunnels within the manor's walls, emerging at last in the coachhouse, where a magnificent coach stood, a team of fine horses and a driver in hat and greatcoat at the ready. Nostalia explained that this conveyance would carry Camille to safety in Levkarest, where she could rally her supporters and return to reclaim her throne.

But when the grateful matriarch ordered the coachman to open the carriage door, the supposed servant suddenly removed hat and cloak to reveal—Ivana's face. As Camille turned to her companion, her face pale with shock and horror, Nostalia stepped forward with a smile and kissed the older woman, who crumpled dead at her feet to the sound of Ivana's cruel laughter.

Ever since that time, Nostalia has found herself haunted by the face of the woman she betrayed and killed. Nightmares in which Camille Dilisnya rises up as a ghost to destroy her are not uncommon. Nostalia is unable to escape the feel of Camille's lips on her own, even when she kisses another. For this reason, Nostalia loathes the touch of female flesh. While she will gladly use her poisonous embrace to destroy men, she is sickened by the thought of actually touching another woman. Therefore, she depends upon her *dagger of venom* when Ivana orders her to assassinate a woman.

She soon found herself at the head of a growing clan of ermordenung. Although there were fewer than half a dozen of the deadly creatures in those early days, it quickly became clear that their usefulness to the lord of the domain would lead to the creation of more. Gradually, Ivana began to place more and more power in the hands of her deadly childhood friend.

In the years that have passed since that time, Nostalia has grown detached. She no longer feels any remorse over her deeds and has come to savor the pain and suffering that she brings to others.

Ecology: Like all ermordenung, Nostalia Romaine is deadly to all that she touches. As such, she can never take a lover, marry, or raise children. While she claims to hold such things in contempt and boasts that she holds no desire for them, the intimacy that is denied her gnaws at her soul.

For several years now, Nostalia has been employing an elixir that prevents her from aging. Only she knows the secret ingredients of this concoction, though it is believed to require the "harvesting" of no fewer than three young men each month. Nostalia must create and consume a new draught each new moon or her aging will resume at a greatly accelerated rate.

Nostalia is Ivana Boritsi's closest adviser and has a great deal of influence in the selection of new ermordenung. As such, she is often thought of as the mother of that race, despite the fact that she had no part in actually devising the formula that made her what she is today.

Adventure Ideas: Nostalia's vanity and hunger for eternal youth is a fine source for adventures. She might easily be encountered while investigating some new tonic or elixir. Further, the "harvesting" of young men for her monthly draught of youth might well bring her to the attention of the heroes.

Ghoul, Ghast (Jugo Hesketh)

CLIMATE/TERRAIN:	Tepest
FREQUENCY:	Unique
ORGANIZATION:	Pack
ACTIVITY CYCLE:	Night
DIET:	Corpses
INTELLIGENCE:	Very (11)
TREASURE:	Q, R, S, T (B)
ALIGNMENT:	Chaotic evil

NO. APPEARING:	1
ARMOR CLASS:	4
MOVEMENT:	15
HIT DICE:	4 (24 hp)
THAC0:	17
NO. OF ATTACKS:	3
DAMAGE/ATTACK:	1d4/1d4/1d8
SPECIAL ATTACKS:	Paralysis
SPECIAL DEFENSES:	Stench
MAGIC RESISTANCE:	Nil
SIZE:	M (6′ 3″ tall)
MORALE:	Elite (13)
XP VALUE:	650

Long ago, Hesketh was a senior priest in the cult of the false god Zhakata led by Yagno Petrovna, the lord of G'henna. As Petrovna's chief Inquisitor, among his horrid duties were dreadful acts of torture and sacrifice; secretly, he practiced cannibalism on the corpses of his hapless victims. Over the years, these unholy practices warped his soul and, upon his death, transformed him into an undead fiend.

Prior to his demise, Hesketh was a tall, slender man. He had sparse black hair and piercing dark eyes that seemed to look deep into the hearts of those he met. He was congenial and polite, if inwardly sinister, and quite possibly the most charismatic man in G'henna.

The accident which claimed Hesketh's life and the terrible transformation to undeath has left his appearance greatly altered. His skin, now dried and mummified, has drawn tight over the bones and turned a sickly gray-green. His fingernails are long and black, taking on the appearance of dreadful claws. His tongue has grown long and rasplike, perfect for drawing the marrow out of bones. Hesketh's eyes gleam in the dark with a searing red not unlike the glow of a burning ember; his teeth are sharp, black, and utterly deadly.

Whatever languages Hesketh knew in life have been forgotten in death. He communicates with the ghouls that follow him through guttural grunts and growls. It might be possible to speak to Hesketh with magical means, but this is mere speculation; to date, no one has tried—no one who survived, at any rate.

Combat: While much of Hesketh's brilliant intellect has been lost, he retains a cruel and deadly cunning. When he attacks, he does so savagely, with tooth and claw.

Each of his two claw attacks inflicts 1d4 points of damage; the horrible bite causes 1d8 points. Anyone injured by Hesketh must make a successful saving throw vs. paralysis or be unable to move for 5 to 10 (1d6+4) rounds. This affects all humans and demihumans, including elves. A priest can free anyone stricken with this curse by means of a *remove paralysis* spell.

As a ghast, Hesketh gives off a foul odor of rotting flesh. Anyone who comes within 10 feet of him must make a successful saving throw vs. poison or become so ill that he or she suffers a –2 penalty at all attack rolls for the duration of the combat.

Hesketh is not without his vulnerabilities. He can be harmed by any weapon, be it magical or mundane, and weapons forged of cold iron will inflict double damage with each hit. He can be turned by clerics of high enough level (at least 3rd) and can be held at bay with a *protection from evil* spell, but only if powdered iron is used in its casting.

Hesketh leads a band of common ghouls, and he is seldom encountered without 1 to 4 of these loathsome creatures in his company.

Any human or demihuman slain by Hesketh will become a ghoul; only if the body is blessed is this horrible fate averted. If the victim is raised or resurrected without being blessed, he or she will rise at once as a ravening ghoul. Of course, if the body is destroyed—for example, if Hesketh and his associates eat their victim—it cannot become a ghoul.

Hesketh is immune to all manner of *sleep* and *charm* spells. Poisons and diseases cannot harm him, and the dark powers have even granted him immunity to the touch of holy water.

Habitat/Society: Jugo Hesketh was, in life, a high-ranking priest in the service of Yagno Petrovna, the lord of G'Henna. Jugo Hesketh was the first man Petrovna encountered when he first left Barovia and entered

G'henna in 702. The two became friends, primarily because of Petrovna's *charm* ability, and worked together to forge the cult of Zhakata. They spent months traveling through the newly formed domain, gathering loyal followers to their false religion. Once the cult was well established, Yagno installed his trusted lieutenant as its chief Inquisitor, responsible for seeking out unbelievers and doubters ("blasphemers"); many a visitor to G'Henna escaped Zhakata's altars only to wind up in the Inquisition's dungeon ("question chambers").

As the years passed, one of Hesketh's primary responsibilities was the conducting of secret and terrible rituals designed to gain the favor of the false god Zhakata. These obscene services frequently ended with gruesome acts of sacrifice and cannibalism. It is said that more than half of the pitiful mongrelmen who roamed the Outlands of G'Henna were captured and brought to a grisly death at Hesketh's hands.

Then, in 725, Hesketh met with an unfortunate mishap. He and a number of his acolyte followers were scouring the wilds around Dervich for a family suspected of blasphemy. It was Hesketh's mission to apprehend these fugitives and bring them before Petrovna for transformation into mongrelmen.

Hesketh found the family attempting to flee north into Darkon. With the aid of his servants, he captured the whole clan and threw them in chains. The prisoners were tossed into a wagon and Hesketh began to lead them back to Zhukar, where they would meet their ghastly fate.

Shortly after the conveyance passed the halfway point in the trek, it was attacked by a band of mongrelmen. They had no idea who was in the wagon, thinking only that they might find food and useful equipment. When they discovered that fate had delivered the hated Jugo Hesketh into their hands, they were ecstatic. The acolytes tried to defend their master but were torn apart by the attackers. The mongrelmen freed the chained prisoners who, it is said, managed to make good their escape into Darkon, where they lived out the rest of their days.

Hesketh, however, was not so lucky. The vengeful mongrelmen carried their prisoner deep into the heart of the G'hennan Outland, where he was slowly tortured to death. His body was then tied to a raft and set adrift upriver of Zhukar.

When the raft arrived in the city, it was empty. But the bloodstains and clothes found on it were more than enough to convince Petrovna that his friend and follower had been killed. Enraged, the lord of G'henna ordered a brutal pogrom against the mongrelmen south of the city. It is unknown how many of the pitiful creatures were killed, or how many of Yagno's own men were slain in turn, before the carnage came to an end.

In the weeks following Hesketh's death, however, reports began to arise that the bodies of the slain acolytes returned from the slaughter for burial rites were being disfigured in their crypts.

Shocked, Petrovna decided to investigate the matter for himself. Much to his horror, he discovered that the half-eaten corpses were the work of his old friend, now an undead monster. For all his sinister evils, Yagno Petrovna could not bring himself to destroy his former friend, even in the terrible form he had assumed. Instead, he drove the creature out, forcing him to flee into the wilds of Tepest.

Ecology: When Hesketh died, a terrible curse fell upon him. The origins of this curse may lie in his own taste for human flesh or in the dying oaths of his countless victims. Whatever the source, this curse saw him transformed into a foul thing of the night. Hesketh now roams the lands of Tepest, searching eternally for flesh to satisfy his unnatural hunger.

Over the years, he has created a band of dreadful undead who follow him loyally. With these sickening acolytes, he seeks out and devours the newly dead.

While Hesketh and his minions do not go forth by day, they are not injured by sunlight. They tend to make their lair in places of death where they hunt for a few weeks before moving on. Often, they leave one or more ghouls behind that must be hunted down and destroyed if evidence of their passing is to be erased.

Adventure Ideas: Hesketh and his ghouls make excellent adversaries for lower-level heroes. A good scenario might involve the PCs being called upon to investigate a number of corpse mutilations or brutal murders. Because Hesketh is very cunning, he will disguise his activities as those of a madman or wild beast. Heroes investigating further will doubtless be shocked to learn the truth.

Hesketh could even be introduced following the demise of an important NPC or even a PC. As the body lies in state awaiting burial or resurrection, Hesketh and his ghouls could attack it. While this might be just another meal to them, it represents a great affront to the other player characters. Adventures that hit so close to home can be particularly terrifying.

If the DM wishes to make Hesketh more dangerous, he could be given some clerical spellcasting ability. In this way, he might be made suitable for use as an enemy confronting higher-level adventurers.

Golem, Half (Desmond LaRouche)

CLIMATE/TERRAIN:	Nova Vaasa
FREQUENCY:	Unique
ORGANIZATION:	Solitary
ACTIVITY CYCLE:	Any
DIET:	Omnivore
INTELLIGENCE:	High (13)
TREASURE:	Nil
ALIGNMENT:	Chaotic evil
NO. APPEARING:	1
ARMOR CLASS:	9
MOVEMENT:	9
HIT DICE:	7 (50 hp)
THAC0:	13
NO. OF ATTACKS:	1
DAMAGE/ATTACK:	2d8 or 1d6+2
SPECIAL ATTACKS:	Nil
SPECIAL DEFENSES:	+1 or better weapon to hit; spell immunities; regeneration
MAGIC RESISTANCE:	Nil
SIZE:	M (6'6" tall)
MORALE:	Champion (16)
XP VALUE:	5,000

Both medical science and healing magic can accomplish wonders. Often, the application of a poultice infused with curative herbs or the weaving of a mystical spell can save the life of an injured or diseased person. Sometimes, however, these noble pursuits of healing can be followed too far, and a virtuous intent often ends with tragic consequences. Such was the case with an unfortunate youth named Desmond LaRouche, the dreaded half-golem.

Prior to his transformation, Desmond was a handsome young man. His eyes were a soft and gentle green that reminded his many sweethearts of cool ferns. His long, sandy-brown hair was bound into a ponytail with a silver cord. His smile, quick to flash across his face and often followed by a melodic laugh, was as bright and winning as any in the land.

After that dark December night when tragedy struck, his features were drastically altered. While the right half of his body is as it was, the left is repulsive to look upon. That half of Desmond's face is now horribly scarred and has the pale gray color of death. His left eye is a sightless orb of white set in a puckered socket beneath a half-melted brow. Veins bulge out as the skin has drawn tight over the bone. His left hand is a withered remnant with long, blackened fingers and nails that curve like the claws of a great cat. It is difficult to imagine a more dreadful dichotomy than that presented by this once handsome man. Few can look upon him without succumbing to fear and loathing.

Desmond's voice alternates between the soft tones of his past life and the harsh, guttural sounds made by the left half of his throat. He speaks only the language of Nova Vaasa and may or may not be able to read and write when encountered, depending on which part of his personality is currently uppermost.

Combat: In melee combat, Desmond has two distinct fighting styles. If his bestial self is dominant, he attacks with a savage fury equal to that of a maddened beast. If his human side has mastery of the body, he tends toward finesse and elegant weapons like the rapier and foil. In either case, he is a dangerous enemy.

At the start of any given battle, Desmond has a 50% chance to give in to fury and rage. When this happens, he enters a berserk state, attacking with a single-minded determination that allows him a +2 bonus on his attack rolls and delivers 2 to 16 (2d8) points of damage each time a blow lands. Enemies who attack him while he is in this state gain a +2 bonus on their attack rolls because of the monomaniacal attention he gives to smashing his target.

If Desmond is not in a killing frenzy, he will fight more traditionally, attacking with his favorite weapon, a silver rapier. This medium piercing weapon weighs 4 pounds and has a speed factor of 4. Desmond's rapier, *Phantom*, is magical and gains a +1 bonus on all attack and damage rolls, inflicting a total of 3 to 8 (1d6+2) points of damage to small or medium-size foes and 3 to 10 (1d8+2) points to larger ones. Desmond's left arm has a Strength of 19, enabling him to grapple with enemies or lift heavy weights with ease. When his golem half is dominant, he is fond of using his left hand to strangle enemies or crush their bones in its viselike grip.

Whenever Desmond is hit by an attack or magical spell, it is important to determine whether the left or right half of his body was affected. This is done simply by rolling any die. If the result is even, the attack strikes his normal (right) side. If the number rolled is odd, the golem half of his body receives the blow. A called shot (as described in the *DUNGEON MASTER Guide*) can be made to strike a specific side of his body.

Desmond's left side has the same vulnerabilities and

advantages as a flesh golem. It can be hit only by magical weapons, and electrical attacks actually regenerate 1 hit point per die of damage that would normally be inflicted by such an attack. Fire- and cold-based attacks do no damage to Desmond's left half, but they do cause him to act as if a *slow* spell had been cast upon him for 2 to 12 (2d6) rounds. All other spells have no effect if they are targeted against this side of his body.

Desmond's right side is more or less normal. It can be hit with any weapon and harmed by fire, ice, electricity, and most other attacks.

The unusual biology that has resulted from this unique fusion of natural and artificial life gives Desmond a number of special abilities. Perhaps the most important of these is the fact that he regenerates very rapidly, regaining 3 hit points per round. In addition, he is immune to all manner of poisons, toxins, and disease. He cannot be *held*, *charmed*, or put to sleep by magical means, but these attacks will automatically turn control of his body over to his inhuman side.

If Desmond is killed, he can easily be restored to life. While he does not regenerate after death, a charge of electricity applied to his left side can restore lost hit points (as described above) and return him to life. As soon as he lives again, his natural regeneration takes over and quickly restores him to full health.

The mere sight of Desmond's face is so terrible that it might be considered a weapon. While it does not petrify or have any real magical effect, all who look upon it for the first time must make a horror check. Even those who have had the monstrous visage described to them beforehand must make this check, for no amount of secondhand information can prepare one for this terror.

Just as Desmond's biology was changed by his transformation, so too was his psyche affected. His mind is now a morass of conflicting passions, vibrant life energy, and the eternal blackness of death. Anyone who makes any manner of telepathic communication with him, either by magical or psionic means, must make a madness check (as described in the RAVENLOFT *Campaign Setting* boxed set). Anyone attempting to contact only one of his two selves will find it impossible to separate the two thought patterns.

Habitat/Society: The tragic story of Desmond LaRouche begins in the city of Kantora near the center of the domain of Nova Vaasa. His parents were the household servants of a wealthy doctor named Sir Tristen Hiregaard. They had no idea that their master was also the dreaded Malken, lord of the domain. Indeed, Hiregaard was so kind and generous an employer that the LaRouches could not conceive of him having any vices or evil intentions.

As he grew, the boy found a special place in Hiregaard's heart. Indeed, the surgeon became a second father to him. On spring days they would fly kites together in the park, letting the wind and warm sun carry away their concerns. When spring turned to summer, they would spend hours playing stickball and fishing. When Hiregaard traveled to the other cities in Nova Vaasa, he always brought back some new toy or present for the lad, and holidays were times of great celebration for Hiregaard and his servants.

Hiregaard's love for the boy grew with the youth. When young Desmond entered his teens, the good doctor took him on as an apprentice, teaching him the ways of science and the healing arts of medicine. The doctor was both amazed and delighted by the speed with which his young friend learned the lessons he taught. In no time, Hiregaard was passing along some of his less serious cases directly to LaRouche, who dispatched them with a dedication and skill that made his mentor glow with pride.

During his apprenticeship, the young LaRouche began to take notice of the true shape of society in Nova Vaasa. Although not a member of the upper class, he had been sheltered from the terrible condition of the vice-ridden masses by the kind heart of Tristen Hiregaard. When he begin to see the suffering of the common people, he was horrified. This repulsion was magnified by the recognition that he was actually one of the oppressors. He began to feel ashamed of his sheltered youth and vowed to make life better for those less fortunate than himself.

Hiregaard saw the importance of this to the young LaRouche and offered to help him begin a practice in the slums that made up large sections of Kantora. Desmond gladly accepted the sponsorship of the nobleman and set about his new career.

In no time, the names of LaRouche and Hiregaard became synonymous with compassion and caring to the people of Kantora. For nearly a year, the two physicians cured the ill, tended to the wounded, and oversaw the healthy birth of countless babies. LaRouche was happier than he had ever been in his life.

During this same year, however, the women of Kantora, especially the harlots and trollops who frequented the gambling houses of the city, began to be terrorized by a series of brutal killings. On more than one occasion, LaRouche was called upon to examine one of the mutilated corpses. Despite his medical training, these examinations sickened him.

Hiregaard brought the matter to the attention of Prince Othmar, the political ruler of Nova Vaasa. He hoped to receive additional guards to patrol the city and search for the murdering fiend. Instead, his pleas fell upon deaf ears. Othmar had little concern for the murders of, as he put it, "a few of the city's far too numerous Jezebels."

LaRouche took the news of Hiregaard's failure badly. He could not believe that their monarch would be so insensitive to the needs of his subjects. Finally, the young doctor decided to take matters into his own hands. If Prince Othmar would not help, then he, Desmond LaRouche, would track down the fiend himself and see him destroyed.

His mind made up, Desmond began to spend his evenings in the dark streets and alleys around the gambling houses. For nearly a week he saw nothing more than the usual beatings, violence, and corruption of the city. On the seventh night, however, he saw a sinister shape moving through the shadows of the city. Unwilling to move against the figure until he knew for certain that this was the killer, he moved to follow the suspi-

Golem, Half (Desmond LaRouche)

cious-looking character.

The constant ebb and flow of people in the streets made tailing the man a difficult task. Indeed, he nearly lost sight of the fellow several times. Finally, however, he spotted the man entering a dark alley with a young dancer from one of the bawdy houses. Fearing the worst, he made for the side street, only to find the press of traffic on the streets too thick to easily penetrate.

The frantic seconds it took Desmond to reach the mouth of the alley seemed to last forever. Looking into the darkness, he saw a flash of light on the gleaming blade of a knife and heard a muffled scream. Cursing his slowness, he dashed ahead and drew his wheel-lock pistol.

At the end of the alley he found the murderer bent over the fallen woman. Blood flowed freely from numerous lacerations and LaRouche knew at once that this was indeed the man he had been looking for. He leveled his pistol at the fiend and called for him to drop his knife.

The murderer had been so intent on his gruesome work that he had not heard Desmond charging down the alley toward him. Now, the sudden challenge caught him off guard. He whirled about, his blade clattering to the pavement.

At that moment, the moon broke through the autumn clouds and Desmond saw the killer's face. He gasped at the sight, for the man's features were bestial and ugly, hardly human at all. The face was twisted in hate and the yellow eyes burned with a cruel fire. For a second, the dreadful face froze Desmond in his tracks. Seeing his chance, the killer charged forward and knocked him aside. Desmond crashed against the wall of a building and fell to his knees.

The killer fled into the night, never looking back. Desmond got to his feet, took aim with his pistol, and fired at the retreating figure. The murderer staggered and fell, clearly having been shot. Before the young doctor could reach him, however, he regained his feet and vanished into the maze of dark streets.

Angry at his failure to either save the woman or stop the killer, Desmond knelt beside the victim's body. In life, she had been quite lovely; a fact which made her mangled corpse all the more horrifying. He steeled himself and draped his long coat over the body; only when this was done did he think to recover the knife that the killer had dropped.

To his horror, he recognized the weapon as a medical blade that belonged to none other than Tristen Hiregaard. Unable to accept the fact that his mentor could somehow be connected to the foul, misshapen killer he had seen, he assumed that the blade had been stolen. Pocketing the knife, he summoned the watch and reported the killing to the police.

With that taken care of, he made at once for Sir Hiregaard's house to query him as to when he had last seen the scalpel. He found the front door locked, as he expected at this late hour, and circled around to the office entrance at the side of the building. There, he saw a sight that made his blood run cold: a small pool of fresh blood on the stones by the door. Before he could con-

sider the implications of this, he heard a choking gasp of pain from inside. Without thinking, he burst in to the office where he had spent so many hours learning the healing arts.

To his horror, he saw the killer standing before him. Blood ran from his shoulder, showing quite clearly where Desmond's bullet had struck him.

Before Desmond could act to defend himself, the bestial fiend attacked. He grabbed the young doctor by the collar and hurled him into a rack of glass beakers and chemicals. Pain raced through Desmond's body as the various elixirs and fluids mingled to form a highly corrosive acid. Screaming in pain, he rolled clear of the chemicals just as they ignited and filled the room with flames and choking smoke.

Desmond assumed that this was the end of his life, for he was quickly losing consciousness and the only sensation he had in the left half of his body was a burning pain. He saw the killer clutch at his chest and fall to the floor beside him. With a detached horror, Desmond saw the bestial features of the terrible man soften and shift. Just as he fell into unconsciousness, he saw the murderer's face change to that of his beloved mentor, Sir Tristen Hiregaard.

The next several weeks of Desmond's life were spent drifting in and out of consciousness. Time passed without meaning to him, and the only thing he felt was an endless throbbing pain. Images remained in his mind, but whether they were real or hallucinations he could not say.

Finally, the young man awoke. He found that he was strapped down to a steel table in Hiregaard's operating theater. He was unable to move, and cold fear ran through him. After nearly an hour, he heard a door open. The brisk fall of footsteps clattered across the tiled floor, and the concerned face of Tristen Hiregaard bent over him to fill his field of vision.

Desmond was furious. He demanded an explanation and, to his surprise, Hiregaard complied. With a look of deep sorrow on his face, he confirmed the lad's worst fear: Hiregaard himself was the brutal killer Desmond had been seeking.

In his defense, Hiregaard explained that he did not commit these dreadful crimes willingly. Indeed, he claimed that his transformation into a horrible beast was the result of a most noble experiment. Hiregaard had long ago decided that human nature was the cause of all the suffering in the world. In order to make any major changes for the better, the basic nature of mankind would have to change. To that end, he began to develop a serum that would destroy the evil in men just as other medicines might destroy disease. Unwilling to risk the life of another to test the potion, he tried it on himself.

At first, it seemed to have worked. He felt like a new man, cleansed even of any evil or impure thoughts. Then, he began to suffer blackouts. For days at a time, he would have no memory of his actions. Eventually, he discovered that his evil nature had been isolated, not destroyed. From time to time, without any predictable pattern, it would surface and take complete control of his body.

Desmond listened in horror to Hiregaard's story. Instead of hatred or revulsion, he felt only pity for the tortured man. Eventually, Hiregaard brought his tale to a close with their encounter in his laboratory. He explained that his evil self, Malken, had lost control of their body as the fire spread. When he came to his senses, Hiregaard saw what had happened and was horrified. He extinguished the blaze and carried the dying Desmond into his operating theater.

The prognosis was not good. The entire left half of his body was being eaten away by the chemicals that had been splashed upon it. Even as he despaired of saving the young man's life, a horrible idea came to him. He had several fresh cadavers in the home for his experimental studies. Might they not be raided to replace the most badly damaged parts of LaRouche's body? Desperate to save his young friend's life at any cost, Hiregaard set to work, little realizing that this ghoulish inspiration had come from the deeply buried Malken.

When his work was done, Hiregaard turned away from Desmond. In a voice heavy with sorrow, he lamented the fact that he had not allowed the young man to die as nature demanded. With that, he released the young man and presented him with a mirror. The agonized scream which escaped Desmond's lips as he looked upon his new body was the most dreadful sound Hiregaard had ever heard.

Desmond left Kantora that night. He said not a word to Hiregaard, but simply walked out of his home and into the darkness. His last memory of the man who had been a second father to him was of a frail-looking old man shaking and sobbing on the floor.

From time to time, Desmond LaRouche has considered returning to Kantora to destroy the man who made him into a monster. Inside, however, he feels that letting him live with his curse is a far crueler fate. LaRouche has no desire to reveal Hiregaard's secret self. He recognizes the good that Hiregaard does to make up for Malken's evil and considers this to be a fair exchange.

Ecology: Desmond LaRouche now wanders the domain of Nova Vaasa. The revulsion that greets him whenever he encounters humanity has embittered him. He has been known to come to the aid of the defenseless, but generally he shuns all contact with mankind.

Desmond's unusual biology frees him from many of the concerns of daily life. He eats but one meal a day, sleeps for only an hour or so each night, and takes no notice of the hottest summer day or the coldest winter night.

Many aspects of LaRouche's life now might appeal to a druid character. He lives in the wild and, because it is his home, protects the land fiercely from those who would encroach upon it and his solitude.

Adventure Ideas: Word of a terrible man-beast stalking the countryside is generally more than enough to draw player characters from miles around. In the case of the half-golem, this sort of lure makes an excellent beginning for an adventure.

Initially the PCs might jump to the conclusion that LaRouche is evil because his form is monstrous. Because of all-too-frequent rejection, LaRouche has come to expect hostility from all he encounters. He will not initiate combat, but he will be wary of strangers. Once they prove their goodwill, his strange mix of abilities can make him a valuable ally.

Perhaps the most interesting use of Desmond LaRouche would be as a supporting character in an adventure involving Sir Tristen Hiregaard. It might be that the tortured doctor has discovered a process by which it might be possible to regenerate LaRouche's damaged half, leading Hiregaard to contact the player characters in hopes that they can track Desmond down and bring him back to Kantora.

This might indeed be the case. More likely, however, Malken has duped Hiregaard into believing that his process will work. In truth, the fiend plans to destroy LaRouche in order to protect the secret of his dual nature. After all, Desmond is the only person in Nova Vaasa who knows the truth about the mysterious killer who stalks the streets of Kantora.

Golem, Mechanical (Ahmi Vanjuko)

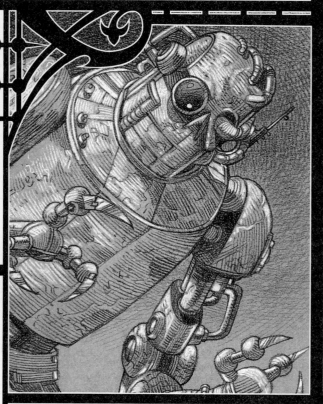

CLIMATE/TERRAIN:	Vechor
FREQUENCY:	Unique
ORGANIZATION:	Solitary
ACTIVITY CYCLE:	Any
DIET:	Nil
INTELLIGENCE:	Average (10)
TREASURE:	Nil
ALIGNMENT:	Chaotic neutral

NO. APPEARING:	1
ARMOR CLASS:	–2
MOVEMENT:	12
HIT DICE:	13 (75 hp)
THAC0:	7
NO. OF ATTACKS:	1
DAMAGE/ATTACK:	4d10
SPECIAL ATTACKS:	Electric shock
SPECIAL DEFENSES:	+2 or better weapons to hit; spell immunities; lightning aura
MAGIC RESISTANCE:	Nil
SIZE:	M (7' tall)
MORALE:	Steady (12)
XP VALUE:	15,000

Of all the tragic and misshapen creatures to survive the nightmare experiments of fiends like the wizard Hazlik or the mad butcher Markov, none is more dreadful than Ahmi Vanjuko. Once a ranger and great explorer, he has been imprisoned in a metal body powered by the sinister magic of Easan, the deranged lord of Vechor.

Prior to his transformation, Vanjuko was a strong and sturdy ranger who stood just over five and a half feet tall. His skin was a rich, earthy brown worn rough by his years of exploring the wilds of countless worlds, while his hair was coffee-colored and his eyes were the cool, crisp green of fresh mint leaves. His smile, it is said, could charm man and beast alike, while his charisma earned him the love of a thousand maidens in a hundred lands.

All that changed when Vanjuko was drawn into Ravenloft. Under the careful attention of the dark wizard Easan, his spirit has been implanted in the metal shell of a mechanical golem. Vanjuko's new body stands just over seven feet tall and looks more or less humanoid. It has long legs that might be likened to those of a bird and gangly arms that look vaguely apelike. The arms end in three-finger gripping devices that incorporate deadly razors into each digit. Atop the cylindrical body of the machine rests a head shaped not unlike a human skull. Despite its slender, framelike build, Vanjuko's mechanical body is far stronger than any known alloy.

Vanjuko is utterly unable to speak, although it may be possible to communicate with him via magical, clerical, or psionic means. If spoken to, he understands the Common Tongue of Oerth, the world of Greyhawk. During his travels in Ravenloft, he also learned the languages spoken in Barovia and Vechor, as well as a sprinkling of the Vistani tongue.

Combat: Vanjuko shuns humanity and has no natural enemies in the wilds of Vechor. As such, he is seldom called upon to defend himself. When he does fight, however, he is a deadly nemesis, for the mad Easan intended that his creation be a killing machine.

Like all of the mechanical golems created in Ravenloft, Vanjuko is immune to attack by weapons with less than a +2 enchantment. Similarly, he is immune to all manner of life-affecting spells (like *hold person*). He does not, however, retain the standard golem immunity to mind-affecting magics and can be *charmed* or the like as a normal man. He is immune to all manner of poisons and diseases. Vanjuko is vulnerable to *dispel magic*, which stuns him for a number of turns equal to the caster's level. During this time, he appears to have been slain. A *detect magic* or similar spell will reveal a magical aura lingering about the golem which grows stronger as he begins to recharge himself.

Vanjuko's primary attack is made with the retractable razorlike blades hidden in his "fingers." Each round he strikes with these weapons, he causes 4d10 points of damage to anyone unlucky enough to be hit by them.

Any natural roll of 20 on an attack made with his razors indicates that a powerful electrical current has been shunted into the victim's body. When this happens, the victim must make a saving throw vs. spell. If the save is failed, the victim takes 6d6 points of additional damage; a successful save results in half damage. In addition, the victim must make a successful saving throw vs. paralysis or be incapacitated for 2d4 rounds due to muscle spasms triggered by the discharge.

Any natural roll of 20 on an attack made against Vanjuko with a metal melee weapon indicates that he has been able to channel an electrical current through the weapon and into the body of the attacker, who then suffers damage just as if he or she had been hit with the electrical attack described above. Again, a saving throw vs. spell reduces damage by half, and a successful saving throw vs. paralysis will allow the attacker to avoid incapacitation. Vanjuko still suffers normal damage from the attack.

On every third round of combat, Vanjuko can trigger a lightning aura that surrounds his mechanical body with a deadly electrical field. Any living creature within 20 feet of Vanjuko that round will be struck with numerous filaments of lightning for a total of 3d6 points of damage. A successful saving throw vs. breath weapons reduces this damage by half; no incapacitation check need be made in any case. Any exposed items carried by a character who fails his or her saving throw must save versus lightning or be destroyed.

As a ranger, Vanjuko had many useful powers and special abilities. In his new mechanical form, however, most of these have been lost. He retains the ability to cast some clerical spells, but only those he had memorized at the time of his transformation. Thus, he can use the following spells once per day: *entangle*, *pass without trace*, and *warp wood*. He casts these spells as if he were a 3rd-level cleric.

For their part, animals will have nothing to do with this unnatural construct. No creature will come within 50 feet of Vanjuko unless trained and held or *calmed*. Any animal, even the most devoted dog or warhorse, will refuse to come within 20 feet of him. If forced to do so, they will become violent and do whatever they must to free themselves and leave the abomination's presence.

Habitat/Society: Ahmi Vanjuko was born in the wondrous City of Greyhawk but quickly learned that urban life was not for him. Before he had reached the age of 10, he vanished into the wilds and started a new life among the animals of the green forest.

In time, he came to know every creature that shared his wilderness home with him. He learned to hunt and stalk like the wolf, to sing and play like the bird, and to lurk and pounce like the cougar. By the time he reached adolescence, the forest was very much a part of him.

One day, a strange figure came to the lands Ahmi called his own and began to build something. Although he resented this intrusion, Vanjuko took no action against this intruder. In time, the construction took the shape of an elegant manor house surrounded by a virtual wall of tangling vines laced with poisonous thorns. To anyone else, these thorns might have been a barrier. To Vanjuko, who knew the ways of the wild, they were nothing more than a challenge.

Determined to see what was going on behind this living fence, Vanjuko made his way through the thorns and into the lands beyond. To his horror, he found that the splendor of the forest had been decimated near the manor. Pools of deadly poisons littered the landscape, the plants were withering away in toxic soil, discarded trash lay everywhere, and the air carried an unnatural stench that made him retch. The animals trapped within the barrier's circuit were sick, dying, or dead.

Vanjuko vowed to see to it that the monster who had done these terrible things left the forest before it could do any more harm. Filled with righteous fury, he moved quickly to the manor's entrance and burst inside. He saw no immediate sign of the place's builder and began to search the house. At every turn, however, he was confronted with mechanical traps designed to kill unwanted intruders. In the end, these proved too deadly for him, and Vanjuko was forced to leave the building.

To his surprise, however, he found that the grounds outside had been engulfed with a rolling, macabre fog. Before he had traveled half the distance to the thorn barrier, Vanjuko was utterly lost and all but blinded by the blanket of mist. He settled down to wait for the passage of this heavy shroud. When it cleared an hour later, he found that he was no longer in his forest. Instead, he was in the domain of Kartakass.

Vanjuko began to explore the strange new land in which he found himself, hoping to uncover a way back to his native land and the forest he loved. From the domain of Harkon Lukas, he traveled north into Gundarak and then east into Strahd's own Barovia. For a time, he lived among the rustic folk of that mountainous domain, enjoying their simple way of life and learning their language.

While in Barovia, he met a young woman named Tanya, and the two fell deeply in love. She and her family were traveling performers who moved from city to city, entertaining the townsfolk before moving on. One night, Tanya came to him and told him that her people were leaving just before dawn. She kissed the ranger gently and bid him farewell, weeping at the thought that they might never meet again. Vanjuko pleaded with her to remain with him in Barovia and become his wife. She smiled, clearly tempted by the idea, but refused. Hers was the wanderer's life, she explained, and her people were the Vistani.

Despite the warnings of his newfound friends, Vanjuko decided that he would not lose the woman he loved. Shortly before sunrise, he went to the clearing where Tanya's family had camped, only to find that they had already left. He dashed off in pursuit, following their trail to the east. He caught sight of their wagons as they rolled into a bank of fog. Without pause, he spurred his horse to greater speed and dashed into the mists after them.

Emerging from the rippling vapors, Vanjuko found no trace of Tanya or her clan. Instead, he discovered that he had again been transported by the whims of Ravenloft's mists. This time, he was in the domain of Vechor. Attempting to get his bearings and learn what was going on, Vanjuko made his way to Abdok on the shores of the Nostru River. In the distance, high atop the Cliffs of Vesanis, he saw the elegant manor house where, he was told, the madman Easan lived. To his horror, Vanjuko realized that this was the same house he had seen in the wilderness of his native Oerth.

Blaming Easan for his original abduction by the mists of Ravenloft, the ranger began to plot revenge against the mad wizard. When he learned that he could not rally the people of Vechor to overthrow their foul lord, he left them and returned to his life among the plants and animals of the forest.

Golem, Mechanical (Ahmi Vanjuko)

In Vechor's wilds, he found all manner of pathetic creatures that were unknown to him. The majority of these things, he learned, were the result of Easan's horrible experiments. He also learned that the mad wizard's machinations did not end with animals. He found countless species of plants, many evil and deadly, which were the result of no natural evolutionary process.

By far the most dreadful of the creatures that he encountered, however, were the twisted men and women who had survived Easan's experiments. Most were contorted and broken, tragic things known as broken ones. A few, however, emerged from the caverns at the base of the Cliffs of Vesanis with mechanical parts grafted onto their bodies. Most of these, thankfully, didn't live long. Those that did, Vanjuko mercifully destroyed to end their pain and suffering.

Vowing to end this madman's butchery once and for all, Vanjuko entered the labyrinth of caves and began to make his way upward to the manor house. The trek took him nearly two days, during which he fought countless creatures more terrible than any he had seen in the forests. By the time he neared the underground entrance to Easan's laboratories, he was sick with revulsion.

Steeling himself to face whatever foul things might lurk beyond, Vanjuko entered. As before, he found the place to be a maze of traps designed to keep intruders out—or perhaps to keep prisoners in. Try as he might, the ranger was no match for the terrible mechanisms and deadly spells that Easan had set up. Shortly after he began to explore the house, Vanjuko accidentally triggered the release of a cloud of toxic gas. Expecting nothing but death, he closed his eyes and collapsed.

Much to his surprise, Vanjuko awoke. He found himself strapped to a metal table in the center of a room that looked like a cross between a wizard's laboratory and a torture chamber. For a long time, he lay still and feigned unconsciousness as he looked about the place. He had hoped to spot some escape from the dreadful place, but instead he found himself speculating as to what many of the terrible devices around him might be used for. It wasn't long before he had his answer.

High overhead, two great metal spheres hung on slender poles. Without warning, a great surge of eerie blue-white light flooded the room as a steady stream of lightning began to flow between the mysterious globes. As Vanjuko watched in horror, the globes descended until they were suspended only a few feet above him. The electrical flow passing above his body crawled across his skin like stinging ants.

Then, as if from nowhere, Easan appeared. He was a short man, almost gnomish in his compact little features. His beady eyes reminded Vanjuko of the predatory gaze of a ferret. With a cruel smile, the wizard began to examine his prisoner's restraints. After a few minutes of this, Easan bent low over the ranger's face. His breath smelled like rotting fish, but Vanjuko's bonds were far too tight for him to turn away.

"Hello, my young friend," he hissed. His voice was slippery and hushed, barely audible above the cacophony of the lightning machine. "I'm so glad that you came to visit me."

Vanjuko tried to spit in the madman's face, but found that his mouth had gone dry. Easan found the gesture amusing and chuckled softly to himself. Turning away from his captive, he continued to talk while working with several arcane devices.

"For a long while, I have been planning to complete a great experiment. Time after time, I have attempted to conclude this great exploration of the soul and its ultimate origins, only to have the patient die before my work was completed. Indeed, I began to despair of ever finding someone who might have the stamina to help me draw this grand investigation to a close. Imagine my delight when I found an intruder in my own home who could survive exposure to one of my most deadly toxins. If you don't survive this experiment, I dare say that no one will."

With that, the shriveled man waddled over to a large winch and began to turn it. Slowly, a panel in the floor beside Vanjuko slid open and a second table rose. Whatever was on the table was covered with a white sheet.

With something of a flourish, Easan swept aside the cloth and revealed a metal body that, although roughly humanoid, was a mechanical nightmare. The wizard laughed when he saw the fear fall across Vanjuko's face.

"I shouldn't worry yourself," he chuckled. "When we are finished here today, I shall have transported your soul into this metal body. You will be the father of a new race! I trust that you appreciate the honor that I'm granting you. Ah well, let's begin, shall we?"

As Easan chuckled his weasel's laugh, the metal balls began to descend again. The lightning engulfed Vanjuko and the mechanical corpse beside him. The ranger cried out in agony as he felt the arcane energies ripping his body apart. The pain was more incredible than anything that he could have imagined. He tried to succumb to it, hoping to lose consciousness or even die rather than endure the seemingly endless torment. As blackness rose up around him, the echoing laughter of Easan rang above the roar of the lightning.

And then it was over. Vanjuko was exhausted. The pain was gone, but so was his strength. Unconsciousness claimed him.

Vanjuko had no idea how long he swam in the blissful darkness of catatonia. Finally, he came to himself and the blackness fell away. The ranger was momentarily confused to discover that he was on a metal table. He attempted to sit up, and found that he was strapped down. Then, slowly, the memory of what had happened returned to him.

Praying that this might be some dreadful nightmare, he turned his head and looked along the length of his arm. When he saw the mechanical limb that lay there, he tried to scream. No sound issued forth from the mute metal giant that was now Ahmi Vanjuko.

Enraged, he fought to free himself from the shackles, only to find them too strong. As he thrashed about, Easan returned. He was smiling, if the twisted grimace on his face could be called a smile, and paid little attention to Vanjuko's struggles.

"Ahhhhh," he hissed, sounding almost cheerful, "is it not as I told you?" Vanjuko tried to lunge at the wizard, but was held in check by the chains on his limbs. Easan seemed genuinely surprised by his behavior. "Don't you understand?" he asked. "I have made you immortal. More than that, I have freed you of the burdens of life. You'll never grow sick or old. You should thank me for the great gift that I have given you!"

That was more than Vanjuko could bear. He tried again to break free, and this time the chains could not restrain him. Metal fragments shattered around the chamber, and Easan sprang back in surprise. Vanjuko sprang forward, his metal body moving smoothly and flawlessly in response to his thoughts. With a great lunge and a whirring of gears, he threw himself at Easan, determined to destroy the madman. When he reached the spot where the wizard stood, however, there was nothing there but smoke. Through some magic, Easan had fled.

Vanjuko tore the laboratory apart, vowing that he would destroy the beast's lair if he could not have the beast himself. Leaving the building a burning ruin, he fled into the tunnels and made his way back down to the forest.

Ecology: Easan has since rebuilt his home. Vanjuko has returned to living in the forest, but he no longer draws the happiness from it that he once did. All around him are vibrant living things, animals that now flee from him in terror and flowers that he can no longer smell.

As a mechanical creature, Vanjuko has no hunger or thirst and never sleeps. He lives in a cave hidden away beneath the cascade where the river Nostru tumbles off of the Cliffs of Vesanis.

Each day, he moves about the forests in a search for more products of Easan's twisted work with the black arts. He destroys them when he finds them, ending their suffering as quickly and mercifully as he can.

As mentioned in the Combat section of this entry, animals cannot bear the presence of Vanjuko. They recognize that he is not a natural thing and abhor him. This is perhaps the most tragic aspect of Vanjuko's life, for the love of animals meant as much to him as the embrace of his beloved Tanya.

Adventure Ideas: Vanjuko is a tragic figure. While he retains a good heart, he is bitter and angry about what has happened to him. He loathes his existence, feeling alone and alien in the world. If it were not for the fact that he feels compelled to destroy Easan and all his works, Vanjuko would certainly have taken measures to end his life long ago.

It is this very deep commitment to his task that can lead to excellent adventures. The people of Vechor have seen the mechanical golem moving through the woods from time to time. Not knowing its history or origins, they assume it to be evil.

Any group of heroes who come into the domain is likely to hear of the creature as well. With the villagers speaking of it as a deadly enemy, the player characters are likely to attempt to hunt down and destroy Vanjuko. If they discover the true nature of their supposed enemy, they might proceed along one of two lines.

First, they might choose to join Vanjuko and attempt to destroy Easan. Although a powerful ally in combat, Vanjuko's hulking form will make it difficult for the PCs to approach the dark lord's manor house without being seen. Vanjuko's knowledge of Easan's methods might be helpful as well. Further, he can act as a guide in the exploration of the tunnels that run from the forest to the plateau on which Easan's manor stands.

Alternately, they might begin a search for some technique which might return Vanjuko to a living body. One obvious solution might be the use of the Apparatus, a terrible artifact originally described in module I10, *Ravenloft II: The House on Gryphon Hill* and most recently seen in the adventure RQ2, *Thoughts of Darkness*, and the *Book of Artifacts*. With the help of this bizarre device, the player characters might be able to arrange for Vanjuko's personality to be implanted in another body. Of course, locating and recovering the artifact (which is the size of a house) will not be easy tasks. Finding a suitable body and deciding what to do with the life force that currently inhabits it might be problems in themselves.

Human, Cursed (Jacqueline Montarri)

CLIMATE/TERRAIN:	Barovia
FREQUENCY:	Unique
ORGANIZATION:	Solitary
ACTIVITY CYCLE:	Day
DIET:	Omnivore
INTELLIGENCE:	Varies
TREASURE:	(F)
ALIGNMENT:	Neutral evil

NO. APPEARING:	1
ARMOR CLASS:	10
MOVEMENT:	12
HIT DICE:	5 (20 hp)
THAC0:	15 (12) or better
NO. OF ATTACKS:	1
DAMAGE/ATTACK:	1d8+3
SPECIAL ATTACKS:	Decapitation
SPECIAL DEFENSES:	Regeneration
MAGIC RESISTANCE:	50%
SIZE:	M (5'10" tall)
MORALE:	Fanatic (19)
XP VALUE:	Varies (2,000+)

The quest for eternal youth has driven many to deeds of great heroism and terrible despair. For some, it is a noble calling that leads to the discovery of great medical advances. For others, it is an obsession that leads to the most heinous of crimes. In the case of Jacqueline Montarri, it has become the basis for a series of crimes as horrible and bizarre as any in Ravenloft's whole sordid history.

Jacqueline maintains a collection of some three dozen severed heads. She is able to remove the head she is currently wearing and replace it with one from her collection at will. Because she changes heads with every shift in her moods, her facial features are constantly changing. She no longer has her own original head, so her true appearance is long forgotten.

Jacqueline changes her clothes as frequently as she changes heads. Her vanity dictates that she wear only the finest garments, always chosen to complement the head she is currently wearing. The only consistent feature in her attire is a ribbon of crimson velvet worn around her neck. Because this magical item secures her various heads to her body, she is never without it. In cases where it clashes with her clothing or chosen head, she covers it with a scarf or jewelry.

Jacqueline's native language is Balok, the common tongue of Barovia. Each of her heads knows one or more other languages, making it easy for her to communicate with almost any visitor.

Combat: Jacqueline's favored weapon is *Ironfang*, her *vorpal sword*. *Ironfang* was fashioned ages past from meteoric iron by the drow of Arak, from whom she stole it long ago. She is able to use this weapon even when wearing the head of a wizard or other character class which might normally be unable to employ such a

sword. This weapon functions in all ways as described in the DUNGEON MASTER *Guide*. Jacqueline has made it a practice to "harvest" new heads only with this blade.

This is not to say that she has no other weapons at her disposal. Indeed, whenever she dons a new head, she gains the class and level abilities formerly associated with it. Thus, if she opts to wear the head of a psionicist, she gains its mental powers. In the case of spellcasters, she cannot master new spells but can cast any known to the wizard or priest from whom she took the head. In each case, the spells are assumed to be freshly memorized each time she puts on the head.

The curse of eternal life under which Jacqueline lives has given her many special abilities. For instance, she regenerates lost hit points at a rate of 1 per turn, even after death. The only way in which she can be wholly destroyed is by the incineration of her original head. Because no one, not even Jacqueline herself, knows where it is hidden, she seems in little danger at present.

In addition to her regenerative powers, she is immune to any manner of poison, disease, or magically induced paralysis. Thus, spells such as *cause disease, hold,* or *sleep* have no effect upon her. Spells and items that affect the mind, like a *charm* spell, affect her normally. Jacqueline is not undead, so attempts to turn her or the use of spells designed to combat such horrors have no effect upon her. These immunities are in addition to the 50% magic resistance that the magical energies with which she has been infused give her.

Whenever Jacqueline is called upon to make a saving throw, she does so as the class and level of the head she is currently wearing. Thus, when wearing the head of a 10th-level fighter she saves as a 10th-level fighter.

It takes Jacqueline a full round to change heads. So long as she wears her crimson ribbon, the head remains fully attached to her body—that is, it cannot be pulled or knocked off. If the ribbon is removed (it is impervious to all damage and cannot be destroyed), the head instantly rolls off and Jacqueline loses access to its powers.

Even without a head in place, Jacqueline's body is able to move and act normally; the curse she suffers enables her to see and hear (but not speak) when headless.

Habitat/Society: Jacqueline was born in the domain of Barovia some 200 years ago. She grew up in the village of Krezk, learning the craft of thieving from her parents, both of whom were master thieves, but she soon surpassed her teachers. By the time she was 16 years old, she had become one of the most skilled rogues in the domain—and one of its most beautiful women.

Like so many others of Barovian blood, Jacqueline found her beauty began to fade slightly as she entered her late twenties. Tiny lines began to appear around her eyes, and the first few white hairs showed in her raven tresses. To Jacqueline, who had been so proud of her beauty and the power it gave her over men, this change was unbearable.

In an effort to find some means of preserving her beauty, Jacqueline traveled to the Vistani compound on the banks of the River Ivlis. She sought out Madame Eva, the matriarch of Barovia's Vistani population, and begged for some means to remain eternally young and beautiful. When the old Vistani refused, Jacqueline offered to buy the secret from her, promising to steal anything that the other might need. Again, Madame Eva refused, telling Jacqueline that the secrets of the Vistani were not for sale.

This enraged the desperate thief. In a flash, she grabbed the elderly Vistani and held a knife to her throat. As a thin trickle of blood ran from Madame Eva's neck, Jacqueline demanded her help. Calmly, Madame Eva told her there was a way to ensure her beauty would never fade, but she would be wiser not to seek it. When Jacqueline insisted, the old woman said that she would find what she wanted waiting for her in the library of Castle Ravenloft.

Relief flooded through the thief from Krezk at the thought that the object of her desire was within reach. The fact that she would have to sneak into the castle of Barovia's sinister lord to gain it meant nothing to her. In order to ensure that the old woman would do nothing to betray her, Jacqueline drew the blade across Madame Eva's throat. Leaving the body on the ground, she slipped her knife back into its sheath and vanished into the deep Barovian night. Had she bothered to look behind her, she might have noticed an evil grin on the dying woman's face.

Jacqueline wasted no time in making her way to the ominous Castle Ravenloft. Not fully comprehending the terrors that dwelt within the great stone structure, she scaled the outer walls and crossed the parapets, entering the keep itself through the belfry. As she explored the darkened halls of the great castle and searched for the library, she failed to notice the silent shadow that haunted her steps.

At last, the thief found what she was looking for. Cautiously, she slipped into the library and began to examine the tomes and manuals that lined the walls of the great room. But as she reached out her hand to take a book from the shelves, she froze at the sound of evil laughter behind her.

Whirling, she found herself face to face with Strahd Von Zarovich. Panic-stricken, she turned and dashed for an exit, but the vampire was upon her before she had gone more than a few feet. Screaming in horror, she felt her life being drained away to satisfy the hunger of the foul master of Ravenloft. As the numbing cold of his touch spread throughout her body, blackness folded itself around her and Jacqueline lost consciousness.

When her eyes opened, she found herself in a great cage that was rocking back and forth. As her senses gradually returned, she realized that she was weak and fatigued, but that the vampire had left her alive. The cage around her proved to be mounted on a wagon which was heading down the narrow road from Castle Ravenloft to the village of Barovia.

The wagon came to a halt in the center of the town. A tall, dark man dropped down from the driver's seat and sounded a loud, mournful call on an iron horn. As the people of the village gathered around, the driver brandished a scroll. "Let it be known," he read, "that this woman was found trespassing in the halls of Castle Ravenloft. By the order of Strahd Von Zarovich, master of Barovia, she is to be put to death. Let others who might be foolish enough to consider such a course of action take heed of her fate."

With that, the man opened the cage and dragged Jacqueline out. She struggled to break free but was far too weak from the vampire's life-draining attack to offer any effective resistance. Sobbing and begging for mercy, she was forced to her knees and her head forced down onto a wooden block. As the people of Barovia watched, a great axe was brought forward and Jacqueline Montarri was beheaded.

As the silent crowds began to disperse, a representative of the Vistani stepped forward. She told the tale of Madame Eva's death and asked that the body of the thief be turned over to the murdered woman's kin. On behalf of Strahd, the driver agreed, and the Vistani carried away the mutilated corpse.

For several days, the Vistani wove intricate magics over the corpse. Then, one week after she died, Jacqueline was restored to life.

When awareness returned to her, Jacqueline found that she was locked in the back of a great Vistani wagon. The clothes she had died in, the leather tunic and dark cotton pants that she favored when on a thieving expedition, were gone. Now, she was dressed in the wild colors and ruffles of a Vistani woman. Her hair had been drawn back and tied with a red cord, a wide band of crimson velvet encircled her neck, and the heavy odor of exotic perfumes hung thickly about her.

To her horror, Jacqueline realized that these were the same clothes Madame Eva had worn when Jacqueline killed her. There was no sign of blood upon them, but the patterns and decorations sewn on them were unmistakable.

Her mind hazy, Jacqueline tried to recall the events that had brought her to this place. She remembered her

Human, Cursed (Jacqueline Montarri)

meeting with Madame Eva and her attempt to burgle Castle Ravenloft. With a shudder, she recalled her capture by Strahd Von Zarovich and the chilling touch of the vampire. Then, as a wave of cold fear swept through her, she remembered the events that followed. She saw the carriage, the executioner, and the townsfolk of Barovia. She even remembered the falling axe and the burning darkness that followed it.

Jacqueline knew that she must be dead. There was no way for her to have survived the beheading. Somehow, the Vistani must have restored her to life—but was it life? Terrified, she considered the possibility that she might now be among the ranks of the foul undead. A quick check revealed both pulse and respiration to be normal, so she set aside fears that she might no longer be truly alive.

Certain that whatever fate the Vistani had in mind for her would be terrible, she decided to escape, drawing on her experience as a thief to ease open the wagon's door and slip quietly out into the night.

To her surprise, she was quite alone. There was no sign of the reception committee that she had expected to find outside the carriage. Instead, a broad clearing spread out around her. The Vistani had been here—that much was obvious from the burned-out campfires and such—but they were long gone.

Relieved, and more than a little confused, Jacqueline left the clearing behind in the event that the Vistani might return. She quickly came across the Old Svalich Road and discovered that she was not far from her home. With a lighter heart, she quickened her pace and made for Krezk.

The streets of Krezk were all but empty, and Jacqueline made her way to the front door of her home without difficulty. She slipped inside and bolted the door behind her.

Trying to forget the nightmares of the past several days, she stoked a fire and set about heating some washing water. She decided to take one last look at the outlandish Vistani dress she wore before removing the thing and burning it in the fire. She stepped in front of a silvered glass and let out a scream of terror that some say can still be heard in the back alleys of Krezk.

In the mirror, she saw the lithe figure that she was accustomed to. Her long, slender arms and legs, as fit and smoothly muscled as those of any athlete, were flatteringly accented by the gypsy costume she wore. Her face, however, was shriveled and old. Indeed, the head upon her body was none other than that of Madame Eva.

Disgusted, Jacqueline tore off the bright clothes, ripping buttons and hooks in her haste. She pulled the cord from her hair, and found that the dark rolling tresses she was used to had been replaced with the wiry gray of old age.

It was only when she pulled the ribbon from her neck that the true enormity of the Vistani punishment was revealed. As soon as the crimson band fell away from her neck, the room seemed to tilt wildly around her. She had the sensation of falling and tried in vain to catch herself. When she could focus again, she saw her new head seeming to grin up at her from the floor, while above her neck she could feel nothing at all.

It is a tribute to the iron will of Jacqueline Montarri that she did not lose her sanity then and there. Instead, she tried to calm herself and learn to understand the curse that was upon her. For instance, she found that she could control her body normally even without a head. When she lifted the shriveled head of the old Vistani and placed it upon her neck, it fell to the floor again. Only when she placed the head on her neck and bound it with the velvet ribbon did it remain secure.

When Jacqueline had at least come to accept what had happened to her, she vowed to undo the curse. She sought out the Vistani camp again and demanded to know what they had done to her. From most, her only answer was laughter and mocking.

One old woman, who claimed to be Madame Eva's daughter, deigned to speak with her. She was bitter, as one might well expect, and seemed delighted with the agony burning in Jacqueline's soul. She told the thief that her only chance to be free of the curse was to find her own head and restore it to its place. If this was done, she explained, the girl's desire for eternal youth and beauty would be granted. When Jacqueline demanded to know where her head was, the old woman only laughed and walked away. Despite the centuries that have passed since that encounter, Jacqueline has never been able to locate her original head.

In the long years that have passed since that day, Jacqueline has learned a great many things about her curse and its subtle ramifications.

The most important of these, perhaps, is that she can wear the severed heads of others as well as that of Madame Eva. Indeed, she has found that she begins to develop terrible headaches if she wears any single head for more than three days in a row. Because of this, she has accumulated a great library of heads collected in a series of brutal murders over a period of many decades.

Whenever she wears a head, she gains the class and abilities associated with it prior to beheading. Thus, if she were to don the head of a 10th-level wizard, she would gain the spellcasting ability of such a character. The variety of heads she owns gives her a great assortment of skills and abilities.

Most of Jacqueline's heads are chosen not for their special abilities, but for their physical attractiveness. The same vanity that lead her to challenge Castle Ravenloft has caused her to assemble a collection of the most beautiful heads one could imagine. She spends countless hours making them up, changing their hair styles, and primping them.

Jacqueline has experimented with her special ability over the centuries. She has discovered that she cannot wear the heads of anything but human females. Males, and females of other races (like elves and even half-elves), are of no use to her. She prefers to claim new heads with her *vorpal sword* (due to the neatness of its cut), but this is by no means a requirement of her curse.

Ecology: Every day that Jacqueline spends wearing a given head ages it one year. When the head is not on her neck, it does not age. This rapid aging causes even the most beautiful head to quickly waste away. Because Jacqueline's vanity demands that she wear only the most beautiful heads, she is constantly seeking to replace her old heads with new ones.

Rather than destroying the heads that she no longer uses, Jacqueline simply tosses them into a great basement beneath her lavish home in Krezk. Because these heads do not die and remain fully aware, this chamber has become a pit of suffering as black as any found in the Abyss. Heads discarded here are kept in glass cases and stacked in row upon row as if they were crates in a great warehouse. The room is filled with an endless cacophony of screams, moans, and sobs as madness gradually claims the minds of those trapped here. Persons entering this foul area and gazing on the hundreds of eternally living and tormented heads must make a fear check at the very least. Spotting a friend's head among the heads is call for a horror check.

Neither Jacqueline nor her many heads has any need to eat or drink. Jacqueline herself still does so in the company of others, however, as this helps to maintain the illusion that she is a normal woman.

Adventure Ideas: Jacqueline's quest to recover her original head makes a fine focus for an adventure. She will welcome any information which might lead to its discovery and might well commission a company of adventurers to locate it for her.

Of course, her unending quest for new and beautiful heads might well bring her into conflict with a group of player characters. She could set her mind to claiming the head of a comely PC for herself. If this is not the case, she might also prove to be a threat to a PC's romantic interest or henchman.

Characters called upon to investigate her home will find it to be a macabre and gruesome place. While the vast majority of the mansion might seem normal enough, the "library" where she keeps her selection of heads will be more than enough evidence that they have stumbled upon something truly terrible.

The PCs might also discover Jacqueline's original head quite by accident while on some other adventure. Its location has deliberately not been specified here in order to enable the DM to place it anywhere in Ravenloft—that is, wherever it would best fit into his or her campaign. It could even be inserted into an existing module. For instance, the adventure RQ3, *From the Shadows* makes mention of several disembodied heads kept by Azalin of Darkon; Jacqueline's could easily be among them.

Of course, once the PCs have Jacqueline's head, she will stop at nothing to get it back. Because it can be used to destroy her, she will consider anyone who holds her head to be a deadly enemy.

Human, Madman (The Midnight Slasher)

CLIMATE/TERRAIN:	Invidia (Karina)
FREQUENCY:	Unique
ORGANIZATION:	Solitary
ACTIVITY CYCLE:	Night
DIET:	Omnivore
INTELLIGENCE:	Average (10)
TREASURE:	Nil
ALIGNMENT:	Chaotic evil

NO. APPEARING:	1
ARMOR CLASS:	8
MOVEMENT:	12
HIT DICE:	5 (17 hit points)
THAC0:	18
NO. OF ATTACKS:	1
DAMAGE/ATTACK:	1d4+1
SPECIAL ATTACKS:	Triple damage on backstabs
SPECIAL DEFENSES:	Hide in shadows 90%
MAGIC RESISTANCE:	Nil
SIZE:	M (6'2" or 5'8"; see below)
MORALE:	Unsteady (7)
XP VALUE:	650

The city of Karina lies nestled in a wooded valley carved by the sparkling waters of the Musarde River. Its cobblestone streets are kept clean and in good repair, flowers decorate window boxes throughout the town, and the weather is generally mild and pleasant.

One night each month, however, a thick fog boils from the river and flows through the streets. When this happens, people fear to leave their homes. They hide behind locked doors until the sun rises and burns off the hated mists. From behind barred windows, they peer nervously into the night and listen for the chiming of the great clock in the center of town. Almost without exception, the last bell of midnight is followed by a scream of terror somewhere in the city. As the echoes of this cry fade into the fog, people make holy signs and offer thanks that the Midnight Slasher has chosen someone else as his victim that night.

Though few have caught more than a fleeting glimpse of the Slasher, there are enough scattered reports of sightings to piece together a fair description of the fiend. The Slasher is tall, rather over six feet in height, and slender. He wears a wide-brimmed hat and a billowing cloak of some black fabric that seems to drink up the light, making him hard to see. The lower half of his face is obscured by a black cloth, above which maddened eyes stare out from a narrow band of pale skin. When he strikes, he uses a long, razor-sharp blade.

None have ever spoken with the Slasher, so it is not known what languages he might speak. The folk of Karina assume he is a native of Invidia, and thus understands the local language, although a few insist this fiend is a foreigner, probably one of those sinister Vistani outcasts known as darklings.

Combat: The Midnight Slasher is not a man who likes to stand for a fair fight. However, when he is able to strike with surprise, he is a deadly assassin. The black cloak that he wears was crafted by the drow of Arak and is said to have been fashioned from darkness itself. When the Slasher wears this cloak, he is able to hide in shadows with 90% effectiveness. In addition, he wears drow *boots of elvenkind* which enable him to move silently with a 95% chance of success. Both of these items work only in darkness; together, they give the Slasher triple the normal chance for surprise. If he attains surprise, the Slasher's attack roll is made with a +4 bonus and inflicts triple damage. In addition, the Slasher has the following thiefly skills: Pick Pockets 50%; Open Locks 42%; Find & Remove Traps 42%; Move Silently 40% (95% with boots); Hide in Shadows 31% (90% with cloak); Hear Noise 20%; Climb Walls 90%.

The Slasher limits his attacks to individuals foolish or unlucky enough to be caught outside when the hour of midnight arrives. He never attacks groups of people nor anyone who looks as if he or she may pose a serious threat. If he fails to attain surprise, the Slasher will usually flee, using his drow cloak to vanish into the night.

Habitat/Society: The Midnight Slasher's greatest secret is that "he" is in fact a woman—a fact which the good folk of Karina do not even begin to suspect. Part of the reason for this is that the cloak, hat, and boots not only hide her features but also make her appear taller than she really is. Another is that they cannot conceive that the shy and silent sneak thief they scoff at and curse by day and the brutal murderer they so fear by night could be one and the same.

The story of the Midnight Slasher begins not with the young woman herself, but with her parents. She was barely five years old when her father, a strong and handsome woodsman, drew the attention of the lord of Invidia, Gabrielle Aderre. After her first chance encounter with him, she learned that he was married with a wife and daughter to whom he was utterly devoted. Aderre vowed that his happiness would be destroyed and began to visit the woodsman regularly. Eventually, the temptress lured him into her arms with her unnatural charms.

As she toyed with the entranced woodsman over the next several weeks, she saw to it that his wife learned of her husband's infidelity. The tension that was growing between the young couple culminated when the wife and daughter returned home early from errands about town and discovered the lovers together. As Aderre stood by and watched with mocking laughter, the young couple plunged into a violent fight. With the prompting of the beautiful but evil witch, the argument grew into something that neither could control. In the end, husband and wife killed each other, utterly consumed by their overwhelming rage.

Aderre left the bloody scene well satisfied with the tragedy she had wrought. She paused in her departure only long enough to kneel beside the almost catatonic child and kiss her gently on the forehead. From that moment on, the young girl's sanity was destroyed.

For the next several years, the young orphan lived as a beggar on the streets of Karina. She stole food and clothing when she could, starved and shivered when she could not. She found shelter in the darkest sections of the city, a neighborhood inhabited by criminals, beggars, and harlots. She saw the latter as kin to the vile woman who destroyed her parents and began to develop a burning hatred for them. Gradually, she became more and more detached from the human race.

Years passed and the girl grew to adulthood on the streets. She spoke to no one, hid from others, and was all but invisible in the heart of Karina. One night, when a thick fog had rolled in from the river to fill the night with misty shapes, she happened across a traveling adventurer in the arms of a trollop. The scene reminded her so much of the one that she and her mother had walked in on that she flew into a wild rage. Over and over she tore at the woman with her dagger as the adventurer fled into the night. When she finished her butchery, the young thief stood over her kill and listened to the distant chiming of the city's great clock tower. As the last echoes faded, the Midnight Slasher was born.

Ecology: The Midnight Slasher lives in the darkness, just as she always has. She moves about the city; hiding, watching, and stalking her next victim. She survives by stealing food and drink. Her knowledge of the city's darkest corners—its dank alleys, abandoned buildings, and forgotten culverts—is unmatched, making her as deadly as any spider in its web.

Adventure Ideas: A Dungeon Master who plans to present the Midnight Slasher in his or her RAVENLOFT game must be very careful. With a foe of this type, the line between horror and gore can be difficult to judge. If the Slasher is presented simply as an insane killing machine who leaves a trail of bodies behind her, then the atmosphere of gothic horror which distinguishes the Ravenloft game has been lost. Instead, the DM should take care to play up the Midnight Slasher as a stalking, macabre character. By using her knowledge of the city and her magical cloak, she can strike and then seem to vanish into thin air.

The most logical adventure to center around the Slasher would be one of detective work. The PCs are called upon to investigate the mysterious killings which have haunted the people of Karina for many years. The best hook to begin this adventure with would be a killing of someone important to the PCs.

I am the night.
I am the fog.
I am the knife.

You cannot hide from me.
You cannot run from me.
You cannot escape me.

The darkness is mine.
The anger is mine.
The vengeance is mine.

I live in your city.
I lurk in your nightmares.
I strike in your sleep.

Let those who live in filth tremble.
Let those who walk the streets weep.
Let those who hurt the children die.

—An assortment of verses found written in blood near the bodies of the Midnight Slasher's victims

Human, Voodan (Chicken Bone)

CLIMATE/TERRAIN:	Souragne
FREQUENCY:	Unique
ORGANIZATION:	Solitary
ACTIVITY CYCLE:	Night
DIET:	Carnivore
INTELLIGENCE:	Exceptional (16)
TREASURE:	S, V
ALIGNMENT:	Lawful neutral

NO. APPEARING:	1
ARMOR CLASS:	10
MOVEMENT:	6
HIT DICE:	1 (3 hit points)
THAC0:	See below
NO. OF ATTACKS:	1
DAMAGE/ATTACK:	1d2
SPECIAL ATTACKS:	Voodan rituals
SPECIAL DEFENSES:	Voodan rituals
MAGIC RESISTANCE:	Nil
SIZE:	M (5' tall)
MORALE:	Average (8)
XP VALUE:	120

The Voodan are a race of humans who are found only in the misty domains of Ravenloft. Some say they are an offshoot of the Vistani, but there is no real evidence to support this claim. Little is known about them, because they keep to themselves and never reveal anything of their pasts.

Chicken Bone is an old man who lives in the domain of Souragne. His real name is lost to the mists of history and none now speak it. When the people of Souragne speak of him now, they do so in hushed tones, for Chicken Bone is a Voodan—a master of dark and mysterious forces that most would not dare to contemplate, let alone attempt to control.

Chicken Bone looks for all the world like any other shriveled old man. His hair is cut short and frazzled, looking as if it has never seen a comb. His gray eyes are set back beneath protruding brows and divided by a long, straight nose. He has no beard or moustache, save that his wrinkled chin is covered with a scattering of wiry whiskers. He wears bright, colorful (some would say gaudy) clothing. He may or may not be typical of the Voodan; so few of them have been encountered that it is impossible to say.

Chicken Bone walks with the aid of a long staff which he leans on heavily. Countless bones dangle from this staff. Despite his name, these bones come from many types of small animals, including lizards, chickens, squirrels, chipmunks, fish, and snakes.

Chicken Bone speaks in the language of the common folk of Souragne. Further, he claims to know the language of the dead and can *speak with dead* (or undead) at will. If there is a language native to the Voodan, Chicken Bone probably speaks it, but this is impossible for outsiders to judge.

Combat: Chicken Bone is exactly what he appears to be, a half-crippled old man. As such, he is hardly suited to melee combat. If forced to defend himself, he strikes with his staff, hitting only on a natural roll of 20 and inflicting merely 1 to 2 (1d2) points of damage with each blow.

However, this old man is able to call upon the forces of the undead to defend him. At any time, he can call 2 to 12 (2d6) zombies to come to his aid. These creatures will be normal zombies (85%), monster zombies (10%), or ju-ju zombies (5%). The ritual to summon these defenders requires 1 hour to perform, so it is of little use if he is caught unawares by danger. However, if he is attacked in sight of any undead creature with no higher than Low intelligence, that monster will come immediately to Chicken Bone's aid.

Chicken Bone is able to employ a number of magical spells. In order to invoke any given power, however, he must complete a complex ritual. Given enough time, the old man can cast any spell from the schools of Necromancy, Enchantment/Charm, or Greater Divination. The ritual required to invoke these spells is quite involved and requires no less than 1 hour per level of the spell. During this time, the Voodan must be left undisturbed. The rituals by which Chicken Bone invokes his spells require him to set alight numerous candles, burn certain incenses, and offer up the lives of one or more small animals as sacrifices—to what, he will not say. In addition to whatever material components the actual spell might require, Chicken Bone must have a sympathetic token from both the person hiring him to cast the spell and the person to be hindered or harmed by it. These tokens can range from things like a lock of hair, some nail clippings, or a drop of blood to personal possessions like a favorite weapon, a wedding ring, or an important lucky charm. Range is not a consideration, for the use of the sympathetic token negates all such concerns.

Neither of the sympathetic items are destroyed in the casting of the spell and Chicken Bone retains them afterwards as part of the contract for his services. In this way, he is able to cast spells on his patrons if they later threaten or refuse to pay him.

Habitat/Society: As has been said, Chicken Bone's origins are utterly unknown. Indeed, it is said that he himself no longer remembers them. So far as Souragne is concerned, the story of this gnarled old man begins some 20 years ago.

It was a cold night and the last full moon of the year hung in the sky like a great jaundiced eye when word spread through Souragne that a strange man had appeared in the swamps west of Port d'Elhour. He had assembled a shack of sugar cane, bamboo, and reeds on an island in the center of Lake Noir. At the same time, a rickety raft appeared near the shores with a long pole that could be used to navigate the open water and reach the island.

Word quickly spread that this old man was a master of strange spells. For a price, it was said, he would use these powers to strike down enemies. As payment for his services, he required only that supplicants perform some service for him. As a rule, these services were minor. On rare occasions, however, the task required might be quite extreme. The severity of the required payment seemed to have no relationship to the action that Chicken Bone performed.

Those who failed to repay their debt to the old man soon fell ill and died. No magical or natural healing seemed able to save them. Once dead, these sorry souls are said to have risen anew as ju-ju zombies who now wander the marshes around Lake Noir. They are now the minions of the Voodan, repaying their obligation with an eternity of servitude.

When someone hires Chicken Bone to cast a spell, the task that he requires of them should be decided upon ahead of time by the Dungeon Master. Like so many aspects of Ravenloft, this seemingly random event ought to be controlled to promote the overall flavor of the game and to drive the plot forward. It is important to note that the old man does not reveal his price until after his ritual is completed and the spell cast. The price for his services, he insists, comes to him during the ritual.

Ecology: The Voodan are an unusual people. They seem to have no homeland, instead settling in many diverse places. There are reports of them living atop mountain peaks, in remote caves deep beneath the surface of the earth, or at the heart of impassible swamps. Wherever they dwell, however, they make their homes difficult to reach. While they are not selective in their customers, those who wish to employ their services must prove their desire by surmounting whatever obstacles might stand between them and the Voodan. Chicken Bone is no exception; the swamps around him are alive with deadly monsters. Reaching his island home can be an adventure in itself.

It is worth mentioning that Chicken Bone seems to have some immunity to the horrors living in the swamp around him. None of the terrible creatures that lurk near him, whether they be magical or mundane, will attack him. Indeed, most will come to his aid if he is attacked. Thus, while it is impossible to say for certain, it seems likely that anyone who kills the old man will stand little chance of escaping the swamps of Souragne alive. In addition, rumor has it that a major curse will strike anyone who harms the Voodan; the truth of this rumor, and the nature of the curse, is up to the Dungeon Master.

Adventure Ideas: Seeking out Chicken Bone to have him cast a spell upon one's enemies is generally not something any group of player characters will want to do. After all, such actions may well require them to make Dark Powers checks. Further, they will then have to leave some sympathetic token in the old man's possession and do him a service, probably not something the average PC will find palatable.

On the other hand, someone might well use the old man's powers to hamper the efforts of the PCs. If this happens, the adventurers may find themselves forced to seek out the hermit and confront him to learn the nature of their enemy. It might also be necessary for the party to recover the sympathetic token(s) used against them. In addition to the fact that Chicken Bone will be very reluctant to part with the items he has acquired, the PCs may find it difficult to locate the specific thing they are searching for, as the old man's home is cluttered and strewn with a bizarre assortment of things.

The land of Souragne is featured in the novel *Dance of the Dead* and in the module RQ1, *Night of the Walking Dead*. Dungeon Masters running that adventure might find Chicken Bone an interesting addition to it. He could serve as an ally to the player characters, providing them with useful information and magic if they are having too tough a time with things. Conversely, he could aid the forces of darkness if the adventurers are finding the adventure insufficiently challenging.

Lich, Bardic (Andres Duvall)

CLIMATE/TERRAIN:	Any in Ravenloft
FREQUENCY:	Unique
ORGANIZATION:	Solitary
ACTIVITY CYCLE:	Night
DIET:	Magical energies
INTELLIGENCE:	Genius (17)
TREASURE:	W
ALIGNMENT:	Neutral good

NO. APPEARING:	1
ARMOR CLASS:	0
MOVEMENT:	12
HIT DICE:	9 (45 hit points)
THAC0:	11
NO. OF ATTACKS:	1
DAMAGE/ATTACK:	2d4
SPECIAL ATTACKS:	Magic absorption
SPECIAL DEFENSES:	+1 or better weapon to hit; *fear* aura
MAGIC RESISTANCE:	Special
SIZE:	M (6′ tall)
MORALE:	Champion (16)
XP VALUE:	13,000

Throughout the domains of Ravenloft and in countless other worlds, there are few creatures more terrible than the lich. In most cases, these diabolical creatures sought out the means by which they attained undead status, willingly sacrificing their humanity in the quest for forbidden knowledge and unchecked power. In rare cases, the curse of eternal life has been thrust upon someone quite accidentally. Such tragedies are few and far between, but sadly they do occur.

Combat: Andres Duvall is not a true lich. Still, his powers resemble those of these foul undead so strongly that it seems best to classify him among their number.

Like a true lich, Duvall radiates an aura of magical terror that causes all creatures of fewer than 5 Hit Dice (or 5th level) to make a successful fear check or flee in terror for 5 to 20 (5d4) rounds.

In melee combat, Andres strikes with a chilling touch. This effect is somewhat less potent than is common in true liches. As such, it inflicts only 2 to 8 (2d4) points of damage. Anyone struck by Duvall must make a successful saving throw vs. paralysis or be unable to move for a number of rounds equal to the number of damage points inflicted. This paralysis can be dispelled normally. In addition to his chilling touch and the paralysis it causes, Duvall can drain the magical energies of spellcasters in the manner described in more detail below.

Duvall is immune to injury by weapons which are not of at least +1 magical enchantment. He is immune to all manner of *sleep, charm, hold, cold, enfeeblement, polymorph, lightning, insanity,* or *death* spells. Duvall can be turned as any other 9 Hit Die undead.

As a 9th-level bard, Duvall has the use of some magical spells. On any given day, he can employ three first-level, three second-level, and two third-level spells, with the following being his favorite choices: *color spray, phantasmal force,* and *sleep; glitterdust, improved phantasmal force,* and *pyrotechnics; fireball* and *wraithform.* Duvall also has the thieving abilities to Climb Walls (80%), Detect Noise (50%), Pick Pockets (50%), and Read Languages (45%). He has lost his ability to influence crowds, inspire friends and allies, or counter magical songs, but does retain his 45% chance to know the history or lore of any magical item he comes across.

Because of the unusual way in which Andres Duvall became undead, he does not have a phylactery or similar vessel containing his life force.

Duvall's transformation resulted in the creation of a special ability unknown among true liches. Magical energies directed at him do not affect him in any way. Rather, these energies are absorbed and serve to strengthen his life force. When Duvall is injured, he does not regain hit points through normal healing or any form of regeneration. Rather, he must absorb spell energy. He can do this in two ways. The first, and easiest, is through spells cast at him. Any spell, regardless of its nature, will have no effect upon him other than to restore 1 lost hit point per level of the spell. Thus, a 5th-level spell like *magic jar* cast upon him will restore 5 hit points. Spell effects from objects work the same way, with the DM having the final word in deciding the effective level of any such spells.

Alternatively, Duvall can absorb spell energy by touching a wizard, cleric, or other spellcaster. In combat, this requires an attack roll; in other situations (such as if the victim is sleeping or unconscious) it might not. As soon as the victim is touched, the highest level spell he or she (or it) had memorized is lost and Duvall gains its energy in the form of regenerated hit points. If more than one spell of the highest level is available, the one absorbed should be determined by a random die roll.

Duvall is able to absorb spell energy even when he is at his maximum hit point total, but he gains no additional hit points from this process.

Habitat/Society: Andres Duvall was a half-elf born in the domain of Darkon some 150 years ago. He was born to an elf mother and a human father in the community of Sidnar, south of Lake Korst. The status of his parents was great enough that he was accepted by the community. Indeed, the young Duvall was so sweet a child that he was cherished and loved by all the elves. Duvall loved the elves in return. He learned their songs, their stories, and their legends. As a young man, their love of beauty and magic drove him to wander the world, seeking out its majesty.

As he traveled, Duvall mastered his skills as a bard. He learned many things, most bright and happy, some dark and sinister. It was his unending search for new stories and songs that brought the terrible curse of undeath upon him.

While visiting the elves of Neblus, he came upon the fragments of an ancient tome. This mysterious document told the tale of a young wizard who sought greater and greater power. At first, he found the story distracting. As he read more, he found it engrossing, though horrifying. In the end, he knew that he had found an account detailing the process by which Azalin, the Lord of Darkon, had become a lich.

Unable to believe what he had read, he destroyed the book and tried to forget it. His soul, however, had been tainted by the evils he had studied. Every night, terrible visions haunted his dreams. Every night, he awoke in a trembling fit with the image of Castle Avernus searing his mind.

At last, he traveled to the terrible fortress where Azalin dwelt. Timidly, he approached the door and, to his surprise, it swung open to admit him. All but entranced, he wandered in and the door slammed shut behind him.

For the next week, Andres was both a prisoner and a guest in Castle Avernus. By Azalin's command, he told stories and sang songs, lightening the dark mood of the domain's master. In return, the lich told him the tale of his life and his years in Ravenloft. It seemed to Duvall that Azalin found it almost a relief to tell another his morbid story.

Duvall was certainly fascinated by the story of Azalin's life, death, and unlife. He was also convinced that the dark lord was not telling him all that there was to know. He decided that he must learn more and slipped quietly into the lich's inner sanctum.

As Duvall explored this terrible place, Azalin discovered his trespasses and confronted him. Enraged at this violation of his hospitality, the lich unleashed a stroke of magical lightning at the bard. Reacting quickly, Duvall attempted to shield himself with the great book he had been about to examine. The lightning struck the tome, which happened to be one of Azalin's most potent books of spells, and a terrible explosion shook the castle. Showers of blazing fragments ignited fires around the room and thick, acrid smoke boiled into the air.

Dazed, but amazed that he had survived at all, Duvall fled. Azalin, intent on saving his magical laboratory, did not pursue. Thus, Duvall escaped and went into hiding.

As the days passed, it became more and more clear to Duvall that the accident in the laboratory had made some great change in his body. To his horror, he found that his heart no longer beat and that he did not breathe. He had not survived the attack, after all. Gradually, Duvall's appearance began to change as well. His skin dried and stretched tight across his bones. He began to look more and more like the withered Azalin. Within a week, he was so horrible to look upon that most folk fled from him in terror at first sight.

Ecology: Duvall survives by feeding upon magical energies. Each day, he must absorb a minimum of one level of spell energy to satisfy his hunger.

Adventure Ideas: Despite his transformation into an undead creature, Duvall remains a force for good in Ravenloft. He is one of Azalin's most hated enemies, for he knows many of that lord's secrets from his time in Castle Avernus. As such, any group of heroes planning to confront the dread master of Darkon might well find a powerful ally in Andres Duvall.

On his own, Duvall recognizes that he can not hope to survive a direct confrontation with the lich lord. Because of this, he wanders the domains and islands of Ravenloft looking for allies and weapons that he can turn against his nemesis. It would not be out of character for Duvall to act as a patron of the PCs in any manner of adventure that might require the discovery of lost secrets or the recovery of an ancient weapon.

Although he is not mentioned in either RQ3, *From the Shadows* or its sequel RM1, *Roots of Evil*, Duvall could easily be inserted into either of these modules. His hatred of Azalin has led him to side with the enemies of Darkon many times over the years, so he just might even be able bring himself to strike some bargain with Strahd Von Zarovich if he thought it might enable him to finally destroy his foe.

Lycanthrope, Weretiger (Jahed)

CLIMATE/TERRAIN:	Sri Raji
FREQUENCY:	Very rare
ORGANIZATION:	Pack
ACTIVITY CYCLE:	Any (Commonly night)
DIET:	Carnivore
INTELLIGENCE:	Exceptional (15)
TREASURE:	Q×5 (D)
ALIGNMENT:	Lawful evil

NO. APPEARING:	1
ARMOR CLASS:	3
MOVEMENT:	12
HIT DICE:	6+2 (42 hit points)
THAC0:	15
NO. OF ATTACKS:	3 or 5
DAMAGE/ATTACK:	1d4/1d4/1d12 (1d4+1/1d4+1 if rake attack)
SPECIAL ATTACKS:	Forces morale check by shapeshifting
SPECIAL DEPENSES:	Hit only by silver or magical weapons
MAGIC RESISTANCE:	Nil
SIZE:	M (5′10″ tall)
MORALE:	Fanatic (18)
XP VALUE:	2,000

Jahed came into Sri Raji as a young adult. At that time, he was a specimen of physical fitness blessed with strong limbs, keen senses, and a quick mind. In the years that have passed since his arrival, the rigors of life in Ravenloft have left their mark on him. His once gentle and laughing features have hardened and become cruel. His green eyes smolder with an anger that is constantly ready to erupt into acts of physical violence. The flowing mane of copper hair that he sported as a lad has been replaced with a savagely cropped crew cut.

Jahed prefers to wear dark clothes, for they enable him to move about in the shadows and alleys without being seen. He has spent some time in the lands of Kara-Tur, and his garb is based loosely on that of the ninjas that he met there. He carries no weapons, being well able to defend himself without them.

Jahed speaks the common tongues of the FORGOTTEN REALMS campaign setting, Kara-Tur, and Sri Raji, having learned the last since his arrival in the domain.

Combat: Jahed will almost always revert to his weretiger form before engaging in combat. In this shape, he strikes with his deadly front claws (1d4/1d4), bites with his keen fangs (1d12), and rakes with his rending rear claws (1d4+1/1d4+1). His combination of intelligence and brute force makes him a deadly opponent indeed. Jahed himself is immune to attacks made with weapons that are not silver or at least bearing a +1 enchantment.

In those rare cases where Jahed is forced to engage in combat while in his human form, he will seek to disengage as quickly as possible, falling back to buy himself the time to transform into a tiger.

Jahed uses his shape-shifting ability as something of an attack in itself. When fighting untrained or easily spooked people (that is, the average peasant or green

guardsman), he makes certain that his enemy sees him transform. In most cases, such people must make a morale check, if not a fear or horror check.

Jahed seldom travels anywhere without a pair of body guards. Like himself, these two will be deadly weretigers.

Habitat/Society: Jahed is a stranger in Sri Raji. He was born to a tribe of wanderers in the Dalelands of the Forgotten Realms. His parents were skilled entertainers and not a little bit larcenous at heart. Because he knows all the tricks and sleight of hand that they use to appear mystical and mysterious, Jahed places no stock in stories of Vistani power. On those few occasions when he meets these folk, he treats them with scorn and contempt.

Jahed's father, Mercurio, was a cruel and prying man. He delighted in the suffering of those they passed in their travels and, whenever it was convenient, took a hand in making such circumstances even worse. Jahed's mother, Antelucia, was timid and sickly, having been battered into submission by her abusive husband long before Jahed's birth.

When Jahed was still a teenager, he met and fell in love with a girl named Milissa. Because Milissa was an elegant young lady, Jahed was careful to avoid letting her know of his family's lowly status.

Mercurio, however, noticed his son's secret departures from their camp and decided to find out what the youngster was up to. He followed Jahed's path into the heart of a thick forest and there found the embracing lovers. Furious, he charged forward and struck Jahed with his heavy walking stick. The boy was sent spinning away from Milissa and fell to his knees.

With his son too dazed to interfere, Mercurio turned his attention to Milissa. At first he verbally abused her, questioning her virtue and demanding that she leave his son alone. He drifted into insults, calling her a tramp and a harlot, and then struck at her with his cane.

Much to his surprise, the girl nimbly avoided the blow and sprang at him. In mid-leap, she became a snarling tigress. Landing fully upon Mercurio, she snapped powerful jaws down on his windpipe and tore his abdomen open with her raking claws, killing him almost instantly.

Jahed, hearing his father's dying cry, recovered his senses enough to realize that some creature was attacking his father and rushed into the fray. Still somewhat dazed from his father's blow, he had no idea that the monster before him was actually his beloved. Drawing his slender dagger, Jahed stabbed at the tigress.

Instinctively, Milissa whirled about and ripped at him with her claws. Badly wounded, Jahed collapsed and lost consciousness. Hours later, he awoke to find himself lying beside a stream that trickled along under the stars of a cloudless autumn night, his wounds carefully tended. Nearby he found a note from Milissa explaining that she would never be able to see him again.

Jahed, whose life had been one of broken promises and harsh punishments, took the heartbreaking news well. The traumas of his life had been such that he assumed she had simply considered their love a dalliance.

In time, his wounds healed and he returned to the traveling life that he had always known. He thought no more of his lost love and devoted himself to caring for his mother. With Mercurio dead, Antelucia began to brighten and take an interest in the world around her. When she died nine months after her husband, Jahed buried her with a remorse he never felt for his father.

Three months after his mother died, on the anniversary of Mercurio's death, a strange transformation came over Jahed. He had become a weretiger. Once he overcame his surprise, over the course of the next several months Jahed fought to understand the strange legacy of his first love.

With time and effort, he found that he was able to control the metamorphosis and become a tiger whenever he wished. However, he also found that he would transform every year on the day of Mercurio's death and that nothing could cause him to resume his normal form save the taking of a human, demihuman, or humanoid life.

Over the years, Jahed's personality changed. The occasional harshness which he had inherited from his father took on a more calculating edge. Recognizing the wild and chaotic nature of Mercurio's life, he sought to give his own a sense of order. While he was unable to throw off the burden of cruelty and wickedness that was

his legacy from years of mistreatment, he lifted himself above his father's brutality.

Years later, traveling through a region of thick jungles in search of an ancient treasure said to lie hidden there, Jahed came across a ruined temple and entered it. Inside, he found tiger mosaics, figurines, and other items that led him to believe that this place had once been sacred to others like himself.

He felt strangely awed by the ruins. Here, he felt, was a home such as he had never known in the lands of normal men. Jahed quickly made up his mind to make this place his den from that day forth. He swore to restore it to its former glory and spend the rest of his days in this tropical land.

The first night that Jahed spent in this temple, he had an unusual and terrifying dream. He found himself in the company of Ravana, the rakshasa god to whom the temple had been sacred. The god charged him with the task of hunting down and destroying Arijani, the god's own son who had become a traitor to his people. The idea of serving another greater than himself had never occurred to Jahed before, but—impressed by the sheer power that seemed to engulf this ancient god—Jahed eagerly agreed and vowed not to die until the betrayer was repaid for his crimes.

He awoke to find himself in Ravenloft, in Arijani's own domain of Sri Raji. When he began to explore his new home, Jahed found himself hunted by the priestesses of Kali, allies of Arijani who seek to destroy any visitor to the realm. Lucky to escape alive, he was forced to flee into the jungles as his temple was razed.

Jahed found survival difficult at first, even for someone with his great powers. Eventually, however, he learned to blend in with the natives of the domain and sought for ways to carry out his mission. For the past several years, he has devoted himself to the creation of The Stalkers, a secret society devoted to bringing down Arijani's reign. By spreading lycanthropy to a select few, he has built up a small but powerful group united by a common hatred of Kali's priestesses.

Adventure Ideas: Jahed is featured in the module RM3, *Web of Illusion*, which details his latest attempt to destroy the rakshasa lord Arijani. Because he is both evil and opposed to the lord of a domain, Jahed can be cast as either a friend or foe to the adventurers. Any scenario that involves him should center around his efforts to defeat Arijani or thwart some plan of the dark lord.

Meazel (Salizarr)

CLIMATE/TERRAIN:	Darkon
FREQUENCY:	Unique
ORGANIZATION:	Solitary
ACTIVITY CYCLE:	Night
DIET:	Carnivore
INTELLIGENCE:	Low (6)
TREASURE:	(B)
ALIGNMENT:	Chaotic evil

NO. APPEARING:	1
ARMOR CLASS:	8
MOVEMENT:	12
HIT DICE:	4 (13 hit points)
THAC0:	15
NO. OF ATTACKS:	2
DAMAGE/ATTACK:	1d4/1d4
SPECIAL ATTACKS:	Strangulation; disease; thief abilities
SPECIAL DEFENSES:	Thief abilities
MAGIC RESISTANCE:	Nil
SIZE:	M (4'6″ tall)
MORALE:	Steady (11)
XP VALUE:	270

People have always feared the darkness, often with good reason. After all, there are things in the black shadows of night more horrible than any vision that might come to a person in sleep. When this dread is combined with the creeping anxiety that comes with travel underground, it becomes a gnawing terror that quickens the pulse of even the stoutest hero. In the dread domain of Darkon, in the maze of sewers beneath the great city of Il Aluk, this horror has a name: Salizarr.

Salizarr is a meazel, one of a sly and murderous race. His skin is rough and olive green in color, marked here and there by angry red patches of blisters and sores. His black hair, thick and wiry, juts away from his head as if blown back by a great wind, framing his triangular face. His jet-black eyes are set in narrow slits and gleam as if they were cut from black marble. His mouth is thin and angular, vanishing almost completely when closed but opening to reveal a frightening array of needlelike teeth. Although this terrible creature wears no clothing, he does adorn himself with a piece of jewelry, a dangling earring that connects by a chain to a jeweled nose stud; this is somewhat unusual, as his kind do not generally value such things.

Salizarr speaks the hissing, guttural language of his people, as well as the Common Tongue of Darkon. The latter, however, is heavily accented and can be quite difficult to understand. It is said that he can speak with the rats of sewers, but this may be myth.

Combat: In close combat, Salizarr is a deadly enemy. Like all meazels, his speed and strength give him a better THAC0 than would normally accrue to a monster of his Hit Dice. His ripping claws can strike twice per round, inflicting 14 (1d4) points of damage each. As if this were not enough, the filth of the sewers has col-

lected on his talons. Thus, everyone who is hit by Salizarr's attack must make a successful saving throw vs. poison (with a +4 bonus) or contract a debilitating disease as described under the 3rd-level priest spell *cure disease*.

Salizarr is fond of strangling lone victims who are under seven feet in height. When he does this, he employs a knotted cord that not only cuts off the air flow of the victim but may actually crush the windpipe. Salizarr only employs his strangulation attack when he is attacking with surprise and from behind. Because of his thieving skills and knowledge of the sewers, he is frequently able to catch his victims unawares, gaining a bonus of +4 on his attack roll.

In order to loop his deadly cord about the neck of a potential victim, Salizarr leaps onto his target's back and rolls his attack. If successful, once the line is in place the meazel applies his considerable (18/50) Strength to it. If he is not dislodged within two rounds, the victim's windpipe has been crushed and death by suffocation is unavoidable.

Forcing Salizarr to release his grip is not easy; he will not willingly loosen his strangling line once it is in place except to defend himself. A player character wishing to break free of his deadly embrace must do so in accordance with the unarmed combat rules described in the *Player's Handbook*. Thus, a successful throw, gouge, or hit with a weapon is required, and a victim wearing armor suffers a penalty of anywhere from –1 to as much as –10 on his or her attack.

The meazel's natural agility and knowledge of the sewers gives him some useful expertise similar to that of a master thief. Thus, he has the following special abilities: Pick Pockets (45%), Open Locks (37%), Find/Remove Traps (35%), Move Silently (33%), Hide in Shadows (25%), Hear Noise (15%), Climb Walls (88%), and Read Languages (20%).

If a combat seems to be going against Salizarr, he will attempt to flee. In general, he is fast and agile enough to do this with ease. If he is pursued, he will attempt to lead his enemies into deadly danger. While he does not set traps or similar hazards to protect his lair, he knows where there are patches of green slime or puddles of gray ooze. With his enemies generally unaware of these dangers, he can frequently dodge them while his opponents stumble right into them.

Habitat/Society: Salizarr lurks in the great maze of sewers that curl beneath Il Aluk. No one knows how extensive this labyrinth is, for there is no record of its construction. It may well be that this underground complex was fashioned by the magic of the lich lord Azalin or even some other, darker power. Whoever or whatever the architect of this great place was, there is no doubt that Salizarr is its master now.

Salizarr is a relative newcomer to Ravenloft, having come into the Demiplane of Dread roughly one year ago. Before that time, Salizarr lived in a series of catacombs not far from the city of Suzail in the Forgotten Realms. One day, a stranger wandered into his underground realm and Salizarr attacked him. The man broke free of his grip and bolted away into the shadows. Enraged and ravenous, the meazel pursued him. After countless twists and turns, Salizarr had to concede that his victim had escaped him. He slowed from a run to a trot and then realized that he had no idea where he was.

The natural complex of caverns that had been his home for so many years was gone. Now, he found himself moving through a series of man-made sewers. After several days of trying to find his way home, it became obvious that his efforts were futile, so he determined to make this new place his own.

At that time, the sewers were home to a tribe of kobolds, living in an alcove near a nexus of two major tunnels. It wasn't long before Salizarr had hunted them down and destroyed them all, one by one. Once they had been removed, Salizarr claimed their quarters for his own, scattering the previous occupants' bones around in various geometric patterns by way of decoration. He has since forgotten his original home, and now believes that he has always lived in these sinister tunnels.

Salizarr collects the gold and silver carried by his victims, but has no interest in accumulating other treasures. He wears an unusual earring, but keeps no other jewelry or art objects. What this or any other meazel plans to do with his hoarded treasure is anybody's guess.

Whenever Salizarr makes a kill, he strips the body of coins. Items that he does not deem valuable, including weapons, armor, and magical items, he carries to a nearby pit and tosses in. At the bottom of this 80-foot hole is a foot-deep pool of green slime. In this horrible bath, not even magical items can survive for long. However, because green slime is unable to dissolve them, dozens of valuable gems are likely resting at the bottom of the pit. Anyone capable of defeating the slime and recovering them might find this quite a valuable treasure.

Ecology: As a meazel, Salizarr seems to hunger constantly for the flesh of humans, demihumans, and humanoids. Because such folk seldom come into the sewers, however, he is forced to subsist on a diet of rats and similar vermin. When this unsatisfactory board becomes too bland for him, he ventures out of the sewers to strike at the folk of Il Aluk. On those dark nights, the screams of his victims can be heard as he drags them back into the sewers to torture and destroy.

Adventure Ideas: Salizarr lurks like a bogeyman in the sewers. Stories about this terrible creature abound, though many people do not believe that he really exists. Few have seen him, and those who have are troubled by nightmares of his evil visage for the rest of their days. The player characters will find him a cunning adversary, and the sewers in which he dwells a horrible lair. Exploring these dreadful tunnels can be quite an adventure.

The PCs might be introduced to Salizarr when one of their henchmen vanishes, dragged into the sewers to satisfy the meazel's carnal hunger. Because of his craven nature, Salizarr is not above stalking children as well. It could be that the PCs will be called upon to rescue some young innocent who has been taken by the fiend.

Once the PCs are in the sewers, they will find themselves in a hostile, alien domain. These tunnels are littered with vermin, slimes, and other disgusting menaces. While Salizarr is not an overly intelligent creature, he is shrewd and has come to know his new home quite well. He will use his familiarity with the sewers and the menaces that dwell there to lead the player characters into dangerous places.

Medusa (Althea)

CLIMATE/TERRAIN:	Lamordia (Demise)
FREQUENCY:	Unique
ORGANIZATION:	Solitary
ACTIVITY CYCLE:	Day
DIET:	Omnivore
INTELLIGENCE:	Very (11)
TREASURE:	P, Q×10, X (Y)
ALIGNMENT:	Lawful evil

NO. APPEARING:	1
ARMOR CLASS:	5
MOVEMENT:	9
HIT DICE:	6 (27 hit points)
THAC0:	15
NO. OF ATTACKS:	1
DAMAGE/ATTACK:	1 or 1d6
SPECIAL ATTACKS:	Petrification; poison; blindness
SPECIAL DEFENSES:	Nil
MAGIC RESISTANCE:	Nil
SIZE:	M (6′ tall)
MORALE:	Elite (13)
XP VALUE:	3,000

Northwest of the domain of Lamordia, beyond even the terrible Isle of Agony, lies a small island known only as Demise. Those who pass near the island have reported hearing songs of great beauty drifting out across the waves. Sailors who travel to this island seldom return, however, for the only thing to be found of the island of Demise is death at the hands of Althea.

Althea is a medusa, one of that terrible race of women who sport tresses of deadly vipers instead of hair atop their heads. Like all her kind, Althea's body is that of a slender, even shapely human woman. Her countenance, however, is dreadful, having the general features of a human face but possessing the scales and texture of a reptile. Her eyes are nothing more than black beads, her mouth but a lipless slit through which her forked tongue slips in and out to taste the air for odors.

Althea's senses are, on the whole, similar to those of a normal human. However, her eyes are somewhat weaker and are bothered by bright light. Her sense of smell, conversely, is far better than a human's. These two tend to balance out, making modifications to surprise rolls and the like unnecessary.

It is impossible to say with certainty which languages Althea does or does not know. While she seems to know the language of Lamordia, she speaks it with a pronounced accent. What her home language is, or where she might have originated, is unknown.

Combat: Althea's primary weapon is, of course, her petrification attack. Anyone who looks into her snake-like eyes is instantly transformed to stone unless he or she can make a successful saving throw vs. petrification. This attack can affect a single enemy per round and has a maximum range of 30 feet.

The power of Althea's gaze is so great that it extends even into the Astral and Ethereal planes. Indeed, she is able to see creatures moving about in these nether regions as plainly as she sees those on the Prime Material Plane.

Even death does not instantly halt the effect of this deadly gaze. Looking into the eyes of a slain medusa still requires a saving throw, although this is made with a +1 bonus per day that has passed since the creature died. Indeed, because any natural roll of 1 is an automatic failure on this saving throw, this gaze weapon still has a 5% chance of functioning for centuries after the actual death of the creature.

Althea is vulnerable to her own petrifying gaze. For that reason, she abhors mirrors and similar objects. Any brightly polished metal surface can be used to turn her gaze back upon her, forcing her to save or be petrified. Nonmetal reflectors will not serve to destroy her; the *gaze reflection* spell is similarly impotent. The gaze of another medusa cannot petrify her, but that of a different type of creature (like a basilisk) can. If she is turned to stone, looking upon her petrified remains no longer carries the risk of death.

The snakes atop her head are able to attack each round. Althea's asps can bite for a single point of damage, but anyone bitten must make a saving throw vs. poison or die instantly.

In addition to this bite, Althea's snakes can spit their venom at a range of up to 10 feet. Each combat round, every enemy within this range will be attacked in this manner and must make a successful saving throw vs. breath weapons. Failure to make this save indicates that the snake has scored a hit on the target's eyes, permanently blinding him or her. The victim is unable to see, with all the penalties and disadvantages that might normally be associated with such a state, until he or she receives a *cure blindness* or similar spell.

In melee combat, Althea attacks with a slender-bladed short sword. This weapon does inflicts 1d6 points of damage against medium targets and 1d8 points of damage to large ones. While it is quite ornate and valuable (being worth some 500 gold pieces), it is not magical in any way. Althea has also been known to employ a short bow in combat, attacking targets as far as 150 yards away and causing 1d6 points of damage per arrow that strikes its mark. From time to time, Althea will use her asps' poison to make these weapons more deadly.

Habitat/Society: Demise, the island on which Althea lives, is far from hospitable. Indeed, it is little more than a great outcropping of rock amid the gray-blue expanse of the Sea of Sorrows. Those who approach by sea will find no safe anchorage near the rocky cliffs that pass for Demise's shore. A small boat might reach the coast safely, but only the most experienced seaman would stand much chance of surviving such an attempt.

The first report of Althea's appearance dates back about 50 years. The *Doma Ordana*, a small merchant ship running north from Ludendorf to Martira Bay, found itself caught in a terrible storm which hung above the sea south of The Finger. In an effort to avoid the brunt of the storm, the ship's captain, a Lamordian named Johan Wehner, decided to sail around the Isle of Agony rather than risk the turbulent channel.

All went well until the voyage was half-over, when the ship rammed something beneath the waterline and split open. Most of the crew died when *Doma Ordana* vanished beneath the storm-tossed water. Wehner and five of his men managed to cling to floating debris and make their way to the shores of a rocky island. They found the coasts utterly inhospitable, being nothing but rocky cliffs and crushing surf. With some effort, they managed to come safely ashore, becoming, so far as they knew, the first men ever to step upon the island known as Demise. Wehner's records of his exploration of the island were found adrift in a wooden keg several months later.

His account begins with the scaling of the cliffs. At the point where he and his men went ashore, this formidable climb was no less that 50 feet. Further, the rock was broken and loose, making it a very dangerous ascent. Good luck was with them, however, for the entire company completed the climb safely.

Wehner described the surface of the island as resembling a rocky plateau or region of badlands. One of his men had spent some time in Kartakass and likened the area to the neighboring region of Bluetspur. Those familiar with that foul domain will certainly understand the unflattering image that such a comparison conveys.

The explorers reported no vegetation of any merit on the island, and the only fresh water they found were pools and puddles from the recent storm. Determined to find food and drink, they headed farther inland.

Again, luck was with them. The center of the island was a great depression, hinting at possible volcanic origin. Within this large crater, life had indeed taken hold. Springs of hot water boiled up from deep underground, filling the air with a thick sulphurous steam. Plants had taken vigorous hold here, transforming the region into a rich, tropical jungle. Animal life, however, seemed nonexistent, a fact which troubled Wehner and his crew greatly.

For two days, the castaways found life in the caldera of that ancient volcano pleasant, if dull. They ate and drank, recovering from the abuses of the storm and their trek across the rocky island. When they were well again, they began to explore their temporary home. While his men began to build the boat that would carry them back to the mainland, Wehner set about exploring the place.

Near the center of the great forest, he came across a strange structure. Built of some incredibly hard white stone, it seemed endless as he walked along its perimeter. At last, however, he came upon an arch in this mysterious barrier. Runes unlike any he had seen before adorned the portal, and he decided to proceed no farther on his own.

The next day, Wehner returned to the portal with his men. They had fashioned spears to defend themselves and carried the knives they had brought with them from the ship. None of them could make anything of the inscription. Together they entered the large, flat structure.

Inside, they found the place to be a great maze of featureless halls. It wasn't long before the company had gotten turned around and become hopelessly lost in this labyrinth. Once again, the men found themselves wandering and without adequate provisions.

From time to time, they came across fine statues of men, women, and demihumans. In every case these were so lifelike and intricate that Wehner and his men thought they might suddenly come to life. The statues seemed to represent a great variety of explorers, adventurers, and sailors. Despite their many differences, they all had one trait in common: Without exception, the faces of the statues were twisted in horror and revulsion. Wehner thought the sculptor's taste and technique odd, and wondered what mortal hand had crafted these ghastly icons.

When Wehner estimated that they had spent ten hours exploring the web of white stone, he called for them to hold up and make camp. His men were tired and further exploration was likely to yield nothing without rest. One of the men stood watch while the others slept soundly.

When Wehner awoke, he saw that some horror had come upon them in the night. The guard had been transformed into a statue. Like all the others, his face bore the unmistakable mask of someone whose last thoughts had been consumed with nightmarish fear and dread. Unable to do anything for their lost companion, Wehner and his crew redoubled their efforts at escape.

For several days this sad company wandered the labyrinth. From time to time they caught sight of some dreadful shadow flashing across the smooth walls. Not long after such a sighting, one of the men would let out a cry of agony and become petrified. In the end, only Wehner himself remained.

Wehner made ready to face the thing that was stalking him. He tied a band about his eyes so that he could not look above the creature's waist. When it came to destroy him, however, Wehner was surprised to find that it did not charge forward like a mad beast. Rather, the

Medusa (Althea)

medusa spoke to him, her words ringing softly off the walls of the labyrinth.

"You need not fear me, brave sailor," the husky, seductive voice sang. "I shall not harm you. I, Althea, have chosen you above all others. You and I are meant to be together. Look upon me—am I not attractive in your eyes?"

Wehner's blindfold allowed him to see Althea from the waist down. The perfection of her body was greater than that of any woman he had ever seen. When combined with the sheer perfection of her voice, the temptation was almost more than he could bear. In his heart, a sudden passion burned that called for him to pull away his blindfold and look upon the woman.

Althea stepped closer and Wehner could see that she was holding out her arms to him. Only then did he hear the hissing of asps and regain his conviction. Blindly, he struck at her with his blade. The cry of agony that echoed through the labyrinth was more than enough to tell him that his aim had been true.

Although wounded, however, Althea was not defeated. She grabbed at Wehner, ripping the blindfold from his face. Before he could look away, the asps upon her head spat their deadly venom into his eyes, leaving him blind.

Althea hissed at him, vowing that he would die slowly and in great pain. Wehner, his nerve shattered by the horror that he had faced, turned and fled. He didn't know how badly he had wounded Althea, but she did not pursue him. He hoped that his attack would prove fatal, but something in his heart knew better.

To his surprise, the blinded Wehner found his way out of the labyrinth. He surmised, correctly, that the place was built as much of illusion as of stone. Without his eyes to guide him, he was far less vulnerable to the labyrinth's magic.

Wehner's account ends with his escape from the labyrinth, and his ultimate fate is unknown to the outside world. Most assume that he died trying to escape the rocky Demise or that he returned to the labyrinth and fell victim to the deadly Althea.

No one can say for certain how Althea came to be in Ravenloft. It seems certain that she is not a native of the Demiplane of Dread. The architecture of the labyrinth is classical in nature, calling to mind images of the Acropolis and similar structures. The runes above the entrance have no meaning in any known language; even magic has failed to reveal their hidden message.

Among the sailors who travel through The Finger and along the coast of the Sea of Sorrows, the story of Demise and its lone inhabitant is told with many variations. Some common threads have emerged, however, and may well be bits of Althea's true story gleaned by scrying and scholarly investigation.

Whatever Althea's original home, she seems to have been cast out from it. Indeed, the volcanic nature of the island clashes so greatly with the rest of the northwestern lands that Demise itself may be a relic of this unknown world. Some of the oldest charts in Lamordia do not show the island, a fact that lends credence to this theory.

As for the medusa Althea, she is very much a pris-

oner of her labyrinth. It seems certain that she did not build it, nor did she design the enchantments described by Johan Wehner. Presumably, however, she has acquired some degree of wealth over the years. Who can say what treasures might have been brought to Demise by explorers and castaways, only to fall into the hands of this terrible she-devil?

Althea's isolation has driven her mad. She desires freedom and, if the stories are to be believed, a mate.

I know now the nature of the beast that stalks me. After the petrification of Varshon, I knew that I must confront the thing or die myself. Escape, it seems, is no longer an option.

I hold no illusions about my fate. I have little chance of overcoming this dreadful creature, but I must try. The souls of my men have been lost; can their captain do less than seek vengeance for them? I think not.

It is death to look into the eyes of this creature; that much I have surmised. To that end, I have bound my eyes. I have left myself some vision, but I can see nothing above the level of my waist. With luck, I shall be able to see enough of my enemy's movements to defend myself somewhat. What weapons it may have beyond this gaze I cannot say.

I have my knife, the blade that was my mother's, and I cannot help but think that it will not fail me. The creature comes for me now; I can hear its footfall. I must make ready to strike.

Heaven guide my knife that I might end the life of this horrible creature once and for all.

—From the journal of Johan Wehner

Indeed, the account of Captain Wehner may well lend credence to this assumption. It seems that Althea always selects a single individual from among any party that enters her lair. All others in the group are then treated as prey, to be stalked and killed at her whim. The chosen one, however, she desires as a mate. It seems certain that anyone who might succumb to the charms of this woman would soon die.

Ecology: The island on which Althea lives is indeed a wonder of nature. From the sea, it looks like a cone of rough black stone rising out of the waves. Newly landed mariners will find its shores bleak and desolate.

Ascending the cone, however, will bring one to the lip of a great caldera. Looking down into this crater will reveal a thriving jungle of plants, hot springs, and rolling banks of steam. Exploration of the jungle will undoubtedly lead to the discovery of the labyrinth at its heart. The lack of animals larger than insects is further proof of this place's unnatural history.

A fact not known to the outside world is that Johan Wehner still lives. Over the years, he has regained the ability to distinguish light from dark, but he cannot make out shapes. He lives in a cave near the sea, where he survives by fishing. He will offer what help he can to those who visit Demise—besides being familiar with every inch of the island, he knows that Althea cannot leave her maze. Those who encounter him will certainly think of him as a mad hermit, for decades of isolation have left him a broken, tragic figure.

Adventure Ideas: Demise is an excellent place for the creative Dungeon Master to stage a shipwreck adventure. The player characters begin the scenario aboard a boat, either in or out of Ravenloft. Through some mishap, they come across the dreadful island and are forced (or choose) to go ashore.

Once on the island, the heroes might encounter Wehner, from whom they will learn much about the creature at the heart of the island. For his part, the old hermit has lost touch with reality and the information he provides might be hidden in riddles, sea chanties, or vaguely coherent reminiscences.

Exploring the labyrinth, which is liberally treated with illusion and similar magics, will be a dangerous and baffling task. Althea will, as mentioned above, pick one of the characters as a would-be mate and then proceed to destroy the others. She takes great delight in tormenting her victims, so she will use hit-and-run tactics whenever possible. She knows the maze well, knowledge that makes her an even deadlier enemy.

Those who survive to reach the center of her maze will find Althea's lair waiting for them. This is a magnificent place with fountains of sweet water, gardens of fruit, and luxurious furnishings. It is also, however, a place of deadly peril. Althea will be quick to deal with intruders who delve this deeply.

Because the labyrinth is a prison designed to contain Althea, her death may result in its partial destruction. Dungeon Masters might want to rule that the entire building crumbles into ruin, leaving the player characters to scramble for safety amid the chaos. Less spectacularly, the magical illusions that serve to make exploration of the place so difficult could fail, leaving it simply a maze of stonework. The DM might also wish to rule that the building remains unchanged, leaving it like a great spider's web that waits to trap the unwary at the heart of the island.

I have been blinded. I do my best to write this clearly so that others might read it, but I must rely on the memory of my hands in the making of these letters. I had expected to die in battle with the creature, but this is far worse.

Still, the deed is done. I have met the creature and survived. My knife struck true, for the blade is slick with blood. I managed to avoid meeting its gaze and have been spared the fate of my companions.

Curiously, I was able to escape the maze fairly easily after losing my sight. It could be that some magic made things appear differently inside the structure; without my eyes, such enchantments could have no effect upon me. Whatever the case, I am back in the jungle.

I must sleep now, for I am exhausted. Thank the Sea Goddess that there are no beasts in this place so my sleep should be undisturbed. When I awake, I shall make my way to the top of the caldera, if I am able. From there I shall descend to the edge of the island and commit this journal to the sea.

Once that is done, I do not know what will become of me.

—The final excerpt from the journal of Johan Wehner

Mummy, Greater (Senmet)

CLIMATE/TERRAIN:	Har'Akir
FREQUENCY:	Unique
ORGANIZATION:	Solitary
ACTIVITY CYCLE:	Night
DIET:	Nil
INTELLIGENCE:	Genius (17)
TREASURE:	V (A×2)
ALIGNMENT:	Lawful evil

NO. APPEARING:	1
ARMOR CLASS:	2
MOVEMENT:	9
HIT DICE:	8+3 (45 hp)
ThAC0:	11 (10)
NO. OF ATTACKS:	1
DAMAGE/ATTACK:	3d6
SPECIAL ATTACKS:	*Fear* aura; disease
SPECIAL DEFENSES:	Immune to normal weapons; half-damage from magical weapons; immune to cold, nonmagical fire
MAGIC RESISTANCE:	Nil
SIZE:	M (6′ 3″ tall)
MORALE:	Fanatic (18)
XP VALUE:	8,000

The so-called Children of Anhktepot are a horrible and sinister lot. Most were created by the dread lord of Har'Akir himself and are wholly loyal to that vile creature. Senmet, however, was given his power and undead stature by Isu Rehkotep, a priestess who stumbled upon a magical scroll. Now free to act as he will, Senmet has vowed to bring down Anhktepot and replace him as the lord of Har'Akir.

Like all mummies, Senmet is a desiccated corpse wrapped in funereal cloth and bearing an unholy symbol on a chain around his neck. An odor of spices and herbs lingers in the air about him. In places Senmet's wraps have fallen away, revealing withered brown flesh stretched tightly over a skeletal frame. It is impossible to distinguish Senmet from a normal mummy.

Senmet is highly intelligent and speaks many languages in addition to that of Har'Akir. Further, he has a natural ability to command all normal mummies that he might encounter. This power is telepathic, requiring neither words nor motions, and functions on any mummy of whose presence Senmet is aware.

Combat: Senmet is a terrible enemy. Like all greater mummies, he radiates an aura of fear that forces everyone who sees him to make a *fear* check at a −1 penalty. If this check is failed, the normal results are doubled due to the great power with which Senmet has been infused. Spells like a *cloak of bravery* or *remove fear* can enable adventurers to overcome this power.

When Senmet attacks in close combat, he does so by striking with his powerful fists. This allows him to make a single attack (at +1 bonus) that delivers a staggering 3d6 points of damage with each blow that lands.

Anyone hit by Senmet will contract a terrible rotting disease that will prove fatal in 1d12 days. On the day

after the disease is contracted, the victim begins to suffer uncontrollable shaking and tremors, making spellcasting and feats requiring fine Dexterity impossible. Further, the victim loses 1 point of Strength and Constitution from the debilitating effects of the disease and 2 points of Charisma as his or her skin begins to flake and wither away. Ridding oneself of this disease is only possible through use of a *regeneration* spell. A stricken character without access to regenerative magic can be kept alive with *cure disease* spells, one for each day that has passed since the disease was contracted. Note, however, that this merely halts the rot from progressing, and the disease remains in the victim's system until a permanent cure is effected.

In most cases, a diseased person crumbles into dust when he or she dies. If Senmet chooses, however, he can convert someone infected with his rotting disease into a unique breed of zombie or an actual mummy. In either case, the newly created horror is completely under Senmet's control.

When he wishes to create a zombie, Senmet strangles his victim. Within 8 hours, the body rises from the dead as a desert zombie. These creatures are described fully in the adventure RA3, *Touch of Death*. For those who do not own that product, desert zombies are similar to common zombies except that they are faster (MV 9) and do not suffer initiative penalties. Desert zombies are able to burrow through sand at a rate of 6 feet per round; their favorite method of attack is to hide beneath the sand, grab passing characters (who are considered AC 10 for purposes of this attack; Dexterity bonuses do apply), and drag them to their doom. Desert zombies resemble desiccated corpses.

In order to create a mummy, Senmet captures someone infected with his disease and takes his victim to his hidden temple. Here, he mummifies the person alive (a terrible and gruesome fate, to be certain). When the process is completed, the victim dies and promptly rises again as a mummy.

Unlike other greater mummies, Senmet is unable to employ clerical spells, having sacrificed this ability for the power to make and control desert zombies. The means by which he made this exchange is unknown and may well tie into Isu Rehkotep's dark worship of the evil Set. If any have learned this secret, they did not live long enough to share it with the world.

Senmet is immune to attacks made with nonmagical weapons, while magical weapons inflict only half their normal damage. Spells and other attacks that depend upon cold, ice, or nonmagical fire to inflict damage do not harm him at all. However, Senmet is very vulnerable to lightning-based attacks, which do half again their normal damage when used against him.

Like all undead, Senmet is immune to *charm, hold, sleep,* or similar spells and cannot be harmed by poisons or disease. He is further immune to damage from holy water, although contact with a nonevil holy symbol burns him for 1d6 points. Contact with an unholy symbol of Set actually restores 1d6 hit points per round. For this reason, Senmet always wears a coiled cobra medallion around his neck and regenerates 1d6 hit points per round so long as it remains in place.

Habitat/Society: Long before the domain of Har'Akir was drawn into Ravenloft, Senmet was a priest who served the powerful Anhktepot. An ambitious man, he was not content with his servitor's role and began to plan the downfall of his master. When Anhktepot discovered Senmet's treasonous plotting, he had him mummified and entombed alive. In order to provide the illusion that his reign was unchallenged, Anhktepot buried Senmet with full honors and cast him as a martyr who died to support his pharaoh.

Centuries later, long after Anhktepot's evil earned him a domain in Ravenloft, a young priestess named Isu Rehkotep discovered a magical scroll. She saw at once that it was the process by which Anhktepot created his dreadful greater mummies.

As a noble priestess of the god Osiris, Rehkotep attempted to destroy the scroll, recognizing that it had great power for evil. Her attempts failed, for the magic of the thing would not let it be so easily cast aside. Anxious to see that none should find and use so terrible a treasure, Isu hid it away, naively thinking that it would be lost forever.

Over the years, the power of this evil began to gnaw at her heart. She began to study the works and teachings of Set, the blackest of the dark gods. At first, she believed that she did this only to learn how to recognize evil and thwart it. Gradually, these sinister writings began to take their toll on her. In the end, she began to worship Set as devoutly as she had venerated Osiris.

Now a minon of evil, Rehkotep recovered the mysterious scroll that she had hidden away so long ago. She began to study it and to make plans for its use. What Rehkotep did not fully understand at the time was that her scroll fragments were incomplete. She was able to awaken Senmet, but not to exercise complete control over his actions as she had expected. Still, she does have a limited power to force her will upon Senmet, commanding him for 2 to 8 (2d4) rounds each day. The rest of the time, Senmet is free to do whatever evil deeds he pleases.

Once he was reanimated, Senmet set about plotting to destroy Anhktepot and claim Har'Akir for his own.

Ecology: Unlike all of the other greater mummies that guard Har'Akir's temples and tombs, Senmet was not created by Anhktepot. As such, he cannot be commanded by the lord of Har'Akir.

Adventure Ideas: Senmet is featured in module RA3, *Touch of Death*. It is quite possible that he will survive the end of that scenario, although his foul plans will have been thwarted. Being a creature of great determination and ambition, however, Senmet will look upon any defeat as nothing more than a set-back.

His desire to rule a land of his own may lead Senmet to travel beyond the domain of Har'Akir. He would certainly find the land of Sebua or Kalidnay (as presented in RR1, *Dark Lords* and the *Forbidden Lore* boxed set) to his liking.

Because he seeks to destroy the lord of Har'Akir, player characters might be inclined to help and even trust Senmet. Those who do will quickly learn that they have made a dreadful mistake: The sinister machinations of this undead fiend have no place for mercy or kindness. Senmet is a harsh and cruel creature whose hunger for absolute power makes him as deadly a foe as Anhktepot himself.

As his evil continues to grow, Senmet will become more and more interesting to the dark powers. Indeed, it may not be long before the Mists reach out to grant him his own domain, no doubt to the dismay of PCs who thought him destroyed. If she survived the events of *Touch of Death*, Isu Rehkotep (P8, LE, 35 hp) will accompany him to his new domain; if she perished, she might still be encountered in undead form.

Night Hag (Styrix)

CLIMATE/TERRAIN:	Darkon
FREQUENCY:	Unique
ORGANIZATION:	Solitary
ACTIVITY CYCLE:	Night
DIET:	Carnivore
INTELLIGENCE:	Exceptional (16)
TREASURE:	Nil
ALIGNMENT:	Neutral evil
NO. APPEARING:	1
ARMOR CLASS:	0
MOVEMENT:	9
HIT DICE:	8 (40 hit points)
ThAC0:	13
NO. OF ATTACKS:	1
DAMAGE/ATTACK:	2d6
SPECIAL ATTACKS:	Disease; magical sleep
SPECIAL DEFENSES:	Spell immunities; cold iron, silver, or +3 weapon to hit
MAGIC RESISTANCE:	65%
SIZE:	M (5′ tall)
MORALE:	Average (8)
XP VALUE:	16,000

From time to time, the misty tendrils of Ravenloft reach out into other lands and draw in unsuspecting beings. Often, these creatures are innocents, pulled in seemingly at random. Others are pulled in because of the evil things that they do. In rare cases, however, someone already trapped within the confines of Ravenloft reaches out to snare an outsider. Such is the case with the dreadful Styrix, a native of the lower planes. She was summoned into Ravenloft by one of the few people powerful enough to contain her: Azalin of Darkon. Desperate to escape, Styrix has created a device called the *Rift Spanner,* which, she hopes, will see her clear of Ravenloft's misty borders.

Styrix is a night hag, a member of the foul and horrible race that rules Hades. In her normal form, she appears as a withered old crone with tangled black hair, skin the color of a fresh bruise, and eyes that burn a bright red in the darkness. Her lips are puffy and blistered, giving her a sickly look. Her teeth and nails are sharp and pointed, though the former look crooked and uneven while the latter are cracked and broken.

Like all her evil kind, Styrix is able to *polymorph* at will, so few ever see her true form. The shape that she most commonly takes is that of an elderly, gnarled human woman. In this guise, she often passes herself off as a kindly old soul who is alone and without family. Those who seek to comfort or befriend this poor creature run the risk of a dreadful fate.

Styrix seems to be able to speak any language known to those she encounters. Whether this is an aspect of some magical item in her possession or the product of some enchantment is unknown.

Combat: In melee combat, Styrix generally attacks with a frenzy of ripping claws and biting fangs. This is taken as a single attack that inflicts 2 to 12 (2d6) points of damage. Anyone hit by her must make a successful saving throw vs. poison or be infected with a debilitating disease. This ailment is treated exactly as if it had been produced by the 3rd-level priest spell *cause disease.* While this disease runs its course, the victim's skin is mottled with patches of purple and black that look like open sores and bruises from a dreadful beating. Despite its vile appearance, the disease is not contagious.

In addition to her melee capability, Styrix is able to use many spell-like abilities. At will, she is able to employ *know alignment* and *polymorph self* (although the former is of limited use in Ravenloft because of the detrimental effect that the demiplane has on all detection spells).

As many as 5 times per day, she can release a volley of four *magic missiles,* each of which does 2 to 5(1d4+1) points of damage. Styrix usually targets all of the missiles at a single foe, hoping to destroy that opponent utterly and to cow his or her companions in one stroke. Thrice per day, she is able to project a *ray of enfeeblement.*

Perhaps her most dreadful ability is her power to cast an unusually potent *sleep* spell. This spell can be targeted at any person of up to 12th level (or any monster with up to 12 Hit Dice). A saving throw vs. spell is allowed, but failure indicates that the target has fallen into a deep magical slumber.

Once the victim is unable to defend himself or herself, Styrix will do one of two things. Most of her victims are simply consumed to satisfy her hunger for human flesh. When this happens, the life essence of her victim is torn from the body and transformed into a larva (as described in the MONSTROUS COMPENDIUM *Outer Planes Appendix*). In Styrix's home plane of Hades, these pathetic creatures are used as a sort of macabre currency. Because such things have no value in Ravenloft, Styrix employs them as mindless guardians. It is said that there are vast catacombs beneath her lair filled with these disgusting creatures.

Styrix's other victims are fed into her *Rift Spanner*, and this terrible device absorbs their life energy to power itself. Styrix plans to use the *Rift Spanner* to escape from Ravenloft as soon as it is fully charged.

Those who make their saves against the *sleep* spell will become targeted for special torment and destruction later on through her use of a special ethereal *dreamform*. This state is similar to that induced by the *wraithform* spell but actually allows her to enter the dreams of others.

When she does this, an otherwise normal dream becomes tainted by her foul presence and turns into the vilest nightmare. As soon as she enters the dream, she leaps upon the back of the victim and begins to ride him or her like a horse. Throughout the night, the merciless hag beats and pokes at her mount to keep him or her running until dawn. When at last she leaves the dream and the victim awakes, Styrix has permanently drained away 1 point of his or her Constitution. No natural healing occurs on those fitful nights when Styrix intrudes upon a dream, nor can spells be memorized or psionic strength points be regained from such uneasy slumber. Once someone's Constitution is reduced to 0 by this draining attack, his or her body dies and the spirit is transformed into a larva. The only way to halt this draining process is to destroy Styrix while the victim still has Constitution points left.

There is one restriction on the use of Styrix's *dream-form*: She cannot enter the dreams of anyone whose heart is pure. Thus, only those who have been forced to roll a Ravenloft powers check can be attacked in this manner. Whether or not the check was successful does not matter; only that the character committed some act which required the check in the first place.

Styrix wears a special amulet known as a *charm of blackness*, or *cob*. This periapt is made of dark iron cast in the shape of a 10-pointed star. This pendant has several magical powers and is Styrix's most prized possession. Anyone wearing the charm is instantly cured of any disease that he or she contracts. In addition, the periapt gives its wearer a +2 bonus on every saving throw he or she is required to make. Without her *cob*, Styrix is unable to assume her *dreamform* state. Curiously, the amulet does not bestow this power upon others who come into possession of it. Each time a good-aligned creature uses the *cob*, 1 of its 10 points will break off. When the last point cracks off, the amulet loses its power and becomes worthless. Creating a new *charm of blackness* requires one month of dedicated labor and the destruction of no fewer than 100 larvae.

In addition to her 65% resistance to any type of magic, Styrix is totally immune to any manner of *charm, sleep,* or *fear* spell, nor can she be injured by any fire- or cold-based attack, whether magical or mundane in nature. Most weapons are unable to harm Styrix as well, for only those cast from silver or cold iron, or those which have an enchantment of +3 or better, can "bite" on her withered skin.

Night Hag (Styrix)

Habitat/Society: In the lower planes, Styrix and her foul kindred are the *de facto* rulers of Hades. This is not through any plan or action of their own but is the result of their being the most numerous and most powerful natives of that plane.

Styrix was dragged from her comfortable home in Hades by the power of the lich Azalin. Knowing that the night hags frequently visited the Prime Material Plane seeking souls for the creation of new larvae, he realized that their knowledge of planar travel must be quite extensive—perhaps even sufficient to allow them to enter and leave the Demiplane of Dread at will. No longer able to learn new magics himself, Azalin hoped to cajole a night hag into helping him escape. With this in mind, the lich lord cast a potent spell and opened a gate to the depths of Hades and randomly drew one of the night hags into it.

Much to the surprise of them both, the night hag he summoned, Styrix, proved unable to escape Ravenloft. Like Azalin himself, she was now a prisoner of the demiplane. Although she was enraged by the lich's summoning, she dared not attack him; being an intelligent creature, Styrix recognized that she could not hope to defeat Azalin in a direct confrontation. Thus, she agreed to work with him in his attempts to escape from Ravenloft.

Unbeknownst to Azalin, Styrix made not one but two vows on the night she entered his service. The first was

to devise a method by which she could escape from Ravenloft. The second and secret one was to see to it that Azalin both knew about her escape and was unable to follow.

Months passed, during which Azalin became less and less interested in Styrix's researches. It seemed quite clear to him that she was accomplishing nothing of any importance and that she was draining a great many resources in her efforts. At last, the lich tired of her and cast her out of his dark castle.

What Azalin did not realize was that Styrix had spent her time learning a great deal about the fabric of Ravenloft. Indeed, she had conceived of the design for a machine that might actually be capable of escaping the Demiplane of Dread. Day after day she conducted magical research and unearthed the carefully hidden secrets of the dark realms. In the end, she undoubtedly knew more about the composition of the demiplane than any other living creature.

Free of the lich's yoke, she traveled to the city of Martira Bay on the coast of the Sea of Sorrows. Here, she assumed the guise of an old woman and set up a lair in an old manor on the outskirts of town. For nearly a year, she labored away and built the mysterious *Rift Spanner*.

Recently, she completed work on the dark and terrible machine. It rests in a vast chamber deep beneath the manor house she lives in. The labyrinth of tunnels that encircles the central cavern is filled with larvae created in the months she has lived here. These foul

creatures serve as Styrix's guards, keeping intruders from exploring the caverns. Thanks to them, no one has yet discovered the night hag's true nature or the details of her labors.

Ecology: As a night hag, Styrix is eternally hungry. Each day, she must kill and consume one person. Such a high mortality rate would certainly be noticed were it not for the fact that Martira Bay's waterfront district has a highly transient population. When she hunts in this area, Styrix polymorphs herself into the shape of a comely harlot or a rugged sailor. In either of these forms she is able to move freely through the waterfront district and seek out victims either to satisfy her hunger or fuel her evil machine.

Adventure Ideas: Styrix's plan to escape Ravenloft requires that she fuel her diabolical machine with the life energy of roughly 100 people. This, in addition to her normal hunger, is certainly likely to attract attention. She will gladly claim higher-level characters to power the *Rift Spanner* because they provide correspondingly greater amounts of energy. If she can manage to feed ten 10th-level characters into the machine, for example, it will be fully charged.

Players anxious to find a means of escaping Ravenloft may well covet the *Rift Spanner* themselves. Of course, charging the machine is as evil an act as one is likely to commit. The number of powers checks that must be made to get the machine functioning ought to persuade any player that his or her character would be lost in the attempt to escape Ravenloft. If they come into possession of the charged machine, however, it might well be a fine means of egress.

Player characters can become ensnared in Styrix's activities if they somehow become aware of the disappearances in Martira Bay and search for the cause. Alternatively, they could hear vague rumors of the *Rift Spanner* and come to investigate.

The Rift Spanner

The *Rift Spanner* is a huge device which was designed and built to puncture the fabric of Ravenloft and allow escape from the Demiplane of Dread. Its ability to do this makes it one of the most powerful magical objects ever constructed. When it is fully charged, it can carry up to three human-size creatures across the misty fabric of Ravenloft's ethereal border and back to the Prime Material Plane. However, the very ties with the demiplane that give them their special powers prevents domain lords from being able to escape with this device. They are too firmly tied to Ravenloft, and would simply be left behind when it makes its way clear of the misty borders.

This magical contraption, triangular in shape, comprises a brass framework that stretches some eight feet on a side. The most obvious feature of the device is the great *Iridium Orb* that stands at its center. Fully five feet in diameter, this opalescent sphere glimmers and pulses with the tremendous energies trapped at its heart. Three brass seats, positioned at the corners of the triangular base, face toward the *Orb* with a small bank of controls before each. Leather straps on each seat can be used to secure an occupant.

Although it usually rests in an inert state, the *Rift Spanner* has two operational modes. The first is used to charge the device in preparation for travel. The second is engaged when the machine is ready to attempt transit across the planes.

Charging the *Rift Spanner* is a very difficult, time-consuming, and gruesome operation. In order to operate, the *Iridium Orb* must be charged with life energy. The more energy in the orb, the better the chance that the spanner will reach its intended destination. Anyone who is seated in one of the brass chairs when the spanner's recharging mode is activated will be instantly slain, drained of all life energy. If the victim is not strapped in, he or she may make a successful saving throw vs. death magic to leap out of the chair before being killed. When this happens, the victim is reduced to one half his or her current level (rounded down). If the victim is strapped in or otherwise unable to escape the brass chair, no saving roll is permitted.

Each level the device absorbs gives it a 1% chance of operating successfully when its transit mode is engaged. Thus, if the machine is able to drain ten 5th-level characters of life, it will have a 50% chance of functioning when engaged. Anyone overseeing the charging of the device must make a powers check for each life consumed by the machine.

The orb can hold up to 100 levels of life energy safely. As insurance against negative die modifiers, however, it can be overcharged. Each life energy level beyond the 100th creates a cumulative 1% chance per level of the device exploding when activated, however. If it is ever charged to 200 energy levels, the device will instantly explode. This detonation will be incredible, utterly annihilating everything within 100 yards (no saving throw) and forcing every creature or object between 100 and 1,000 yards to successfully save vs. breath weapons (or disintegration, for items) or be utterly destroyed.

Once the orb is charged, anyone familiar with its operation can set it to travel to a specific point on the Prime Material Plane. Activating the transit mode requires an operator in each of the three chairs to engage a specific control at the exact same time. Failure to trigger all three switches at once bleeds off the energy stored in the orb and forces the machine to be recharged before another travel attempt can be made.

There are three steps in any journey made with the *Rift Spanner*: dematerialization, transit, and rematerialization. Each of these requires a 1d100 roll against the energy level of the orb. Failure on any one of these three checks indicates that the voyage has been aborted. If this happens, the spanner and its occupants are returned to their starting point with the orb utterly drained of energy.

The journey across dimensions is quite perilous. Anyone who is not strapped in when the *Rift Spanner* begins its voyage has a good chance of being tossed clear during the voyage and lost somewhere between the planes. Each time that the dice are rolled to check on the machine's operation, an unsecured passenger must make a successful saving throw vs. death magic or be torn free of the buffeting spanner and lost.

Spectre (Jezra Wagner, The Ice Queen)

CLIMATE/TERRAIN:	Barovia (Mt. Baratok)
FREQUENCY:	Unique
ORGANIZATION:	Solitary
ACTIVITY CYCLE:	Winter nights
DIET:	Body heat
INTELLIGENCE:	HiBh (14)
TREASURE:	(Q×3)
ALIGNMENT:	Lawful evil

NO. APPEARING:	1
ARMOR CLASS:	2
MOVEMENT:	15, Fl 30 (B)
HIT DICE:	7+3 (47 hp)
THAC0:	13
NO. OF ATTACKS:	1
DAMAGE/ATTACK:	2d8
SPECIAL ATTACKS:	Heat drain
SPECIAL DEFENSES:	+1 or better weapon to hit
MAGIC RESISTANCE:	Nil
SIZE:	M (5'1" tall)
MORALE:	Champion (16)
XP VALUE:	7,000

Winters in Barovia are not pleasant things. Icy winds blow down from the peaks of the Balinoks carrying heavy snows and bitter cold. But frostbite and avalanche are not the greatest dangers to be found on the slopes of Mount Baratok. For as the days grow short and the nights stretch out, the ice queen Jezra Wagner rises from her seasonal grave.

Jezra is a spectre, and similar to her undead kin in many ways. She retains the appearance of a living woman, save that light passes through her as if she were some manner of projection or image. Although short, just over five feet in height, Jezra is incredibly beautiful. She has fair skin, silver hair, and pale blue eyes that glint like frozen pools. Jezra's clothes are of the finest manufacture, making it clear to all that she was one of Barovia's most wealthy nobles.

Jezra is able to speak just as she did in life. Her voice is sweet and melodic, but carries a tone of authority. She knows the language of Barovia but not of any of the surrounding domains, as she died before they came into existence. Jezra is fond of singing, and the haunting beauty of her fine voice conveys the misery and suffering of unlife so clearly that it is said to have driven more than one person to an early grave.

Combat: Like all spectres, Jezra's primary attack is made with her chilling touch. Most spectres inflict damage with their touch because of the life-sapping energies of the Negative Material Plane. The ice queen's touch draws its wintery power partly from this source, but also from the manner in which she died. Because of this enhancement, Jezra's touch inflicts 2 to 16 (2d8) points of damage, twice that of the normal spectre's attack.

Jezra does not have the normal level-draining powers of a spectre. Rather, she draws the heat from the bodies of her victims in an attempt to drive off the endless chill that aches in her ghostly bones. Thus, anyone who suffers damage from her touch must make a saving throw vs. death magic. Failure indicates that the body of the victim has been instantly frozen, transforming it into something not unlike a perfect ice sculpture.

Persons who have been frozen can be revived only by great magical power. A *wish* or *limited wish* will be sufficient, but lesser spells will generally fail. By a curious twist of fate, the *simulacrum* spell can be used to restore a body frozen by Jezra to life.

Those who die by falling prey to Jezra and her heat-draining attack do not rise again as spectres but are simply dead; Jezra has no ability to create more undead.

As an undead creature, Jezra is immune to *sleep, charm, hold,* and all manner of life-affecting spells. She has no physical body, so spells designed to affect solid enemies (like a *web*) will not hinder her in any way. Similarly, she is immune to poisons, toxins, diseases, paralysis, and the like. Holy water splashed upon Jezra will inflict 2 to 8 (2d4) points of damage. She can be turned by clerics and paladins, provided that they have attained sufficiently high levels of experience.

Jezra is unusually vulnerable to some magics and utterly immune to others. Any attack which normally inflicts damage with cold or ice has no effect upon her. A *raise dead* cast upon her requires Jezra to make a successful saving throw vs. spell or be instantly destroyed.

As a spectre, the light of day is too pure and true for Jezra to bear. Although it does her no harm, she is powerless to attack or defend herself when caught in its rays. Because of this, she hides herself away and strikes only after the sun has gone down.

Habitat/Society: Jezra Wagner died at the age of 27 some 75 years after the domain of Barovia came into Ravenloft. She was well known among the nobility and common folk alike, for she was as kind and loving a woman as anyone was likely to meet in such a dark land. The tale of her accidental death, and the terrible fate that awaited her on the other side, is one of Ravenloft's most tragic stories.

Jezra's parents were wealthy boyars, or land owners. Their property was considered to be something of a wilderness holding by most of the gentle folk of Barovia because of its remote location on the slopes of Mount Baratok. This unspoiled land was a source of both joy and wealth to its owners, for a fine vein of silver ran amid the stone. For decades, the Wagner clan has overseen the operation of this mine and been well rewarded for their efforts.

Jezra loved the wild lands of her family's ancestral estate. She cherished each season for the special gifts that it brought to the land. Indeed, no matter what the month or how harsh the weather, she and her older brother, Giorggio, could almost always be found exploring the wilderness. Indeed, even after her brother vanished while climbing Mount Baratok, her love of the land remained to console her.

In the spring, she explored the forests, watching as life returned to the land. She would slip quietly up to the nests and lairs of the woodland beasts, marveling at the tenacity that pulled them through the winter. When the wild flowers bloomed, she brought them back to decorate her home.

As spring drifted into summer, she would watch the trees bear sweet fruit, and swim in the chilly waters tumbling down from the mountain top. It is said that she could mimic the call of any bird native to the area and that the thrushes and finches would come at her call to sing for her.

With fall came a shock of spectacular colors. The countryside of Barovia was afire with orange, red, and yellow foliage. This was the harvest time, and few relished the gifts of nature more than Jezra Wagner.

Winter, however, was the season that she loved the most. With the coming of the first snow, she would dash outside to dance and frolic in its chilling embrace; how ironic, then, that it was the snows of winter that claimed her life.

Jezra's end came as the winter solstice drew near one year. She and several of her friends were climbing the slopes of Mount Baratok, hoping to reach its summit and look out across the grandeur of the Balinoks. It was their hope to see the distant spire of Mount Nyid, which was said to be visible from the highest reaches of Baratok. Their expedition was ill-fated, however, and doom claimed it before they reached the mountain's crest.

Jezra was the first to hear the rumbling. Indeed, this is probably what saved her from the sudden death that claimed her companions. Shouting a cry of alarm, she forced her body into a narrow fissure as the avalanche swept past her, ripping her companions from their ropes and sending them down to their deaths. Those who were not slain by the long fall were crushed to death by the weight of the snow that fell upon them.

Jezra, perched in a narrow cleft, was unhurt. She found that the crack she had taken shelter in was in fact a small cave that ran some 20 or 30 feet back into the cliff. The avalanche, however, had sealed the entrance behind her. With horror, she realized that she had been entombed alive.

Several time she tried to dig her way out of the dark cave. Each time, she gave up the futile effort as more snow fell to seal the entrance. It was not long before her small stock of provisions ran low. The candles she had stored in her pack were all used up, the air in the cave was becoming sour, and her food was gone. Soon, she knew, she would die. Cold fear began to grip her heart as she grew drowsy with the approach of death.

What happened next might be accredited to many things. Perhaps the air was growing thin and she was beginning to hallucinate as her brain slowly starved for oxygen. Perhaps the forces of evil saw their chance to claim this young innocent for their own and sent some dreadful agent to treat with her.

Whatever the truth, Jezra found herself bathed in a ghostly light. Her arms and legs had grown numb and frozen, the first victims of her frosty prison, and she sadly noted that this light brought no warmth with it. If anything, the temperature in the cave fell even lower.

Her interest aroused, she tried to draw herself back from the brink of death. Whatever this mysterious phenomenon was, she longed to know its cause before she died. Her eye focused on the source of the glow and delight welled up inside her. Giorggio, so long presumed dead, stood before her.

The vision moved forward. Short and stocky, with the same charismatic smile that she herself had, this was indeed the exact image of her brother. He wore the traveling clothes that she had last seen him in, but they were tattered and torn.

She reached out her hand to the shimmering vision, grimacing at the frigid fire in her lungs and hardly able to move her arm. The image of Giorggio knelt before her and looked at her with curious, almost unrecognizing eyes.

"Save me," was all she could manage to whisper.

"I cannot," came the reply.

Jezra began to cry, the tears freezing before they could fall from her face. The spirit faded away, leaving her alone and isolated in the darkness of her icy tomb. With her last breath, she cried out for someone, anyone, to save her from death, swearing that she would do anything to keep her existence from ending like this. Then she closed her eyes and felt the bitter cold around her steal the pitiful remains of her body's warmth.

Somewhere in the darkness of Ravenloft, her pleas were heard. A strange darkness, deeper than the blackness of the cave, seeped out of the soul of the mountain. It coiled around the young woman's body like an ebony snake. Two pinpoints of red light like eyes smoldered to life, yet drove away none of the darkness. Then, like a cobra striking, the blackness plunged into Jezra's body.

As the last traces of the shade vanished into the corporeal flesh of the woman, Jezra twitched and her face contorted in agony. Unseen in her tomb, her body

Spectre (Jezra Wagner, The Ice Queen)

thrashed about violently for several seconds and then was forever still.

Gradually, a cold glow filled the cave. Jezra blinked and opened her eyes. She could feel her hands and her feet again. The air no longer choked her. The cold, however, was redoubled. Her flesh seemed to tremble endlessly, and her bones pounded with an arthritic ache. She cried out in agony and rose to her feet.

Her only thought was to somehow escape from this icy darkness; had she looked down, she might have seen her own body, unmoving in death. Instead, she plunged desperately into the rocks and ice blocking her escape, passing through them as if they were but fog to her.

Not realizing that she had died in the frozen cave, Jezra spent the next several days wandering the slopes of Mount Baratok. Although her heart longed to return to her family estate, she delayed while she searched for her brother, not realizing that she had now become an undead creature, as had he. Alas, search as she would, she found no trace of him.

At last, Jezra descended the mountain. She was not far from her home when she happened upon a furrier whom she knew slightly. Normally, she would have passed him by with just a cheerful greeting. For some reason, however, she now found herself fascinated with the rough-looking man. She drew near him, feeling the warmth of his body even across a distance of several yards. Suddenly, an intense desire overcame her. She rushed forward and caught the man up in an ethereal embrace. It is unlikely that he ever saw her coming or knew what was happening to him.

For a brief moment, as the body of the furrier crystallized in her arms, she felt a relief from the agony that throbbed in her bones. With a sigh, she stepped back and almost wept with delight. This sensation faded quickly. The agony returned, but she knew now how to ease it for a time at least.

Jezra continued on. She came at last to the home where she had been born and, indeed, where she had lived her entire life. She longed to see her parents again, and imagined to herself their surprise and delight when they learned that their beloved daughter had escaped her companions' fate and survived such hardship to return home once again.

Locating them was not difficult. Ironically, she found them just as they were learning from a group of hunters that their daughter had been claimed by an avalanche. Jezra longed to go to them, to tell them that she had survived, and that they should not mourn.

Instead, she found her attention drawn to the heat flooding off of their bodies. She could taste it like the aroma of fine food. It called to her, urging her to leave her hiding place and attack. The ache in her bones was enough to drive her mad.

At last, she could stand it no more. She tore herself away from the window and fled, launching herself into the night. By the time the sun rose, she had left no fewer than a dozen people dead. With each frozen corpse Jezra's pain was lessened, only to return again as biting as it had ever been.

Three long centuries and more have passed since that terrible day. All that time, Jezra has roamed the frozen slopes of Mount Baratok in search of warmth. She does not realize that she died in the cave, believing instead that she is suffering from some strange curse. From time to time, she escapes the agony of her frozen unlife by drawing the heat from a living body and leaving a crystallized corpse in her wake. When she does this, her pain subsides for a number of minutes equal to the level of her victim.

Ecology: As a living thing, Jezra's influence on the natural world ended long ago. Now, she is a terrible aberration. As an unliving thing, she pollutes the world around her with unnatural death and suffering.

The story of the young girl's death and transformation is not unknown in the land of Barovia. Indeed, the Vistani sing a song called *Regina d'Ghiaccio* or *The Ice Queen* which retells the event almost exactly as it happened. This tragic story is often told as a folk story and is frequently taken to be apocryphal by the scholarly and uneducated alike.

The famous vampire hunter Rudolph Van Richten knows better, having encountered the spectre of Jezra Wagner on at least one occasion. It was his assertion that she might be destroyed by anyone who located her frozen corpse and set it atop a funeral pyre. He attempted to do this himself but found the task beyond him. With remorse, he was forced to abandon his quest to lay this unusual spirit to rest.

Jezra's unlife is tied to the coming of winter. As soon as the snows end and the first rays of spring begin to warm the earth, she is forced to retreat to the mountain cave where her body lies. Here, her spirit reenters the frozen corpse and she sleeps until the last leaf of autumn falls. Thus, the sight of living things that she held so dear in life is lost to her forever.

Adventure Ideas: The obvious adventure here revolves around the destruction of the spectre. There can be much more to such an adventure than a direct confrontation, however. Indeed, when facing the undead, such a rash act is likely to result in the death of one or more party members.

The careful DM will make the adventure revolve around the investigation of Jezra Wagner's life, death, and terrible resurrection. An excellent set of guidelines for such ghost hunting is set down in chapter six of RR5, *Van Richten's Guide to Ghosts*. Using this as a framework, the creative DM ought to be able to construct a great tale of terror to chill the hearts of his or her players.

There are numerous ways that a group of heroes might be drawn into the search for Jezra Wagner. They could be contacted by the modern-day descendants of the Wagner family, who still live in northern Barovia and mine the silver of Mount Baratok. To these people, the story of Jezra and her fate hangs over the head of the family like an ancient curse.

They might also be called upon to complete the quest begun by Dr. Van Richten. With or without his presence, the investigation would follow along the same lines as under the auspices of the Wagner family. Indeed, it is quite possible that the two patrons might come together and seek out the PCs as allies. Van Richten feels that the best way to destroy the spectre is by the cremation of its corporeal body. Thus, he will recommend that this be the focus of the investigation. If the players are acting without his counsel, they are free to act in whatever way they think best.

The adventure might also be set with a more mild beginning. Players who like to explore the world in which their characters live might find the idea of scaling Mount Baratok quite appealing. Of course, they would be certain to encounter the spirit of Jezra Wagner as they climbed higher and higher.

If the PCs are not the type to explore for the sake of exploration, the DM might present them with some reason to travel into the mountains. It might be that a series of murders takes place in Vallaki and the adventurers are called upon to capture the criminal. When he or she flees north toward Markovia, they will have little choice but to follow.

This adventure has the advantage of focusing the attention of the heroes on a red herring. As they battle the snows of the Balinoks, they will expect to confront only the villain they are hunting. Imagine their horror when they find him or her dead and then become themselves hunted by something that must surely have risen from their worst nightmares.

My dear Countess,

For two weeks now we have labored on the treacherous slopes of Mount Baratok. Of the six men who left your so-fine home a fortnight ago, three are now alas dead. Two were slain in an accident and we have laid them to rest beneath the ever-frozen snows of the mountain.

The third, however, has been attacked by the creature we seek. It came upon us suddenly as we rested in camp. So beautiful and angelic was the creature that my heart went out to it. Such is always the case when the fair and innocent are claimed by darkness. In any event, there is no doubt in my mind that this silver-haired phantom was indeed this spirit we sought.

She moved with great speed, flashing through the air and coming to a halt near the fire. It seemed to me that she was attempting to warm herself by it when she threw her head back and let out a cry of suffering. Never have I heard anything so tragic as the agony and longing that hung in the air after that great wail.

Ahmbrose, our cleric, grabbed up his holy symbol and held it out to the creature. She turned to face him, seeming to take no notice of the sacred star that he wielded. Indeed, it seemed only to draw her attention to my beloved Ahmbrose. With the speed that I have already described to you, her hand reached out to touch his cheek.

The contact was slight. Indeed, it seemed that she might almost have been stroking his flesh as might a lover. The effect of the touch on Ahmbrose, however, was terrible. He cried out in pain and tried to pull away. Even as he did so, ice crystals formed along his body. Before any of us could react, he had been transformed into solid ice. His inertia sent his now-brittle form tumbling into the fire. With a great hiss of steam, Ahmbrose's body shattered and the fire was extinguished.

Andreas was the first to get a light going, but it was too late. The spectre had vanished and our companion was dead.

We shall remain on our quest for another week. At the end of that time, however, we shall be forced to retreat. Winter is coming quickly, and I do not intend to give my life to the mountain, as so many others have over the years.

With all respect and admiration,
Rudolph Van Richten
—found among the papers of Lady Catherine Wagner after her death

Thrax (Palik)

CLIMATE/TERRAIN:	Kalidnay
FREQUENCY:	Unique
ORGANIZATION:	Solitary
ACTIVITY CYCLE:	Night
DIET:	Water
INTELLIGENCE:	Very (12)
TREASURE:	K, L, M
ALIGNMENT:	Neutral Evil

NO. APPEARING:	1
ARMOR CLASS:	2
MOVEMENT:	24
HIT DICE:	9 (52 hit points)
THAC0:	11
NO. OF ATTACKS:	1
DAMAGE/ATTACK:	2d6
SPECIAL ATTACKS:	Dehydration; psionics
SPECIAL DEFENSES:	Psionics
MAGIC RESISTANCE:	Nil
SIZE:	M (6'8" tall)
MORALE:	Elite (15)
XP VALUE:	4,000

PSIONICS SUMMARY:

Level	Dis/Sci/Dev	Att/Def	Score	PSPs
2	1/2/4	—/—	12	66

Psychometabolism—*Sciences:* Complete Healing and Shadow-Form. *Devotions:* Aging, Cause Decay, Displacement, and Double Pain.

Several years ago, the Mists of Ravenloft reached out to the strange and alien land of Athas. Moving across burning sands that stretched endlessly beneath a smoldering crimson sun, the dark powers settled over the city-state of Kalidnay. There, a terrible magic was being worked by the twisted templar Thakok-An. His spell failed, and he and his city were drawn into the Demiplane of Dread (the details of this tragedy are presented in the *Forbidden Lore* boxed set). Most of the folk of Kalidnay and the neighboring town of Artan-ak died that day, but some survived and rebuilt the city-state under Thakok-An's guidance. Unknown to the templar, however, the dark powers brought other foul horrors of Athas into Ravenloft with him, one of the most dangerous of whom is Palik.

Palik is a thrax, one of the most terrible creatures to be found on Athas. From any distance more than a few feet away, he looks much like a mul: the unique hybrid of dwarf and human found only under the dark sun. His skin is dark and ruddy, a trait not uncommon in Kalidnay, and his ears are pointed like those of an elf. His body is greatly muscled, indicating a tremendous strength that would give even the greatest wrestler pause. His pale blue eyes shimmer like a desert oasis; when not maddened by his all-consuming thirst, they reveal him as a rational, intelligent being.

A closer look at Palik, especially an examination of his hands, reveals his inhuman nature. Palik's fingers are unnaturally long, fanning out at the tips to end in disgusting suckers. It is this vile adaptation that marks him as a predator of the sands.

Thrax speaks the language of Kalidnay, but knows no other tongue. He can neither read nor write.

Combat: Palik tends to stalk his prey in shadow-form, for, while this reduces him to a movement rate of 6, it makes him both difficult to detect and attack. In this state, he cannot cross open, well-lit areas, but he is impossible to detect without magical or psionic means. He cannot be attacked while in shadow-form, but neither can he himself strike at an enemy. Once Palik has found a victim, he resumes his normal form and attacks with his incredible speed.

If Palik's chosen target wears armor, he will use his psionic ability to Cause Decay in an attempt to destroy it. This requires him to make an attack roll, for he must touch the armor to affect it. A successful use of this power (as described in PHBR5, *The Complete Psionics Handbook*) causes the armor to corrode into useless debris instantly unless it passes an item saving throw vs. acid.

If the victim has no armor, or after his or her armor has been destroyed, Palik moves in for the kill. Palik's great blows inflict 2 to 12 (2d6) points of damage each. An unarmored victim who is successfully hit must make a saving throw vs. petrification. Failure indicates that Palik has attached his deadly suckers to the victim's exposed flesh and can begin to drain away the water in his or her body that same round.

If the target's armor has survived Palix's psionic attack, or if the victim has Armor Class bonuses due to Dexterity or magical items (for example, a *ring of protection*), then there is a chance equal to 10% times the target's AC that the thrax will make contact with bare flesh (thus, Palik has only a 30% chance of using his special attack against someone in plate armor). Anyone with an AC of 0 or less is safe from Palik's water-draining attack, but such a person might still be beaten to death by the enraged thrax.

Once his suckers are attached, Palik begins to feed by absorbing the water from his victim's body. It takes roughly 1 minute per 20 pounds of body weight for a victim's body water to be drained away. Thus, it takes Palik roughly 10 minutes to fully absorb the moisture from a 200-pound man.

The absorption process is extremely painful for Palik's victim. At the end of each round, the victim loses one-fifth of the hit points he or she had when the feeding process started and must make a saving throw vs. death magic. Failure indicates that the pain has been too great and the victim loses consciousness. As the process continues, the victim suffers a cumulative –2 penalty to the save each round after the first. Any attack or other action made by a character who is currently being drained by the thrax suffers this penalty as well. Once the draining process is 75% complete, the victim always loses consciousness due to the severe dehydration. The pain of Palik's feeding is so great that it is impossible for his victim to cast spells or employ psionic powers while his suckers are doing their evil work.

Those who die from Palik's attack become dried-out husks. From a distance, they look withered and mummified. At the slightest touch, however, the body crumbles away into fine, powdery dust. Once the integrity of the corpse has been broken, resurrection is impossible.

Those who escape from Palik's deadly attack after he has tasted the fluids of their body are in a far more deadly danger. Such persons must make a successful saving throw vs. death magic or become a thrax. The transformation of a living man or woman into a thrax is terrible to behold. The process takes 2 to 4 (1d3+1) weeks, during which time the victim is driven almost mad with thirst and pain. A *remove curse* spell cast upon the victim during this period will instantly end the process. Once the change is complete, however, nothing short of a *wish* can save the victim. Only humans can be transformed into thrax; all other races are immune to the process.

Habitat/Society: When Thakok-An and the city of Kalidnay were drawn into Ravenloft, Palik was stalking a wandering merchant near what is now called Bleak Knoll. He was about to strike when the young man cried out in pain and toppled over. Indeed, Palik himself felt a brief instant of agony. Curious, the thrax moved nearer to the body and examined it. He had clearly been robbed of a victim, for the fellow was dead, but the cause of death was impossible to determine. Palik shrugged and set the matter aside as he drained the corpse of water, leaving a dried-out and withered body.

After feeding, Palik stood and looked around. So his horror, he saw that the entire landscape of Kalidnay had changed. No longer could he see the splendid stone spire of the Great Spear to the north or the low, jagged ridge of the Cracked Spine to the west. Now, the city was an island at the heart of the Sea of Silt. What terrible magic might have caused this he could not imagine.

In the years that have passed since Kalidnay became a domain of Ravenloft, Palik has watched the population of the city grow from the handful that survived the mysterious transition into a great host. He has managed to survive and to keep his presence fairly secret by feeding on escaped slaves, lone travelers on the road to Artanak, and the occasional adventurer. Secrecy and concealment are foremost in his mind when he is hunting.

He has learned something of the nature of Ravenloft from encounters with outsiders. He has decided that he must escape the close confines of Kalidnay and travel through these other lands. He believes, correctly, that there are few (if any) of his kind in this strange demiplane besides himself. This anonymity would enable him to move freely about and hunt openly again, something he desires more than anything else.

Ecology: Palik's kind have long been known and hated on Athas. As such, he knows that a concerted effort will be made to destroy him if the people of Kalidnay learn of his existence. Because of this, he is always careful to destroy the bodies of his victims and to make certain that no one he attacks escapes to tell the tale. On the latter note, he is also very careful not to allow the creation of another thrax.

Adventure Ideas: Palik's burning desire to escape Kalidnay is a fine source of adventure scenarios. Arranging for the players to meet him is easy enough once they are in Kalidnay City. Every so often, strong-looking men and women are "recruited" by the templars there to serve as gladiators in the arena. In addition, any wizards spotted in the domain are hunted down and killed in an ongoing effort to root out defilers. Either of these events is likely to send the PCs fleeing from the city and into the wilds to the north where Palik stalks prey. He almost always takes time to converse with outsiders before killing them in hopes that they can help him leave behind this island in the Sea of Silt.

Treant, Evil (Blackroot)

CLIMATE/TERRAIN:	Tepest
FREQUENCY:	Unique
ORGANIZATION:	Solitary
ACTIVITY CYCLE:	Any
DIET:	Carnivorous
INTELLIGENCE:	Very (11)
TREASURE:	Q×5, X
ALIGNMENT:	Chaotic evil

NO. APPEARING:	1
ARMOR CLASS:	0
MOVEMENT:	12
HIT DICE:	12 (84 hit points)
THAC0:	9
NO. OF ATTACKS:	2
DAMAGE/ATTACK:	4d6/4d6
SPECIAL ATTACKS:	Animate trees; spells
SPECIAL DEFENSES:	Spells
MAGIC RESISTANCE:	Nil
SIZE:	H (18′ tall)
MORALE:	Elite (14)
XP VALUE:	14,000

The domain of Tepest has long suffered under the evil of the three hags who rule it. Their wickedness has seeped into the land, permeating it and poisoning even the plants and beasts of the forests. Perhaps the most awful example of this corrupting taint is the dreaded Blackroot. This evil treant dwells southwest of Lake Kronov, near the borders with G'Henna and Markovia. None who pass through these woods do so without attracting his notice and, if care is not taken, his wrath.

Blackroot is a foul and terrible thing. He stands just over 18 feet tall and looks like an ancient oak. His bark is grooved and rough, providing excellent protection from physical attacks. His branches are long and gnarled, never sprouting leaves or showing even the faintest hints of bud or blossom. When he wishes to be seen for what he is, a gnarled face appears to form from the fissures and grooves of his bark. A great and terrible maw, shaped like an inverted V, opens up beneath two knotty eyes.

Blackroot, like most treants of any alignment, is able to speak with the animals of the forest. His evil is so pervasive, however, that the traditionally neutral animals of the forest near him have become neutral evil. Thus, even the most innocent creature in Blackroot's realm can be a potential enemy for PCs, reporting their every action back to their treant master. Blackroot speaks the languages of Tepest and each of its neighboring domains. He seems to have no understanding of writing, not recognizing it as a form of communication.

Combat: Those who enter the forest attempting to destroy Blackroot are seldom seen again. If they are not destroyed by the wilderness which he commands, they usually perish in combat with this ancient, evil creature when they find him. Blackroot can attack twice per combat round, inflicting 4d6 points of damage with each blow that strikes its target. His tremendous strength and mass is such that it enables him to crumple even plate armor as easily as if it were cardboard.

Blackroot's thick bark provides him with excellent protection from most attacks. However, his plantlike biology makes him very vulnerable to attacks made with magical or mundane fire. Any weapon or spell that employs fire gains a +4 bonus on the attack and inflicts an extra +1 point of damage per die. In addition, any save that Blackroot must make against fire-based attacks is made with a –4 penalty.

Because of this vulnerability, Blackroot will quickly attempt to destroy anyone who is careless with fires in his woods. As he is well aware of the danger that such enemies pose, he prefers to act indirectly against them, directing the savage wolves of Tepest and other animals of the forest to destroy fire-wielding enemies for him. Only if these means fail will he seek a direct confrontation.

All evil treants are very dangerous; Blackroot is even worse than most, having grown in soil tainted with the evil of Tepest's three hags. This infusion of evil has given him several magical abilities that most of his kind do not possess. Once per day he may cast the following spells as a 12th-level druid: *animal friendship, animal growth, animal summoning I, animal summoning II, anti-animal shell, anti-plant shell, call woodland beings, charm person or mammal, create water, entangle, hold animal, hold plant, locate animals or plants, plant growth, putrefy food & drink, repel insects, snare, speak with animals, speak with monsters, speak with plants, spike growth, summon insects, wall of thorns,* and *warp wood.* Blackroot has no need of components for his spells; they are all simple acts of will.

Blackroot has the ability to animate the trees of his

forest, causing them to obey his mental commands. It takes one round for an animated tree to uproot itself, but once this is done it is fully mobile. At any given time he may have two such followers doing his bidding. These trees conform to the statistics for mature treants, having 10 Hit Dice and inflicting 3 to 18 (3d6) points of damage with each of their two attacks. They are not actually intelligent but do serve as extensions of Blackroot's own consciousness. Trees under his control must remain within 60 yards of their master, or they revert to their normal status.

Habitat/Society: Blackroot began his life as a tree, not a treant. He was a majestic and noble plant towering above the other trees of the forest and fairly radiating health and stamina. Indeed, so wondrous was this fine oak that a sect of druids settled around it to protect and nurture the ancient plant.

It was not long, of course, before the hags who rule Tepest took notice both of the tree and its protectors. They saw that more and more people were turning to the ways of the druids, venerating nature and its "balance." Such a shift in attention away from the action of the vain and terrible coven was unacceptable.

In order to set things straight, the hags decided to destroy the druids. In order to make certain that others learned the druids' lesson, the hags set down a powerful curse on them. One by one, each of the druids was transformed into a twisted and putrefied tree. So sinister and terrible to look upon were these new trees that the people of Tepest began to avoid the woods. They took to calling the regions southwest of Lake Kronov *Brujamonte* or *Witches' Wood*. As these newly created trees took root, the other flora and fauna of the wilds began to change until they too were twisted and corrupted.

The great oak, however, they reserved for special attention. In their horrible iron cauldron, they brewed a special draught. Composed of things dark and dreadful, it was practically liquified evil. When their brew was done, they took it out to the forest and dribbled it on the roots of the tree. Every night for a month the trio gathered around the tree at midnight and repeated their dark ritual. In the end, as a full moon the color of blood rose into a cloudless sky, the great oak's transformation was completed. With the hags dancing and cackling over their success, Blackroot was born.

Over the years, this once-great tree has become more and more evil. Now shriveled and twisted, a nightmarish reflection of the resplendent plant that he had once been, Blackroot rules the Witches' Wood. Through the plants and animals of the forest, he keeps a careful eye on all that transpires in that vile place. While he is not under any form of mental domination, he does the bidding of the hags out of respect for their greater evil and in the hopes that he might one day replace them as the master of Tepest.

Ecology: Blackroot survives on a diet of human, demi-human, and humanoid flesh. Because of the large number of goblins that infest the woods of Tepest, he is frequently able to satisfy his hunger without molesting travelers on the Timori Road. From time to time, however, he becomes hungry for sweeter, human flesh. Generally, this happens about once a month.

Anyone who enters the forests of southwestern Tepest will instantly become aware of that place's evil nature. The trees produce bitter fruit, the streams are brackish, stinging insects are everywhere, and thorny undergrowth hinders progress in every direction.

Adventure Ideas: The players might come into contact with Blackroot and his forest entirely by accident. Such an encounter could easily occur as they traveled the Timori Road into or out of Tepest. Blackroot frequently orders his trees to attack caravans and parties traveling on that highway to satisfy his hunger for flesh.

On the other hand, the destruction of the druid cult could also be used as a motivation for the PCs to enter the Brujamonte. The very nature of this corrupted wood should entice any druid in the party to examine its mysteries. Groups without such a person in their company could easily be contacted and hired to learn what happened to the druids who once lived in Tepest.

Adventures centering on Blackroot should focus not only on the destruction of the evil treant but also on the restoration of the area. This was once an area of great natural splendor and, with a great deal of effort, it might someday be restored to that state.

Of course, the hags who rule Tepest (detailed in RR1, *Dark Lords*) are certain to take notice of anyone who attempts to destroy their handiwork. They take great pride in the malignant ugliness of the Witches' Wood, and player characters attempting to set right the changes that they have made in the *Brujamonte* are certain to be looked upon as challengers to their authority. As such, the hags will simply seek to destroy them.

Vampire, Illithid (Athaekeetha)

CLIMATE/TERRAIN:	Bluetspur area
FREQUENCY:	Unique
ORGANIZATION:	Solitary or pack
ACTIVITY CYCLE:	Night
DIET:	Brains; life energy
INTELLIGENCE:	Insane (1)
TREASURE:	Nil
ALIGNMENT:	Chaotic evil

NO. APPEARING:	1
ARMOR CLASS:	1
MOVEMENT:	12
HIT DICE:	8+3 (55 hit points)
THAC0:	11 (9)
NO. OF ATTACKS:	4
DAMAGE/ATTACK:	1d6+4
SPECIAL ATTACKS:	Mind blast; energy drain
SPECIAL DEFENSES:	+1 or better weapon to hit; regeneration
MAGIC RESISTANCE:	90%
SIZE:	M (6'4" tall)
MORALE:	Fearless (20)
XP VALUE:	14,000

One of the most terrible domains in Ravenloft is the dread Bluetspur. Located in the far south of the core lands, it is a land of madness and insanity. The vile illithids (or *mind flayers*) who dwell there keep great herds of intelligent creatures as cattle, feeding on their brains. For these wretched creatures, life is only a period of waiting before an agonizing death. But there are creatures here that even the illithids fear, things made all the more terrible by the fact that the mind flayers themselves created them.

Athaekeetha, like all of the vampire illithids, was created in a foul experiment conducted by the vampire Lyssa Von Zarovich and the High Master of the mind flayers. The experiment was part of an ultimately successful attempt to transform the latter into a vampire. The "prototype" vampire illithids created by these experiments were believed to have been destroyed, but their regenerative powers enabled them to survive and escape into the wild, where they have flourished.

While they look much like normal illithids, this undead species wears no clothing and moves about like wild beasts. Their craniums are smaller than those of their living kin, perhaps a sign of their lower intelligence. Vampire illithids have feeding tendrils that are much longer and thicker than those of normal mind flayers; in addition to their primary purpose of boring through the skull to extract the brains within, these tentacles make excellent bludgeoning weapons, striking with great strength.

Like all vampire illithids, Athaekeetha is unable to speak or communicate with other races. It does seem to be able to convey information its fellow vampire illithids, however; possibly by some manner of rudimentary telepathy. Attempts to communicate with Athaekeetha by magical or psionic means have always failed and always require a madness check (as described in the *Forbidden Lore* boxed set).

Combat: Vampire illithids are able to employ the combat tactics of both vampires and illithids. Their undead nature makes them physically powerful (Strength 18/76), granting them a bonus of +2 to hit (for an adjusted THAC0 of 9) and +4 to damage in any melee attack.

As a rule, Athaekeetha begins any attack by unleashing a powerful *mind blast*. This attack takes the shape of a cone some 60 feet long with a 5-foot-wide base and a 20-foot-wide mouth. Anyone caught in this area must make a successful saving throw vs. wands or be stunned for 14 rounds. Further, any creature which is at least semi-intelligent must make a madness check (see the *Forbidden Lore* boxed set or module RQ2, *Thoughts of Darkness* for details). Dungeon Masters not using these additional rules should substitute horror checks instead.

Once its victims have been stunned, Athaekeetha charges into melee, attacking with its four feeding tentacles. Each tentacle strikes for 5 to 10 (1d6+4) points of damage and drains two levels of life energy from the victim. A stunned or helpless victim's brain can then be consumed in 4 rounds.

As a vampire, Athaekeetha regenerates 3 points of damage each round. In addition, every time it drains life energy from a victim, it instantly heals 2d8 hit points of damage it has suffered.

Many types of attacks have little or no effect upon Athaekeetha. Like most undead, the vampire illithid is immune to any form of *charm, hold,* or *sleep* spell. It cannot be harmed by poisons or disease, and its mind flayer heritage gives it a staggering 90% magic resistance. Further, nonmagical weapons will not bite upon its rubbery skin.

In spite of its many powers, Athaekeetha is burdened with the weaknesses of the undead as well. It can be turned by clerics or paladins of sufficient level, but only at a –6 penalty. It is not held at bay by holy symbols but can be burned by holy water, which does 1d6 points of damage per vial.

The degenerated state of Athaekeetha's mind keeps it from using many of the special powers that mark both vampires and illithids. For instance, it cannot *charm* enemies or use any of the illithid spell-like or psionic abilities besides *mind blast*. It cannot change shape, as most vampires do, and is unable to summon lesser creatures for aid. Because Athaekeetha is a product of magical experimentation and not a true undead, it cannot create more of its kind.

Destroying Athaekeetha is no simple task. Most vampire illithids are forced into gaseous form if reduced to zero hit points and must spend the next 24 hours reforming their corporeal bodies, during which time they are extremely vulnerable and can be slain by any attack. However, while Athaekeetha's physical form can be temporarily destroyed by massive damage, its body continues to regenerate, even if reduced to below zero hit points. Eventually, it will recover from even the most complete destruction; even such foolproof methods as cremation have proved ineffectual. Therefore, the best way to defeat Athaekeetha is to reduce its body to ashes and then imprison the remains in some sort of permanent magical trap.

Sunlight does not harm illithid vampires, although they hate it and will avoid it whenever possible. Other bright lights (including *continual light* spells and the like) offend them, and they will attempt to destroy the source of such illumination whenever they can.

Habitat/Society: Athaekeetha was the last vampire illithid created by Lyssa Von Zarovich and the High Master before they gave up on the experiment; its higher intelligence is proof that at least some progress was being made in the project. Like the rest, Athaekeetha survived the High Master's attempt to destroy these flawed creations and fled into the catacombs that run beneath the entire domain of Bluetspur. With insane cunning, it has since evaded all attempts to recapture or destroy it, remaining free to wreak havoc on any unfortunate enough to fall into its clutches.

While the majority of this debased breed have remained near the mind flayer city, Athaekeetha prefers to haunt the surface, especially along the borders of neighboring domains. Rumors have begun to surface in Hazlan of strange and terrible creatures moving in packs and attacking travelers on the road between Toyalis and Sly-Var. Similar stories have been told in Barovia's village of Immol. These accounts, though unconfirmed, might indicate that Athaekeetha has gathered others of its kind about it and is beginning to look beyond the borders of Bluetspur for prey. If this is the case, it is dark news indeed. Few would deny that these foul creatures are among the most horrible beasts in Ravenloft.

Ecology: Athaekeetha and the rest of its evil breed have no place in the natural order of things. However, since the domain of Bluetspur has only the shattered remnants of an ecology, this is of little consequence. They do not breed and cannot reproduce themselves by preying upon others, as most undead do. They seek to slake their bestial hungers for the blood, brains, and life energy of their victims but can survive for long periods without feeding.

Adventure Ideas: The vampire illithids are introduced in the adventure *Thoughts of Darkness*. Athaekeetha itself is not mentioned by name but could easily be inserted into that storyline to add yet another twist to an already tangled puzzle for the players.

A Dungeon Master wishing to run a highly unusual adventure could arrange for his or her players to receive a plea for help from the mind flayers of Bluetspur. The vampire illithids have begun to become a serious nuisance as they have claimed more and more illithid lives; the Elder Brain decrees that they be stopped. To minimize the distraction, expendable outsiders (the PCs) are brought in to deal with the menace, attracted by extremely generous rewards in the form of magical items harvested from past victims. Mind flayers are highly lawful and will keep their agreement with the PCs to the letter, but they are also wholly evil and will exploit any loopholes in the contract, so the PCs would be well advised to negotiate carefully. . . .

On another note, Athaekeetha and his savage followers might well begin to prey upon the humans, demihumans, and even monsters who dwell in the domains that border Bluetspur. A group of player characters acting as part of a town militia or as guards for a caravan might therefore encounter vampire illithids under the command of Athaekeetha. Such an encounter might be part of a planned investigation or utterly accidental. Imagine the shock of player characters exploring the mysteries of Forlorn or wandering the forests of Kartakass when a pack of degenerate undead mind flayers jumps them from the shadows.

Vampire, Eastern (Mayónaka)

CLIMATE/TERRAIN:	Any
FREQUENCY:	Unique
ORGANIZATION:	Solitary
ACTIVITY CYCLE:	Night
DIET:	Special
INTELLIGENCE:	Exceptional (15)
TREASURE:	F
ALIGNMENT:	Chaotic evil
NO. APPEARING:	1
ARMOR CLASS:	1
MOVEMENT:	18
HIT DICE:	8+3 (43 hit points)
THAC0:	11 (8); (5 with katana)
NO. OF ATTACKS:	1 (touch) or 3/2 (with katana)
DAMAGE/ATTACK:	1d6+7; 1d10+10 or 2d6+10
SPECIAL ATTACKS:	Energy drain; jump; swordsmanship
SPECIAL DEFENSES:	+1 or better weapons to hit; regeneration; invisibility; half-damage from cold and electricity
MAGIC RESISTANCE:	Nil
SIZE:	M (7' tall)
MORALE:	Champion (16)
XP VALUE:	10,000

Mayónaka wanders the domains of the Core, seeking out the greatest warriors in Ravenloft and challenging them to duels. While he hopes that he will die in such a match one day and thus be freed of his eternal curse, he has yet to meet anyone strong or skilled enough to defeat him.

Mayónaka dresses himself in common robes that effectively conceal his oriental arms, armor, and features from the people that he encounters in his travels. Beneath his robes, he wears the armor of a samurai and carries an assortment of unusual weapons. Mayónaka stands just under seven feet tall and has the smooth build of a graceful athlete. His hair is short and dark, matching perfectly the endless night reflected in his midnight black eyes.

Mayónaka speaks the Common Tongue of Kara-Tur, as well as that spoken in the western realms of Toril. He has picked up a fragmentary knowledge of the languages of Ravenloft's various domains, but this is only satisfactory for simple conversations.

Combat: As an expert warrior, Mayónaka is a deadly opponent. With the abilities he gained as a vampire, he is almost unbeatable.

Like all vampires, Mayónaka is tremendously strong. Indeed, he is even more powerful than most of his undead kin. His unnatural Strength rating of 19 gives him a +3 bonus on all melee attack rolls and a +7 bonus to all melee damage rolls, for a total of 8–13 (1d6+7) points of damage for each bare-handed blow.

In addition to the damage inflicted by his crushing blows, anyone struck by Mayónaka is instantly drained of two life energy levels. This is a by-product of the vampire's terrible nature and can be used by Mayónaka whenever he touches the exposed flesh of a victim. He need not employ this special ability if he chooses not to.

Mayónaka does not normally fight bare-handed. Instead, he wields a keen silver katana, or oriental sword, that has been in his family for generations. Oriental runes run down the side of the blade, naming it *Tasogare* or "twilight" in the language of Mayónaka's homeland. The katana is described in PHRB1, *The Complete Fighter's Handbook*; it can be used either one- or two-handed. As a one-handed weapon it does 1d10 points of damage against small or medium-sized targets and 1d12 against large ones. As a two-handed weapon it does 2d6 to both types of targets. The katana is a medium weapon that weighs 6 pounds and has a speed factor of 4. *Tasogare* is enchanted, giving it a +3 on all attack and damage rolls. In addition, once per day it can be used to cast a *darkness, 15' radius* spell. Anyone holding the sword can see normally in the area of darkness, which remains centered on the weapon itself. Mayónaka's Strength bonus of +3 to attack and +7 to damage applies when using *Tasogare*.

Like all eastern vampires, Mayónaka has the ability to render himself *invisible* at will. When in this state, he has all of the normal advantages associated with invisibility (such as a −4 on all attack rolls made against him). When he is about to enter combat, fading from view is generally his first action.

Anyone attempting to attack Mayónaka must employ a weapon that has at least a +1 enchantment. Any weapon of lesser quality will pass through his body without seeming to strike anything. Even if magical weapons are employed and he is harmed, Mayónaka regenerates 3 hit points per melee round.

If he is driven to 0 hit points, Mayónaka is not slain. Rather, he is forced to assume a gaseous state similar to that created by a *wraithform* spell (see below). Once in this state, he has 12 rounds to reach his current resting place. If he fails to accomplish this feat, his vaporous form breaks up and he is destroyed. If he does reach his resting place, he must rest there for 8 hours and will then rise again with his body wholly regenerated. When he is in this vaporous form, no weapon or spell can harm him, he can pass through even the smallest crack or opening, and he appears to be nothing more than a drifting cloud of shimmering fog. Unlike more traditional vampires, he cannot assume this state at will but must be driven to it by the destruction of his physical body. Similarly, he has no natural ability to shape change.

As an undead creature, Mayónaka is immune to all manner of *sleep, charm, hold,* or other spells that depend upon biological function for their effects. Poisons, diseases, and similar things have no effect upon him at all. His undead nature also makes him very resistant to cold and lightning, so that all such attacks do only half damage to him.

Mayónaka has the natural ability to *spider climb* and *jump,* as if he were employing the spells of the same names. He uses these abilities to seek out his victims and to escape from his pursuers when need be. Like all eastern vampires, he lacks the natural charming or summoning abilities of the western vampire.

There are means by which Mayónaka can be held back and even driven away by those who have the courage and wisdom to confront him with the correct tools. He cannot approach anyone who presents a lawful good holy symbol. Instead, he must remain at least 10 feet away from the symbol until some means can be found of removing the offensive object. It is important that the person presenting the icon be a strong believer in the deity to which the symbol is sacred, however, or it will have no effect upon the vampire. Similarly, he cannot bear the presence of ginger root and will not come within 10 feet of it. If an unbroken line of powdered ginger is made on the floor, he cannot cross it.

It is possible, although quite dangerous, to use some of these items as weapons against the vampire. If he is touched with a holy symbol, his flesh is burned for 1d6+1 points of damage. Holy water or ginger juice splashed upon him does 1d6+1 points of damage per vial that strikes his flesh.

Exposure to direct sunlight is just as deadly for Mayónaka as it is for any other vampire. Thus, a single round of exposure to the purifying rays of the sun will utterly annihilate him. However, running water has no negative effect on Mayónaka. Further, he is not required to obtain an invitation before entering the home of a potential victim, nor do mirrors distress him.

Unlike the traditional vampire, Mayónaka's resting place is not dictated by the place in which he died. He has no need to maintain a coffin or similar sanctuary. When the sun lights the eastern sky, Mayónaka must seek out the place where he last killed someone. He must find a lair within 100 feet of the spot on which his victim died in which to pass the daylight hours. If he cannot escape the daylight and remain within the required radius of the kill, his body crumbles away and he dies.

Any human slain by Mayónaka's life-energy drain will become a vampire in turn. The transformation into unlife occurs one day after burial. Those who are not buried will not rise as vampires; thus, tradition dictates that all who die at the hands of these undead be cremated. Mayónaka recognizes the horrible nature of the living death and would wish it on no other, so he never willingly creates new undead. When he takes a life with his level-draining ability, he always sees to it that the body is destroyed. If the victim died with honor, he arranges a very solemn ritual in which great respect is shown for a worthy enemy before a pyre is set and the body destroyed. If the victim died in a cowardly or dishonorable way, then no such courtesy is shown and the body is merely tossed onto a fire and forgotten.

Habitat/Society: Mayónaka was born nearly a century ago in the lands of Kara-Tur in the FORGOTTEN REALMS campaign setting. He came from a noble family, having a father and mother who were both samurai of great distinction. As the youngest of three children, Mayónaka lived in the shadow of his two older sisters, who were proving themselves to be masterful warriors. Their growing fame simply made Mayónaka more determined to win a name for himself as a samurai greater than any who had ever lived before.

His chance came when he was seventeen years old. Both of his sisters had vanished while exploring an island that was said to be haunted. It was generally assumed that anything deadly enough to defeat them was more than a match for anyone else, so few were interested in investigating the matter. Mayónaka, however, took up his sword and set out for the island.

As he explored the island, he discovered that it was indeed the lair of some horrible, undead creature. Further, he found that the beast had captured his sisters and was subjecting them to horrible tortures and temptations in an attempt to corrupt their honorable souls.

Sickened by what he saw, Mayónaka vowed to free his sisters and see to it that the monster was destroyed. Moving as quietly as he could, Mayónaka crept into the monster's lair and reached the cages where his sisters were held. As he worked to free them, the sisters told him of their capture and the hideous vampire spirit that had tortured them. Working quickly, Mayónaka managed to free them and the three began to flee the villain's cave.

Suddenly, the invisible vampire attacked them. In the confusion that followed the surprise attack, Mayónaka was sent tumbling over what appeared to be an almost bottomless fissure. His sisters, enraged by the loss of their brother, drove the monster off and escaped from the island in Mayónaka's ship, little knowing that their brother still lived.

Hours later, Mayónaka awoke on a ledge that protruded from the walls of the endless shaft. With much effort, he climbed the rough stone face and reached the vampire's lair. Much to his horror he found that the creature was fully recovered from its earlier wounds. Delighted to discover that it might still have a prisoner to torture, the vampire attacked. The battle was long and terrible. In the end, the samurai was triumphant. Sadly, he too was dying. The vampire had tasted his life essence and left his soul drained and tainted. With a final prayer to his ancestors, he died.

Vampire, Eastern (Mayónaka)

To his surprise, he awoke a day or so later. His wounds, it seemed, were completely healed. Indeed, he felt better than he ever had before. He left the vampire's lair and headed out of the cave. With luck, he hoped to rejoin his sisters before they left the island. As he reached the cave's mouth and stepped out into the sunlight, he found himself wracked with horrible pain. He turned and tossed himself back into the cool darkness of the cavern just in time. With horror, he realized that he himself had become undead.

Mayónaka spent the next several days coming to grips with his new condition. While any lesser man would have collapsed in despair and given in to the bestial urges that now burned within him, the samurai did not. Instead, he meditated and prayed, seeking the council of his ancestors. At last, he decided that he must return to his home. With luck, the priests there could drive this curse from his body.

Mayónaka fashioned a crude boat and set sail. He spent the next few days at sea. Each morning, he would retreat into a coffinlike wooden box until the daylight passed. Because he had not yet slain anyone, he was not bound to rest in a given area. The voyage was difficult, not because of bad weather or lack of seamanship, but because Mayónaka was beginning to feel the vampire's hunger for human life. By the time he reached the shores of his native land, he found himself weak with hunger.

Because he was left without navigational instruments, Mayónaka was not certain where he had come ashore. He began to explore, coming across a monastic encampment of monks. Careful not to reveal his nature to them, Mayónaka presented himself to them shortly after nightfall and asked for their help. They took him in and answered all his question. Much to his delight, he found that he was within 30 miles of his home.

The night passed quickly, for the monks saw many travellers and had news of Mayónaka's sisters and their return. He learned, as he had expected, that he was believed to have died in the battle with the vampire. Indeed, it seemed that his sisters were being hailed as great heroes for their valor in destroying the beast.

Had his mind been clear, the young vampire should have known that this was to be expected. However, the darkness that is vampire's blood burned in his veins now. Reason faded before an onslaught of sinister emotions, jealousies, and hatred. Soon he had convinced himself that his sisters deliberately left him for dead, fleeing before the threat of the vampire so that they could return home and claim victory. Indeed, had it been only an accident that sent him tumbling into that chasm? Probably not. Perhaps they had even struck a deal with the vampire to lure their brother out to the island. No doubt they knew that he was destined to become a far more skilled warrior than they and devised this scheme to see him destroyed.

At last, the rage and hunger proved to be too much for the samurai vampire. He flew into a wild frenzy and killed the monks, feasting on their lives and laughing at their pathetic attempts to drive him off. When the sun arose, he hid himself away in their ravaged camp and

slept. In his heart, now, he knew that he must rest near the site of his last kill. He saw now the pattern that his life must take.

The next evening, he began to move back toward his home. His tortured soul hungered for the hour when he would stand before his sisters. They would cower before him, aware at last that their plan had failed. Their treachery would be exposed, and then they would die. Somewhere, deep in his heart, a voice of reason cried out that his sisters were women of honor, but the hunger of his vampire's nature was far too potent to be swayed.

As the sun began to lighten the horizon, Mayónaka found a small home that belonged to an elderly couple. As they slept, he descended upon them and drained them of their lives. By the time a cock crowed to greet the sunrise, he was fast asleep in their peasant's bed, nestled between the two cooling corpses.

The next night brought him to the edge of his family's ancestral lands. Aware that he had no time to act before the coming of the sun, he found the home of a young couple and entered it. They recognized the young man as their lord, expressing relief that he was still alive when all around them thought he was dead. Scoffing at their false protestations of happiness, Mayónaka killed them and fed. Inside his fading soul, the tiny spark of his humanity flickered and grew dim.

The next night, Mayónaka went to his parent's castle. He had learned that walls were no obstacle to him in his vampiric form and quickly scaled them. As the night passed, he moved from room to room, killing everyone in the fortress. At last, he came to the rooms occupied by his family. He moved to the large gong that was used to call the castle to alert in times of crisis and struck it with his fist. To his surprise, his new strength was so great that he shattered the thing. However, the tremendous sound that it made brought his parents and sisters racing into the hall, ready for battle.

At first, Mayónaka watched them. Lurking invisibly in the background, he watched as they discovered that everyone else in the castle was dead. At last, he became visible and confronted them.

His father, normally a reserved and quiet man, was so happy to see his lost child that he began to weep. As he rushed forward to embrace his son, Mayónaka struck with his katana. The keen blade flashed in the night and beheaded the old samurai with a single stroke. His mother cried out in horror and his sisters drew their weapons. They advanced on Mayónaka, under the impression that he was some form of monster that had taken their brother's shape.

Mayonaka scoffed at them. He attacked them and, with the aid of his new vampiric abilities, easily killed them both. As he stood over their bloody corpses, he turned to his mother and faced her in single combat. Despite the passing of many years since her last duel, she was an expert swordsman. Time after time, Mayónaka struck, only to have his blows fended off. At last, his great strength snapped the blade of her katana and left her defenseless before him. As she calmly awaited death, he stepped forward and beheaded her. As her body fell across her husband's and her blood mingled with that of her daughters, the last spark of humanity in Mayónaka's soul faded and was gone.

Mayónaka looked around at the carnage he had sown. All around him was death and desolation. With disgust, the vampire samurai remembered the battle against his family. For all their supposed skill and might, they had been no match for him. His skill as a warrior was, as yet, untested. He vowed to wander the world until such time as he found a worthy enemy: to make it his lot in life (or death) to seek out the mightiest warriors and test himself against them. When he found someone whose blade was faster and whose skill was greater, he would accept death with honor. In the interim, many lesser foes would die and feed his newly discovered lust for life energy.

The next evening, when he left the desolate castle, he stepped through the gates and into a rolling fog. He had not gone 20 paces before he knew that something was amiss. Whirling, he saw that the castle was gone. Somehow, he had been transported to another land.

In the years since he was drawn into Ravenloft, Mayónaka has traveled throughout the Demiplane of Dread. He has fought werewolves in Kartakass, battled the illithids of Bluetspur, and triumphed over the Drow of Arak. While he has never faced the lord of a domain, he has battled some of Ravenloft's most powerful creatures and, in every instance, defeated them.

This has left him somewhat despondent. He has grown tired of his unlife and is now desperate to see it ended. Yet he still holds to his vow and refuses to put forth less than his best effort in battle. If he is to die, it must be at the hands of someone who is truly his superior in combat. The longer he lives, however, the more certain he becomes that his ultimate reward will be forever denied him.

The Vistani know of this wandering creature, and speak in pitying tones when they are asked about him. They call him *Rittenuig*, which means the eternal warrior, and say that an old prophecy of their people holds that no man's hand will ever bring him the ending he seeks.

Ecology: As with all vampires, Mayónaka is not an aspect of the natural world. He feeds on that world, draining away the life energy of its creatures, but gives nothing back to it. He is an obscene aberration, the likes of which is seldom encountered by man.

The aura of evil and unlife that surrounds Mayónaka is so absolute that animals and similar creatures can sense it. Horses will snort and bay at his presence, dogs will howl and bark at him, and cats will hiss and spit.

Mayónaka's existence is nomadic at best. Each night, he travels in search of a warrior to challenge. If he does not find one, he kills someone just before dawn so that he may rest near the site of his or her demise. It is not difficult to follow his progress across the lands of the Core, for he leaves a fairly regular pattern of bodies in his wake.

Adventure Ideas: Mayónaka makes a fine opponent for any character who feels that he or she is the best warrior in the land. Such a person will attract the eternal warrior like a beacon in the night, for he or she promises a chance at release that Mayónaka cannot pass up.

Mayónaka lends himself well to adventures that are cast in the "most dangerous game" mold, where one of the heroes is to be hunted like an animal for the satisfaction of the vampire samurai's hunger for life energy. He might capture a group of heroes and release them at separate points in a thick forest or vast underground maze. As they seek to find their companions and a way out, he moves about and tries to destroy them one by one.

The players could stumble across Mayónaka's trail of corpses and decide to follow it to its source. This is especially useful if they have a natural tendency toward being vampire hunters or righters of great wrongs. For his part, Mayónaka will be fascinated at the thought that someone is actually stalking him. He will assume that these must be great warriors and will begin to stalk them as well, turning the hunters into the hunted.

Vampyre (Vladimir Ludzig)

CLIMATE/TERRAIN:	Falkovnia
FREQUENCY:	Unique
ORGANIZATION:	Pack
ACTIVITY CYCLE:	Night
DIET:	Blood
INTELLIGENCE:	Exceptional (16)
TREASURE:	F
ALIGNMENT:	Chaotic evil

NO. APPEARING:	1
ARMOR CLASS:	4
MOVEMENT:	12
HIT DICE:	8+3 (46 hit points)
THAC0:	11
NO. OF ATTACKS:	3
DAMAGE/ATTACK:	1d4/1d4/1d6
SPECIAL ATTACKS:	Charm
SPECIAL DEFENSES:	Nil
MAGIC RESISTANCE:	Nil
SIZE:	M (6′ tall)
MORALE:	Steady (12)
XP VALUE:	3,000

Nature takes great care to insure that there is always a balance of predators and prey. In the oceans, there is the ever-present shark, constantly seeking to satisfy its dreadful hunger. In the jungles, the great cats are always lurking in the shadows, ready to strike down the unwary. Even humankind cannot escape this inevitable fact, for nature has seen fit to create the vampyres, a deadly race of predators who move among humankind and strike down the careless.

Vladimir Ludzig lives within the walled city of Lekar. Here, his cunning and unmatched bloodlust have made him the master of that city's vampyre population. In appearance he is very much like a normal human, although he looks as if he might have a touch of elven blood somewhere in his past. His dark hair, seemingly bottomless eyes, and perfect physique make him one of the most physically attractive people any group of adventurers is ever likely to meet.

Ludzig is fond of wearing harsh clothing fashioned from supple black leather. He often adorns his outfits with chains made of silver or platinum and a sash of crimson worn as a belt. He never carries a weapon, needing none beyond his own teeth and claws.

As a native of Falkovnia, Ludzig speaks the common language of that domain. He has picked up fragments of the dialects spoken in Mordent, Darkon, and Lamordia, although his command of these languages is adequate only for the most basic of conversations. When he speaks, Ludzig always adopts a snobbish tone.

Combat: Ludzig's bloodlust sets him apart from even the most horrible of his kin. When he enters combat, he does so with a zest and glee that is almost impossible to describe. He delights both in ripping enemies apart quickly and in leaving them to linger in painful agony for long periods of time.

In melee combat, Vladimir Ludzig strikes with his long, sharp fingernails. These terrible claws are unnaturally keen and hard, ripping through flesh as if they were razors. He is able to make two such attacks each round, inflicting 1 to 4 (1d4) points of damage with each successful hit. In addition, he is able to deliver a savage bite. His fangs, every bit as long and sharp as those of the most savage nosferatu, inflict 1 to 6 (1d6) points of damage with each successful attack.

Anyone bitten by Ludzig must deal with the foul chemicals in his saliva. These enter the bloodstream and quickly attack the brain of the victim. If a saving throw vs. poison is not successful, the person *bitten* is charmed by the vampyre. The more damage inflicted by the vampyre's bite, the more toxin is injected, and the harder it is for the body to resist. Thus, every 2 points of damage inflicted by the bite imposes a –1 penalty on the victim's saving throw. Once a victim is charmed, he or she will no longer resist Ludzig's attacks, eliminating the need for the vampyre to make additional attack rolls. If other vampyres are present, the victim will still resist their attacks until such time as he or she fails a saving throw for each attacker.

Habitat/Society: Unlike the majority of Ravenloft's vampyre population, Vladimir Ludzig is not a native of the Demiplane of Dread. He was born and raised in an all-but-unknown world where the race of vampyres long ago brought down humankind. Here, Ludzig was a great warlord who, like any vampyre of importance, kept a large stock of human slaves to feed himself and his followers.

Ludzig's treatment of his captives was far from humane, but probably not much worse than was the norm for that world. If he was slightly more evil and cruel than his peers, the corruption of that world was such that only his unfortunate slaves noticed.

Then one night, as the crimson moon stood high above his palace, Ludzig's human slaves revolted. He mercilessly crushed the uprising and captured its leaders. To his surprise, the architects of the failed coup proved to be outlanders. They were human, but not natives of his world. He found them far more aggressive and dangerous than the cowed race of humans his kind kept as slaves.

Before he had them killed, Ludzig tortured them to learn all that he could about their past. He discovered that there were whole worlds where the existence of his race was undreamt of. Looking upon these as hidden gems, objects for future conquest, he ordered his wisest followers to begin studying the ways in which access to such lands might be had. It was clear the captured outlanders had employed some manner of magical ship to reach his world, but no sign of their vessel was ever found.

After years of research, Ludzig's scholars claimed to have isolated a means by which a magical *gate* could be opened to another world. They sent for their master and arranged for a demonstration of their new magic. Ludzig watched with glee as they drew mystical symbols on the floor, set magical candles alight, and chanted mysterious spells. When the sages completed their work, a shimmering portal appeared in the air.

Beyond the magical opening, Ludzig saw a great city that looked very much like his own, but populated by humans. As he watched its folk pass before his eyes, his mouth watered, and he thought of a whole new world of unsuspecting prey waiting for him and his kind to feast upon. Then, without warning, the spell went disastrously wrong. The portal suddenly reached out like the jaws of a great gaping mouth and swallowed Ludzig and the sages whole. Ludzig found himself falling in seemingly endless clouds of fog. A surge of energy swept through his body and he lost consciousness.

When he awoke, Ludzig found himself in the city of his vision. Two of his sages lay nearby, but they had not survived the journey. He quickly disposed of their bodies and set about learning as much as he could about the world he was now trapped in.

Within a year, he found that his initial conceptions about this world were wrong. Other vampyres did exist here, but they were far fewer than on his world and were forced to hide their activities for fear of retaliation from the humans, who vastly outnumbered them. Ludzig made contact with the vampyres in Lekar and, before long, was the head of that sinister band.

Resigned to the fact that he will never again see his homeland, Ludzig envisions a day when his kind will overwhelm the humans first in Lekar and then in all of Falkovnia. He is still coming to grips with the unusual nature of Ravenloft and doesn't fully understand that it is a demiplane and not a true world.

Ecology: Vampyres are an ancient race of predators that have fed upon humankind since before the dawn of recorded history. Ludzig takes great pride in his heritage and looks upon humanity as nothing but cattle upon which he can feed. He sees himself as the deliverer of his people, who will raise them back to their rightful position as masters of these human cattle. His followers believe as he does, making the band a pack of savage hunters with no regard for human life or the suffering they cause.

Ludzig's plans are grand indeed, but they may not be as far-fetched as they sound. In the decade or so since he came to Falkovnia, the vampyre population of Lekar has trebled. While this has resulted in an increase in the number of killings that his folk must make to support themselves, careful management of "the herd" has kept it from becoming an overwhelming concern of the city officials and the domain's master, Drakov.

One way in which Ludzig has kept the body count low is through the use of horrific feeding houses. Here, captured humans are kept alive so that the vampyres may feed upon them day after day. To be certain, this brutal existence soon drives the captives utterly mad, but that means little to the vampyres. These disgusting places are so vile and repulsive that anyone entering one for the first time must make a horror check immediately.

Adventure Ideas: Player characters might be drawn into conflict with Ludzig and his followers when one of their number or associates is captured and taken to a feeding house. Because of the large scale of vampyre operations, and the ease with which vampyres blend in with their prey, PCs will have a difficult time convincing city officials that the menace is as great as it truly is.

Any attempt to battle the vampyres will result in a great counteroffensive by the sinister creatures. This can be especially effective if the players do not realize the enormity of the plot their characters have stumbled upon. The shock and horror they experience when they discover that they face not a pack of a dozen or so vampyres but a veritable horde of over a hundred should be most rewarding.

A TREASURY OF RPG INFO
you can't get anywhere else!

Dragon MAGAZINE

The leader of the role-playing world offers gaming advice, reviews, monsters, cartoons, and treasures not found anywhere else!

Dungeon ADVENTURES FOR TSR ROLE-PLAYING GAMES

The module magazine for AD&D® and D&D® game players leads you to the limits of the gaming universe!

If you want the latest info on all the hot new AD&D® gaming products . . . if you want information that will make your world the best it can be . . . and if you want it at the best price around . . .

SUBSCRIBE!

Fill out subscription form and mail today!

- -